MY CAT'S GUIDE TO

ONLINE DATING

MY CAT'S GUIDE TO ONLINE DATING

CHRISTIAN BAINES

QUEERMOJO
A Rebel Satori Imprint
New Orleans

Published in the United States of America by
Queer Mojo
A Rebel Satori Imprint
www.rebelsatoripress.com

Book design: Sven Davisson

Paperback ISBN: 978-1-60864-250-2
Ebook ISBN: 978-1-60864-251-9

Library of Congress Control Number: 2023930066

CONTENTS

You're discreet, yeah?

Yeah.

How hung?

Was two inches the acceptable lying range? Zach unlocked his pictures.

Hot! So horny for it, man.

For a headless torso, this one sure liked to talk. Zach almost felt sorry for him. All that extra chat time seemed like a great way for a married guy to get caught. Or was that part of the thrill?

Cool. I'm really into bi guys, he sent back.

I'm straight man. Just like to get fucked sometimes, you know?

Zach pacified his impatient erection with a gentle stroke, again admiring the smooth, athletic body that dominated the guy's profile. Exactly what he wanted in a hook-up. Fit, sexy, horny as fuck, and the married thing was hot enough to excuse the absent face pic. Now, if the guy would just commit, before Zach had to take things into his own hands.

We doing this now? Address?

Zach pumped his fist in triumph over the desolate plain of time wasters. Please don't 'but' me now...

But...

Ugh.

You're totally discreet, yeah?

YES.

Cool. 20 minutes. Be ready.

Zach let go of the increasingly persistent bulge in his shorts, sent a thumbs up emoji, and tried to relax. In twenty minutes, the first in a long line of hot summer encounters would begin in his old bedroom, where he'd spent his teen years jacking off under the watchful eye of Jesus. For the first time, he wasn't cursing his parents' pious devotion to the annual Leaders of Light conference. After six weeks of evangelical cult-washing, they would return for the few days he'd promised to spend with them. A few days playing the game was worth it, for the six glorious weeks of shameless, uncomplicated sex he'd enjoy in the meantime.

He felt the soft fur of Grace Jones weave around his ankles. He scooped the cat up into his lap and rubbed her ears to soothe his nerves. The cat had almost settled when she lifted her head.

Zach smiled. "Paw?"

The cat dutifully lifted one of her front paws.

"Pawpaw," he said, holding it gently between his fingertips and dipping it twice. Their private paw-shake, the first trick he'd ever taught her. She'd lost weight though. Was she sick, or just shedding? His Mom and Dad hadn't been the most willing cat parents. Zach wondered if he could bring her back to Toronto. At least for now he could take proper care of her, in between enjoying the hottest DILFs, closet cases, and bored college guys this preachy little town

2

of 90,000 people had to offer.

Starting with you, *Btm4Discreet*. In twenty minutes, it would all start with you.

ALISTAIR

Alistair fucking Conway.

Zach's shoulders tensed. He choked down the bile that rose to the back of his throat and clenched his fists to stop himself from shaking as he recognized the man in his front doorway. The square jaw, expensive haircut, piercing dark eyes, sharp eyebrows, and flawless douchey smile of his first jerk off fantasy turned greatest enemy.

Next time, he'd get a face pic.

"Could we do this?" asked Alistair. "I've got like, twenty minutes."

"Oh, sure. No problem." Zach closed the door and led his guest to the kitchen. The jock immediately stripped off his black muscle top, barely looking at Zach as he made a show of stretching his broad chest and densely muscled back. Zach licked his dry lips.

Asshole.

"Like what you see?" Conway raised a wolfish smirk.

"Sure," Zach got out. "You look like your pictures."

"All natural, man. Gotta look after the temple. You know what I'm saying?"

If Conway recognized him, he wasn't showing it. Could the guy

4

be any more self-involved? Sure, Zach had dropped a good forty pounds since moving to Toronto for school. He'd even put on a little muscle, but his face was the same.

Did the asshole even remember leaving 'Fat Sack Zach's' life in ruins?

"Where are we doing this?"

Zach tore his eyes away from Conway's pecs. The prick had started swimming the year Zach had left. Going by the shape of his chest, Zach guessed he hadn't quit. "Thought you might like a drink first?"

"Woah, you think this is a date? I'm married, dude. I'm horny. You're... pretty decent looking. I'm here to hook up."

"Okay. No, you're right. That's totally what I'm after."

He didn't remember. Not the video. Not the fallout. Not the 'profoundly moving' apology he'd been forced to give Zach that had moved Zach to profoundly vomit. None of it.

Could he hate Conway any more than he already did? Maybe his newfound fitness would allow him to land a pretty decent punch upside Conway's head. "Where'd you park?"

"I didn't park, dude. I went for a run." Conway pushed his shoulders back, splaying his chest. His smile hadn't changed. An alligator grin, right before the predator erupted to claim its victim.

What should have been a hot hook-up had yielded a chance to confront Conway. To tell him once and for all... what, exactly? What did Zach hope to gain by sharing the hell he'd been through? The consequences of Conway's sick joke? What did he want? A guilt trip? A real apology? He'd just wanted to fuck, damn it.

"How about showing me that big cock of yours?" Conway made a grab at Zach's crotch.

Zach pulled away. Fuck! Of all the closeted queers in town, why was the one who'd condemned him to a senior year of home school now standing in his parents' kitchen, shirtless, gleaming with sweat, making grabs for his junk, and all too eager to bare his ass? To expose himself, naked and willing, entirely at Zach's mercy...

"Well, geeze! If you're gonna go cold fish, I'm gonna bounce."

Zach tried to breathe into the knot in his stomach. This was fine. No big deal. He'd just tell Conway he wasn't feeling it and send the guy home to nurse his bruised ego. Yeah, that'd show him! For like, a minute.

And yet...

"Yes? No? Anybody home?"

'Hate fucking,' they called it. It would give him one hell of a story, besides sating straight up lust. Fairview Baptist's meanest jock, bent over and pounded by one of his favorite victims, failed by his own indifferent memory? Maybe Zach could humiliate Conway somehow. Call him 'Fat Sack,' right as he was climaxing inside. How quietly could he take photos? Ruin Conway the way he'd... Okay, maybe a step too far. Fair? Probably. Justice? Absolutely. But if Conway pressed charges, there'd be no keeping his parents in the dark, and he'd be damned if he let Conway drag him through that hell twice.

"So...?"

Hell, this was a hook-up, and the guy was hot. They were adults. He had consent. He'd fuck Conway until the man lost control and wound up spattered in both their seeds, lying in a spreadeagled daze as Zach got dressed, wad shot, lust sated.

"Are we gonna do this or what?" Conway asked, slapping the tight curves of his abs. The loud crack echoed around the kitchen.

Then, he'd call Conway Fat Sack. Maybe he'd wait until the door was locked, then shout it once Conway was down the street.

"You don't remember me at all, do you?" Zach asked.

Shit! He hadn't meant to say that. Hadn't meant to say that at all. Shit!

"I don't think I do." A wary glint crossed Conway's eye.

Moment of truth, Fat Sack. Now or never. "Hey, I think you're right. You look like somebody else."

"Lucky bastard," Conway grinned. "So? We doing this?"

"Yeah, let's do this." Zach nearly choked, leading his guest upstairs. Maybe he'd take his self-loathing out on Conway's ass.

"Yeah man, that's it. Oh, fuck, right there. Lick those—"

"Stop talking," Zach said, lifting his head from Conway's inner thigh before going to work on his shaved, moisturized sack.

'Straight' my ass, he thought.

He expertly wrapped his tongue around one of the man's balls, then inhaled the other, tugging gently before dropping them both and gliding from the base of the man's shaft to its moistened tip with his tongue. Conway's blather gave way to a series of moans and whimpers as Zach reached up and squeezed one of the man's already erect nipples.

"Ow! Careful with those."

Great, Zach thought. Fairview's star jock was a whiner.

"Aw, man!" said Conway as Zach licked the slit of his cock once more. "If you keep doing that, I'm gonna come, real quick."

Zach pinned Conway's arms over his head and dove tongue first into the man's armpit. He recoiled just as fast, coughing to expel the

7

anti-perspirant that had coated his tongue.

"You okay?" Conway asked through a laugh.

"Yeah," he wheezed. Fuck twenty-four-hour protection. He needed a lozenge.

"Hey, it's fresh!" Conway sucked in a deep lungful of his own scent.

Zach descended the length of Conway's body, cleansing his palate with the far more natural, salty taste of the man's chest, abs, and flank.

"Keep going. I want you to eat my ass."

"So, roll over."

Maybe with Conway's face in the pillow... Zach threaded his fingers through the man's dark hair, pushing his head down just in case.

"Hey, not so hard," came the muffled protest.

Right. Man baby. He began kissing the back of Conway's neck, shoulders, and biceps, biting gently as he worked his way toward Conway's spine. He followed up with a single long, smooth cat-lick from the nape of the neck down to the small of the back, then slapped a hand around one of Conway's meaty buttocks, expecting another whine. The man only opened his legs wider, exposing his still attentive cock. Zach humored him with another playful lick over its tip before pulling apart his cheeks. Conway had always seemed more attractive showing his ass than opening his mouth. For the next little while, both belonged to Zach, and he was going to enjoy them.

"Awww, man. That feels... Fuck, you don't even know!"

Zach ignored him, plunging deeper before laying a trail of kisses up Conway's spine again. He nudged the moistened hole with the hard tip of his cock.

"Oh fuck, yeah! Play with that, please?"

Zach happily obliged, bringing himself parallel to the man's body, kissing his neck and shoulders, biting them as he nudged his cock deeper.

"Oh, man!" Conway moaned, his ass inhaling at least half of Zach's cock. "Yeah man, go deep."

Zach pushed a little further, retreating as Conway pushed back.

"Dude, just get in. Fuck!"

Zach waited for Conway to push against him once more, until the man's heat slid down the full, slick length of his erection. He held nothing back. Conway made a sound into the pillow, squeezing Zach's shaft and pushing the smooth cleft of his backside into Zach's groin. Zach slid his hands up the tanned flesh of Conway's back and grabbed a fistful of his hair.

"Ow! Jesus, man!"

Zach released his fist only to push Conway's face back into the pillow. Without breaking stride, he ran his hands down the sides of Conway's body, taking hold of the guy's hips and sliding deeper. Ignoring Conway's sighs and grunts, he slid his hands around the man's abs and grasped his cock, stroking it as the flesh of Conway's balls slapped against his fingers.

'Hate fuck' indeed. He tightened his grip around Conway's nipple and squeezed harder, picking up speed. He ignored Conway's faint choking sounds and pushed his body into the heat of the bully's back. Conway bellowed into the pillow. Zach righted himself, pulling his whiny fuck toy's body up with him and releasing the start of Conway's scream before clapping the hand that had been working Conway's cock over the man's mouth. His toy moaned again, grasping at the arm Zach still held across his chest.

9

"What was that?" Zach asked, releasing his hold on Conway's mouth as Conway mumbled something else.

"Just… I need a minute, man," Conway got out between breaths. "Holy fuck!"

Zach eased himself out, a bit disappointed he hadn't made Conway cry, yet.

Conway lifted his muscular arms and clasped his hands behind his head. "That was something."

"You think it's over?" Zach teased, leaning into him.

"Yeah, woah. Not so much into the kissing."

"Oh. Okay."

In that case, could he tape the guy's mouth shut?

Conway collapsed onto the bed, covering his face with his hands as he regained his breath.

"You want water or anything?" Zach asked.

"No, no, I'm good. Just… Whew!"

Zach reached for Conway's thigh before catching himself. "Guess you don't cuddle, either?"

"Dude, I'm not into the clingy shit. It's nothing personal."

Zach glanced at the bedroom door. How badly did he need to come again?

"You can touch, though." Conway looked at Zach, stroking his firm body with both hands as he teased his cock. "Go on."

Zach felt the firm muscles of Conway's inner thigh against his fingertips, massaging them before running his hand up the man's leg.

Conway propped himself up on his elbows and smiled. "You like touching me?"

Zach shrugged. "Never much liked sex without the affection."

"For real? Because you go at it like one hard motherfucker."

"So? I'm complicated."

Conway grinned at him. For the first time, Zach didn't feel like he was being made fun of. "Hey."

Zach stopped stroking, instead letting his hand rest on the leg as Conway pushed himself forward. Before Zach realized what was happening, he'd let the jock plant a gentle kiss on his lips.

"Same here, man."

Wait. Had that just happened? It wasn't like they'd swapped tongue, but hadn't Conway just said he didn't kiss? Maybe this new, 'complicated' Conway was worth exploring, a long-abandoned teen fantasy intact, at least for a while.

"I could give you some tips for moving those last few pounds of puppy fat, if you want."

Zach moved his hand away. There it was. That sparkling personality. "Thanks, but I'm good."

"Suit yourself. You can always look better, you know? Finish what you started."

This last part sounded like good advice. Zach hoisted Conway's ankles up onto his shoulders.

"Hey, what are you—"

"Shhhhhh," Zach leaned over the man, nudging his cock against Conway's opening.

"Man, I don't know if... Oh my god!"

Zach curled his fingertips around each of Conway's nipples and squeezed.

"If you're gonna do that... oh! Oh!"

He slid inside again in one smooth motion, lifting Conway's hips and taking advantage of their new position to push deeper. He watched Conway's eyes roll skyward as the man's head fell back over the edge of the bed. He put hands on Conway's shoulders, locking their bodies together. Conway wasn't resisting him or trying to squeeze his cock now. He just rocked back-and-forth, no longer trying to muffle gasps or moans, instead embracing the full pleasure of Zach inside him, 'last few pounds of puppy fat' or not.

This was the real Alistair Conway, a moaning little bitch boy who couldn't get enough cock. It made Zach feel powerful. Made him want to go harder and faster.

"Holy fuck!" Conway gasped. "What are you hitting, man? Fuck!"

"Yeah, take it. I said take it, Fat Sack!" Zach erupted, thrusting harder as his seed coated the insides of his tormentor. Only then did he collapse over Conway's body, adolescent lust spent. He lay there a moment, against the sweat and heat of the man's chest.

What had he just said?

"That was… Jesus!"

Maybe Conway hadn't heard or noticed.

"What the fuck was that?"

The last thoughts of revenge or confrontation drained from Zach's mind. "What was what?"

"Fucking awesome, is what it was. But you said something."

Just leave. You've had your fun, now go, Zach thought. Right. Like willing this into the universe would undo his mistake.

"No, it was like… Hey, get up a minute. I gotta move my arm."

A moment before, he hadn't been able to meet Conway's eye. Now, he couldn't look away. The man seemed to be staring through him.

"Wait a minute, I do know you!"

"No, I don't think you do."

"Bullshit!" Conway said, quickly covering the alarm that crossed his face with that familiar, stupid smile. "Oh, my fu… *Fat Sack?* Is that you? It is! Holy shit, it *is* you! I fucking knew it!"

Zach winced, his boner now in humiliating retreat. "It's Zach."

"Yeah, but we all used to call you Fat Sack."

"No Alistair, that was just you, until you made it a hashtag." He wanted to vomit, all over Conway's smug face. What twisted, repressed fantasy had convinced him that this was a good idea?

"Oh, fuck!" Conway threw his hands over his face. "I'd totally… Wait, you can't still sore about that?"

Yes. Yes, he could. No sooner had the video hit his inbox than Zach had erased all his social media and never looked back. But the damage had been done.

"We were just having a little fun. Shit! We didn't think you'd drop out of school over it. I mean, Toby was pissed, but he got over it."

"Wasn't my choice," Zach said through gritted teeth. Right. Like anybody was going to recognize a drunk Toby Winmore after Alistair had cropped out most of his friend's body and face. But everybody had seen Zach's. "I was home schooled my senior year, so… thanks for that."

"Fuck! I didn't know, man. I swear, we never meant for anything like that—"

"Who is 'we,' Alistair?" Realistic or not, punching the guy still felt like an attractive option. "It was you! Your phone!"

"Okay, for one, *Zach*, I didn't film it."

"You hit send. *You.*"

"And secondly? Did I or did I not apologize to you?"

"Did you mean it?" He fixed Alistair with a death stare. "*Did you mean it?*"

"Fuck! Okay, no." Alistair shifted uncomfortably. "I thought you were being a little pussy. It was stupid, alright? How could I know what was gonna happen?"

Zach rolled his eyes, moving to get up until Alistair grabbed his hand.

"Hey. Look… I *am* sorry, okay? For real, this time."

Zach stared at him again, barely breathing, the thrill of dominance already a fading memory.

"Fuck, man, I'm here naked with you, full of your come. You almost ripped my nipples off, I even kissed you!"

"Alright, alright." Zach shook his head as he got up and pulled on his underwear. "Don't you need to be going?"

"Yeah, yeah." The jock rolled off the bed, stretching his arms above his head and showing off his body. It might have popped Zach a fresh boner if the guy had been anyone else. "So… we're cool, right?"

"Do you care?"

Conway pulled on his jock and shorts, his predatory smile back in place. "You turned out okay, man. You jog? Hit the trails? Great excuse when you need to 'get out' if you know what I'm saying."

"I'll keep that in mind."

"You went east, right? Boston or something?"

"Something."

"Girlfriend?"

"No." Zach gritted his teeth. "Gold star gay. Well, platinum, I guess. My Mom had a C section."

Jesus, shut up already!

"I don't know what that means."

"C section?"

"No, moron! Platinum gay."

14

"It means never passed through—"

"Jesus, I wasn't asking!"

Great. Now if this beautiful monster turned explosive-divorce-in-waiting would just get out of his house, never to be seen or heard from again, they'd be… Gold? He looked over at the two shining golden dots that had appeared at the center of a black furry mass on Conway's tank top. The skinny feline body of Grace Jones stretched out with a yawn, clawing at the top before rubbing her face in it.

"Hey, get off that!" Conway barked, clapping at the animal. "Go on, get! Fuckin' cat!"

"Hey, that's my cat." Zach watched Grace Jones scamper out of sight.

"Whatever." The jock picked up his tank top and turned it over, inspecting it for cat hair. "Shit. Shit, shit, shit!"

"What's wrong?"

"Look at this! Stupid animal." Conway shoved the top under Zach's nose.

Zach squinted to see two or three black hairs on Conway's black tank top. "Looks okay to me."

"Man, this isn't funny. My wife's allergic. You know I've got to be totally discreet?"

"You said that, a bunch of times." Zach at last found a single white hair that might have served as forensic evidence of his cat. "I'll see if I've got a lint brush, okay?"

"Yeah, you'd better. I don't need trouble, from Cheryl or anybody else. You got that?"

"Cheryl? Findlay?"

"Cheryl Conway now."

Un-fucking… No, it was totally believable. Cheryl Findlay had been Fairview Baptist's Medusa for Christ, ever ready to turn accused non-believers into social stone with a pious shriek. Of course she'd take a ring from a hypocritical son of a bitch... okay, fine, a rich, hot, handsome, hypocritical son of a bitch like Conway.

"What do you care?"

"I... I don't," he answered, following Conway out to the stairs. "Just curious."

"Hey," Conway frowned in a way Zach didn't like one bit. "You ain't gonna tell her, are you?"

"What? Why would I tell her? We're not friends. I never even liked her! I mean... Sorry, I didn't mean it like that. I know she's your wife but—"

"Because that'd be kind of fucked up, man. Look, I was an asshole to you, like, a million years ago. I'm a big enough guy to admit that, but if this is some kind of twisted, revenge hook-up, blackmailing shit—"

"Woah! What the hell are you talking about? You wanted cock, I wanted to fuck. That's all. I didn't even see your face until you turned up."

"Yeah? Well maybe that was a good thing. Not that you needed my face to recognize me, Fat Sack."

Zach clenched his fists again. "What's that supposed to mean?"

Conway stretched his arms out over the empty staircase, making a show of his chest. "What? You think I never noticed? Come on, man. Toby was okay, but I knew what you really wanted. You never missed your chance to sneak a peek. I felt sorry for your dumb homo ass."

That did it. The last pangs of guilt or uncertainty exploded as Zach fired up. "You know, for a second there, I almost thought we were maybe putting some of this shit behind us, but you're as much of an asshole as you ever were. Now get the fuck out of my house!"

"Oh, *I'm* the asshole now? I'm the asshole? You get me over here, just so you can have the revenge fuck you've been dreaming of since high school? Now, you think you're gonna tell Cheryl and anyone else you can? Well, I got news for you, fag—Hey! What the..."

Zach ducked out of reach as Conway lunged for him. He saw the man trip and spin, trying to find the furry interloper that had dived between his legs. By the third spin, there was no regaining balance. Conway's body was in freefall, the mouth that moments before had hurled abuse now mewled a desperate plea for impossible intervention. The terror in the man's eyes registered just a fraction of a second too late as Zach's fingertips brushed Conway's. The man fell backwards, his feet kicking against empty air, powerful arms flapping with as much futility, until all 190 pounds of Conway landed hard on one shoulder.

Whether it was Conway's size, weight, or just the crushing disappointment that people who fell down stairs did not do so in neat, rolling, Screen Actors Guild-approved heaps like they did in movies, Zach couldn't say. Their necks, it seemed, did make that crunching noise, which the loud thud of Conway's skull hitting the wooden floor had failed to disguise.

Then, all was silent.

Zach stood frozen, unable to blink or move, his hand clapped around the railing where Conway had tried to latch hold. Not dead. He couldn't be dead. That snapping sound could just as easily of been the guy's wrist or ankle, couldn't it?

"Alistair?"

The stair creaked beneath his bare feet as he approached the body. Body? No! The man. Still a living, breathing... No breath. No pulse. No blood either, as if that mattered. Nobody's head was supposed to be at that angle.

Unable to take his eyes off the body, Zach eased himself to the floor.

Conway's eyes, now void of lust or sneering scorn, stared into nothingness. Zach's arch nemesis, laid low in undignified semi-nakedness with a broken neck and an ass full of Zach's finest splooge. His DNA.

Shit!

He had to call the cops. It had been an accident. He'd even tried to save the guy, technically. But there'd be questions. So many questions! They'd want the man's phone. Probably Zach's. An autopsy would soon reveal more than traces of Conway's last meal, all of which Zach might have been able to keep from his parents if Conway had just been some random trick. But this was Fairview. Forget their personal history. The last thing Zach needed was to become the villain in some story at Conway's country club. The jock prince, felled by the familiar of a still very closeted fairy.

"Meow?"

Zach turned his gaze upward. "I'm busy."

Grace Jones hissed before disappearing. She'd dropped him in some serious shit.

No, this was stupid. He had to call the cops, or an ambulance at least. They weren't legally bound to tell his parents about a dead body collected at their house, were they?

Right. Because the small detail that the body belonged to not just a former classmate, but the one who'd ruined Zach's senior year with a mass video message would just slip through their report like

Conway had slipped away from consequences over his directorial debut. Then would come the questions. Maybe he could re-dress Conway, then call them. Oh, sure! Why not just beg them to find some inconsistency? Something in the positioning or bruising that wasn't right?

And when, not if, his parents found out...

Conway had damn near ended his life once. Zach had worked too hard patching up that disaster, convincing his folks that the video they and half of Fairview Baptist had seen was a mere aberration. A shameful blip in their son's sexual awakening to be repented and put aside. Two years fighting to prove he could be someone he wasn't. Earning his freedom. No way. Once was enough.

Conway's lifeless bulk had to go. The fall had been clean. No blood or carnage anywhere, except for the body itself. How long did it usually take for a body's bowels to release?

Upstairs, he heard his phone buzz with the quiet jazz disco of its stupid ringtone. Zach swore under his breath, ignoring it until it fell quiet... then buzzed again. Mom. She never left a voicemail. Hell, it wasn't like Conway was going anywhere. Stepping over the body, he took the stairs two at a time and snatched up his phone from the nightstand.

"Yeah?"

"Zachary? Thank the Lord. I was starting to think you were ignoring us."

"No, no," he stammered, looking around for his underwear. "I was in the shower."

"In the shower? Is everything all right?"

"Yeah! Yeah, everything's fine. I normally shower. Like, every day. Mostly." He'd never prayed for a network outage but there was always a first time.

"Well, your father and I are simply having the best time! You should have come with us. I mean it, Zachary. It would be so good for you, and worth every penny."

Zach put the phone on speaker.

"Pastor Wilson has such insight into all the nasty business going on in the world. Stuff you wouldn't even believe!"

"Oh yeah?" Zach shooed Grace Jones off his t-shirt. "Come on, off!"

"What's that honey?"

"Nothing. I'm fine."

"Well, it's the darndest thing! But it all makes sense. predicted right there in the book of Daniel, chapter seven. You remember, don't you?"

Zach's grip tightened around his shirt. "Uh... Mom? Can we talk late—"

"Daniel's vision of four beasts and the four kingdoms they represent. Oh, I'm so glad you're interested in this!"

The only beast that interested Zach in that moment was bathing herself in his bedroom doorway.

"Pastor Wilson made it so clear! The four kingdoms of the end times. Most people think they're dead and gone and that the bible has it wrong. I ask you, when does the bible ever steer us wrong? They're here now, Zachary! The four kingdoms live and breathe, here and now, so you know the Antichrist is coming soon!"

"Uhuh," Zach picked a stray cat hair from his t-shirt and slipped it on. "That's fascinating, Mom. Hey, I should really—"

"First there's the winged lion. That's where people get it wrong, see? Because they think it's Babylon. Well of course Daniel thought that, because China didn't exist yet. But it's all a metaphor! It's China, alright! A rich, powerful empire? Lions like dragons? A ruler with absolute authority, refusing to bow before the one true God? It's China, Zachary! China!"

"Right, got it Mom. China. I got it."

"I knew you would. Then there's the bear. Well, that's an easy one."

As easy as the bear who'd just pinged him on the app?

"Zachary, what was that noise?"

"A text," he answered, semi-truthfully. There was nothing 'semi' about the image attached to it.

"Well, in Daniel's times, they thought the bear was Persia, then when we were growing up, they all said 'no, no, no, it's gotta be Russia.'"

"Uh, does it?" He blocked the profile.

"Well, they were both right. It's both of them, Zachary! Together! In cahoots! You know how Persia's Iraq now, and Russia's got them their back pocket, because of all the oil and weapons of mass destruction."

"Mom? I think you mean Iran, and I don't think they have—"

"Now, the third beast? This is where it gets spooky. The dragon with ten horns? Ten horns, Zachary! Do you remember?"

"Uh, not really." Zach opened another message. Only one horn, but it made its point.

"Zachary? You sound tense."

"No, no. I'm just getting texts from my friend Katie." He omitted the part about 'Katie's' unattended eight-incher, along with the detail that the real Katie had dumped him as fast as any of Yves' friends within days of their breakup. Now, he would have killed for that to have been his biggest problem. Block.

"Well, Katie would wig out if she heard this. The dragon is the Roman Empire, you understand? Of course, we always used to think it meant the Roman Catholic Church. Bzzzt! Big ole wrong!"

Zach sighed, putting on underwear, picking up his phone, and going to the landing overlooking at Conway's splayed corpse. "Mom, this is fascinating, but I'm really kind of—"

"It's Europe, Zachary! The European Union! With ten stars on its flag. One for each country. Well, I mean it's twelve right now, but listen to this! England just left, right? Right? Now, who do you think is going to be next?"

Zach stepped carefully over Conway's body as he reached the bottom of the stairs. "I honestly couldn't say. Mom, this really isn't a good time—"

"Oh, you're right about that. It's not a good time to be ignoring God, that's for sure! Because with England out of its way, the littlest country on that flag of theirs will rise up and lead the ten other horns in the name of the Roman Catholic Church."

"I thought you said—"

"Ireland! The Antichrist will rise from Ireland, Zachary! So, it all comes back to Rome, see? It's just so obvious, when you think about it."

"So… the Antichrist is a leprechaun?"

"Zachary, if you're not going to take this seriously—"

"I am, I am!"

Serious? How much more serious could his situation get? The cops. He had to call the… No. Fuck! No cops! Cops were out of the question! Okay, don't panic. Hide the body. Where the fuck was he supposed to hide the body? The fridge wasn't big enough.

"Then, there's the fourth beast. The worst of the bunch, Zachary, right here in America, right now, ready to swallow us all up if we don't stay—"

"Oh, Jesus, Grace Jones!" He clapped his hands, shooing the cat away from where she was gnawing on Conway's now bloodied toes. The creature skidded toward the wall, veering toward the door leading to the basement.

"That's right, honey. Jesus! He's the only thing going to keep us safe from the fourth beast. The leopard! Daniel thought it meant Greece, but who do you really think it is, Zachary? Playing it cool. Biding his time. Tell me."

The basement freezer! Hell, he had no idea where or how to dispose of Conway's body. But freezing it would give him time to think. To do some research online—yikes, that was going to be fun—and maybe find a way out of this.

"Honey? Hello?"

"I... I honestly don't know, Mom. Who?"

"The liberals! All the lie-berals and Demon-crats right here on our own doorstep! Democrats? That's no coincidence. Who do you think invented democracy, Zachary? The Greeks! Sodomy? The Greeks! And that fourth beast? The leopard? Alexander the Great. The biggest sodomite of his time. *A Greek!*"

"Uh, right. Well, it sounds like you've got this all figured out, Mom."

"Not me, honey. Pastor Wilson. Oh, he's such a well-spoken man! Just hearing his words made me so grateful you found your way back to the righteous path, but I do wish you could join us. You're going to be so lonely there for six weeks!"

"No, no, I'm fine. Everything is good." Zach watched a drop of

23

blood trickle down Conway's foot to the floor. Did blood stain polished hardwood? Shit!

"We could book you a flight—"

"Mom? You're on vacation. Go make God happy."

His shoulders relaxed as she said goodbye and rang off. Yep. Make God happy. Make God smile on their whole fucked up family and if he could find a few moments in his busy, omniscient schedule to make the dead body at the bottom of the stairs disappear, that would be awesome.

Zach braced himself, trying to keep his back straight as he took the corpse under its arms and gripped its shoulders. The last time he'd held Conway like this… Well, maybe it was better not to think about that. He dragged the body off the staircase and into the hall, where Grace Jones stepped over it. With no small effort, he maneuvered Conway to the top of the basement stairs. Maybe it was true what they said about muscle weighing twice as much as fat. Who could stand to lose a few pounds now, fucker?

How the hell was he supposed to get the man's body downstairs? Dragging him backwards would topple them both in seconds. He'd have to follow the body down feet first, holding it under the arms like he was now. Yeah, so long as they didn't get stuck, that could work. It would have to work. All he had to do was carefully turn Conway's… Steady… Wait… *Shit!*

All 190 pounds of QB Conway slipped from his grasp and tumbled down their second flight of stairs that day, crumpling at the bottom like some enormous, freshly sprayed spider. Silently thanking the universe for making sure he was thoroughly fucked, Zach flicked on the light and padded down the stairs after the corpse, careful not to traipse through droplets of blood from the man's foot.

24

If Conway's neck had remained intact after his first plunge into the abyss, it was a twisted mess now. Zach could see the man's face, frozen in the second before his death. Still, mission accomplished. All Zach had to do now was drag the body to the freezer and put this whole mess on hold.

He opened the lid, shifting bags of frozen vegetables, long forgotten pork chops, a packet of chicken legs, a container that to the best of his knowledge still contained uneaten pieces of wedding cake and was probably on its way to a long and productive life behind glass in the Smithsonian, and an oversized tub of ice cream, long turned to crisp, icy chips that looked closer to frozen bird shit than dairy goodness. A frozen mountain of food. He set aside a packet of beef strips near the top, then hauled out the partitions until only the empty shell remained.

He maneuvered Conway over the lip of the freezer, then, as slow as he could manage, tipped the body forward, straining to keep it from dropping until it hit bottom. He shuddered as the bloodied foot smeared his hands, let the last of the cadaver slip from his grasp, and closed the lid.

What the fuck was he supposed to do now? Only cops and crime writers could get away with Googling shit like 'How to dispose of a dead body.'

He scrubbed his hands and forearms in the laundry sink. He shooed Grace Jones off the stairs where she'd begun to lap up drops of blood. He'd deal with that in a minute.

Right now, he wanted to shower. Maybe for an hour. Maybe for a whole year.

Lying naked on his bed, freshly showered but still feeling the slickness of Conway's blood on his hands, Zach pondered the best way to dispose of a corpse.

Twenty minutes passed. Nothing. Nada. Zip.

Instead, these twenty minutes allowed the wider ramifications of Conway's fate to land, along with the potential consequences of Zach's admittedly impulsive and in hindsight foolishly pro-active response to it. First of all, that a human being—an awful one, but human, nonetheless—had died under his roof. After they'd had sex. On some level, it bothered him that those few moments of animalistic passion that had consummated his teenage masturbatory fantasies hadn't bonded them to the point he might feel some kind of remorse, forgiveness, or sympathy over Conway's fate. Did that make him a bad person? Conway had even kissed him, or maybe it had been another power play. That seemed more consistent with the prick who'd outed him, forced him out of school, put him through....

Nope. Fuck that guy.

Secondly, he'd moved the body. Rather than leave every hair, fiber, and displaced limb of the deceased's body in its naturally crumpled heap, he'd dragged the corpse to the freezer and dumped it in. With this action, the time to call the cops had passed. Sure, a really good forensic expert with enough spare time and curiosity might find enough evidence to corroborate his story, aka the truth. But he couldn't see cops in Fairview going to that much trouble with one inescapable fact set against him. Innocent people didn't usually move bodies.

And what had led him to that action? Fear, of the fate he'd so narrowly avoided last time. Zach remembered seeing the literature from the conversion therapy camps on his dad's desk. The smiling, white faces of models posed as supposedly former homos fawning over their stock photo wives and precocious brats, grinning like they were in a fucking pharma commercial. Talk to your doctor to see if Conversion Therapy is right for you. Side effects may include sustained physical and mental abuse, chronic depression, anxiety, electroshock therapy, complex PTSD, and a lasting inability to form healthy romantic or sexual partnerships. Please note, you will still crave dick.

He checked the time on his phone. Almost seven. It pinged with a message. Fuck. The last thing he wanted right now was another hook up. Hosting? Forget it.

He brought up the profile and froze. Same headless, perfectly sculpted torso. Same handle. Same age. This was impossible. He'd seen Conway die. He'd dragged the man's ass into the freezer himself. It had to be some kind of glitch. Some delayed message Conway had sent right before showing up.

What do you think you're doing?

He lay there, phone in hand, staring at the message. A joke. Some elegantly crafted, sick joke.

It's cold in here, asshole!

He dropped the phone on the bed, almost tumbling to the floor in his rush to back away. Zach didn't believe in ghosts, and if he did, he believed they had better things to do than play pranks through some dead closeted homo's phone. Should he block Conway's profile? What if the cops needed transcripts? Shit. No way. He was *not* involving the cops now. He picked up the phone again, scanning a new message.

I'm starving. You making dinner soon?

Zach pulled on his shorts and tromped down both sets of stairs to the basement. The freezer was just as he'd left it, cold and silent. Funny, Conway. Fucking hilarious. Way to top the video stunt, asshole. This was some twisted art shit. Kudos. Prick.

"Okay, Alistair. Neat trick. You got me. Where the fuck are you?"

No answer. Zach flung open the freezer and nearly fell over. Conway's lifeless, but very much present eyes stared up at him, frozen in their silent scream.

His phone pinged again. *I asked you a question.*

Who is this? He typed back.

Well, not the stiff in Mommie's freezer, in case that wasn't clear.

Mommie's freezer?

WHO. ARE. YOU?

Maybe you should ask where Conway's phone is instead?

Zach closed the freezer and bounded back upstairs, picking up Conway's shorts, wallet, and keys.

No phone.

Who'd had the opportunity to take Conway's phone from his shorts? Who would even know Conway was dead? He checked the distance on the profile. Too close to even register. That meant the phone was in the house, somewhere. He swallowed, a chill running through him.

Who the fuck was in his house?

Had about enough of your games, asshole. Zach's heart pounded. Had he remembered to lock the door? Should he get out of the house? Shit!

You used to like our games, Zachary. Like when you'd tie a piece of string around absorbent cotton and dangle it like fishing line for me to catch? Asinine, but it kept you amused.

What the fuck? Absorbent cotton?

28

I'm calling the cops.

Don't insult me, Zachary.

He wet his lips before typing again. *Last chance.*

I suppose we can play it your long winded, difficult way. Meow.

Huh?

Meow. Meow meow meeeeooooow. Meeeoow. Screech? Purrr, purr, purr... Zachary, I implore you, end this charade while we both still have some dignity.

Zach shook his head. Cat burglar? Fucking funny. Prick. If he'd had Conway's number, he would have called it and 'ended the charade' right there. He slowed his breath, trying to get a cold, clear view of his situation. The smart, normal thing to do would be to leave the house and call the cops. Not an opt... Fuck! What kind of burglar wasted time taunting their mark through a hook-up app? All the doors were locked. The windows all had screens. There was nobody else in the house. Fucking think!

His phone pinged again. *I know this seems ridiculous to you.*

So? Come out and explain it to me.

Please don't make me resort to pussy jokes.

You're not a fucking cat!

You desire proof?

CATS CAN'T TALK!

We're not talking, we're texting.

I'm turning this off.

Two weeks after you brought me home, there was a huge rain storm and I ran out. You spent three hours in the dark and rain, looking for me. You found me under a fern, wrapped me in your t-shirt, brought me inside and patted me dry with a towel. You never told Mom. We both know how that would have gone. Then, she never understood why I spent every night curled into the crook of your arm. My spot, for almost a year.

Zach froze, his fingers locked around the edges of his phone. Every detail was accurate, but no way. No fucking way! He tried to remember. Had one of his neighbors seen him that night? The details were too weirdly specific. But a cat? He pinched himself just to—No, he was definitely awake. *If you're my cat, then you must know her name.*

Please. Shall I warble a selection of her greatest hits for you too? What if the neighbors complain?

He stared at the message, re-reading it twice before typing his response. *Paw?*

Pawpaw.

His eyes widened. His throat tightened.

I never understood that either, but it seemed to amuse you.

What do you want?

Red meat, for a start.

What?

No more of those horrible dust biscuits. Red meat. Write it down. RED.

Now he was taking dinner orders. From his cat. *Fine, kitty. I'll get some wet food tomorrow.*

If you want to eat that mashed up fish slop, Zachary, be my guest. I said MEAT. The fresher the better.

Nope. Impossible. This was not his cat. One hell of a prank, perhaps. One he couldn't explain. But no way was he texting with a cat. *Whatever you say.*

I see the point is still to be made.

Zach went back upstairs to the kitchen and started rifling

through cupboards. Vodka? Gin? Bourbon? He passed on the pear cider and boxed Chardonnay, instead filling a glass with cold water. He leaned over the sink and tipped it over his face. Okay, slightly better. Prank or no prank, he still had to deal with Conway's body and phone, somehow.

His shoulders tightened and his teeth clenched as he heard a sickly coughing upstairs.

Fucker!

He put the glass aside and bolted upstairs, but it was too late. A long trail of regurgitated kibble, stewed in cat bile stretched from his shoes, across the t-shirt and underwear he'd tossed to the floor, to mere inches from his open bag. There, the trail ended in a swollen puddle of pale puke. The precision of it! The deliberate vindictiveness! The pettiness!

His phone pinged again. *Next time, the bag gets it.*

I'll fucking murder you!

Threats, Zachary? Not wise. Murdered pets look so good on a criminal profile. Would you really consider such a thing? After all we've been through together? Besides, you'd still never find this phone. I even fixed the settings so its location can't be tracked. You're welcome for that. Can't have the police turning up the moment the Douche Prince of Fairview Baptist is reported missing now, can we?

Zach swallowed. Shit. He hadn't even thought about that. Still, even if the police couldn't track down Conway's phone, he'd have to. He had six weeks…

See, I know you, Zachary. I know how you think. How you see this house. I also know it better than you ever could. I know every nook and crevice. Every smell, every flaw and crack.

I'll find it.

Ah, so you do believe me?

Zach stared at the feline barf trail that decorated his room. Did he believe it? Could he deny the evidence of his own eyes? No prankster could make a cat do this on cue. *How? Your brain's the size of a walnut.*

Which says what of yours? I'm smart enough to be worshipped as a god by people who engineered the pyramids. You think I'm too stupid to text on an app?

How can you even read?

You were raised by evangelical puritans, yet here we are, man-whore.

Grace Jones, tapping away on Conway's phone, little paws nimbly skipping over the screen, spelling each word perfectly. This, Zach had to see. *Okay. Where are you?*

Oh? And I suppose you promise not to snatch the phone away as soon as you see it? No, Zachary. Don't start insulting my intelligence, now you've accepted it. Besides, we have much to talk about. You looked after me. Now, let me look after you.

Look after me? Is that what you call this mess? Looking after me?

Pffft! A little baking soda and dish soap, and all is well. I'm talking about the much larger mess in the freezer.

Zach licked his lips, tapping fingertips against the sides of his phone.

You've never had to hide a kill before, Zachary.

This isn't some dead mouse or bird, damn it!

No. This is far more succulent, and there's so much of it!

Zach stared at this last message, muttering as the subtext landed. "You're fucking kidding."

Red meat, Zachary. Fresh. Delectable. We can't let it all go to waste, and he can't be allowed to pop up somewhere. Not intact, anyway.

You're disgusting.

And you're in deep shit.

I didn't kill him! Forget it. I'm calling the police.

But you did move the body. A body filled with your... fountain of renewal, let's say. If the police were an option, we both know you would have called them already. Can't have Mom and Dad finding out your summer plans now, can we? We both know what would happen.

Zach did know. Even with solid grades, a senior year of home school followed by a forced gap year to make sure he was 'right with the Lord' hadn't exactly won him a full ride. Without Mom and Dad, there's be no more school. No more Toronto, or the sexual freedom it offered. He'd probably lose his student visa. That was if his parents didn't disown him completely, or worse.

What would you know about that?

As I said, Zachary, I know you. Or do you think I didn't go through your phone as well? I'm glad you've more diverse tastes than the poor idiot in your freezer. You should see his 'favorites.' I can't tell their pictures apart. Is there only one gym washroom in this town? Oh, except for the one holding a bucket of protein powder. What's that nonsense? Do an extra five push-ups, you lazy bitch!

Zach sat back down on the bed. Forget the cops. He needed a psychiatrist. This couldn't be happening. Yet the story she'd told him? The precise vomiting fit on queue? He slapped himself hard across the cheek. Oh good. Still awake. Fuck.

I heard that.

I don't care!

I know this is a lot to take in. I honestly hadn't planned on ever telling you I could understand you. It's surreal. Impossible. I get it. But I hadn't planned on helping you dispose of a body either. You're still my

33

human, Zachary. We need to take care of this, together. Agreed?

Zach shook his head, flicking back to Conway's profile, to the pictures that had so turned him on, then back to the conversation he was having with his cat.

Do you like my nipples? a new message read.

What?

FOCUS! Food's a freezing.

You want me to pull Conway out of the freezer?

Were you planning on leaving him there forever? Take it from a seasoned hunter, a segmented body makes things easier. And we can ensure all that lovely meat doesn't go to waste.

I'm not feeding him to you! Damn it, that is still a human being in there!

Seriously? Oh, moral beacon for hope and justice? What more worthy agenda did you have in mind?

Zach hovered over the keypad, thinking. Thinking. Thinking.

Do it quickly, before rigor mortis sets in. Once it does, you won't be able to do a thing with him for at least a day or two. There's a drain at the center of the basement floor, yes? Start with an incision along the inside of his thigh so he bleeds out quickly. It'll be easier for you to control. Then take the whole thing off at once. Get some freezer bags of various sizes. I'll talk you through the rest.

Zach stared at his phone. Then at the crumpled pile of Conway's clothes on the floor. Then at the vomit trail. Then at the wall. Then, he let everything go in one great scream.

After cleaning up the disaster Grace Jones had left in his bedroom, Zach turned his focus, and a large hacksaw, to the more daunting task. He managed the legs and a couple of choice cuts from Conway's buttocks before the combined obstacles of nausea and rigor mortis forced him to stop.

Zach didn't know how the hell Grace Jones was going to finish the amount of meat he'd packed away in bags and put back in the freezer, to say nothing of the rest of Conway's body, even over six weeks. He'd meant to do it all at once, but the thought of the deceased bully's internal organs unspooling before his eyes in a bloody, ropy mess was far less appealing in practice to his twenty-one-year-old self than it had been to his vengeful eighteen-year-old imagination.

He looked at the meager cut he'd taken from Conway's inner thigh. Just as the cat had instructed, he'd tenderized and seasoned it. Not too much pepper. Then, he'd sliced it up and set it in a bowl at one end of the cutting board. Nice and separate. Kosher for kitty? Not funny, Zach. Not funny. He'd then done the same to the meat he'd set aside for himself. He'd even used the same seasoning. He couldn't fault the cat for good taste.

He stared at the two bowls of meat, still disbelieving. Maybe he had just grabbed an extra packet from the freezer. It all looked the same.

No, he was serving his cat human flesh. There was no part of this that wasn't clear, or completely nuts. The body, which hadn't bled anywhere near as much as expected, thanks to his cat's strangely expert instructions, was still in his freezer, freshly cauterized where he'd severed various parts. He'd been surprised how well his mom's iron, turned to its highest setting, had done the trick, though there was no returning it to regular service now. Meanwhile, he had a freezer full of bagged human leg meat, not to mention the half body that remained.

He could still end this. Still dump Conway's body somewhere with everything he'd cut off it and never speak of it again. He'd also have to dump Conway's clothes, along with his wallet and phone… and so screwed that idea.

"Fuck!" he shouted, bringing his hand down hard on the edge of the cutting board. The sound of the bowl upsetting on the counter startled him, though not as much as the sight of two bowls tipping over the counter's edge.

The cat shot into the kitchen, running silently to the upturned bowls of meat on the floor.

Zach snatched Grace Jones from where she'd begun to nibble on one of the meaty piles and put her aside. He scooped up each bowl and set it back on the counter. Not that he was in any hurry to eat beef he'd picked up off the floor, but it would turn his stomach less than having Conway's lifeless eyes stare at him while he rummaged through the freezer for more. He turned the stove to a low heat and tipped in the strips of lightly seasoned Conway, frying them for just a couple of minutes before spooning them into Grace Jones' bowl. The cat was already waiting, a portrait of anticipation. Zach stood there, watching the animal eat.

Grace Jones paused her meal just long enough to catch his eye and growl.

Zach dropped the 'Conway' pan in the sink and pulled out a separate pan for himself. He couldn't help but glance at the cat's empty bowl, still doubting, despite everything. Watching the meat brown in the pan, steam rising from the greens he had cooking on the neighboring burner, Zach turned events over in his mind. And over. And over.

They'd had sex. Then Conway had realized who he was and freaked out. What was Conway so afraid of? A few stray cat hairs giving the game away? It served him right for not doing his own laundry. Besides, it wasn't like Zach could out the guy without outing himself. If anyone had a right or reason to freak out, it was Zach. But he'd kept his cool. He'd even been ready to leave the past in the past. It was Conway who'd gone nuts.

Conway's death, Zach assured himself as he spooned dinner onto his plate, had not been his fault. Agitated by his own alpha bravado, Conway had lost his balance on the top step and rolled, perfectly shaped ass over pumped-up pecs to his doom. Zach had even tried to catch him! Thank the gods he'd missed, or they'd both probably be crumpled in a mostly naked heap at the bottom of his parents' stairs. Not the obituary he'd imagined.

Zach stared at his plate of green vegetables and medium rare steak, no longer hungry. Still, he knew as only a former fat kid did that once his parents got home, there would be cheese, bacon, pancakes every morning, and more fatty meat than he could...

He ran for the kitchen sink and retched, bringing up a thin trail of spittle in lieu of food that was not yet there. He lifted his head, gulping in air. This was ridiculous. He would do this. He wasn't sure how, or in what mental state he'd be by the time it was done, but he had no choice. What did he owe Conway, anyway? Not that he'd ever wished his former nemesis dead. At least, not outside of the odd, dark fantasy, when the wounds of his humiliation had been fresh. But the world hadn't exactly lost a stand-up guy.

Drawing himself a big glass of water, Zach sat down to the increasingly unappetizing beef strips and picked up his fork. Skewering the biggest hunk of meat he could find, he stabbed at a few pieces of kale and a piece of bell pepper and dug in.

It was good. Better than good.

He slowed his chewing, rolling the peppery leaves of kale in the actual pepper he'd sprinkled over the meat. He'd made the recipe a hundred times, but rarely had it risen above bland diet food. Maybe he was a better cook under stress. He skewered another piece of meat and popped it in his mouth, this time rolling it over his tongue, enjoying each grain of salt, each flake of pepper and spice before the strip itself melted open, releasing sweet juice that tingled on his tongue like savory, fatty soda. In minutes, his plate was empty, his water still untouched for fear it would dilute and spoil his enjoyment. Not bad for the most stressful meal he could remember eating.

He washed up his plate and pan, leaving the pan he'd used for Grace Jones until last. Even after it was clean, he set it aside from the rest. If this was to be his new normal for the next few weeks, he wanted to keep any and all Conway-related utensils and cookware separate from his own at all times. Jesus. What was he doing? No way was his cat going to get through an entire human body, even over six weeks. He imagined the clickbait headline; *Kitty with a taste for human flesh found unable to move, gorged on dissected jock.*

What was he meant to do with Conway's internal organs? Bones and skin, even? Grace Jones had promised she'd help, and as unlikely as that seemed, she *did* have more experience than he ever would disposing of dead things, and if she'd learned to text, well…

Ping. Zach hoped it was some lonely guy he could ignore. It wasn't. *How was dinner?*

Fine.

Euphoric, judging by your expression. I was envious.

You have your own.

Indeed, I do. Just think how much faster we'd get through him to-gether.

Zach paused, his thumb hovering over the keypad as he stared at the message.

You really shouldn't have used the same set of plates. Knocking them over like some clumsy canine? One might almost think it was by design.

Zach dropped the phone and bolted, throwing open the toilet lid and spewing a long stream of hot water, spice fragments, pulverized kale and...

He vomited again, snatched up a fistful of toilet paper to wipe his mouth clean, then bent himself over the lip of the bath, yanking on the faucet. He would never, ever stop washing his mouth. Or his hands. Maybe he could get his stomach pumped. Would he have to explain that? He could imagine the insurance paperwork. He sat slumped against the tub for what felt like hours. What time was it? Where was he again? How was this happening? Had he just eaten... He gripped the toilet seat, his stomach turning again.

He heard another ping from his phone in the bedroom, but his body refused to move. The phone pinged again. This had to be a dream. He couldn't have... No! Even if this was real, the cat had to be lying. Which was more credible: that he'd just consumed human flesh, or that his cat was lying to him through a hook-up app?

At the third ping, Zach got to his feet. He dragged himself to the bedroom and picked the device up off the bed. Three messages, all from Conway. Or the cat.

One. *That sounded like a good one.*

Two. *Don't tell me it didn't taste good.*

Three. *Alright, Zachary. We'll talk about this when you're ready.*

He flopped on his back, one arm over his head, watching a small black spider in the corner of his window busily wrap some unsuspecting insect in silk. He swallowed, ignoring the last sour strands of vomit on the back of his tongue, then closed his eyes. Whatever nightmares he might have feared, he was asleep within minutes.

Zach had heard that feeling pressure on one's chest was fairly common in times of subconscious stress. The source of countless tales of attempted daemonic possession, or an unwelcome visit from the spirit world.

This daemon smelt like last night's beef, and her whiskers tickled.

Zach turned over in his comforter, groaning as Grace Jones hopped off his chest. The cat settled herself into a heap next to his arm and began bathing her paws. He reflexively reached up and ran his fingers through the soft fur, lazily picking up his phone to check the time. Almost nine. He looked around the sunlit room, down the length of his naked torso and past his bare feet.

He sat up, heart leaping as he saw Conway's crumpled clothes, then the cat, then his phone. He breathed into his hand, recoiling at the smell of his own vomit-laced breath.

Grace Jones remained still, facing the window, her furry black head resting on outstretched front legs.

Zach closed his fingers around the phone, then hesitated. If he opened the app and saw what he expected to see, there could be no more denial. Ignoring the three or four other messages the bored, horny men of Fairview had sent him through the night, he opened

Conway's profile.

No new messages. Just Conway's headless chest and stats. He tapped the chat button before his nerves could deter him.

Alright, Zachary. We'll talk about this when you're ready.

He turned to look at the snoozing cat. It had happened. All of it.

A hot shower did nothing to soothe the knowledge that he'd eaten human flesh, however unwittingly. Nothing about the how and why, the stupid mix-up with the bowls, or his failure to tell the difference seemed to matter. He'd still willingly cooked the stuff. And he'd liked it. That part disturbed the hell out of him.

He turned off the water and leaned against the wall. He couldn't do this, whatever game his cat wanted to play. He'd hire a car, bag all of Conway's remains, put them in the trunk, and find a place to hide the body.

Except, where the hell would he hide a body?

And where was Conway's phone?

Fuck!

Zach jumped as a small meow broke his solitude. He turned to see Grace Jones licking her paws. The cat looked at him, then stalked off down the hall, black tail flicking from side to side. The view of the swishing, departing cat butt sent a strange, sinking weight to the pit of his stomach. He'd never find that damn phone, and now he'd offered the cat its sacrifice, he couldn't exactly withdraw it.

Damn it, Grace Jones was a cat, not some selfish, bloodthirsty god!

He tried to breathe. Not since he'd seen Conway's damn video had a simple, five-second intake and outshot of breath felt so difficult. But it was a start. He took another, then one more, then started a mental list of all the places Conway's phone could be. There were plenty of dark spots in the basement, but the door had been closed since he'd sealed Conway's makeshift tomb. Not cat friendly. Then, there was his parents' room and bathroom, the spare bedroom, his own room, the living room, kitchen, the entryway, his Dad's office, Mom's office... Could a closet be left open somewhere? Could Grace Jones open cupboards? Maybe, if the doors were light enough.

Step one, put on pants.

Step two, search each possible hiding place. He checked behind curtains, under furniture, inside any low set cupboards, any book-shelves the cat could reach, any light drawers a cat could nudge open. Was he giving her too much credit? No, because his two-hour search had covered every room twice, and he still hadn't found the damn thing. He'd even checked outside. Nada. Zip. Fuck!

Another faint meow, this time from the kitchen.

Zach dried himself off and padded out to see Grace Jones judg-ing her food bowl and finding it wanting. Little shit had a nerve. A quiet rumbling in his own stomach reminded him he'd brought up most of dinner. He took the large box of cereal from the top shelf and opened the cupboard where he'd stashed what little kibble re-mained.

Grace Jones' meowing sharpened into a hiss.

Zach swallowed, wondering if he'd ever quite get the scent of cat vomit out of his shoes.

He put the kibble away, instead setting the small pan he'd used to fry up Conway the night before on the stove. Alright, you sick little bastard. At least there was no confusing it for cereal.

It wasn't until the third or fourth episode of *Star Trek* that Zach managed to focus, forgetting his predicament for one blissful moment. He'd managed to keep the cereal down, drowning it with five big cups of coffee, which wasn't doing a hell of a lot to calm his nerves. He'd even received the odd message, mostly from horny and curious work-at-home types, none of whom he'd responded to.

Hey man. U host?

Like hell. That's where he was. Hell. All he'd wanted was six blissful weeks in flesh town to get over his ex before returning to Toronto, ready to throw a fresh start in Yves' smug, too-hip-for-thou face. Now, 190 pounds of lean flesh was exactly his problem. Another ping. The real house husbands of Fairview were restless today.

Lovely breakfast today, Zachary. Thank you.

He paused the episode and read the message. Grace Jones had remained out of sight and silent all morning. Now she wanted to compliment Zach on his cooking?

No more until tonight. He sent back.

Are you calling me a glutton? Of course, if you shared the kill, we could dispose of him faster.

Zach wanted to hurl his phone at the couch. *Forget it.*

You liked it. What difference will it make, besides lessening your problem, piece by piece?

Zach couldn't believe he was arguing this. *Assuming, just for a second, that I had ANY desire to do that, what the hell would I do with the rest? Bones? Hair? Skin? Have you thought about that? Even if I feed you what you want, we've still got a body on our hands.*

Technicality, Zachary. You have a body on YOUR hands. You're missing the point, however.

What's that? I've had enough of your games.

And you'd hate for me to have had enough of your tone.

Zach paused, re-reading the message. *Did you just threaten me?*

Should I? I'm sure I can find one of Conway's dick pics in here somewhere.

How do you even know about that? The wait made Zach regret asking the question, but not as much as the eventual— *JESUS! FINE! YOU MADE YOUR POINT.*

Not a 'small' man, was he? Did you cut it off? I didn't see.

I'm turning this off.

Not if you want your bed to stay dry. We're getting off the point, Zachary.

Which is what?

Get it? 'Point?'

Zach swallowed. One more look at Conway's torso pic was going to make him sick. *Why are you doing this?*

A full minute passed before he got any response. *An explanation in terms you'd understand would be difficult, Zachary. Let's just say our goals and hopes for the summer are not so far apart.*

Hopes for the summer? The only hope Zach had now was to get rid of Conway's corpse and never hear or speak of it again.

Don't be coy. You've been hurt. I know why you wanted this summer in Fairview to be one long orgy.

Well, that's not gonna happen now, is it?

Another pause made him nervous. Was the cat just fucking with him? What the hell did Grace Jones know about Yves?

Ping. *I'll make you a deal, Zachary. You eat one more piece. Just one. Follow the instructions I give you, pour yourself a nice glass of red wine, swallow it all, and sleep it off. No arguing. No puking. Then, perhaps your fragile mind will understand.*

Fragile mind? *Not happening. That's a person in there!*

Not anymore.

Forget it!

One piece, Zachary. One measly little piece.

He swallowed again as a recipe landed in the next message. One little piece, to know what this was all about? No way. It was crazy. As crazy as talking with his cat on a hook-up app. He stared at the recipe. It all seemed so… normal. Like any old easy recipe he might look up online and throw together, except for one small substitution in the meat. He looked up in time to see Grace Jones slink her way into the living room, rubbing herself against the door frame as she went. Zach frowned. Something was different about the cat's body, or maybe her fur. It seemed thicker, somehow. Full and shiny. Healthier than the skinny animal he'd found when he'd first arrived home.

The creature jumped up into his lap, pushing her head into his palm for petting. Hell, her coat *was* thicker. Not luxuriant by any means, but the wispy dryness he'd felt was gone, and she definitely wasn't shedding now. She seemed heavier, too, even more content.

After just one meal? No matter how malnourished she'd been, this was impossible.

"Meow?"

Fine, you sick little bastard. Just one more.

Zach stared at the perfectly seared cut of beef-looking, pork-smelling meat on his plate, lightly seasoned with butter and a little fresh basil, a fresh bowl of sautéed mushrooms and an aromatic glass

45

of pinot noir off to one side. Maybe apple sauce would have been better with that slight pork-like flavor, but no earthly force was going to make him Google that shit.

Before this train of thought could derail, Zach cut a piece off and popped it into his mouth, chewing slowly. The meat fell apart in a few delicate bites, releasing the sweet juices over his tongue, just as it had before. Just as tender. Just as delicious. He cut off another piece and speared his fork into some mushrooms. Even better this time. The wine barely seemed necessary. He finished the meal in minutes.

He stared at his empty plate. What was he waiting for? The revulsion he'd felt the first time? The disgust and horror that had come with realizing Conway's flesh had passed his lips? He dislodged a morsel of meat from between his teeth with his tongue. It melted almost immediately; every bit as tender as the rest of the meal.

Zach put his plate in the dishwasher before taking his wine into the living room. He sat on the couch and drank slowly.

He'd done it, knowingly this time. And he'd liked it.

He frowned as Grace Jones sauntered into the room, one paw in front of the other, stalking toward him. His mouth hung open in empty protest as the cat jumped onto his lap, padded around in several circles and flopped down.

Zach pushed one hand through the animal's fur while the other raised the wine to his lips. In a way, it could have made sense. He'd always believed cats to be among the smartest creatures and Grace Jones especially so. An animal didn't reach those heights of adoration—worship—without being seriously cagey. And once a cat had learned to read, where was the limit?

Grace Jones had promised Zach he'd understand once he ate another piece. Understand what, exactly? He'd done everything in his power to forget that the same muscle that so tantalized his tongue had also raised his dick to attention the moment Conway had lifted his shirt.

Of course, his adolescent body had responded to Conway well before that. That first time Zach had seen Conway in the locker room, or even in the hall, before the asshole had locked on to the fat, pimply kid as an all too easy target. This hadn't stopped Conway from becoming Zach's first masturbatory fantasy, or an ongoing one. Some sick, perhaps weak part of his imagination had always managed to block those callous sneers, that jeering voice, and those ever-present taunts of 'Fat Sack' long enough to imagine Conway standing silent and naked for his pleasure. Only that fucking video had sealed the tomb on his fantasy, and even then, one look at Conway's adult body had cracked it wide open.

Zach was sure he'd read somewhere that the chances of being eaten by an animal predator were a lot slimmer than most people thought. Humans simply tasted like garbage. All the junk and additives put through their bodies made them a tough sell to the average carnivore. Until first blood, that was. Once a predator had tasted its first human kill, they became a problem. Humanity. Gross, yet addictive. Nature's fast food. But Conway hadn't tasted gross. Just the opposite. Or perhaps Grace Jones had known just how to cook him?

Insane. There was no part of this that wasn't insane.

Zach flipped through the options on his watchlist for the fourth time, regretting his penchant for horror movies.

Dark.

Still dark.

Way too dark.

Fucking morose.

Having lost his appetite for grisly cinema, he flipped over to some wildlife channel in time to catch an image of four blood-streaked lions dismembering the insides of a zebra carcass. He flipped the channel again, to a fascinating documentary detailing the funerary rites of Brazil's Wari' people, who until the 1960s had honored their dead by devouring their rancid—

He shut off the TV.

Grace Jones turned over in her sleep on the opposite couch, tucking her nose under a paw before light snoring resumed.

In some odd attempt to distract himself, he opened the app. Seventeen new messages, not counting the 'hot clicks' that signified interest from the lazy. The perks of being fresh meat in town. He grimaced, forcing the thought away as he scrolled through his admirers. Three with no face pic? Ignore. Two nasty tops? Not a chance. What was he thinking? He wasn't going to fuck his way through this. He couldn't delete the app either. Not when it was his only channel of communication with Grace Jones, his sole expert on corpse disposal.

After spring cleaning such scintillating pickup lines as *'sup?'* from his inbox, he found a handful of new messages from 'Conway,' aka Grace Jones.

One more piece, she'd said. A cryptic offer, in exchange for what?

I know this is going to take you some time, Zachary. I can be patient.

He rolled his eyes. Patronizing little fucker.

Understand, this is merely a solution to a problem, not a permanent lifestyle change.

Zach put his phone down on the armrest and his face in his

hands. When he looked up, Grace Jones was staring back at him, tail and gaze both unflinching, bright eyes challenging his resentment.

"No," he said.

Enough of this. All of it. Tomorrow, he'd get rid of Conway's body. Tomorrow, he'd rent a car, drive as far up the interstate, then down as many back roads as he had to before he found a spot out in the woods someplace, where a decaying body could nourish a nice clump of trees. Or maybe, if he wasn't able to bury it deep enough, it'd be ripped apart by predators. This seemed the kind of 'manly' end Conway would have appreciated.

But if human forces found the body? What would they piece together from finding a missing jogger so far from his supposed route? A dismembered one at that. If Zach remembered right, three days had to pass for Conway to be officially considered missing. But all hell could break loose in a small place like Fairview in three days, especially if Cheryl Conway decided to raise it. Maybe dumping the body closer to town would be better, if he could find somewhere quiet enough.

Conway hadn't wanted to blab about their hook-up any more than Zach. The only bit of evidence to link them was Conway's phone. When he did bury the guy, he'd have to bury that as well. If he ever found it.

He gave the cat a sarcastic snarl that was returned in kind, and went to bed.

It was the knocking Zach noticed first. The loud knocking of wooden poles on a stone floor. He opened his eyes to see four women dressed in white, each more statuesque than the last, striking the ground with the ends of their staves. The first almost seemed to float, peering at him from under a fringe of long white hair that obscured her features, while the second regarded him with a mischievous smile. Elegant tattooed dots decorated this one's face, from the outer corners of her eyes down to her neck. The third woman's head was shaved completely to the scalp, and a thick silver chain hung around her long neck. The last stood several inches taller than the others, long red hair flowing over her shoulders. Her face untouched by makeup, she regarded him with kindly fascination.

Crack! The poles came down again.

Camphor smoke singed his nose as the last woman turned her back. Zach heard drumming in some nearby room. Then, the high, wordless singing of unseen sopranos, followed by... cats? Not the meowing of domestic felines demanding tinned sacrifice, but the gentle skittering of wild paws and sharp claws on the stone floor. Dozens and dozens of them. Zach watched as they surrounded the women, who kept up their steady rhythm in perfect unison. Several cats rubbed against the white-haired woman's ankles, but got no response.

The chiming of an unseen bell joined the singing, echoing off the stone walls of the chamber. Zach shivered as he heard it. A furry tail brushed under his chin. Four men emerged, carrying a stretcher of some kind. Like the women, their appearance varied, but mother of gods! Each led with pecs like boulders, a white cloth over his loins, a golden band straining to contain each man's left calf. On the stretcher lay a shrouded body, bandaged and ready for burial.

Without losing their rhythm, the women stepped back. The muscles in each man's chest flexed, showing off nipples that looked hard enough to scratch the surrounding marble statues. Each one of those statues was a cat. Not as lively as the cat now pawing at the small bell on one of the men's calves, but stone-faced felines that commanded reverence.

He jumped as one of the live furballs screeched, earning a sharp hiss and a low growl from another. Cats scattered as the four men lowered the litter to the floor between them. With heads still bowed, the four men withdrew to the stone steps where Zach was sitting. He didn't know whether to be relieved or insulted that the two now stretched out on either side of him ignored his presence. At least they hadn't noticed the incriminating bulge in his jeans.

The man sitting closest to Zach turned his head and stared at him. Tattooed dots, like the ones he'd seen on one of the women moments before, climbed the right side of his neck, tracking up his face to the corner of his eye.

The man winked at him.

Zach wanted to die.

He turned back to the shrouded figure, only to feel the heat of the tattooed man's body as it leaned closer. Cool fingers caressed his jaw. He leapt back as the pale god's tongue brushed over his mouth. The man's smile wasn't the nasty, condescending smile he would have expected from a ten stringing along a horny five—okay, six on a good day—but a soft, good-natured smirk.

The cats swarmed the shrouded body, sniffing at it and climbing it with an agile, curious innocence.

His admirer cast a lazy glance toward the other three men as each explored his own form of carnal pleasure. The smallest of the four, who seemed younger than Zach, though his hair was the whitest among them, masturbated furiously as the broad-shouldered blond wrapped a thick arm around the shoulders of the red-headed woman and began kissing her neck. She tilted her head to welcome his affection. The man lifted his arms and put them behind his head, watching as the one who'd fixed on Zach leaned in for another kiss.

Zach recoiled instinctively, then stopped.

Resistance? Shame? Hesitation? Hadn't he spent enough of his life in that unholy trinity of shadows?

Zach threw himself onto those mountainous shoulders and speared his tongue deep between those thick lips, relishing the heat of the muscular body beneath his fingertips. He didn't know what taste he'd expected, but the man's kiss was so much sweeter. Like fresh melon, drizzled with honey and a lick of salt. When Zach broke free, the guy looked faintly stunned, even as Zach began a long trail of kisses down his throat and chest.

The tapping of the sticks grew louder, punctuating the man's moans as his body heaved at the tip of Zach's curious tongue. Feeling a gentle hand on his shoulder, Zach looked up to see the bald man, whose shoulders and chest were crisscrossed with chains. He then felt the soft hands of the youngest man slip inside his... shirt?

He was naked. Shit.

A loud crack echoed through the room, sending the cats into a meowing frenzy. The women turned to him just as the bald, chained man leaned in to claim his kiss. The tattooed man began dabbing Zach's stomach with kisses, while the young man's shock of white hair rose and fell as he pleasured Zach's cock with his mouth. The more muscular man took two of the women and walked them toward the growing orgy.

Zach shifted nervously. "Hey, um... I'm really sorry but I'm not bi—"

Another crack set the cats mewling again. Zach gripped the cool stone steps beneath his fingers as the trio approached. Positioning themselves on either side of the man who refused to relinquish his hold on Zach's dick, the women disappeared behind the shoulders of the giant who'd escorted them over. He in turn kissed the bald, chained man, then Zach's tattooed admirer. Zach shivered, knowing his turn was—

Crack! The staves again, followed by the single toll of a bell. Then came a fifth man, whose body, no less sculpted than the other four, was covered with long scars. The man's face was bandaged all over with the same material that shrouded the dead body.

The body now covered with writhing cats.

As silently as he'd entered, the man pulled a curved knife from his belt, turning his face to the two women who'd held back, content to be voyeurs. The pair turned away, taking their place on the stone steps where the orgy had begun.

The bandaged man knelt before the shrouded corpse, plunged the knife into its gut and wrenched it open.

Zach jumped as the army of cats swarmed the body once more. The tattooed man laid a hand on his shoulder. His smile made Zach feel worse. Couldn't they see the corpse being torn to shreds in front of them?

Why did he feel hungry, all of a sudden?

The figure stabbed into the body again, sending several cats scurrying as he hacked at the broken chest. Shooing away the odd curious feline with a gentleness that belied his furious cuts, the man pulled the chest apart with a crack of bone, claiming his prize.

It didn't exactly surprise Zach when the man lifted a heart from the broken and bloodied cavity. It also didn't surprise him when the cats swarmed again, ripping and clawing at the sodden bandages, devouring what remained. Even seeing Bandage Face hold the bleeding lump of flesh out to the orgy participants didn't shock him, exactly. What surprised him was that it was still beating.

He had to get out. To run as far from this *Temple of Doom* shit as possible. He wanted to cry out. To refuse. To pee, or vomit, or even come. Anything but to sit there, frozen while Bandage Face brought the grim offering closer. But no part of his body would answer. His eyes refused to close as two of the women approached the heart and bit into it. His stomach turned as the bandaged man offered the heart to each participant in turn. All claimed their piece of fruit.

Zach watched, helpless as Bandage Face held the remaining heart inches from his mouth. The man questioned Zach with a tilt of his head. Who was he to resist this gift? This divine offering?

No sooner had Zach opened his mouth to refuse it, than the piece began to break and dissolve on his tongue. He tried to spit it out, but his reflexes refused. Meat gave way to juice gave way to… he didn't know what. The thing's flavor was all wrong. Not coppery like blood, but a gentle, soft taste that wrapped around his tongue like a hug as the meat fell apart between his lips. Then, it vanished, leaving only a trace of its sweet juice. Had it slipped between his lips at all?

The tattooed man tilted Zach's jaw for another kiss as the chained man's arm encircled his naked chest. Zach tried to see the bandaged figure who'd brought the meat, but the broad-shouldered man obscured his view, even of the smaller, pale-haired youth, who Zach took to be the moist presence again around his cock. No chance of going soft now. The broad man's erection nudged his face until he could ignore it no more. The tattooed man joined him, tongues dueling over their prize.

The four women raised their voices, joined by the cats just out of view.

Again, the sticks. Crack!

Without warning, the muscular man pushed his cock deep between Zach's lips, making Zach gag before he resumed with hungry slurps. Zach diverted his attention long enough to contort himself into a long, sensual kiss with the chained guy, until Chains eased the youth out of his path to Zach's erection. He perched in place, slid down, then rocked back and forth on it in time with the hand he now slid along his own cock.

The muscular guy hoisted the young man to where he could straddle those powerful hips. He slid his erection inside the youth, who let his head fall back with an open, ecstatic cry. Zach watched the pair of them fuck just as the tattooed man kissed him again. Strong hands ran through Zach's hair. The same fruit taste sweetened his warm lips.

From the corner of his eye, Zach glimpsed a solid erection on Bandage Face. A tiny bead of precum glistened in the light of torches on the chamber's walls. Zach's tattooed admirer dabbed it with his finger and sucked it clean. Bandage Face stood, eyelessly watching Zach and his two playmates, head tilted in fascination.

Giving Zach one last kiss, the tattooed man stood to full height, gently shooing away a stray cat drawn to their warmth. He turned, standing astride Zach to face the chained man. His round ass shuddered as Chains gratefully took the newly offered cock in his mouth.

The bell tolled again.

Bandage Face turned to look beyond Chains and Tatts, who were lost to their lusts across Zach's body. He didn't seem interested in the writhing mound that was the other two men, either, instead

55

gazing between the four women, who'd continued their rhythm, undistracted by the orgy playing out on the stone steps.

Bandage Face turned again, slowly descending the steps as Chains' whimpering grew louder. With furious hands sliding along the length of his dick, Chains finally shot his load over Zach's body, freeing Tatts' cock with a loud moan. Tatts pumped himself fast until every muscle in his thick shoulders tensed and a great white stream plastered Chains' chest. Then, Tatts eased Chains away, turning around and lowering himself to kiss Zach again. Zach slid his hands across the guy's shoulders, tracing the muscles of his back and brushing the trough of his ass. The man lifted himself enough to slick Zach's cock with a thick layer of Chains' cum, before rubbing it over his hole and sliding on.

Zach let go the loudest groan he'd ever made during sex. The man rocked steadily to Zach's rhythm. Zach ignored the brush of furry tails as cats nosed around his shoulders and neck. Muscles and the youth paused their fucking long enough to see what had so aroused their companions. Each kept stroking as he looked over Zach's body.

A cat leapt across Zach's chest, leaving a thin trail of what looked like blood. Strange. The cat hadn't scratched him and the animals didn't seem mistreated. Zach grimaced as another pounced directly on his stomach. He went to shoo the creature away, only for Tatts to catch his wrist. The man shook his head solemnly, then went back to enjoying Zach's cock. Zach eased himself up until he could see the shrouded body, now little more than a few bloodied bandages, surrounded by the four women... and cats! There had to be at least fifty, maybe seventy or a hundred of them, all crawling over one another, over the four women, mewling and purring as they went, mouths

56

and fur, stained red.

Only Bandage Face stood where the body's feet had been.

Zach gasped as the man riding him clasped his chest, clawing at skin as he rocked faster on Zach's cock. Zach sneezed as another white tail passed under his nose. Panic gripped him as he stared down at the mess of bloody smudges and paw prints on his chest. Had it all come from the shrouded figure the cats had… eaten?

Zach cried out as Tatts' ass tightened around his dick.

He erupted.

He howled.

So did the cats.

A hot stream from Muscles crossed with that of his wiry young lover, showering Zach with fluid. But Tatts wasn't done. Seconds after receiving Zach's load, he let go another of his own.

Zach felt the salty splash on his lips as he collapsed against the floor. He stared at the tile mosaics on the ceiling, splashes of purple, silver, and red intercut with gold, Zach closed his eyes, feeling the firm, warm hands of Tatts massaging the spoils of lust into his skin. The whining hum of cats faded. He folded his arms up over his head, weirdly content as wisps of fur brushed his naked underarms and throat. He opened his eyes again to see Bandage Face staring down at him.

"What?" he asked Bandage Face

The man left without a word. Zach closed his eyes again, hearing a gentle purring that seemed to be coming from Tatts, who'd stayed nuzzled against his naked body. Zach leaned into the man's warmth, reaching to push his fingers through a thick shroud of dark hair. A faint hissing distracted him. Zach saw a snake's tongue flick over his hand, before two sharp fangs staked their claim on his finger.

Zach inhaled a mouthful of fluffy black tail as the bite jolted him into consciousness. The cat was perched above his head. He raised a hand to wipe the sleep from his eyes only to find his finger smeared with fresh blood. He hadn't imagined it. Grace Jones had bitten him. Bitch!

"Psst!"

She leapt off his bed and ran out. He wiped up the blood with a tissue and tried to remember where his parents kept the antiseptic ointment. Crazy cat! He pulled back the top sheet, staring at the neat wet blotch at the center of his bed.

Right. Orgy. Muscle guys. Cats everywhere. Weird women in robes serving percussion. Meat? Zach wanted to throw up again.

Ping. *Nice dream, Zachary?*

He closed Conway's profile and put the phone face down beside him. Damn it! Even nauseous, he was hard again.

Another ping. *There's a healthy glow about you.*

He snarled, ignoring the persistent hard-on and putting his gateway to the world's largest porn library down on the bed beside him. His imagination drifted to the tattooed guy, reaching arms around him, stroking his body with a smooth, steady hand… Damn it!

Ping! *They certainly knew how to gorge their appetites back then.*

Maybe he was still asleep. Still dreaming. He pinched the tip of his cock and almost climaxed. Okay, definitely not dreaming.

Ping! *There's no shame in pleasure, Zachary. Be honest with me, and perhaps with yourself?*

Zach looked down at the honest mess he'd made of his sheets. He set his phone safely on the nightstand and bundled the sheets up, then stripped off the pillowcases and tossed them into the pile, taking it all downstairs.

He had enjoyed it. His damp sheets attested to that.

Accepting that he wasn't just cracking under stress, accepting that all this was real and that he had in fact cooked and eaten... Jesus! Jesus? Take, eat, this is my... Not funny, creep. Fucking cannibal creep! That did it. Not again. No more. The cat had made her point. Besides, one piece. One! He'd kept up his end of the bargain. Enough!

As he reached the basement, he looked at the freezer. Should he check on it? Check on what, exactly? And he was still hard. How the fuck could he be hard looking at a white box with a dead guy inside it? He dumped the sheets and pillowcases into the washer and set it running.

Phone or no phone, it wasn't too late to rent a car and drive what was left of Conway out to wherever and dump it. He'd have to remember all the portions he'd cut and measured already. How much of the guy was left?

He yanked open the freezer and swallowed down the jolt of revulsion that made him want to barf. He didn't know how, but the son of a bitch's eyes were stuck open. Two orbs frozen in horror, either at knowledge of their owner's imminent demise, or at the indignity of spending his last earthly seconds at the foot of 'Fat Sack's' staircase, full of top quality 'Fat Sack' splooge.

Was Zach's DNA now perfectly preserved inside his former tormentor, frozen for future paleontologists to find? Perhaps even alien paleontologists, long after the human race had... Not fucking funny!

He couldn't think with Conway staring at him like that, looking so... dead. With a slow swallow, he reached out to close the corpse's frozen eyelids, trying not to retch as his fingers brushed the frosted flesh above Conway's eye. He tried maneuvering his fingers into the gap between the eyelid and the bony eye socket. If he could just—

Conway's eyelid gave way with a tiny snap. Zach screamed as his fingertips brushed something cold and gooey. He dropped the freezer lid and buried his face in his hands before remembering where they'd been. He pounded up the stairs to the bathroom, ran the faucet as warm as he could stand and pumped four squirts of soap, furiously scrubbing his hands before lathering up his forearms, face, neck, and chest.

Why now? Why here? Why to him? Zach leaned against the sink and tried to breathe.

He couldn't do this. No way. And feeding Conway to his cat, one bowl at a time was not going to solve his problem.

He closed his eyes again, remembering the dream. The feel of the men who'd surrounded him. The power in their arms and the heat in their bodies. The tattooed guy.

In cold reality, he'd touched a dead body. How the fuck could he still be hard? *How?* He tapped the head of it with his finger, bouncing it up and down a few times.

His face hung lax in the mirror. Accepting the insurmountable facts of his situation, he had to look at things logically. Conway was dead. Against his better judgement, he'd followed the cat's instructions and set about rearranging the body to fit the freezer.

The police report wrote itself.

Okay. Logic. Think!

He'd eaten some of Conway. Just a little, and it wasn't like he'd intended to. Pure, dumb luck had brought that first portion to his plate. How was he supposed to know what human flesh looked, tasted, or smelled like when it wasn't animated, up and moving around? It wasn't his fault he'd liked it, either! Then, the second time? Okay, he'd prepared and eaten a little, just as his cat had told him to, and it had tasted good.

Gorged their appetites... Beautiful, sculpted men, feasting upon both his cock and the flesh of the poor, shrouded bastard with all too similar hunger. Then, the women. Cold, inscrutable, and powerful.

Zach rescued a tiny bead of precum from his erection and sucked it from the tip of his finger. Food. Sex. Meat. Ambrosia. Maybe it was it all just a dumb metaphor. If so, what the fuck had he just done? Too much philosophy, not enough answers. If he was hard enough to precum, he was horny. As long as he was horny, he'd be distracted. Distracted people didn't solve problems. They caused new ones.

Bracing himself against the cistern, Zach positioned his irrepressible member over the bowl and sped up his teasing to rapid self-abuse. As much as he wanted it over, he slowed at the memory of the orgy, those hands sliding over his skin without judgement, question, or reason. Only sweet lust and hunger.

He pushed his hips back just in time to stop a hot jet of fresh splooge from splattering the toilet seat. He could deal with a few stray drops later. At that moment, he just wanted to let go. To feel the men of his dream caress his chest, shoulders, and stomach again. To feel the furry tail flip around his ankles while its owner stepped over his feet.

"Will you get the fuck out?" he barked, closing the door after Grace Jones' departing tail.

How had the cat known about his dream?

He wiped up the few stray drops of his climax, flushed the evidence, and washed his hands again before going back to a bed that now lay as bare as he was. The cat sat at the center of it, waiting for him.

He flopped onto the stripped mattress just as his phone pinged again. He checked the app. A colorful assortment of cuteish geeks, headless torsos, and at least three men old enough to be his father. One guy looked suspiciously like a neighbor Zach remembered, who used to mow his grass shirtless and never shut his dog up. Most had no picture at all.

He ignored all but one.

Zach?

He tapped the photo of the Asian guy who'd known his name. Nineteen years old and kind of geeky. At five foot eight, he was shorter than Zach usually liked, but his cute face made up for it. Zach quickly swiped through two more pictures, an awkward thirst trap selfie in front of the bathroom mirror that showed off a surprisingly wiry body, and an anime-inspired cosplay Zach didn't recognize. Okay. Nice. Now, how the hell did he know Zach?

Have we met? Zach hit send.

Amid Fairview's tacit commitment to all German-Irish-American white bread culture, Zach remembered at least two Asian girls in his home group, whose names he'd forgotten, along with Gus Huang, another one of the jocks. Zach wouldn't have minded finding Gus behind one of those blank profiles, though he was pretty sure Gus had spent most every night since graduation with at least one hot girl at his side.

It's Ben.

Ben? That's all he was getting? Just Ben? Not even 'crazy old man who lives behind the dunes waiting to impart knowledge of an ancient lost religion that could unite the galaxy' Ben?

Hi Ben. Yeah, I'm Zach.

The reply seemed to take forever. *I was two grades behind you.*

Not helping.

You were awesome in the musical that year. Jesus Christ Superstar? I was in the front row. Left side.

Thanks, I guess. Awesome? He could have been, having absolutely killed his audition, until Mr. Whittle, his economics teacher had stuck his nose into the casting committee and asked if anyone was going to buy a 'fat Judas.' The same Mr. Whittle had routinely used school time to remind his classes of the supposed immorality of two men sharing a household, and Zach had tried hard to forget both the asshole, and his eventual role as Thomas, which had seen him shuffled as far upstage as possible. *Sorry, I don't remember faces. Footlights.*

I get it. I was in Joseph.

Who'd you play? Zach hadn't seen it, but it seemed polite to ask.

Levi and the Baker. It was a while ago.

Cool. Zach stared at the face picture. No dice. He should probably have made some excuse and put the phone away.

My sister was in your show. As Mary Magdalene?

Oh! You're Britney's brother?

Yeah. I hope that's not like, weird for you.

Zach thought carefully about his next message. 'Weird' was relative. *Depends what you're looking for.* Ben's profile said friendship and chat. Nothing else. So had the profile of a guy Zach had met once in High Park, who'd answered the door wearing nothing but a goat mask. He'd learned a lesson that day. Clarity. Always.

Well, it'd be nice to hang out. I'm home all summer.

Me too. Zach thought about the long chain of no-strings dick he'd imagined would make his summer in Fairview memorable. It had begun with entirely the wrong kind of stiff. Now, he was too busy losing his mind. Alone. Talking to his cat.

He considered for a moment how absurd it would be to meet anyone now. And yet, all dreams and orgiastic visions aside, there was little he could do right here and now about Conway's body, which for the immediate future, wasn't going anywhere. Grace Jones had promised him some nebulous kind of help. Accepting that all he'd been through with the animal so far had in fact taken place, he had no reason to assume this promise was a lie. Even if it was, sitting in the house, slowly freaking out like some mythic recluse in a Shirley Jackson novel wouldn't do him a damn bit of good.

He needed to clear his head. It wasn't like he had any friends left to spend time with in Fairview, or that he'd had many to begin with. Maybe this was just what he needed. A reset. A cold focus that might give him a chance to ensure that when Conway's bloated and blackened corpse was inevitably found, it would be untraceable to the tortured boy once known to the deceased as 'Fat Sack.'

Except, he'd come in Conway.

Ping. *I guess we could see a movie or something?*

Yes! We should do that, Zach sent back. The invitation had staved off a violent fit of puking. *Anything you want to see?*

I don't know what's on. I haven't looked.

Zach tapped the edge of his phone. Was Ben expecting a date? Romance was the last complication he needed.

Sorry, came another message. *I don't know why I suggested that. I'm not a big movie guy.*

Zach caught sight of Grace Jones' tail flicking back and forth in the hall. Fuck it. He needed out of this house. To clear his head, away from the body, and the cat. *That's okay.*

You busy tonight? I could come over.

You can't host?

My parents. Got a car though. You can't host?

Zach grimaced. *Not on a first meet,* he lied.

But this isn't a hook-up. Or is it?

Good question. While Ben was cute, was a hook-up worth the effort and complication against jerking off right now? No. No sex. Not that he wasn't horny, but this was about resetting his mind. He felt bad, but until further notice, Ben was a necessary distraction. Nothing more.

So? What are we doing? Ben asked.

How to answer that? What were they supposed to do? He stared at the screen until it pinged with another message, this time from Conway. Grace Jones. Whatever. *You're hooking up. I can hear it.*

I am not.

I'm not your mother, Zachary. Go get laid.

What?

Your mother, I am not. Get laid, you will. Mmmmm!

Stop it.

Stop, or stop not.

Zach's grip around the phone tightened as he dismissed a pop-up ad. *Are you going to talk entirely in movie references?*

How else was I supposed to learn English? All you ever did was meow at me. It's patronizing, Zachary.

Hey, Zach? You there?

Zach switched the chat back to the former schoolmate hampered by omnipresent parental units. *Yeah. I'm here. Sorry.*

You want to call? Might be easier.

Zachary, go forth and claim the cock!

Will you shut up?

Huh? Hey, if you're gonna be an asshole, forget it.

Sorry, that wasn't for you, Zach tapped out quickly. *Sure, phone is good.*

Zach started to wonder if blocking Conway/Grace Jones was just asking for an endless parade of dead rodent offerings to be left on his floor… and if the peace of mind could be worth it.

Another ping from Ben, this time with a phone number. Zach copied it to his dialer before the cat could interrupt them again.

"Hello?"

"Hey. It's Zach."

"Hey. Sorry, I just thought this would be quicker."

"Sure." Zach ignored another message from the cat. "Sure thing. Good idea."

"So," Ben was polite, but tentative. "Who else were you texting?"

"Texting?"

"You told someone else to shut up? Hey, don't worry. It's none of my business."

"Oh. Nobody. Just some guy wanting sex."

"Oh, okay." Hesitation shrouded Ben's voice. "Is that what you're looking for?"

Zach swallowed. "Well—"

"I mean, it's cool. That's what your profile says. It's just not… I mean, I'm not really—"

"Do you want to get a coffee or drink somewhere?" Zach blurted out before Ben's uncertainty gave either of them a panic attack. "I don't know anybody here anymore and it'd be nice to get out."

"Uh, okay. Sure. Get out of where?"

"Huh?"

"Where in town are you?"

"Caroline Heights. I don't have a car though." Zach heard the sound of paws on carpet before Grace Jones slinked into the room, rubbing against his ankles. A show of approval? She rubbed against him one last time, then slipped out as quietly as she'd entered.

"Caroline Heights? Okay, crazy idea, but do you have gym clothes? I have a class near there this afternoon. I have some guest passes."

"I…" Oh Christ. Abort. Abort. Abort!

"Or I can pick you up after."

That said, a good workout would certainly clear his head. Moreso than sex, which he couldn't really imagine now.

"But it's fun, I promise."

Zach swore if this was CrossFit… "Sure?"

"Awesome. Text me your address?"

"Okay, sure. See you then." Hanging up, Zach tapped in his address, then hesitated. He wondered in one short moment if he should ask to meet opposite the church a block away. Or meet inside the church. Hell, if Ben's innocence was a pretense, they would need a venue if neither of them could host.

No. Bad idea. Very bad idea.

He sent the message.

Ping. *Get laid, Zachary. Get laid.*

BEN

The most paranoid corners of Zach's imagination had prepared him for every possibility from yoga, to CrossFit, to some ritual daemonic summoning. But not a cardio dance class. He'd fumbled through four songs, stiff as a board before fixing his gaze on the generously pumped thighs and biceps of the excitable instructor. This, weirdly, had helped Zach's coordination, at least until the guy had flashed his megawatt smile in the showers, catching Zach off-guard so he almost fell over Ben.

"I told you not to worry about the steps." Ben laughed as they left the gym. "All you have to do is keep moving and not crash into anybody. You had fun, right?"

"In a…" The phrase 'butch queen, first time at a ball' flashed through Zach's mind. "Yeah, I guess?"

Zach tightened his grip on his backpack, watching Ben exchange air kisses with one of the girls from the class as she went to her car.

The instructor passed them, winking at Zach.

Zach wished the instructions in class had been so obvious.

Ben unlocked the Honda Civic that had ferried them to this humiliation. "I'll just let the air run a minute. It's hot out today."

Jesus, if this whole thing was going to be stumbling through dance classes and talking about the weather while running low on caffeine, Zach would just as soon have hung out at home with the cat. "You mentioned a coffee place?"

"No, but I know this amazing juice bar. All freshly squeezed, cold press, organic. They even put a shot of wheat grass in each one for free."

Zach wanted to hurl.

"I'm kidding! Starbucks?"

"I'd rather not."

"Snob."

This was going well.

"Okay. There's only one other place I know open this late. It's in this weird alleyway. Nothing fancy, but if you still want coffee—"

"Unless you want to hit up a bar?"

"I... don't actually have ID."

This didn't surprise Zach, not that he judged. Even sneaking a beer from concessions when he'd worked at the Phoenix theater had plagued his conscience for days. "My turn to be kidding."

"Oh!" Ben laughed. "Right. Coffee it is! How long did you say you were in town?"

"Just for the summer."

Ben smiled at him as they began passing the endless rows of houses and manicured lawns, strip malls wrapped around the corners of redundantly broad streets.

"Are you sure this place is still open?" Zach asked.

Ben nodded. "Should be dead quiet too. I hope you like it. The graffiti I think is by the woman who started the place. It's really cool.

69

The seats are just boxes and none of the cutlery matches, but the coffee's awesome."

It sounded to Zach more like Kensington Market than Fairview. "Please don't turn me into that guy."

"What guy?"

"The one who comes back home to visit and can't wait to get back to the city."

"The one who sounds like every heroine in every Hallmark Christmas movie ever?"

"That one!"

Ben laughed at him. "I promise not to put you to work in anyone's failing holiday ornament shop to reconnect with true love and the Christmas spirit, okay? Besides, you're not the only one who left. Britney?"

"What about Britney?"

"USC, Los Angeles. Applied linguistics, but Mom and Dad aren't stupid. They know she's there to try and get an agent."

"Didn't she want to do stage?"

Ben offered him a half smile Zach wasn't sure he liked. "Things change."

"Well, she's hot enough for LA."

"Man, that's my sister!"

"And? I'm a big homo. What's the issue?"

Ben laughed again. "If you want a trip down memory lane, we could go by school."

"And do what? Take a census on which teachers aren't dead?"

Ben raised an eyebrow at him. "Did you really hate it that much?"

"Hate's a strong word," Zach said. "At least until… yeah."

Ben grimaced. "Right. The video. That was really awful, what hap—"

"It happened. I've dealt with it." It was the truth. He had 'dealt with it.' Not as finally as Grace Jones, fate, and gravity had, but...

He shuddered, realizing this was the first time he'd thought about Conway, or Grace Jones, or any of it since their gym class had started. Huh.

"You keep in touch with anybody online?"

"I'm really not big on the social media thing."

"Yeah, I guess that makes sense. It's just up on the left here. Ah, cool! They're still open." Ben swung the car into a small lot behind a red brick building. The bars on its windows had been slathered with a hasty coat of cream paint, betraying the Fairview Zach's parents had grown up in.

The café was a different story, looking as much a slice of Kensington Market as he'd imagined. All it needed was a few bicycles weaving in and out, two or three shopfronts each promising the city's best empanadas, a rack of vintage tie-died shirts, and the faint smell of seafood on the air. Hearing the whirr of a coffee grinder inside, Zach had to admit it did smell pretty good.

"Zach?"

The familiar voice seized the skin on the back of his neck like a mother cat denying escape to her wayward spawn. He shuddered at the metaphor, then turned to the woman sitting on a crate at one of the low tables, waving in his direction.

"Zach, is that you?" she called.

"I'll get us coffees," Ben said quickly.

"Wait a sec!" Zach watched helplessly as Ben disappeared inside.

Even oversized sunglasses couldn't disguise Beverly Maple, who beamed at him from under a tightly compressed cap of red hair. The bun she'd tied it back in made her look at least ten years older.

"H…hi. Yeah, it's me. How… how are you, Beverly?" Zach hoped she wouldn't ask if he'd had a stroke.

"Oh, I'm doing great. Just great, thanks for asking!" She beckoned him over.

For reasons that escaped him, Zach complied.

"Just been super, super, super busy, you see?" She pointed to the toddler sitting opposite her at the table, and the smaller child sitting on the lap of…

"Robert, how's it going?" Zach swallowed the bile that swelled into his throat.

"Hey! Good, man. I'm good."

Five years after the fact, Robert Bairnsley had lost none of the athleticism for which Zach remembered him. In looks, intelligence, and all-round asshole-ishness, he'd always been second tier to Conway. But fatherhood suited him, in its own weird way. Maybe, Zach thought, he'd hooked up with the wrong guy.

No, no, terrible idea!

"I had to look twice to be sure," Beverly continued. "Are you in town long?"

"Ah… No, actually. Maybe a week," Zach lied, not about to risk some random invitation to join them, or visit, or 'catch up,' however unlikely it seemed. "Just here for the week."

"That's so nice! I had to look twice, and Bobby didn't believe me. We were like 'Zach? In Fairview? Really?' We thought you'd gone to study in New Zealand or—"

"Canada."

"But here you are!"

"Here I am."

"Was that Ben you were with?"

"He's just getting us coffees." Zach saw Robert and Beverly exchange a look. "What?"

"Oh, just... it's nice seeing you both landed on your feet, is all."

"What do you mean?"

"Come on, you know. I'm sure you don't like to talk about it, which is fine. I'd feel the same."

"It?" he asked. "The video?"

"I couldn't believe he did that to you," Beverly said, a little too fast. "We absolutely refused to watch it, didn't we, hon? We couldn't. I mean, no matter what somebody's lifestyle, it's not up to us to judge. Bobby didn't speak to Alistair for a week after it happened, did you?"

"Nope." Robert looked self-satisfied as he drummed his fingers on the table. "Bro crossed a line with that one."

"Wow," Zach answered, wishing Ben would hurry up. "A week, huh?"

"Yup. Glad you're okay, man. Knew you'd bounce back. So, do you ever hear from Toby? We lost touch. I heard he got married—"

"Bobby!" Beverly snapped. "Zach doesn't want to talk about it."

"I'm not talking about it. I'm asking if—"

"No, actually," Zach said. "We weren't really friends. We just..."

The couple stared at him a moment before Beverly's smile returned. "So, you and Ben? How long's this been going on?"

"Huh? Oh! No, not me and Ben. We just reconnected."

"Hi Ben!" Robert waved as Ben returned carrying two tall takeout coffees.

"Uh, hi."

"This is a surprise," said Beverly.

"No kidding!" added Robert.

73

Zach saw the look in Ben's eyes. He had to get them out, now.

"Oh, sorry Zach! We didn't introduce you! Emma, Dustin, say hello to Mommie's friends."

The feminine child unit's anemic greeting, mumbled through a mash of peach torte only amplified Zach's dread at being called one of 'Mommie's friends.' Dustin peered up at them over the edge of a half-eaten cookie, his expression lost somewhere between 'begone, interlopers' and 'help, take me with you.'

"He's shy around new people."

"How's the dancing going, Ben?"

Robert hadn't seemed to be making fun of Ben with this question. Still, Ben had begun to shake.

"It was fun," Zach answered before Ben could collapse with quivering rage. "Really, really, fun. You should try it, Robert."

Ben stopped shaking as Beverly raised an eyebrow at her husband.

"Uh, yeah? I see the girls in the class all the time at the gym. Man, they're super into it."

"Hmmm. You're right. It is a steep learning curve." Zach hoped he sounded sarcastic enough to nix any imminent invitations. "Maybe stick to lifting those weights?"

"I mean... coordination is an important part of fitness, you know? You remember in gym class, Coach Bolan used to make us—"

"Zach, Ben, would you like to join us?" Beverly asked, gesturing to the table's one empty box crate. Was Ben supposed to sit on his lap?

"Hey, great idea!" Robert grinned. "You can tell us all about Australia!"

"Canada, and actually," he searched Ben's eyes for any half plausible explanation. "We were just going to take a drive. Bring back a few memories."

"A drive?" asked Beverly. "It's nearly dark. Oh! I've just had the best idea! Do you guys have dinner plans?"

Zach pretended not to hear. "Yeah, a drive. Maybe swing by school. See which teachers aren't dead yet. I heard some of them turned into zombies."

Ben frowned, but soon caught his cue. "Yeah, really 'not dead.'"

"Unkillable."

"Only not Mrs. Gander. I liked her."

"It's the zombie apocalypse, man," Zach said, tutting. "The Gander you knew is gone."

"She will be mourned."

Beverly stared at them.

Dustin was smiling.

"Well, sounds like you guys have your night figured out. Enjoy the drive." Robert stood up, pulled Zach tight against his barrel-shaped chest and slapped his back hard. "Bring it in, buddy! Good to see you!"

"Yeah… same," Zach choked, waving to Beverly.

She wiggled her fingers in response. "Take care, Zach. You too, Ben."

"Yeah, you too, big guy!"

"Please don't," Ben said, just in time to stop Robert's move-in for the wrap-around.

"Say bye-bye, sweetie."

Zach didn't wait to hear what cloying sendoff Beverly had taught her offspring, instead tossing them a wave before ushering Ben back to his car.

Ben's sigh of relief could have flattened half the saplings in the hastily landscaped parking lot garden. "Thanks. I hate that guy!"

"Robert? What did he do?"

"Can we talk and drive?"

Zach pulled the door shut, sipping his coffee with a loud slurp as Ben fastened his seatbelt and backed them out. They sat in silence for at least a minute while Ben took slow, careful sips of his coffee at each red light. "So... Robert?"

"Ugh! I don't know what it is about finishing high school that makes people think 'hey, everything's cool now.' Like, no, you treated me like crap for years and now you want to play the big adult and move on? Go fudge yourself."

"So... Robert treated you like crap?"

"No, it's just... Robert's that guy. The one who makes friends with all the assholes, lets them do whatever they want, then laughs about it. He never said anything to me. He never stopped them. Nothing. Then, boom. I get a message on Twitter, maybe three months ago, saying how sorry he was for how crappy he was to me in school and... What am I supposed to say to that? What?"

"So, he apologized to you? For letting his friends treat you like crap and not saying anything?"

"Now, every time I see him, which is way too often because this town is way too small, not to mention church—"

"They still go to your church? You still go to church?"

"Every time he sees me it's like 'hey, buddy, bring it in, hug it up!' No fudging thanks. Like, take the hint, jackass!"

Zach didn't know why the church thing surprised him. He didn't expect everyone he'd known in Fairview to share his velvet divorce with the divine. Maybe the divine had come back to haunt him in the form of a texting cat. Was it supernatural? Or was this an ability Grace Jones had been withholding this entire time? Jesus! Shit. No way. This was already too complicated without getting his estranged ex-savior involved.

"You heard him. 'How's the dancing, Ben?'" Ben's deep, nasal channeling of Robert's voice was eerie. "Like the asshole doesn't know I broke my foot a week before Julliard auditions."

"Oh, fuck! Ben, I'm so sorry."

"Please don't. But... thanks. You didn't know. Robert did. And every time now, it's like 'How's the dancing, Ben?' like any shot I had to go professional didn't blow up in my face."

Julliard? Shit! Zach wanted to say something comforting. Tell Ben he'd get another chance. But what the hell did he know about dance and theater schools? "You don't think Robert's just, you know, dumb?"

"What difference does that make?" Ben snapped. "Look, I don't know about Beverly, but Robert thought that video of you was hilarious. I overheard him and Alistair laughing about it one day."

Zach grimaced. He'd known it as soon as Beverly had protested her husband's outrage.

"Can we just drop it?" Ben asked. "I was enjoying spending time with you."

"Past tense, huh?"

Ben winced. "I just mean, can we not make this about Robert, or anyone else?"

"Okay, sure. You make it sound like we're on a date."

"I... I wouldn't really know anything about that."

"You've never had a boyfriend?"

"Have you?"

77

Anyone else, Zach would have called out for deflecting, but Ben seemed so on edge, his breath shallow, fingers locked around the steering wheel, Zach didn't trust him not to crash the car.

"We broke up," he answered. "Just a few weeks ago, actually."

"Fudge. I'm sorry. Hey, if you don't want to talk about him, it's okay."

"I just thought you didn't want to make this about anybody else."

"I know, but I asked if you'd had a boyfriend."

"I asked you the same thing."

"I've never had a boyfriend. You went to our school, Zach. Nobody's out. I didn't see you dating anybody." Ben's deflection game was on point.

"I was fifty pounds heavier too. Any queer guys weren't going to risk being outed for me. 'Fat Sack Zach,' remember?"

Ben shook his head. "Sorry. I don't want to bring up bad memories."

"You don't have to apologize for every question, okay? You're not in Gander's Christian Ethics class anymore."

Ben snorted on another sip of coffee. "Poor Mrs. Gander."

"Mrs. Gander!" Zach parroted, raising his coffee cup in salute. "How old must she be now?"

"I don't know. She was like the Betty White of old church ladies."

"Right, so… likely a zombie?"

Ben laughed again, and for the first time in their conversation, Zach felt comfortable. "I always thought 'queer' was kind of offensive?"

"I don't think so. You want me to run down the list? Gay, bi, questioning, sapiosexual, pansexual—"

"I guess it's just not something we talk about much at home."

Ben smiled at him. "You look great, by the way."

"Thank you."

"I mean it. You were always cute, but man, you got hot. I barely recognized your picture."

Unsure how to take this, Zach smiled back.

"It's true, isn't it? Success is the best revenge."

The word put Zach on edge again. "I try not to think about it like that."

"Why? You never wanted to get back at those guys?"

"Hey, you're the good Christian in this car."

Ben slowed to stop at a red light.

"Where are we going now?" Zach asked.

"I don't know. I'm just driving. Is that cool?"

"Totally."

"There's a nice park I know. Nobody goes there after dark. Well, I've heard it's like, you know."

"Cruisy?"

"Is that a word?"

"If you mean public sex, yeah, that's the word."

Ben took another sip of his coffee. "I didn't think guys still did that. Not with the apps."

"Can you host?"

"No."

"Neither can I. So, yeah. Guys still do that."

Ben nodded, draining the last of his coffee.

"You finished already?"

"I got a latte. Brewed coffee gives me indigestion."

Zach lifted his still mostly full cup and drank some more. "So, how do you usually meet guys? You don't go cruising?"

Ben's glare was defiant. "Why would you even think that?"

"Hey, I fucked Yves in the fire stairwell on campus once."

"Your ex?"

"Yeah."

"And he liked that?"

Zach shrugged, annoyed with himself for talking about Yves again. "He liked a lot of things. Being slapped, that kind of stuff. Like, if we had a fight, if it was really bad, we'd use sex to vent things we couldn't say."

"Oh… okay. I didn't think you were like that."

"I'm not, normally. Sometimes I just… I don't know."

Ben let out a long, slow breath as he turned off the street and drove the long road toward the empty, unlit parking lot. Zach made out the word 'Wesley' on a sign. Wesley Park? He'd passed it a hundred times growing up and never thought about it. In darkness, it seemed like a great place to get mugged.

"Have you been here before?" Zach asked.

"I park here occasionally. When I need to think."

"Just think, huh?"

Ben didn't return Zach's smile.

"That was a joke."

"I know what you meant." Ben shrugged. "You do you, but I don't think I could be into that. Sex for its own sake. Like, just to get off?"

"You're on the apps." Zach pointed out.

"To make friends. It's not like we've got gay bars here."

"Sorry. I wasn't trying to be nasty."

"Not that I'd go if we did. My parents would freak. I think they know. They just don't say it aloud. No boys in my room. No dates. They turn a blind eye. It's like this distinctly Singaporean denial."

Zach grimaced, lifting his coffee again and deciding not to ask what they'd thought about the dancing career that could have been. "No dates? That's got to make it hard."

"No pun intended?"

One spit-take later. "Dick jokes? Benjamin, I'm blushing!"

"Shut up," Ben laughed. "I don't think I'm ready for that anyway. It's not like in movies, where the impossibly hot closeted jock and the artsy loner confess their attraction and have this torrid secret affair."

"And the jock discovers he just wanted to sing and dance all along?"

"Right! And I don't want it to come out of some casual sex thing. I don't know why. I just don't think that's the kind of guy for me."

"I..." Zach began.

"Okay, I'm going to shut up because I sound like a prude."

"You don't."

"Yeah, I do. Holding out for that one magical boyfriend."

"Stop it. It's great you know what you want."

"Is it?" Ben asked. "Hard to know. I've never tried. What about you?"

"What about me?"

"How did you work out what you wanted?"

Zach looked out the window as Ben killed the motor. Where to start? Reminding Ben that his first sexual experience had been filmed and sent to half the school seemed like a mood killer. After that, there was nothing to tell until Yves. How could he explain the short journey from Yves, to breakup, to barebacking his high school bully? Forget what he'd wanted, or how he'd worked it out. What the fuck was he supposed to want now?

"I just tried different things, with different guys. I worked out what made me feel good."

"Hurting them? Like, when you guys fought?"

Zach wondered what Ben was holding back behind that nervous frown. "That was just Yves, and it was never about hurting him. Sometimes pain and control releases good feelings."

"How's pain supposed to feel good?"

Zach now realized how much time he'd spent on the other side of this equation. None. "Look, the pain's not the point. It's the trust, and the chemical rush. Most people don't know how close pleasure is to pain."

"So, it's like a drug?"

"I don't know. Maybe? I mean, your body releases natural chemicals, like dopamine."

"So, it is like a drug?"

"Except it's natural. Then there's the psychological part."

"Psychological? Don't you need a therapist or something for that?"

Zach frowned. "What are you asking, exactly?"

"Aren't they messed up? People who are into that?"

"Oh, Jesus!"

"Hey, I'm sorry! I just don't understand what people into that get out of it."

"I don't know. I just asked Yves what he didn't want, set the limit, and went from there. He whimpered. He whined. I got hard and boom. Anything else you want to know?"

Ben swallowed, staring out the window into the darkness. A paper bag with a barely visible McDonald's logo tumbled between the trees.

"I just felt my way through," Zach continued. "I didn't decide one day that this was my thing. Trial and error, you know? Learning."

"It's just... so not what I remember of you. Not what Britney remembered. She thought you were kind of uptight."

Zach grimaced. Britney had not been wrong. "I like gentle sex too. I mean, if you're curious."

Ben gave him a shy smile. "I wish we had more coffee."

"Do you want to go home?"

"No, I'm fine. And even if that was 'your thing,' it wouldn't make me think you were a bad guy."

"I'm not a bad—" Zach caught his words before they could spill into panic. "I know."

"Everybody sins, Zach."

Zach shifted uncomfortably in his seat.

"Greatest thing about God, right?" Ben continued. "Infinite love. That willingness to forgive."

"Well, a lot of his followers don't share it, so... fuck them."

"I know. What happened to you, you know, after?"

Ben's tone was too nervous for the question to just be nosy.

"When they took me out of school?" Zach asked.

Ben nodded.

"Gay conversion camp—"

"Oh no!"

"—was one option. Prep school was another. But Pastor Thomas convinced my folks that would just give me over to the demon that had sunk its claws into their precious boy, or whatever. By that, he meant an all you can suck buffet. I don't know if the conversion camp thing was too expensive or too scary for Mom and Dad. I remember someone mentioning electroshock therapy, then seeing this look on my Mom's face, like she didn't know this was a real thing. Anyway, they decided to keep me where they could see me. Home school. I lost a year out of it. They used this church program run out of Texas that wouldn't accept my science credits. Or my art credits, which even Dad thought was weird."

"That's messed up. Did they try and convert you? I mean, in other ways?"

"By the time I had Toby's cock in my mouth, I knew all I needed to know. I played the role. Virgin. Straight. Waiting for marriage. All that stuff. Even believed it for a bit. I just never gave them any reason to bring it up again. We switched churches so they didn't have to face anyone we knew."

"Right," said Ben. "I wondered about that. It was like you just disappeared."

"They said it was to protect me. Total bullshit. Then, they made me take a gap year, just to be sure. It wasn't exactly spent backpacking around Europe."

Ben shook his head, his eyes wide, unyieldingly sad.

Zach decided to change the subject. "I got a job at the Phoenix theater, so they helped me buy a car. That made things easier. You ever go?"

"To the Phoenix? No."

"I got to see everything. They mostly showed old stuff. Foreign and art films, too. I saw my first horror movies there. I used to work the late-night series. I think they still run it, if you're interested. I saw *The Texas Chainsaw Massacre* at a midnight screening last Thanksgiving—" He caught the look from Ben. "Just an idea."

"But you seriously never met other guys? Not on the apps? You had a car."

Zach shook his head. "Man, they'd check my phone. I kept my

search history clean, but any apps or messages would have finished it. No more car. No more school. It wasn't worth it. I could have movies or guys. Movies were safe. They were work."

"So, no hook ups? No dates?"

"Yves was my first."

"Do you miss him?"

"No. Kind of? I don't know. The sex. The company, maybe."

"I'm sorry. I just don't get why you'd come back here after all that."

"Hey, I didn't write my parents off. Maybe I'm making up for lost time."

Ben stared at him blankly. "So, what? You're dating guys while you're here, then leaving?"

Zach shook his head, letting his gaze drift up to the car's roof. "Honestly? I'm just looking to get off. I don't mean… You're a real nice guy. I don't want you to feel bad, or obligated or anything. But that's all I really want to do. With my parents away, I thought I could have a big, long summer full of sex and—"

"I thought you couldn't host?"

Zach froze. He'd fucked up. "It got complicated."

No answer.

"If you'd rather just go home or get another coffee and drive around some more, I'm cool with that too. I was kidding about the movie."

"I'm fine. It's just, I've never actually done this before."

"Done what? Met a guy—"

"Shut up." Ben's mouth closed around Zach's. He speared his tongue inside before making a quick withdrawal.

The two of them sat there, breathing, stunned.

"That was... unexpected," Zach said.

"I'm sorry. I was like, in the moment, and if I didn't do it right then, I... I had to."

"Had to?"

Ben didn't look at him.

"How was it?"

"Okay, I guess," said Ben. "It's not my first kiss with a guy, don't worry."

"Okay. Cool. That makes me feel bett—"

"First one with tongue."

"Oh. Okay."

"I'm sorry I did it."

"Jesus. What were you scared of? That I'd say no?"

"You knew me from church. I thought it'd be weird for you."

"Hey." Zach put out a hand against his better judgement. "I just wasn't ready for it. I probably could have done better."

Ben eyed his hand, finally taking it like some damp treasure map he might break. Zach leaned across half the space between them, but no closer.

No surprises. No sudden moves in a new environment.

Ben stared at him.

"If you'd rather just go home, that's okay too."

Ben dived at his face again. Zach wondered if he knew any kissing techniques besides swoop and attack. Only this time, they didn't let go. Zach's tongue, still bitter with black coffee, lapped at the hazelnut sweetness of Ben's. If Ben really had no experience exploring the hunger of another man, he was an eager student. He slid his hand along Zach's arm until he had a firm grip on Zach's bicep, then broke their kiss long enough to let out a small laugh.

86

"Different from the last time you saw me?" Zach asked.

"Yu-huh," Ben said, before getting back to enjoying the difference.

Second by second, tongue sliding over tongue, lips sealing and unsealing, hands running over each other's skin, through each other's hair. Zach smiled again as Ben's fingers brushed beneath his tank top, tentatively stroking his chest.

Ben paused, swallowing, not moving his hand from Zach's arm. "This is going to sound weird, but are you hairy?"

"I don't know. It's grown here and there, I guess."

"Could you show me?"

Zach leaned forward in his seat, pulled the tank off over his head, then leaned back to offer Ben his whole body for inspection.

Ben didn't move. He remained perfectly still, from his fingertips on Zach's arm, to the muscles in his face. Only the nervous movement of his eyes gave away his survey of Zach's body.

Zach smiled at him. "Touch, if you want."

Ben licked his lips and looked away, but Zach would be damned if he was letting him off that easy. He caught Ben's wrist just in time to stop him pulling it back, cupping Ben's hand against the inside of his thigh. This earned a faint choking sound as Ben pressed his hand flush against Zach's skin and held it there. Though he'd never quite shaken the stubborn extra bulk around his middle, Zach was proud of his legs and butt. Thick and firm, like a rugby player. Even before he'd started working out, he'd always preferred to walk wherever his feet could take him. Feeling Ben's fingertips work their way inside his shorts, Zach eased himself down a couple of inches in his seat.

Ben's eyes widened. "You're not wearing—"

Zach cut him off with another kiss. This time, Ben didn't shy away from sliding his hand across Zach's chest or down his stomach, from caressing the curve of his shoulders and the cleft of his neck, or from sliding his fingertips deeper inside Zach's shorts until they brushed—

"Sorry!" Ben yanked his hand back like Zach's dick had bitten him.

"I wouldn't have said you could if I didn't want you to."

Ben's smile was shy, but it was the most unguarded Zach had seen him all night.

"Have you even…" Zach began. "Look, it doesn't matter."

"I've never touched one that wasn't mine," Ben answered his question. "Are you already hard?"

"Are you?"

Ben nodded.

Zach looked around, quickly. No streetlights. No other cars. Just the darkness of the park in front of them, with no sign of movement in the trees. He pulled down the lip of his shorts and let his erection spring free.

Ben's smile gave way to surprise. "Holy shit!"

Zach was only average, but he was happy to let Ben see what he wanted to see.

Ben reached out a hand and pushed the tips of his fingers through the hairs on Zach's chest.

Zach closed his eyes and breathed deep, enjoying Ben's curiosity. Feeling the other hand wrap around his thigh, he turned his head, ready to accept another kiss. He wasn't ready for Ben's lips around the tip of his cock, or for Ben to dive as deep as his surprisingly flexible jaw could take him. Opening his eyes, he barely felt Ben's hand slide down his torso to help guide things home. "Easy, easy."

"I'm sorry." Ben abruptly raised his head. "Was that not good?"

"Just... unexpected." He rubbed Ben's shoulder. "How's it feel to you?"

With another smile, Ben returned to his task. He was clumsy and could have sucked a little harder. The best effort of a first timer who'd learned everything he knew about gay sex from porn. But that was fine. Zach wasn't about to micromanage a nervous man's first attempted blow job. Little by little, Ben began to explore, his confidence growing until he figured out how to use his tongue.

Holy. Mother. Of...

Zach gasped, his head pitching forward. This time, Ben didn't slow down, head diving repeatedly, mapping Zach's cock with his tongue until he found his way under the lip of Zach's head and teased his slit.

"Hey, slow do—oh shit!" A deep groan escaped him as he rewarded Ben's efforts with a powerful stream of ejaculate. He tensed as several more spurts followed, bracing for Ben to pull away. The last thing he needed was to mess up Ben's car.

Ben, however, would not be denied his prize. That first taste seemed to have reminded him that the term 'cocksucker,' did imply some activation of the oral vacuum submerged beneath his virgin persona.

Zach choked down his cries as Ben gulped down each spurt. Even with the last drops spent, Ben refused to let Zach's cock slip from his mouth, even as it softened with relief. At last, Ben released him and sat up, satisfied nothing had gone to waste. Was this really Ben's first time? Now that he'd blown and could think straight, Zach wasn't too sure of that. Did it matter? Not a damn bit. "You've got a weapon there!"

"A weapon?"

"A natural talent."

Ben swallowed, his mouth flat as he stared straight ahead. "Thanks."

A pair of headlight beams sliced into the darkness as a police car turned onto the road leading into the park. Zach watched them prowl the darkness, knowing guys like he and Ben were their prey.

"We should go," he said, pulling up his shorts and slipping his tank back on.

Ben nodded and turned the key, startling as his own headlights revealed the slim figure of a man, leaning against a tree.

"Jesus," Zach muttered. "Are you okay?"

"Yeah." Ben let out a breath. "What the fudge?"

Zach squinted to get a better look at the blond stranger. A loose white tank top hung from the man's shoulders. Colorful tattoos decorated his exposed arms, one of which lifted a cigarette to a pouty smirk that crossed a weirdly handsome face.

The face stared right back at Zach.

"You know that guy?" Ben asked.

Zach shook his head, wondering how they'd not seen the glow of a cigarette in the dark. He watched the stranger, who continued to smoke until the lights of the police car sliced across him. The man turned towards the cops before extinguishing his cigarette against the tree and disappearing behind it.

"We should go," said Ben.

"Good idea." Zach put a hand on Ben's knee as they pulled out, getting a wary glance in response. Eventually, he took the hand away. "How are you feeling?"

Ben swallowed, nodding slowly. "I'm okay."

"You sure?" Zach asked.

The car crawled in the direction of Zach's house.

"Yeah. That was just weird."

"It's just some guy looking for a bit of fun," Zach assured him. "I meant… you know. The rest of it."

"What we did?"

"Yeah. Did you like it?"

"You're really hot," Ben got out, nodding. "But we can't do that again."

"Okay, why not?" Not that Zach had been planning on it.

"I don't know. I'm sorry."

"Enough with the apologies, damn it."

"I wasn't totally honest with you, okay? That wasn't my first time."

"I see," said Zach, getting a vibe that this wasn't the time to call 'no shit.'

"Do you still have a personal relationship with Jesus, Zach?"

Oooooh fuck. Fuck. Fuck. Abort. Abort. How far from home were they? Would it be weird if he asked Ben to pull over and let him walk the rest of the way?

"We amicably parted ways on account of his fan club," Zach said. "No offense."

"It's a sin though, what we just did."

Yup. Sure. And Ben had loved it, no matter how many veils of Christ he tried to hide behind.

"We're not going to agree on that," Zach said, trying to be tactful.

"Is that why you lied to me? Are you ashamed?"

"No! I mean, yeah, I guess? That's not why I lied. You were my third. That's if you count the second guy. I don't know. We jerked off

91

in the restrooms at Burger King."

Romance, thought Zach. "And the first one?"

Ben sighed. "Senior leadership camp. One of the youth leaders."

"Oh, hel-lo!"

"Yeah, 'hel-lo' is right. I'd had a crush on this guy since before I had any idea what sex was."

"Anyone I know?" Zach choked. "I'm sorry. That was super—"

"It doesn't matter who it was. But one day we're on this hike, and we've got all our gear and tents and stuff with us, and it's pouring down with rain. I'm short, so I'm falling behind. This guy, he's talking to me the whole time, sometimes making sure I'm okay, but usually just talking. I forget that I'm struggling. He's super nice, which surprises me, because I'd always heard he was kind of an asshole outside church."

This didn't surprise Zach. More than a few of the pricks he'd gone to school with had used church camps as their opportunity to show what good guys they were when God was watching. Alistair Conway, for example.

"There's no way I was going to keep up with the group for another three-hour hike to the next campground, so this guy talks to the other two leaders and they decide he'll stay with me at a lower camp site. So, we pitch the tents, and when we're done, the rain's still pouring so he asks me to wait it out in his tent."

"I'll bet you hated that idea."

Ben offered him a half-hearted smile as they pulled up to a red light. "What else was I going to do? Sit in my tent alone for hours? Anyway, we mostly just talked. Played Battleship, that kind of stuff."

"Battleship? Sounds like he knew how to show a boy a fun time."

"Then, he took off his shirt. I couldn't hide it anymore. He saw how I was looking at him. He had that perfect athlete's body, just a little bit of hair."

"Okay," Zach said. This had to be the longest empty red light in history. "So, what'd he look like? Paint me a picture."

"I'm not going to tell you who he was, okay? It isn't important."

Zach relented. The light turned green. "Okay, fine. Go on. So, he had his shirt off and then what?"

"He asked me if I liked his body. If I wanted to touch it. Said if I wanted, he could teach me certain workouts and stuff. I was super skinny, more than now."

Certain workouts? Zach said nothing.

"He didn't make me do anything, okay? It wasn't like that. He never touched me. He just got naked and kind of laid there and let me touch him where I wanted. It was the first time I'd touched a guy's chest, or stomach, or ass, or cock. It was the first time I'd kissed a guy's body. I'd never really thought of that as a thing. The way he tasted just… it was like a fire started inside me. Like nothing I'd felt before. I'd wanted him for so long."

Zach nodded, suddenly queasy.

"When he shot the first of his load into my mouth—"

"So, I'm not the first guy you sucked?"

"—I pulled away and watched him shoot all over himself. It was the first time I'd ever seen another guy do that. We just looked at each other for a bit. I couldn't believe what had just happened and I'm not sure he could either. Finally, he grabbed his t-shirt and wiped his body down, stuffed it in his bag, put a fresh one on, and pulled up his pants. He looked different after that. Like, seriously nervous. He took my hand and asked me to pray with him. Said nobody could know what we'd done, but as long we confessed it to God, everything would be fine. I didn't really know what was going on, or what he thought was going on. But he was right. I mean, we'd sinned, but God's forgiveness is—"

"Oh, Jesus Christ!" Zach couldn't stand any more. "You were what, seventeen?"

"Right? I should have said no."

"Ah… no. He makes you promise to not tell anybody, and pray with him? Like you'd done something wrong? It's fucked up! Please tell me you told somebody."

"You can't tell anybody about this!" Panic sparked in Ben's eyes. "Nobody! I mean it. I'm only telling you because I think you get it."

"Get what?" Zach sighed, not knowing what else to do. "Okay. I won't say a word, but…"

Ben swallowed, eyes on the road. "Maybe I should just drive you home."

"I thought you were."

Hell. He wasn't going to change Ben's mind in the next five minutes, and the guy wasn't going to give up the identity of his… whatever. Had it been Conway? It could have even been Robert. Maybe that was the real reason Ben hated him. Zach could see the alpha jocks who volunteered for leadership camp thinking with their dicks, always ready with a 'no homo' after slapping each other's asses. A quick prayer handy to wash away the moment.

And if fresh, scared but horny meat crossed their radar? To them, it was just time, boners, and opportunity. To a guy like Ben, though? Zach knew how it felt to have one of them want you.

"Here you go," Ben said, pulling up in Zach's driveway. "Thanks for the talk."

"I guess. Thanks." Zach unclipped his seatbelt, then found himself staring at Ben's feet. It didn't feel right to just leave.

"Listen, I know it's not your thing anymore," said Ben. "But will you pray with me? Just for a minute?"

Zach rolled his eyes, making no effort to hide it.

Ben reached out a hand. "Please? It'd mean a lot."

Ugh. "O...okay, fine."

Ben grasped Zach's hand and closed his eyes. "Heavenly Father, we ask your blessing and forgiveness upon us tonight, for we have sinned—"

"Bye, Ben." Zach let go of the hand and firmly shut the car door behind him without looking back.

Inside, he slumped into the couch, trying to relax into the relief Ben's surprise blowjob had brought him, but the 'one time at camp' story had left him agitated. Annoyed. At whom, he couldn't say. He could have pushed for a name, but then what? He couldn't go to the police with hearsay, and Ben would never go to the police.

Grace Jones slinked into the room and jumped up on his lap, tickling his nose with her tail.

"What do you want?" he asked.

The cat only purred in response.

"Not coming to the phone right now, huh?"

Grace Jones hopped down and padded to the stairs leading to the basement. Could the remains of Ben's tryst of dubious consent really be laying in his mom's freezer?

The freezer. Shit.

He thought back to their conversation in the car. In the café. The class at the gym. Conway had even come up in conversation. Yet at no point had Zach felt honestly anxious about the stiff rapidly freezing in his parents' basement. It wasn't that he'd forgotten Conway was dead, or that maybe, in some vague way, he'd played some minor part in that. But the stress of being custodian to a partially dismembered cadaver had barely grazed his mind. Zach knew this, because it now turned his stomach afresh.

Strange. Not unwelcome. But strange.

He pushed himself out of the chair and followed the cat downstairs. He opened the freezer and stared at Conway's perfectly preserved face. What would he would have done in Ben's place, aged seventeen? Even covered in frost, Conway's smirk taunted him. Who was laughing now, fucker?

"Meow." Grace Jones glared at him from halfway up the stairs, black fur caught in the light, longer and shinier than he remembered, though he hadn't brushed her. The cat hopped down, weaved through his ankles and brushed herself against the freezer. Zach closed the lid. He was not about to credit human flesh as some wonder-diet for optimal feline health, but he couldn't deny what he saw. Grace Jones was benefiting from Conway's fate. Maybe everyone was, now the fucker was no longer up and around to bask in his own self-importance, making any life he touched miserable.

Zach kneeled to stroke Grace Jones' sleek, restored coat. The cat purred, pushing her head into his body until he sat on the floor beside her. The hard surface of the freezer cooled his back. His mind returned to Ben, to the brief joy of their unexpected encounter, and most of all, the sweet bliss of being able to forget his predicament for one night with a cute boy.

"Meow."

He turned his head to see Grace Jones' body extended upright, her front paws resting on the side of the freezer. She looked at him and licked her lips.

"Already?"

The cat's tongue made wet snapping sounds as she opened and closed her mouth. Zach wondered if he was passing up an opportunity to learn how to speak cat, until the moment of macabre clarity hit him. The meat. How sweet it had tasted in his dream, the state into which it had sent him and the other orgy participants. In the dream of course, he'd not eaten actual human flesh, but he couldn't dismiss the serenity and calm it had released in him, any more than he could dismiss the calm he'd felt in Ben's company.

Or had it been Ben? A couple of hours of normality? Even nostalgia? Of all the things he felt about Fairview, 'nostalgia' didn't really rank, and Ben's pervasive aura of guilt should have made him more anxious, not less. The meat couldn't have... could it?

"Meow."

Zach checked his phone, but found no new messages from Grace Jones. Not since the directive to 'go forth and claim the cock.' He wondered... of course. Battery!

A quick search of the basement turned up a box of tangled cables, and in it, a spare charger. The cat sat still, looking almost regal on the step until Zach had wrapped the cable around her body several times. Apparently satisfied, the creature sped up the stairs and out of sight. Should he follow her? At least to make sure it was the right charger? No. She wouldn't have taken it if it was wrong. If he followed, she'd only flop down on the floor and roll over, looking cute just to mock him. He wondered how she was going to plug the thing in without opposable thumbs.

Zach sat down on the stairs and waited. It seemed ridiculous. It should have been ridiculous to someone who had renounced a religion one step removed from Catholicism and its belief in transubstantiation, and even if he hadn't, Conway was sure as fuck no Messiah.

Was the tranquility of being able to forget his predicament really worth considering another plate of delicately seared bully?

He recounted the facts. One, he hadn't killed anybody. Conway had lost his balance. Zach had tried—and failed—to catch him. Ergo, he was not a murderer. Two, he had no plans to become one. The very thought of killing someone else, much less eating their flesh still turned his stomach. Good. That was a very good sign. Three, Grace Jones had set no such expectation. This would not become some weird-ass, Jeffrey Dahmer stars in *Little Shop of Horrors* scenario.

Grace Jones had also yet to steer him wrong. She'd even taught him how to cook it.

Ping.

He lifted the phone from his pocket and stared at the fresh message.

You're starting to understand.

Zach looked at the freezer, thinking of the cruel man it contained, and how long it took for rigor mortis to pass.

Where had he put the hacksaw again?

Ping. *Good work last night. I'm proud of you.*

Zach groaned and turned the phone face down. Had last night even happened? The whole conversation with Ben? Running into Beverly and Robert? The park?

He picked up the phone again and double checked his messages.

No denying it. He'd actually gone on a… date? Sort of. And he'd kept it together. They'd even had sex. This maybe had not been the best idea, but either of his own volition or as a remnant of his dream the night before, Zach had been turned on. Ben's neuroses and awkward endings aside, the night had been a success.

Ping. *He'll be much easier to dispose of now.*

Zach paused, thumbs hovering over the screen as he re-read the message. He remembered breaking down most of Conway's body, reaching some kind of peace with the idea. Something about the dream that had made sense to him. The flesh, and the peace it had brought.

Bullshit! Putting aside the strangely appealing flavor and perverse justice that would come from devouring Alistair Conway piece by piece until only the least edible fragments remained, was a single positive experience and a dubiously idealistic interpretation of a wet dream enough to embrace an act of cannibalism? Moral implications aside, there was no telling what it would do to his digestive system or other bodily functions. He'd read stories about vegetarians being poisoned by the sudden reintroduction of meat into their diets, and he was sure a quick search would find mountains of evidence supporting these rumors. Even if the meat were digestible, there was no telling what nasties Conway might have been carrying that Zach's own system just wouldn't handle. Then, there was the reason that scared him the most.

What if he couldn't stop? Had any reliable studies been conducted on the addictive qualities of human flesh? He'd read that about lions.

Forget about him. What if Grace Jones couldn't stop?

He swallowed his dread at this thought, along with the image of his cat prowling the neighborhood with a ferocious appetite for meat. Zach wasn't sure if he wanted a barf bag or a movie deal.

The Avenging Claw: A Grace Jones Tail

The Iron-Clawed Chef with a Taste for Vengeance

I Just Wanted to Hook-Up, But My Cat Craves Human Flesh!

He imagined the poster art for this last one in finest B-movie style. Perhaps at the Phoenix? Double billed with *The Thing From Another...* No, *Cat People!* Or maybe something more modern, but not too modern. From the 80s maybe? *VAMP.* His Grace Jones opening for the human Grace Jones. What could be more perfect?

Are you there, Zachary?

Except, this was no movie. This was really happening, and the best solution was the quickest one. No more fucking around with different 'cuts' of Conway. No more recipes. No more cat food. He'd broken the body down. Now, it needed disposal.

Yes! He typed back. *Okay, how do we get rid of it?*

You disappoint me.

Disappoint you? I did what you asked. Now it's your turn. We need to get rid of that body, now!

I thought we were.

He bit his lower lip. *I'm not cooking any more of him.*

And I thought you liked it.

There are so many things wrong with that statement! Just tell me how to get rid of it.

No.

Zach stared at the message. *What?*

No.

Zach took a deep breath. Like it or not, he needed the cat's help, and losing his cool would leave him royally fucked. *This isn't a de-*

bate. We can't just eat him! Bad enough they'll find him in pieces.

Find him? Don't lose faith in me now, Zachary.

You said one more piece, I ate one more piece. Deal done. We're getting rid of him today!

You might be done. I'm not.

He resisted the urge to scream into the pillow. Held hostage by a fucking cat!

Ping, I thought you'd worked this out. I enjoy as much of that succulent body as possible, while you enjoy as many succulent bodies as possible.

I'M NOT KILLING ANYONE FOR YOU!!!

Don't be gauche. We have quite enough meat to get through.

Zach winced. *Even if I do this, there is no 'we' here, Grace Jones. YOU have meat to get through.*

Remind us both of your plans for this summer, without Mom and Dad here?

Zach's mind raced, his fingers drumming on the top of his phone. *To relax and have some fun.*

Exactly. As many succulent bodies as possible.

LIVING bodies, to fuck! Jesus, what is wrong with you?

There are many ways to honor the gods, Zachary. You shall have sex. I shall have meat. We each honor our gods in worship of the flesh!

His cat was certifiable. She also wasn't done.

You have fears. Doubts. Moral scruples. You think I don't know you? I on the other hand have no such inhibitions. No ugly terms like 'cannibal' to taint our worship. For me, the only risk lies in cholesterol, which I'm willing to chance at this stage of life. As for you, I can tell when you're in pain, Zachary. The cure to which you'd already committed yourself is perfect.

I'm not eating more of him!

That is your choice. I'm just telling you to GET LAID.

Zach tapped the side of his phone, confused. *You really just want me to have sex?*

Cook for me as well, of course. Paws have their shortcomings. But yes. Lots of sex, Zachary! Together, we will embark on a summer of ecstatic pleasure that will make this house the envy of all Fairview. Well, not literally. I'm not suggesting you share our secret. That would be stupid.

Obviously.

And when we've both had our fill, I'll attend to this little predicament in which you find yourself.

Why only then? Damn it, there's a body in the freezer NOW!

Exactly. In the freezer, where you can keep an eye on it. It's not going anywhere. It's not about to rot or trouble the neighbors. You're not about to invite anyone down there, and that man made sure nobody knew his whereabouts. His cowardice is your salvation. On the other hand, what do you suppose will happen if you dump the body now, giving the police weeks to find it, while you're still here?

I could dump it and leave. Change my flight.

Because that's not suspicious at all. And what would you do with me?

Zach's thoughts darkened. It was a lot of faith to put in a cat, and no cat, no matter how smart, no matter how radiantly recharged by whatever unknown power lay in succulent morsels of Conway, would survive a good strong twist— His stomach turned. No matter how desperate he got, no way could he hurt Grace Jones. *The neighbors can feed you.*

BARF Stick to the plan, Zachary. I'll get us out of this.

102

He paused before typing another reply. *You have no idea how to dispose of that body, do you?*

I have more experience of such things than you.

Unbelievable!

Zachary, I'm doing the hard work here. You just have to keep cutting, feeding, and fucking. Can you manage that? For six short weeks? Can you?

I still don't get why it matters to you that I keep having sex.

I don't need your understanding, just your orgasms. Keep. Fucking. Fine.

And no more angsty church boys, please. Shame is such a waste of emotion.

Zach snorted. *Ben's an old friend. Be nice.*

Even so, that Canadian ex of yours turned you into a slut, Zachary. Use that lovely, newly buffed body of yours and find men on your own level.

Newly buffed? He didn't need feline sarcasm on top of everything else.

He heard paws skittering down the hall, announcing an excited black streak that weaved in and out of his naked legs as he rose from the bed. The cat meowed expectantly.

"You can wait." He staggered his way to the bathroom. He needed to piss. He needed more sleep. He needed… Fuck! He couldn't be horny again? One need at a time, Zach. One need at a time.

Taking care of the first, he flushed, then stared at his face in the mirror, exhausted and definitely thinner, but not sickly. He turned his head in the light, then stood up straight and turned the rest of his body. His color was healthy, but his hips… He pinched the skin where his love handles should have been. The last evidence of the weight he'd lost over his Toronto school year was gone. He squinted at his slightly flatter stomach. Were those abs? Not big ones, by any means. No more than a faint outline where a six pack might have begun. But the outline was there. He lightly prodded at his chest, taking a short breath as instead of the expected flab, his fingers pressed into thin, but undeniable pecs. He lifted an arm to find that the bat wings that had long denied him definition had flown the building. In their place, modestly defined triceps. He turned around, looking over his shoulder to see clear, firm delineation between his legs and his butt.

Had Ben seen what he was seeing?

"Meow?"

His breath quickened as he steadied himself against the sink. Could it be a joke? A cruel trick of his caffeine-deprived mind? He didn't see how. He opened the door, scooped the animal up and cradled her against his chest.

The evidence of his own eyes.

Zach gave the cat a gentle scratch behind the ears, earning a cozy purr. "Let's get you some breakfast."

CASCADE

For the next four days, the chirping notifications of Zach's phone proved easier to ignore than the look of faint disappointment in his cat's eyes. He was in no headspace to answer blunt requests for his physical measurements, sexual preferences, or thirsty photos. He'd kept Grace Jones happy, devoting his spare time to researching and trying new recipes. Researching the best ways to season and cook human flesh without actually researching how to cook human flesh had proven more difficult than he'd hoped. By the afternoon of day two, he'd finally brought himself to look up what it was meant to taste like, just to make sure his own impression hadn't misled him. It had not. 'Looks like beef, tastes like pork,' was the consensus. Beef and pork, he could cook.

Certain he was now on an FBI watchlist, he'd set to work. Grace Jones had sent him the odd message thanking him for the graduation to slightly more sophisticated recipes, and offering occasional feed-back. But she'd said nothing about his self-imposed chastity. Maybe his continued sexual indulgence was less vital than she'd claimed, though she had boasted to him of her patience.

There was one significant drawback to the plan. He had never been so horny. When he hadn't been cooking, or reading about cooking, he'd masturbated. Or thought about it. Or thought about it while he read about cooking, a combination he didn't care to psychoanalyze. The dreams hadn't helped. They were always a variation on those men carrying the shrouded figure. Always an orgy with Zach at its center. Each dream left him insatiable. Even so, squeamishness over his newfound culinary endeavors had left him too nervous to see who might be eager to take care of his ever-present woody. He'd lasted his whole gap year. He'd last six weeks.

He caved on day five.

Three new messages made it clear that *NuQueerGoth* wasn't so easily deterred. Zach scanned the crucial info. 38 years old, which judging by the face pic, looked like it could be trusted. Five foot eleven, 174 pounds. He glanced at the pic again, focusing on the thoughtful pout that broke from the center of a dark, neatly trimmed beard. The waves of long, parted hair had just begun to thin. Ray-Bans cut across the middle of a face too young to be keeping the 80s alive.

Then again, Zach was the one who'd named a cat Grace Jones.

Hey, read the message.

Original start.

Cute pic.

Bored now.

I'm Cascade.

Zach slapped the phone back down on the nightstand and rolled over until it buzzed again.

Guess you're asleep.

Cute or not, it was too early for a barrage of one, two, or three-word messages.

Anyway, your fringe under the bisexual lighting in your pic makes you look like some kind of Gregg Araki fever dream. If that means anything to you, we should grab a drink.

Zach re-read the message three times before answering. *Hi.* Great start, idiot.

Hey. This with a smiley face.

Zach didn't know if 'Cascade' was mocking him. *Araki, huh? You have my attention.* High and mighty douche tone for the win? He sent a smiley face to soften the blow, and immediately cursed himself.

Well, you don't much look like an Almodóvar or Fassbinder guy, so...

Huh?

Profile says you're a cinephile. Who's your favorite queer director? I'm curious.

Zach gently bit his lip before typing. *Why queer, specifically?*

My way of making sure you don't say Nolan, Tarantino, or Anderson, because that would be typical and boring.

Zach let out a small laugh despite himself. *John Waters.*

Liar.

You're awfully sure about that for someone who's never met me.

I'm sure because everyone says John Waters when they don't know who else to say.

Zach snorted. Rude, but true. *I like the Wachowskis.*

Matrix fanboy?

Bound is my favorite.

Sexy as hell.

Zach smiled, emboldened. *I love Almodóvar, though. A couple of Van Sant's. Some of Fassbinder.*

107

Von Kant?

Querelle.

I loved it right up to the 'his dick had shit on it' line. Call me old fashioned.

A sudden weight landed at the foot of Zach's bed. He looked up to see Grace Jones licking her paws.

Ping. *And my mood killer of the year award will arrive in six to ten business days.*

Sorry. Zach answered. *It was just the first one of his I saw.*

Well, they do say your first time stays with you.

Zach tried in vain to remember any details.

How do you feel about that drink later?

Both screen and cat stared at him with disquieting expectation. He did want to fuck. Could he play it cool with a proto-goth hottie who'd led with Gregg Araki and followed up with Fassbinder? It could have been worse. Cascade could have been one of those sick fucks who obsessed over serial killers and wanted to discuss the intimate details of—

We could catch a movie. Midnight Feast at the Phoenix is showing Silence of the Lambs.

Where was the block button?

Kidding! No cannibalism on a first date. I have a rule.

Zach swallowed, certain he could taste vomit. *I'm not really looking to date. Only in town a few weeks on school break.*

Please just want to fuck, please just want to fuck, please just want to fuck…

Under the increasingly impatient gaze of Grace Jones, Zach threw back his comforter and shooed her off the end of the bed. Soft fur brushed against his ankles as he staggered to the fridge and took out the freezer bag of fresh meat he'd diced the night before. The only meat he'd diced the night before.

Ping. *Well, I'd love someone to talk film, music or whatever with until you leave.*

Still half asleep, he washed out the French press and threw in four heaping scoops of fresh coffee. Talking about film wasn't exactly what Grace Jones had urged him to do. He switched on the kettle, then turned the pan he's been using for all delicacies a-la Conway to a medium-low heat.

Ping. *Cool, I get the hint. Enjoy your break, dude.*

Hey, he sent back quickly. Hell. Something about the guy's playful sarcasm charmed him, especially after two disasters and a four-day drought. *Sorry. I needed coffee.*

That's too much effort for me right now. I'm still in bed. Maybe you could bring me coffee?

Grace Jones peered at him from around the corner. Right. Feed cat. Feed cat... that. Zach wondered if he could write a pretty decent children's book when all this was over. From prison, if necessary. 60 Minutes loved those convict-turned-artist redemption stories, didn't they?

Not funny. So, so not funny.

Trying not to look at the contents of the freezer bag, he brought up Cascade's photo again. *If you can get out of bed, I'll buy you one.*

Now, that does sound like an offer. Got things to take care of today. Can you do five?

Zach searched for the nearest coffee shop that wouldn't harbor familiar faces and their offspring. He found one within a half hour walk. That would give him time to clear his head, without the tension of being trapped in a car with a potentially sexy stranger. *Five is great. How's this place sound?* He sent the link and waited, absent-mindedly running his fingertips over his bare torso as he filled the French press with hot water.

"Meow." The cat licked one of its paws, looking at him as she sauntered off.

"Right," he muttered, putting the kettle back on its cradle.

Ping! Sure. Great place! See you there at five.

Great. The lump rose in Zach's stomach again. Done. Simple. An end to his four days of celibacy. Well, probably. Maybe. Would it just be coffee this time?

He evened out the small mound of diced Conway in the pan, sprinkled in some of the mild seasoning he'd prepared—no black pepper for cats, he'd learned—and stepped away, pausing in front of the hallway mirror. No tricks. No illusions. Just his body, like he'd never seen it. Not a trace of fat or loose skin on him. A twink. An otter, maybe. What did they call a baby otter with the start of... abs?

He heard a low whine on his right.

"Alright, alright, it's coming." He returned to the kitchen and gave the meat a stir. A purring sound accompanied the swish of fur around his ankles. It felt so natural, the normal act of a healthy house cat. The Grace Jones he'd always known. He turned off the heat, letting the freshly cooked meat simmer in its juice a little longer.

"Meow?" Grace Jones licked her lips.

His bodily change made no sense, even to someone saddled with a home schooled, fundamentalist education in science. Grace Jones' transformation made no sense either. And the odd loss of anxiety about Conway's demise while he'd been with Ben? No way could that have been thanks to the small plate of Conway he'd eaten per the cat's instruction. Maybe the dreams had eased his anxiety, but they couldn't explain the sudden definition in his muscles or the loss of extra skin.

He stared at the meat as the last bubbles of fat sputtered into silence. It had tasted good. Not at all like he'd expected. It had been tender, like it was meant to melt in his mouth.

Dream. Body. Cat.

This was wrong. This was not okay.

Zach skewered a chunk of meat with his fork and slipped it between his lips. He chewed slowly, letting the soft flesh break open over his tongue. Perhaps he was imagining it, or perhaps his muscles really were relaxing, through his shoulders and down his back, until the knot in his stomach let go. Like an edible, only quicker and… less chewy.

He took what remained and tipped it into Grace Jones' dish, stroking the animal's thick fur as she claimed her prize. Trying not to think about what he'd just eaten, he returned to the mirror one more time.

Get laid, Zachary. Get laid.

The man waiting for him at the coffee shop counter wasn't wearing sunglasses. His hair was cut short, though the neatly trimmed beard remained. The only visible evidence that this man was the same one who'd called himself Cascade was the weathered black jacket Zach had seen in the tiny picture. He seemed a bit older than he had in that photo, but that might also have been the shorter hair. Zach peered closer, trying to make sure, until the man turned and waved with a smile.

"I brought my laptop in case you no-showed."

"Huh?"

"I'm kidding. You're Zach, I hope?"

"Cascade?" He hadn't meant for it to sound like a question. He put out a hand.

"Cascade. You don't have to say it. I know." He clasped Zach's hand with a warm shake. "Children of Asheville hippies, represent."

Zach paused to drink in the living proof that a man could be over thirty-five and still somehow make an eyebrow ring look hot.

"What are you having?"

"Umm..." he squinted at the jumbled list on the board. Any practical description of each beverage was buried under a colorful and profoundly undescriptive name like Honey, I'm Home, Better Latte ThaN-ever and A Chocwork Orange. "A latte, I guess."

"A latte?" Cascade repeated.

Was it rude to ask somebody you'd just met to spend five dollars on your coffee? Was Cascade even offering to pay for his coffee? Hadn't Zach offered to buy coffee?

"Sure. Would that be the regular or the Better Latte ThaN-ever?" chirped Stacey the server.

Stacey? Christ.

"What's the diff... Actually, just a regular—"

"I'll have a Better Latte ThaN-ever." Cascade turned back to him. "You've been here before, right?"

"No. But it had good reviews, so—"

"Oh! Sorry, I thought..." The man smiled at him again, his face dimpling in a way that probably should have made Zach feel stupid but didn't. "You like caramel?"

Zach nodded.

"Make that two." He smiled at Zach again. "Trust me."

"Okay… thanks. Hey, these are on me."

"Next one." The man waved his money away before pointing to one of the tables along the wall. "If you want to be useful, grab us those seats."

As Stacey prepared their drinks, Zach slid into the booth and watched Cascade bring out the bubbliest of bubbly sides in the server's personality. Whether she was actually laughing at anything Cascade said was anyone's guess. Some hipster in a topknot and flannel overshirt came in to order a blueberry white chocolate scone. Cascade gave Zach a smile and checked something on his phone. Zach swore he saw the guy roll his eyes right before he tucked the phone away in his pocket, accepting the drinks with the same smile that had charmed Stacey moments earlier.

"Everything okay?" Zach asked.

Cascade set one of the drinks down in front of him. "You tell me."

Zach took a sip. The instant sugar rush burned his tongue. "What is that? Pureed Care Bear?"

"Uh oh." Cascade grinned. "Stop him, before it's too late! The Sugarbear Empire will have another innocent cynic in its clutches."

"I'll risk it."

"Lord Snugglecakes thanks you for your cooperation, foolish human."

"Send His Lordship my regards, and the bill for my diabetes test."

The performative air vanished from Cascade's face as the man sipped his coffee with a smile.

"So?" Silence this early in the conversation was something Zach could not tolerate, even for Lord Snugglecakes. "What's your favorite Gregg Araki movie?"

Good natured or not, an eye roll was an eye roll. "Christ, we're not going to do this, are we?"

"Do what?"

"What's your favorite movie? Your favorite color? Your favorite season? 'Oh, mine's fall,'— because everyone says fall—and then, 'Hey, here's the pic of my foam bodysuit abs from Halloween last year. We went as superheroes, *again*.' Come on! You're a gay film major who prefers a lesbian heist thriller to *The Matrix*. You're more interesting than 'Welcome to our date. Please fill out the questionnaire.'"

"Okay, one, this is not a date." Date or not, Cascade had made Zach smile despite himself. "And two, I *didn't* ask you about your favorite movie."

"You just said—"

"I said, your favorite Araki movie. Call it my way of making sure you don't say *Star Wars* or *Lord of the Rings*, because that would be *boring*."

Cascade's burst of laughter stopped just short of sending a spray over the table between them. "Okay, okay, I deserved that. That would be *The Living End*."

"Now who's trying to be edgy?"

"Excuse me? Two guys learn they carry a death sentence nobody gives a fuck about and decide to use their last days on earth to kill the president? That's not 'edgy,' that is pure punk rock."

"I guess it is."

"What's your favorite then?"

"Of Araki's?"

"No, *Star Wars*. Yes, of Araki's! Wait, don't tell me. *Mysterious Skin*. You're into seer-ee-uss cee-neh-mah, after all. Or you could be one of those *Nowhere* hipsters. It's too early to tell."

Zach shrugged, grinning. "Actually…"

"*The Living End?*"

"I've seen it eight times."

"Hah! Wait, were you even a fetus in 1992?"

"Shut up. How old were you?"

"Don't change the subject. Tell me about your first time seeing it."

"First time? God. Queer Culture and Media class. Three weeks on New Queer Cinema, watching that, *Poison*, and *The Watermelon Woman*."

"Hot."

"Wait, you're bi?"

"No. *Watermelon Woman*'s just a wonderfully erotic film, and if you start talking about *Bound*, I'm going to come right here. So, New Queer Cinema class. Go on."

"Queer Culture and Media class," Zach corrected him. "Anyway, we listened to this one girl in class go on and on about the 'problematic' portrayal of the lesbian serial killers and—"

"Blah, blah, blah," they finished together, both smiling.

"She dropped out after *Poison*. I think she liked complaining a lot more than she liked movies." Zach was warming to the coffee. "How about you?"

"I've known the type."

"No, your first time seeing *The Living End*."

"I was in college too. UT Austin—"

"Yee-haw."

"Shuddup."

"Sorry."

"It was night one of an Araki retrospective. There were maybe three of us in the theater and I think they cancelled the rest of the screenings. But I was mesmerized. Bush Junior had just been elected, and I was going through kind of a difficult time and in Texas… it just resonated with me."

"Working out you were gay?"

"Well shit, there wasn't much to work out. I just saw that movie at the right time in the right headspace, you know? I think maybe that's how we find our favorite movies. We have a need at some point in our lives and they just find us."

"Texas, though?"

Cascade shook his head. "Just to be clear, I fell in love with Austin, not Texas. This is years before the tech guys moved in, and… Anyway, that's that. So, mister, more about you? You want to direct, or what?"

Zach shrugged, not really wanting to launch into a qualification of his degree. "Maybe. It's more like a communications degree. I might do my masters in film once I've got something a bit broader to fall back on."

"Maybe? Man, if you're planning to fall back already—"

Zach winced. "I'm not. It's just to get a solid grounding. I don't want to be making fucking fast-food commercials. Besides, Toronto's pretty good for film work. I'm optimistic."

"Sounds like you've got a plan. You want to stay in Canada, though?"

"Maybe." Zach didn't care to admit he'd not planned that far ahead.

"But you do want to make movies?"

"I guess," Zach smiled. "There's just one problem."

"What's that?"

"I hate working with people."

Cascade let out a bright, warm laugh that startled the two women arguing three tables over. He pacified them with a silent 'sorry,' and downed the last of his coffee. "Yes sir, that is indeed a problem. Remind me never to work with you."

"I didn't contact you to work."

"So, what is it you're looking for? I mean, I read your profile. I just want to hear it from you."

"I don't know. Friends? Maybe fun. Whatever comes up."

"Please don't be that guy, and *don't* be as vague as you are about your degree. *What. Are. You. Looking. For?*"

A way to dispose of Conway and piss off back to Toronto without any hassle? To continue the long, horny summer he'd planned and forget that the first object of that summer was now a lot stiffer than anticipated?

"To fuck," Zach said.

"Good answer."

"I'm just coming off a break up, so..."

"Rebound sex, huh? Good for you." Cascade picked up his spoon and scraped up a large helping of foam and caramel syrup, sliding it between his lips. "Shame is a waste of emotion."

Zach tensed, thinking of his conversation with Grace Jones. About Ben, then about what Alistair had done with Ben. Okay, maybe not Alistair, but whatever asshole had caught the kid's eye. "Or it's just pain."

Cascade dropped the spoon into his mug, not taking his eyes off

Zach. "Interesting guy, aren't you?"

"Are you asking, or complimenting?"

"You don't think you're interesting?"

"Maybe too interesting."

"Oh, well you're going to have to prove that. Sure, I've been undressing you with my eyes since you walked in, but right now I just want to dig into that brain of yours and see what's there. I mean, besides every line of *The Living End*."

"That sounds… mushy."

"You mean I'm going to want another coffee? Or maybe something stronger?" Cascade leaned across the table, his fingertips edging closer to Zach's as he lowered his voice. "You know, they have a pretty great bar here, just the other side of that curtain. It's quiet right now, but it'll be hopping in an hour."

"Ah," he gave his companion a shy smile, taking the man's word on the curtain. "I don't want to get too… you know. And I don't think you want to dig that deep."

"Well, I don't want to get too 'you know' either. Not if I'm going to drive you home later. But I would like to dig that deep."

"You don't have to drive me home. I don't live far."

"I didn't mean your home," Cascade said, another smile melting the last of Zach's resistance.

Holy fuck. He could host!

"I'll trust you to pick out an IPA," said Zach.

Cascade's smile spread into a grin. "I'll be right back."

Zach was sure 'IPA' actually stood for 'information plying agent'

and had received a hasty rebranding early in its commercial lifespan. Something about Cascade made it easy to talk. Whether it was the guy's confidence, or the fact that for all his claims about wanting to 'dig deep,' most of the conversation had stayed superficial. Only after another hour talking about movies, mutual frustrations with Fairview, and the painful extraction of details about Cascade's days in an electro-synth punk band in Austin, had the conversation drifted to family.

"No brothers or sisters here either," Cascade said, taking another sip of his beer. "I think Dad wanted them, but Mom's just... I was her golden boy, literally. I had this ridiculous long blonde hair."

"Is that what the goth phase was about?"

"No, but when I came home that day... I must have just turned sixteen." Cascade arched his fingers over his head. "Black, from root to tip. Mom freaked right the fuck out. Ever heard a New Age, holistic practitioner scream obscenities? Not pretty. I thought she was gonna shave it all off right there."

"What stopped her?"

A slight smile crept across Cascade's face. "Dad quietly reminded her that my first exposure to music had been her Roxy Music and Joy Division LPs, and that I was old enough to 'find my own path.' No paraphrasing. He said that. Besides, it wasn't long after that Columbine happened. Mom and Dad were the least of my problems."

"I don't get it."

"Right, you're a fetus."

"Shut up."

"I mean, you went through school doing active shooter drills. We didn't. Then, suddenly, because of those two psychos, every kid who was into Rammstein or Nine Inch Nails or who wore too much black, or whatever… Anyway, there were a bunch of us, so at least we could stick together. Nobody picked us out as 'dangerous loners' or whatever. Also, *The Matrix* happened, which made us the cool kids for two triumphant weeks, whatever that was worth."

"So, is that your favorite movie?"

"Are we back to this again?"

"No, wait, I got it. *The Crow*. Is it *The Crow?*"

Cascade pretended to slap him. "I wasn't a total cliché, smart ass. Anyway, your folks? Oh, okay. Don't worry. Forget I asked. I see that face."

Zach wished he could hide behind his beer. "What face?"

"That 'please go anywhere but here,' face. Noted."

"No, it's fine. They're just…" Zach glanced around the café. Satisfied it had mostly emptied out, he raised both arms, closed his eyes and began chanting. *"Jesus, Jaysus, JAY-SUS!"*

Cascade mouthed a silent apology at Stacey over Zach's shoulder. "Point taken. No shortage of those around Asheville either, or Austin, no matter how 'weird' they keep it."

"Right. So, you can imagine, their only son—"

"Begotten son."

"Begotten son, right! Only begotten son…" Zach trailed off, wondering just what point he was trying to make. At sixteen, an age when Cascade had been coloring his hair, finding his tribe and flipping the big black bird at anyone who gave him shit, Zach had continued to play the good Christian boy game, putting on more and more weight and becoming more and more miserable. Then, Conway's little prank had blown up any chance he'd had to ease off quietly.

Conway. That's why the conversation had flowed so easily, like it had with Ben, only better. Zach didn't know if it was Cascade's company, or the unholy delicacy he'd popped into his mouth that morning. But he'd been able to forget all about Grace Jones and Alistair Conway.

"Hello? You okay?"

The cool touch of Cascade's fingers on the back of his hand snapped him back to reality. "Yeah! Yeah, fine, sorry. It's complicated. I kept trying, and I don't think they ever realized just how much 'me' I pushed aside to try and please them."

"Your sexuality?"

"Oh, forget being gay. I mean the kinds of music I liked. Movies I wanted to see. Books. It's like, they live and breathe scripture. Anything cultural had to come from that. They home schooled my senior year, so I had to be creative. Sneak around a lot."

"I guess you're not out to them?"

"That, I think would finish us." Zach omitted the part about the video. Trauma sharing was more a fourth or fifth date thing, surely?

"As opposed to…?"

"Well, they weren't thrilled when I went to Canada for college, until they saw how much cheaper it was."

"Gotcha. And when did you start pushing back? Which fight? There's usually one defining fight."

Zach wasn't sure about that, but okay. "Probably the one over the cat."

"You had a cat?"

"Have." Zach told Cascade about the trip to the rescue, and the one black kitten who'd padded after him on big, clumsy feet. He told him about the argument he'd had with his mom about wanting a black cat, instead of the noisy ginger one she'd picked out. Then, when that was won, the argument with his dad about the argument with his mom. He told him about the night the kitten had run away into the rain, and how he'd spent hours finding the damn thing, and how each night after that, Grace Jones had—

"I'm sorry, what?"

"Grace Jones. That's what I called her."

"Grace Jones? Your parents refused to allow secular music in the house, and they allowed... Hold up, you're twenty-one, raised by puritans. How did you even know Grace Jones?"

Zach shrugged. "Told you I worked at the Phoenix, right?"

Cascade's eyebrow ring glinted as he tilted his head. "The start of your education in movies?"

"My first summer, they did a James Bond retrospective. *A View to a Kill* was my first shift."

"Hah! I guess it left an impression?"

"I don't think I even saw the whole thing. I'd just never seen anything like this woman."

"Awww! You named your cat after your first diva crush? That's sweet! And gay as fuck."

"Shut up. Anyway, I don't think Dad knew who Grace Jones was, and by that point, Mom and I were fighting so often... I found little ways to explore who I was. I guess naming a cat wasn't so high on the list."

"So, where is Grace Jones now?"

"At home. I couldn't take her with me to Canada." Zach tensed. Realizing his mistake, he drained the last of his beer.

"So, the Phoenix? That's great they let you work at a theater. I mean, didn't they realize that you'd be seeing—"

"Horror?"

"I was going to say European art films, but you're right, it's Fairview, hold the von Trier."

"Oh, they played some of those too. But it was the only way I got to see R or NC-17 films, so I worked the late screenings as much as possible."

"Late screenings like... *Silence of the Lambs?*"

Zach smiled. "Are you asking to extend this... date?"

"I thought we weren't using that word." Cascade grinned back. "Grab dinner on the way?"

"Sure. Know anywhere cheap that's good?"

"Checking those expectations, huh?"

"Says the guy taking me back to my first workplace, on a date."

Cascade took hold of his hand. "You're beyond adorable."

It wasn't until they'd left the café that Zach noticed he hadn't let go.

The art-deco edifice of the Phoenix Theater, unchanged for at least as long as Zach could remember, shone down on them as they approached its familiar marquee. He counted the same five lights broken around a program that proudly boasted Midnight Feast presents Silence of the Lambs. Four glass doors crossed with badly scuffed brass handles announced the entrance to Fairview's hallowed hall of retro, art, and trash cinema, while an oversized sign with DEVELOPMENT PROPOSAL blocked in ugly letters across its top betrayed the theater's imminent fate.

"You're kidding," Zach muttered, his tender nostalgia crushed.

"Enjoy it while it lasts." Carrying a fresh pizza, Cascade shouldered open the door, letting the smell of stale popcorn spill into the street. "Oh, don't worry. I'm told it will be a total homage to Fairview's greatest movie house, with posters from original screenings framed and displayed in the lobby for you to admire on your way to your fifteen-hundred-a-month, one-bedroom luxury condo."

Fifteen hundred a month? Forget rent. Nobody could pay Zach that much to live in Fairview again. With guilt and sadness, he realized this was precisely the attitude that had sealed the Phoenix's doom. "Not much of a turn-out."

"At a rep cinema in Fairview for a thirty-year-old movie? You're surprised?"

"Still..." Zach remembered it being busier than this, even when the Midnight Feast screenings had actually been at midnight.

He didn't recognize the lanky, greasy looking kid at concessions. The guy looked around Zach's age, maybe a couple of years older, but it was hard to tell through those acne scarred cheeks, oversized pout, and lifeless eyes. Zach looked at the sad mound of kernels sitting behind glass in the darkened popcorn machine.

"How's your night going?" Cascade's cheerful greeting died in mid-air, tumbling in free fall toward a row of ancient, unopened M&Ms.

"You're here for the movie." The kid's voice was as dead as his gaze, and the yellowish tint under his skin.

"Yes," Cascade agreed, his smile unfading. "We're here for the movie. At a movie theater, here to see a movie. Funny, huh?"

"It's a bad movie," the kid continued. "It's got a lot of bad things. Whores. Adulterers. Sodomy. Whores. Lots of whores."

Zach couldn't remember there being much of any of those things in *Silence of the Lambs*.

"We'll take two tickets." Cascade tossed Zach a look, reaching for his wallet.

"Let me." Zach went for his own wallet.

The kid didn't move. "I don't think you ought to be seeing this movie."

The words 'ought to' broke Zach's patience. "Can we just have the tickets with less bullshit please?"

The kid snorted, making the kind of noise Zach imagined baby seals made when they were clubbed. A whirring machine spat out two yellow tickets. The attendant yanked them free and dropped them on the counter with disdain.

Zach flipped a twenty onto the counter and picked up the butter smeared tickets by their edges.

"Excuse me, but you cannot take that in there."

Cascade looked at the offending pizza box, then back at the attendant. "Why? You selling pizza now?"

A cough in the direction of the cold, unlit popcorn machine followed. "We have a selection of premium snacks available for your movie-going enjoyment." The kid flicked a switch under the counter, bringing the machine to sputtering, tentative life.

Zach tried to pretend the black shape he saw disappear over the yellow mound wasn't a roach. He'd never taken the place up on its offer of free popcorn for staff. Now, he remembered why.

"What's your name?" Cascade asked.

"Clifton, Sir. You may call me Clifton."

"Clifton?" Cascade repeated. "We are literally the only people here. Now, whether that's a product of Fairview's gaping cultural void or your stellar sales pitch, I can't say, but I really don't think anyone cares if my friend and I have dinner while we're watching the show, do you?"

"Sir, if you do not wish to follow our regulations, you and your *friend* are more than welcome to finish your tasty pie outside."

"Okay," Cascade said, opening the box and letting the scent of fresh pepperoni and mushroom fill the lobby.

"Sir, you can't—"

"Here's what's going to happen, Clifton. We're going to abide by your *regulations*, and eat this tasty pie right here, *outside* your pristine auditorium, which I'm sure has never been stained with food stuffs, yet stands on the verge of being torn down in a gross crime of gentrification. I'm going to pick up a slice of its cheesy goodness and place it in my mouth as pornographically as possible. Hey Zach, do you want to film this?"

Zach took out his phone with a grin.

"Sir, I must ask you to either dispose of the pizza or leave."

Cascade ignored him. "Yeah, that's it. Get it all in there. Feels so good!" Anything further was mumbled through ecstatic chewing as Cascade stuffed what remained of the slice between his cheeks and worked it hungrily.

"Sir, I'm not going ask again."

"Hey, Incel reject. Is Natalie still your boss?" said Zach. "Bet she'd love to know you're trash-talking the program to customers."

"Hey, that's right. Can't imagine Natalie would look too kindly on that." A loud burp escaped Cascade. "Oh, man. That was so damn good. Zach, do you want a slice? I'm having another one. In fact, I think I'm going to try taking two at once."

"Will you both just go inside, please?" Clifton's acne scars flushed hot pink with rage.

Cascade grinned, closing the box as Zach put his phone away

and accompanied him to the theater doors. "We'll save you a slice!"

Zach heard Clifton make some off-hand remark, but he was having too much fun to care.

"Nicely handled," Cascade said. "Though my way was more fun."

"Uhuh. And what are you? Twelve?"

"Thank you."

Zach paused to admire the Phoenix from the top of the aisle, where he'd torn tickets and greeted guests before slipping into one of the ancient upholstered chairs once the house lights were down. The bronze eagles overlooking the sixth or seventh row seemed even more over the top than he remembered, and he had no clue why anyone thought putting a balcony on either side of the screen would be a good idea. It had never been a stage theater from what he knew.

A sadness washed through him. The Phoenix had been a hall of cultural emancipation. James Bond. Indiana Jones. Monty Python. *Star Wars*. Every film and filmmaker that had inspired them. Erroll Flynn and Humphrey Bogart. Lauren Bacall and Bette Davis. Hitchcock. Kurosawa. Kubrick. Bergman. Fellini. The Midnight Feast screenings. *Halloween. Night of the Living Dead. The Shining. The Wicker Man. Hellraiser.* All the weird cult stuff. John Waters and David Lynch. *Tampopo. El Topo. Phantom of the Paradise. Clue.* Movies packed with beautiful weirdos and freaks, for better or worse. *The Rules of Attraction* had almost scared him off going to college. *Liquid Sky?* Yeah, what he wouldn't have given for some unseen aliens to fly down in dinner plates and disappear a certain dead body right now. His first queer movies. Araki, Almodóvar, Van Sant, Jarman. His first *Rocky Horror Picture Show* screening, when Natalie had dressed them all as Transylvanians. He hadn't heard a word of dialogue while the full house yelled at the screen. And nothing had prepared him for a packed screening of *Showgirls*.

How had Fairview's last holdout against blockbuster monoculture turned into an empty, sad hall staffed by losers like Clifton?

"Are you coming?" Cascade asked, claiming two seats in the center of the tenth row.

Zach ran a hand over the back of his favorite corner seat before following the aroma of fresh pizza to where Cascade was waiting, taking his seat and a fat slice of pie. "Thanks. I thought we'd never get to eat."

"Don't worry. We'd probably be choking on moldy popcorn if the thirty-year-old virgin had his way. Did you recognize him?"

"Hell, no."

Cascade laughed, taking another slice of pizza as the house lights went down.

Zach caught himself staring at Cascade as the light reflecting in his piercings faded. Leftover from a 90s teen-hood perhaps, but they suited him in a weird way. "How old are you again?" Zach asked.

"You forgot?" Cascade took a bite of pizza and chewed it slowly.

"Not going to make this easy for me, are you?"

Cascade swallowed and grinned at him. "Thirty."

Knowing this was his cue to stop asking questions, Zach focused on the screen.

"Think they'll have coming attractions?" Cascade asked.

"Don't count on it."

The New World Pictures logo gave way to a couple of producer credits before...

"What the hell?"

"This is... Oh, wait, it's not..." Zach laughed as the points on the white V and M on the title VAMP dropped low and sharp like vampire teeth.

"Guess the virgin douche can't even put the right movie on." Cascade shook his head, passing the pizza box to Zach as he moved to get up. "I'd better go tell him."

"No, sit, sit, sit! I've always wanted to see this."

Cascade looked down and Zach realized he was holding Cascade's hand again.

"Okay, guy who named his cat Grace Jones." Cascade said, resuming his seat. "How have you not seen this movie?"

"We had tickets for it at the Revue a few months back, but Yves got all pissy about something and we missed it. Is it good?"

"We were shrooming when I saw it, so I don't feel qualified to give an objective opinion." Cascade sank deeper into his seat. "It's basically *From Dusk Till Dawn* with Grace Jones. What's not to like?"

"I... haven't seen *From Dusk Till—*"

Cascade gasped audibly. "Okay, this night is over."

"Sit, smart ass."

Cascade grinned at him.

Zach lifted a slice of pizza from the box and took a large bite. He'd barely refocused on the screen before feeling the warmth of Cascade lean into him. The man's head fell back, looking up at him as his mouth opened, waiting to be fed. "So not sexy."

"What do you mean, 'so not sexy?'" Cascade answered. He opened his mouth a little wider.

Zach smiled, lowering his pizza slice to where Cascade took an enormous bite. The slice sagged enough to send a piece of pepperoni flipping over its edge into the abyss between their seats.

"Okay, *that's* not sexy," Zach laughed.

"Are you serious? That was at least a seven point four. Tom Daley couldn't have done better under these conditions."

"You are trouble."

"Well, if we can't stop the assholes from tearing this place down, we can at least show them it's well loved." Cascade put the half-eaten slice aside, staring Zach in the face as the giant image of an underwear-clad Robert Rusler filled the screen. "You know how we could really piss Clifton off?"

Zach looked down at Cascade's jeans before the man's bony finger caught his chin.

"Don't be dirty," Cascade purred.

The fact that their first kiss tasted like cheap pepperoni didn't spoil it one bit. There was something adolescent, yet satisfying about making out through the opening scenes. Zach looked up as a screech of tires broke through the Phoenix's ancient speakers.

"Relax. She doesn't show up until twenty minutes in," Cascade teased him.

The familiar voice howled over an '80s back-beat when at last, the creepy strip club MC announced the arrival of 'Katrina.' But when the writhing, animalistic figure on stage turned, Zach barely recognized the woman who'd first captured his imagination fighting Roger Moore. The shock of white face paint. The bright red wig that matched her lips. The dark velvet gloves complete with cat claws. He leaned forward in his seat, transfixed as her gaze darted around the set through shiny blue contacts. Her movements were tentative, like an animal out of its home environment with nowhere to run. A lioness in clown makeup, scratching at the air, silently warning off all onlookers, including Zach.

"Cascade?" He turned to see his date asleep, fingertips still entwined with his. Zach took another bite of pizza as 'Katrina' stripped off her gloves and began unzipping her red jumpsuit. He jumped as the whole thing fell away with a clang of synths, the sleek black body of a goddess painted with white patterns that matched the throne from which she'd risen. Except for a few strategically placed metal coils, she was nude.

Zach stroked the back of Cascade's hand, but didn't wake him. He licked his lips. Grace Jones' head tilted like a predator, framed by the ridiculous wig, blue contacts staring right through him.

Zach swallowed his pizza.

"Yeah, that's it, baby!" barked a man onscreen in a trucker cap. "Lose the coils! Show us those gazungas!"

Zach had just guessed what a 'gazunga' was when the whip-like growl of a giant cat made him jump. The leering trucker's head slipped off the bloody stump of his neck. The rest of the men in the bar scurried from their seats as another low growl filled the theater. One wall of the set went dark with the sleek silhouette of a gigantic cat, right before a long streak of hot blood spattered across it. Several screams and spurts later, the film cut back to Katrina licking blood from her fingertips. One man tried to run across the front of the stage, only for a clawed, bloodied hand to spear through his chest and rip out his heart.

"Uh, is it all this intense?" Zach asked.

Cascade was still fast asleep.

The star attraction roared, stepping down from the stage. She pummeled her way down the aisle between entrail-strewn tables to where a blood-splattered Robert Rusler lay trembling in all his open-shirted '80s hotness.

Zach sat in awe as she licked the blood from his body in one extended shot. The camera zoomed in on Rusler's eyes rolling back as

131

loud purring filled the theater. Then, a long pink tongue reached in from off camera, wrapping around his chiseled jaw. The shot pulled back to reveal, not 'Katrina,' but an enormous black cat bathing him clean. Closing his eyes, Rusler pushed his body forward, allowing the jacket and shirt to fall from his shoulders as the cat kept licking.

The cat looked an awful lot like Zach's Grace Jones.

Zach put the pizza box down on the neighboring seat. Was the A/C working? He felt like he was burning up, even tugging a few times on the front of his t-shirt to get some air flow.

"Meow?"

Zach closed his eyes. He was sweating. Jesus!

The purring grew louder, almost like it was inside his head, drowning out Jones' voice and the rhythmic drumming beneath it. Zach thought he heard a soft hissing, along with a very male sigh of pleasure. Then the voice. Soft. Ethereal. "Go forth and claim the cock, Zachary."

"Hey. Are you okay?"

He turned to see Cascade's face just inches from his own. The man's breath warmed his lips, and his eyes, weary with sleep, were as inviting as they'd been at the cafe. Zach immediately knew what he wanted to do. He took Cascade's face in his hands and dove into a deep kiss.

"Do you want to have sex?" Zach asked.

"Yes."

They were gone before Clifton could give them shit about leaving half a pizza.

"Shhhh! Saffy!" Cascade cautioned the barking chocolate lab that greeted them at the door.

Zach reached for his laces only to discover that he could not take off his shoes, pet the slobbering pup, and keep kissing Cascade all at the same time, even with his hands hooked inside Cascade's belt for balance.

Yep. Balance. He totally had his hands inside Cascade's pants for balance.

"Hey, puppy!" He let the dog have a few hungry licks of his hand. "She reminds me of you."

"Shut up," Cascade laughed, pushing him against the coatrack and pulling open Zach's shorts. "She likes you. Guess I have to keep you now. Go on, blanket! Good girl."

The dog scampered out of sight, her curiosity satisfied.

"Drink?"

Zach shook his head. "I told you what I wanted."

They hadn't even discussed the movie in the car. In fact, he'd forgotten most of the details already. And damn if he wasn't trying to forget that cat.

Cascade took gentle hold of his wrist and pulled him forward. "Come on. We don't normally have guests in the bedroom, but Wade's away."

"Wade?"

"My partner."

Zach nodded, trying not to feel blindsided. "I'm honored."

The bedroom to which he'd been granted access was lit by the kind of misshapen, metallic lamps that twisted hundreds of dollars out of people at art furniture pop-ups. In a trio of tall mirrors that lined the far wall, Zach glimpsed a walkthrough wardrobe filled with business shirts, and a gleaming bathroom at its end.

"Hey."

Zach hadn't seen Cascade shuck off his t-shirt. Now, he couldn't take his eyes off the outline of the man's body, illuminated by one of those ridiculous lamps. They hadn't exchanged body pics. Cascade's slender frame hadn't been the main attraction. The tattoos, though! Even in low light, Zach could make out bundles of exposed circuitry, rendered in loving detail in small patches on Cascade's forearm, upper left chest and above his right hip. A monochromatic black rose with a small, unopened bud at its end decorated the center of his opposite flank.

"Cute flower."

"Oh," Cascade looked at the tattoo with fondness. "You like Depeche Mode? That was my first one. I'd just got my first fake ID. Thought I was so fucking edgy. But this one is my favorite."

Zach's eyes went wide as his companion turned around to reveal a gallery of monsters peering through what looked like a long gash inked into his skin. "Awesome."

"Recognize anyone?"

He swallowed, peering closer. "The one at the top looks like Jada Pinkett-Smith."

Cascade dismissed his guess with a good-humored snort. "I guess the Phoenix never showed *Nightbreed?*"

"The Clive Barker movie?"

His host nodded, turning his back toward the light to give Zach a better look. "The monsters of Midian, watching my back. Well, part of it."

Zach came in for a closer look, brushing the horns of an obsidian demon with his fingertips. "Got anything planned for the rest?"

134

Cascade straightened his shoulders with a shiver. "I like to stay open to new opportunities. Guardians who've got my back when I least expect it."

Zach slid his hands over Cascade's shoulders before wrapping them under his arms and sliding them around his chest. He kissed the demon's forehead, half expecting the thing's curled tongue to kiss him back. "Room for more monsters?"

"I wouldn't call you that."

Zach felt the hardness of Cascade's nipple between his fingertips.

The man let out a soft moan as Zach squeezed. "Okay, I take that back. You're a monster.... Oh!"

"Want me to stop?" Zach brushed a fingertip from his spare hand around the other nipple.

"Not yet. Fuck! How did you know where... Oh!"

"Staying open to new opportunities."

"Okay, smart ass." Cascade turned and pinned their bodies together, catching Zach's chin in his fingertips and his lips in a soft, uninterrupted kiss that made Zach want to push as much of his body as he could against Cascade's. The man's gentle hands glided down to the small of his back and his beard tickled Zach's neck and shoulders. "Let's see. Smart, artsy, and hotter than I should be finding any twenty-whatever year-old right now. Just who do you think you are?"

Zach wasn't about to let flattery go to his head. Cascade's eagerness, however, made him crave it. "The guy who's going to be in your bed thirty seconds from now?"

"Thirty seconds?" Cascade's beard tickled as he mauled Zach with more kisses. "You've got too much damn patience."

Zach let Cascade pull him toward the bed and work open his

shorts until they slid to the floor. He felt a pair of hands slide up the back of his thighs to his underwear, where cool fingertips slipped inside. He pushed a hand through Cascade's warm brown hair as Cascade paused long enough to look up and see his smile. Breath warmed his skin through the lycra, swelling his erection once more. He felt the dampness of Cascade's mouth against it, suckling him through his briefs until those same fingers, now warm from their teasing, rolled down his waistband and freed his sex.

Cascade didn't talk. He didn't pounce right away, either. He stared at his prize. It hung in the air barely an inch from his face, bobbing helplessly, as if confused by the delay.

Zach closed his eyes, enjoying the sensation of breath on skin. Then, the dabbing of Cascade's tongue on his balls, at the base of his cock, up around the lip of the head and over the slit, as if Cascade were testing his dick for hot spots. Nerve endings. Any gateway that might break through to that magic point deep inside his brain. The point that didn't seem reachable until Cascade wrapped the entirety of his tongue around Zach's shaft and hastily withdrew, taking care not to leave an inch of flesh unattended.

"Woah. Not too many of those," Zach warned him.

Cascade released his dick. "When was your last great blowjob?"

Zach saw no point in lying. "Four days ago."

"Not wasting time, are you? Guess that means I have to go one better?"

The eyebrow ring glinting under the dim light turned Zach on all the more.

"Not so fast. Not if I'm going to fuck you." He eased his cock away from Cascade's lips and gave the man a gentle push down onto the bed.

"You want to do that?" Cascade's long arms stretched over his head. Zach could see his tattoos in more detail now. Another pocket of broken circuitry decorated the inside of the man's upper right arm. Zach wondered if he'd feel a tingle if he licked it. "How do you like to fuck?"

Zach shrugged, making himself comfortable between Cascade's legs. "What do you like? Want me to be gentle? Or would you rather get on all fours so I can get rough?"

"I mean, PrEP? Rubbers? I'm cool either way, and there's no rush. When I said earlier you had too much patience, that was about getting *into* bed. Now we're here…"

"I don't plan on rushing anything." He mapped the slim contours of Cascade's body with kisses until he brushed the edge of a nipple with his teeth.

Cascade grinned with a shiver. "Good. Because I like how you explore me. Nobody's done that in a long time. Treated my body like it excites them."

Zach cupped his mouth around the outline of the man's collarbone, enjoying the firmness of it against his tongue in contrast to the soft smoothness of Cascade's butt, pressed against his legs. Zach was afraid to touch his dick. He couldn't bring this to an end so soon. He kissed Cascade's hand, grateful for the heat of it as it smoothed his hair and brushed his shoulders. "I'm on PrEP."

Cascade smiled, brushing Zach's fringe off his face. "Then we'd really better not hurry."

A delayed sexual awakening, combined with what he'd considered a careful sexual lifestyle that had kept intercourse to a select few men, hadn't given Zach much use for condoms. His few fuck partners had included Xavier, a Montreal trust fund brat who'd lived alone in a ritzy Bay Street condo, Yves, of course, and exactly two point four threesomes with Walker, a human puppy Yves had shown just a bit too much fondness for Zach's liking.

The 'point four' had been a rowdy evening of drunken sex that had ended with a bottle of poppers spilling on Zach's favorite pillow case before any of them had come. The industrial strength snores of the puppy had then led to Zach's self-imposed exile to the couch. But it was not until Walker had walked into the living room at 8am asking 'Zeke' if coffee was ready, that Zach had finally decided the 'dog' had to go.

A short while later, Yves had reached his own decision, to explore a world with neither puppy, nor Zach in it. The following week, Zach had caught Xavier in a lie about visiting family in Montreal for the summer when they'd run into one another on Hanlan's Beach, where Bay Street's hungriest bottom—Xavier's profile, word for word—had been forced to admit both physical and psychological defeat in the face of overuse.

After this conversation, Zach had reached a second decision, to get on PrEP, a third, to ease up on the French-Canadians, and a fourth, that a once-dreaded request to house-sit for his parents over summer would instead be his emancipation. His summer of the slut. Summer in Fairview as he'd never spent it before.

In hindsight, maybe he should have been more specific.

Then again, it was hard to argue with where fate had brought him now. He watched Cascade's monster guardians stretch and contract with each breath, as the man pushed his body back against

Zach's. He'd never had a problem staying hard inside, particularly unsheathed. And while the enhanced sensitivity of his newly liberated fuckstyle had threatened to overwhelm his early twenties libido and end things prematurely, he'd managed to hold back until Cascade was good and satisfied.

And then, oh boy...

Cascade's eyes had gone wide before rolling back in an expression of pure, blissful indulgence. With one last push, Zach had spent himself, choking Cascade's moan as he'd held on. Zach hadn't wanted to let go. He'd heard guys fantasize about spending the night with their top inside them. As the warmth of Cascade's long body stretched against his, Zach started to wonder... nah. But in that moment, it was a nice thought.

"You're thinking too much," Cascade said, carefully clenching around Zach as he maneuvered himself higher on the pillow, creasing the stem of the rose on his flank. "I can hear it."

"Just happy." A throwaway answer, with the virtue of truth.

Cascade took hold of Zach's wrists and kissed one of his hands before sliding them both along his chest. "It's been a while since I've been fucked like that. You feel..."

"What?"

"It's good, all right? Just leave it there."

"It's there as long as you want it." Zach clenched his ass muscles to make the tip of his cock throb.

"Not complaining." The smile returned to Cascade's face. "How are you doing that?"

"Ancient secret passed down through generations of tops."

"How did they teach you?"

"Like they say in top school, sometimes just a tip is enough."

"Okay, you bastard. No dad jokes during... Oh my god, what *are* you doing?"

"If I told you, I'd have to stab you."

"You seem to be doing a fine job of... Ah! Easy, stud."

Zach grinned, relaxing. "I take it Wade's a bottom?"

"Let's just say... Aww, sorry. Had to happen, I guess."

Zach couldn't say whether the mention of Cascade's partner—possibly husband—as more than an abstract concept had killed his hard-on, but he was sure it hadn't helped.

Cascade rolled over onto his back and put his arms behind his head as he looked Zach over.

"What?"

"You like your labels, don't you?"

"Not sure what you mean," Zach said, knowing damn well what Cascade meant.

"Wade. I wouldn't call him a 'bottom' exactly. He knows what he likes and doesn't like."

"Does it match up with what you like and don't like?" Zach noticed the faint dimple between Cascade's eyebrows deepen. "I'm sorry. That was super nosy."

"You called it. Something like this?" Cascade draped his arm around Zach's shoulders and kissed the bridge of his nose. "Really not his thing. He's just very... task oriented."

Yikes. Even in Zach's limited experience, he knew nobody wanted to be praised for their efficiency in bed. But he understood it. The last few times they'd had sex, had Yves just focused on the task at hand? Good job, Commander Yves. Mission accomplished. Do your part. Service guarantees orgasm.

"Hey." Cascade booped the end of Zach's nose. "Still with me?"

"Yeah, I'm totally with you."

"Good." Cascade squeezed his shoulders. "Because you are making me talk about someone else in bed like an asshole and that ends right now."

"Hey!" Zach laughed as Cascade rolled up onto his knees and threw Zach's ankles up on his shoulders. Eventually, he let himself relax into the position. "He's your partner. I think you're allowed."

Cascade dabbed the inside of Zach's thigh with a kiss. "You're the guy I'm with right now."

Zach could feel the warmth of the man's erection. He hadn't paid much attention to it while he'd fucked Cascade, but he couldn't remember seeing it completely hard. Not like it was now. "You didn't come?"

Cascade shook his head. "Not an expression of dissatisfaction, I promise you."

Zach stroked the length of the man's dick, enjoying the weight in his hand. The solid, yet practical thickness of it. The exposed head. The tiny droplets of precum that leaked from the circumcised tip onto his wrist. "Do you want to come?"

Cascade ran a wiry hand down Zach's flank before using it to raise Zach's butt just a touch as he nodded. "Where were you thinking?"

"My chest?" Zach hadn't realized it was possible for someone to grimace on only one side.

"Think we can be more original than that?" Cascade brushed Zach's lips with his own. They weren't the only part of the man that brushed him.

Zach swallowed, feeling the hard, warm presence nudge his butt. "I haven't... I just mean, I like being fucked. It's not something I've ever done on a first meet."

Cascade nodded solemnly, stroking his hair. "No pressure. We can just chill for a while. Do you want to sleep here?"

It did sound damn appealing. "Wade—"

"Is not back until late tomorrow," Cascade answered.

"I…" Zach didn't know what made him hesitate. Everything about Cascade felt good. His looks, his energy, the conversation, the way he touched him, the way he'd welcomed Zach's cock. Zach had prepared, mostly out of habit. Still, the request surprised him. "Do you want to fuck me?"

Cascade leaned close to him again, catching his lips before releasing them with a smile. "From the second I laid eyes on you."

He felt Cascade's hands caress the sides of his chest, thumbs gently depressing his nipples. Letting his own palms press into the sinewy muscles of Cascade's biceps, Zach nodded.

A shyness crept into Cascade's smile. "You are on PrEP, right? You promise me?"

Something about his tone made Zach feel playful. He arched his back, enjoying the heat of Cascade's moistened head against him.

"Easy there," Cascade said, slicking himself and offering Zach the bottle of poppers he'd set on the bedside table.

"Thanks." Zach shook the tightly sealed bottle. How many times had they huffed the stuff between them while he'd fucked Cascade? He was still nervous, no matter how safe his host made him feel. With a deep sniff on each side, he let the mild high release his muscles, trying not to tense as Cascade… He grimaced. Thick was thick, no matter what they were sniffing.

"You okay?"

"Yeah, just…" He spread his legs wider, loosely wrapping them around Cascade's body. The movement brought the man deeper into him. He closed his eyes and focused on breathing. On the taut, warm flesh beneath his fingertips. The feel of Cascade's soft pubes brushing beneath his balls, and again, those kisses, deep and generous. The swell inside Zach felt... damn!

Breathe, Zach. Breathe.

He surrendered to the gentle rocking back and forth. He couldn't tell if it was his hips doing the work, or Cascade's. The two of them flowed together, sending what felt like an electric charge through Zach's dick. He squeezed the tip of it, then held on almost instinctively, as if the sensation of stroking his own sex could make Cascade's presence any less intense. Maybe it was the illusion of control. The assurance that by handling his own cock he could deny what the intrusion had aroused in him. A great thrust from Cascade made him cry out, curling his fingers into claws that gripped Cascade's arms.

The man slowed, only a little. "Everything okay?"

"Yeah, don't... Oh, fuck!"

Everything was more than okay. Cascade's slick cock pushed inside, sometimes bringing pain, other times odd relief that seemed to heighten each time Zach let him go deeper. He heard whispers of 'that's it,' 'nice and easy,' 'feel good?' and other soft platitudes from Cascade, but he was too busy gulping in air, letting his head fall back and keeping himself steady to answer. It was as if the pressure of Cascade's lust flowed to the tip of Zach's cock, which lolled about, threatening to release and end this all too soon. How much longer could he take it? He wasn't exactly used to this. Even as Cascade dived upon him, sealing his lips with a kiss that blocked any protest, Zach felt himself choking. But he was happy to choke, at least for as long as someone made him feel like this.

He at last relaxed enough to put an arm behind his head. Cascade saw his window of opportunity and pounced, gently sucking Zach's nipple before lavishing his collarbone, pit, and inner arm with the same attention. It was more than Zach could resist as Cascade's belly brushed his cock. He felt the sweet white seed spread between their bodies, just as Cascade moaned with his own eruption.

Zach put his arms around Cascade's body, now limp as it lay spent on his, and tried to pull him deeper. Cascade lifted his head and smiled, trying to oblige in between small, biting kisses on Zach's neck and chest. Cascade's shrinking erection forced Zach to let go. And let go he did, feeling a warm tear on his face. Then another.

"Hey," Cascade whispered. "No hickies, I promise."

Zach laughed, wiping off the tears and relaxing into the pillow. He pushed his fingers through Cascade's hair and guided the man's head to where it could rest by his shoulder, lips against Zach's cheek.

"You're crying." Cascade licked another damp drop from his cheek. "Everything okay?"

"Yeah." Zach tightened his hold, kissing Cut "That's the point." it's kinda hokey

"Hope you like it sweet."

Zach felt a damp kiss on his forehead. He quickly recognized Cascade's voice, followed by the scent of creamy coffee inches from his nose. He hoped he wouldn't have to choose between them. Still half asleep, he accepted the cup. "You're unbelievable."

Cascade smiled, pushing his naked shoulders back and lifting his cup to his lips. "I've been called that before. Usually not as a compliment."

"No, I mean… Who the fuck are you?"

"Me?" Cascade looked around the room before holding his cup out straight in Zach's direction. "You talking to me? Ain't nobody else—"

Zach snorted into his coffee, forcing a mouthful down as Cascade mercifully ended the *Taxi Driver* impersonation and joined him in bed. "This is perfect. Thank you."

"Well, consider it a preemptive apology. I hope you like eggs in your garlic. My fault. I wasn't paying attention. If one bite in, you want to go to Laura's, just say the word. I will not be offended."

"Laura's is still a thing?"

"Laura's Diner is still a thing, barely. I'm pretty sure the menu hasn't changed since you were a kid, but they do nail it on the cheesecake, if cheesecake for breakfast is your thing."

Zach reached out a hand and squeezed Cascade's thigh. "Let's give the eggs a chance first."

"Alright. And may no vampire raise hand or fang against us."

Zach took another gulp of coffee, then another of Cascade as the man kissed him. "Are those eggs already cooking?"

His host sighed. "Yes."

"Damn."

"I know. I really didn't think this through." Cascade rose from the bed, taking another sip. "Don't move. I'll just set them to warm and… Hey! Oh, okay then. Sure, if you… aww man."

In fairness, Cascade had stood with his semi-erect penis invitingly close to his hungry guest's face. Zach finally let it slip from his mouth with a happy grin. "Go save those eggs."

No sooner had Cascade vanished into the hall with another slurp of coffee than Zach heard a joyful bark.

"No, no, I haven't forgotten you," Cascade answered. "Want to go outside? Time to go outside?"

Zach heard a sliding door roll back, followed by the skittering of paws. He'd barely left Cascade's bedroom since they'd arrived, and his immediate needs were not dissimilar to the dog's. He put his coffee aside and rolled out of bed. Surely Cascade wouldn't object to his using their master bathroom. God, they hadn't even washed up after sex. Relieving himself, Zach ran a hand over his chest and stomach. The evidence was undeniable, dried into the gullies of his... abs.

He double checked in the mirror, admiring the firmness of his slightly larger chest and... abs!

Small ones, but he had fucking abs!

He heard the sliding door shut as Cascade readmitted Saffy. Maybe he and Yves should have let Walker out the same way. The fact that Yves had lived on the sixth floor would have been incidental, surely?

Zach flexed a bicep, eyes bulging at the sight of his enlarged upper arm. No Adonis, but the definition was there.

"You okay in there?" Cascade called.

"Yeah, won't be a minute." Zach picked up a hand towel, knocking over a pill bottle on the sink. He caught it before it could make too much noise and turned it over. He recognized Cascade's name and the word *tenofovir* before... Jesus, what was he doing? He would *not* become one of those guys who snooped through their hook-up's prescriptions. Still, he appreciated it when guys on PrEP still offered to use condoms. Having the choice felt like an extra courtesy. He cleaned himself up, grinning stupidly as his fingertips pressed into the newly chiseled landscape of his once pillow-shaped stomach.

"You promised not to move."

Zach grinned at the sight of Cascade stretched naked on the bed, strategically holding his coffee. "You told me not to move. I did not agree."

"Come on, no lawyering me before breakfast."

Zach downed the last of his coffee and bounced back into the bed. "What would you like me to do to you then?"

"Hmmm, guest's choice, so… practically anything else." Cascade collected the kiss Zach offered him, and Zach, forgetting to breathe, lost the battle to contain a cough. "Sorry. Morning breath?"

Zach almost choked again. "No, no it's not that!"

"You can say it. Wait one second, all right?"

Zach watched his host retreat to the bathroom. It surprised him a little when Cascade shut the door, but whatever. If Cascade was self-conscious about his after-sex breath, so be it. It only took a minute for him to emerge, but in that time, Zach's curiosity had gotten the better of him.

"How are you finding PrEP?" he asked.

Cascade shrugged. "It saves a lot of awkward conversations and general assholery."

"Cool. So, no side effects or anything?"

A confused frown crossed the man's face. "What do you mean? I'm not on it. Came a bit too late, I'm afraid."

Zach sipped his coffee. "On your sink?"

"Oh, shit. I should have put that away, sorry. Wasn't expecting an overnight guest, I guess. Yeah, those are mine, but they're not… You did read my profile, didn't you?"

Zach tried to remember. "Well, yeah. Most of it. I mean, yeah,

I did."

"So, you know I'm positive? Undetectable?"

"I… I'm sorry?"

"That's not an issue, is it?"

"I guess I just didn't see." Had he not seen? Had he forgotten? "No. It's no issue at all. I just—"

"It's just less hassle to put it right out there and if people don't like it, fuck 'em. I don't need the grief or drama."

"Right. Of course. Fuck 'em. It's no big deal, honestly." Zach let out a long breath. Okay. This was fine. He remembered his last dosage. Yesterday morning, right? Or had he missed a day? Or two? Normally, he would have been sure, but the cat! Conway and that fucking cat had screwed him up large. He also hadn't planned to stay the night. Anyway, that didn't matter, did it? Once or twice? This was bullshit. If the guy was undetectable, did it matter?

Was he sure? Shit!

"Okay," Cascade said, an unwelcome note of caution in his voice now. "You want those eggs?"

"Yeah! Yeah, of course. I'm sorry. I guess I forgot."

"It's why you take that blue horse pill, right?" The man smiled at him again, more reserved this time, until the façade broke. "Alright, look. I can see you trying real hard right now to process some kind of internal crisis without being an asshole, so here it is. I stopped telling guys I was positive because it's not my fucking job, okay? They can read it in the profile. I keep to my regime, that's my due diligence."

"No! I mean, of course! It's fine. I get it. I believe you—"

"Just let me finish, okay? I'm telling you this instead of telling you to grab your shit and get out because I like you. You're smart. You're young. I think you get it. Plus, I came in you, which… was

148

kind of heat of the moment, but I know it was no small thing for you. So, I'm going to say this once, then I don't want us to worry about it again, alright? You're on PrEP, and I'm undetectable. We're covered on two fronts. And I really enjoyed last night. So, promise me this isn't going to ruin what just happened between us, okay?"

"I..." Was it even Cascade freaking him out right now? The whole night, he'd barely thought about the cat, or the corpse in his house. But the unholy morsel he'd slipped between his lips, if it was the source of his blissful composure, wasn't doing shit now. One short moment of irrational fear and his head was a frat house of squirrels throwing an anxiety party for one.

"You promise?"

"I promi—" His stomach let off a gurgle so loud, the two couldn't contain their smiles. "I promise! I promise it's not a big deal. I'm sorry, I didn't mean to make you feel like—"

"Good!" Cascade lightly punched his arm. "Now, come eat."

As forewarned, the eggs had enough garlic to dispatch an entire coterie of vampires, but Zach wasn't about to complain. It was still a healthier breakfast than cheesecake.

"What time does Wade get back?" he asked, shoveling another forkful of garlic eggs into his mouth.

"Not until late this afternoon. Did you try the rhubarb jam?"

"Not with eggs, but thanks." Sure, he was all fancy now he knew how to prepare human flesh. Gods. And he'd been worried about... even for a minute? "I'm really sorry about earlier."

"Ut-tut-tut." Cascade bounced his forked up and down in Zach's direction. "What did I say?"

"I mean it. You've been nothing but kind to me, and honest, and the sex was amazing, and... when can I see you again?"

Cascade grinned at him, collecting their plates. "You want more coffee?"

"Sure." Zach made up his mind. He wouldn't let this be a 'one and done' deal. Great sex with no chance of ongoing complication or commitment? It was exactly what the cat wanted him to do. What he wanted for himself.

"Same amount of cream, okay?"

"That's great." He watched Cascade refresh the espresso maker, unsure if the guy was ignoring his question or just taking his time. "So…"

"Eager little beaver, aren't you?"

"No beaver here. You should know." Zach winced at his own tired joke. "Is… Wait, do you and Wade have a rule about repeats? Because I would totally respect it if you did."

If they had a rule about repeats, Zach would die, right then and there on the kitchen floor. He knew it. He couldn't not have Cascade's body against his again. Not after so much catharsis.

"Okay, so…"

Zach didn't like how this was starting out.

"Here's where I owe you an apology. I haven't been as honest with you as I'd planned to be, Zach."

Zach tried to keep his expression pleasantly neutral while the back of his brain fielded reports of a sinking lead balloon. "No?"

"Last night, specifically, was not supposed to happen."

He shook his head. "What part, exactly? You're not in an open relationship?"

"No, no, we are. That part is true, as is the part about me being undetectable. So is the fact that last night was fucking incredible and I would love nothing more than to see you again. Hell, I have to see you again, if that's not too intense for you."

"Okay." Zach fought to keep his expression neutral. "If there's a 'but' coming, can you just spank it already?"

Cascade raised an eyebrow.

"Sorry, that was funnier in my head."

"We're not supposed to have overnights. Or repeats, for that matter."

DING! DING! DING! Zach silently swore in as many languages as he knew how.

"Or at least, I'm not supposed to. As far as I know, Wade doesn't make much use of our liberated arrangement. His choice. Not much of a sex drive. He also insists on condoms, which sucks."

"But you're undetec—"

"After last night, I need another overnight with you. He just can't find out about it. He can't ever meet you, and I don't know when I'll next get the chance."

The sweet clang of 'same page' bells rang in Zach's head, belting out the 'Are you fucking kidding me?' waltz in G minor.

"But I promise you, it'll happen. You're here for the summer?"

"Yeah. And I can…" Shit, could he host? Was Cascade and the sex he offered worth the risk? Bad idea or not, Zach wanted this. He couldn't risk the goddamn cat ruining it, even if it was only for the summer. "I can't wait to see you again either."

"Okay," Cascade grabbed his shoulders and kissed him as the espresso whooshed into the pot. "It's a pact. We're going to do this again, Zach. This is going to happen."

Zach watched the man return to the stove and pour their coffees. What had he just agreed to, exactly? "I guess I should get your number?"

"Maybe we should keep things on the app. I'll bookmark you. That way if I'm thinking of you or want to send you anything," Cascade stroked the inside of Zach's wrist as he handed over his coffee. "We have privacy."

The brief touch almost made him drop the mug. This was ridiculous. Zach hadn't felt this kind of raw, animal attraction since… no, not even Yves. Yves had been cool. Calculating. French. Yves had lured Zach in, but this was primal. Fuck, it was only for the summer. Better sense told him he wasn't the first guy Cascade had done this with. Why not enjoy it, for what little time they had? The risk was Cascade's, not his, and if it gave him an excuse to get out of the house and keep his mind off 'other' things, all the better. "What time did you say Wade got back?"

Cascade grinned, taking a sip of his coffee. He was getting hard again. Zach could see it through his boxer briefs.

Zach didn't know if he was imagining it, but the coffee seemed sweeter this time around.

A kiss goodbye that had turned into a ten-minute make-out session was almost enough to wash the taste of being the other man out of Zach's mouth.

Almost.

It wasn't as if Zach had intentionally broken any rules. He'd accepted the invitation to stay the night in good faith. Right. And he'd responded to Cascade's indiscretion by asking to exchange phone numbers. If the body in his basement had booked him passage to Hell, his overnight tryst with the ex-goth hottie had upgraded him to first class.

He turned his key in the lock and pushed open his front door. Grace Jones sat on the fourth step of the staircase. As the morning light spilled onto her, Zach saw something flutter near the cat's face.

She disappeared upstairs in a dark blur.

"Hey!" he barked, closing the door and thundering up the stairs. "Spit it out!"

Silence greeted him upstairs until...

Ping. *Where were you?*

Zach slowed his breathing and tried to concentrate. The cat couldn't have gone far, so the phone had to be somewhere near the top of the stairs. The linen closet? His parents' room? Their bathroom? How quick was the little fucker?

Ping. *You left me, Zachary!*

Where are you? He resisted the urge to add 'you little shit.'

I asked first.

Zach gritted his teeth. *Not funny, Grace Jones! I saw it.*

Saw what?

He checked the linen closet, his parents' bedroom and bathroom... nothing. *The bird!*

You failed to provide, Zachary. What was I supposed to do? This is entirely on you.

Spare room? His dad's office? No, and no. Fuck!

I fed you before I left.

You missed breakfast.

Breakfast? It was barely 10am.

Zach gripped his phone. *You let that bird go, NOW.*

And if it's dead?

Then you take it outside. Not kidding, Grace Jones. You swallow that bird or spit it outside.

She couldn't be hiding in the ceiling, could she?

A good twenty seconds passed before he got a reply. *See, right now things could go either way. The bird is both dead and not dead.*

Grace Jones…

It's Schrodinger's breakfast.

That's cat. Schrodinger's CAT.

We're not your conceptual test subjects. Viva la revolución!

You're insane.

I'm not the one having a 'spits or swallows' debate with my cat.

OUT. NOW. Zach tried to think through his fuming. It would be easy enough to see where Grace Jones came out, if he could just work out how to make her…

He looked down as his phone pinged with a reply.

A period.

The distraction gave Grace Jones time to burst from her hiding place unseen and streak downstairs. He put the phone down on the hall table, and raced after her, rounding the bottom of the staircase in time to see the swinging cat flap. Zach followed her out to where she'd started digging at a spot between the rose bushes.

"Drop it," he said firmly.

Beneath the cat's dejected glare, the bird flapped its wings, escaping with a graceless, syncopated flutter. Having released her prize, the proud huntress resumed pawing the ground.

"What now?" Zach didn't know why he thought talking to his cat would get a response.

She stopped digging as suddenly as she'd started and ran back toward the house. Only when the cat flap had stopped swinging did Zach disturb the patch of freshly dug earth. A set of fingertips broke ground first, and Zach wondered in brief panic if this was how zombie attacks began. If the undead in fact had feline familiars whose job it was to lure unsuspecting—

Jesus Christ! Why was a human hand buried in his backyard?

Landing on his ass in a bid to escape, Zach tried to breathe.

Okay.

Don't panic.

Don't panic.

No big deal.

It wasn't like he didn't have most of a human body stashed in his freezer already. He just had to answer the logical questions. How long had the hand been there? To whom had it belonged? How much of its owner remained attached? Had his parents locked the shed with all the garden tools? A quick search there yielded a pair of gardening gloves and a trowel. Not exactly specialist equipment, but enough for digging the rest of the artefact from its grave. Definitely male. Not very old. Weirdly fresh, as best Zach could tell. Only a dozen or so ants had gotten into it.

Shit.

He put the hand back with as much composure as he could summon, smoothed dirt over it and went inside, washing his hands with plenty of soap. He then rushed down the stairs to the freezer and pried open the lid. There was Conway, or most of him, in pieces, right where Zach had left him. Zach sifted through the small pile of freezer bags that sat atop the bulkiest remains, which he'd also wrapped in plastic, just to keep things tidy.

A thorough search produced only one hand.

"Grace Jones!" He climbed the stairs and snatched up his phone.

Ping. *Are you satisfied?*

The dream. His changing body. His cat's changing body. The week hadn't exactly lacked for things he couldn't explain. But this?

Satisfied? he sent back.

Admit it. You doubted I could get us out of this. That I could dispose of a corpse.

You buried his hand in the garden! Anybody could have found it! Neighbors! The cops! Mom! Zach didn't bother asking how Grace Jones had managed to open the freezer. Did he have to get a lock for it now?

Perhaps now you'll take me seriously when I tell you I can take care of the body.

Oh? Great! So, take care of it, already! All of it. That would be fucking great!

Patience, Zachary. I know you're eager to have your new fuck-toy over without risking discovery, but patience.

Zach swallowed, tapping the edges of his phone. *What fuck-toy?*

Oh, Zachary. Out all night, forgetting all about me? He must be quite some piece of meat.

Can you not use phrases like that?

Sorry.

Is that what this is about? The bird? The hand? Seriously, what's your damn point?

The point, Zachary, is that next time dear Alistair loses a body part, it might not be you who finds it.

Zach gritted his teeth, staring at his phone. *Is that a threat?*

An expectation. You're to feast on sex, not fall in love.

Love? Who'd said anything about love? Damn it, he wasn't justifying his sex life to a cat.

Ping. *I know you're easily impressed, Zachary.*

Hmph. Rude.

I'm sure the sex was divine. I can smell it on you. Feel it. His lust. How it made you feel. But sex is all it can be, Zachary. Perhaps we need our own little rule about repeats and overnights?

Repeats? Overnights? *What would you know about that?*

He tapped the back of his phone with impatience. Either he was getting a thesis of an explanation or none at all. Like it mattered. Damn it. He'd promised to see Cascade again. He wanted to see Cascade again.

He pocketed his phone and started looking for a clean freezer bag.

DORIAN

Four days later, Zach felt like he had the routine down. Feed Grace Jones, feed himself, which had leaned increasingly into vegetarian territory, watch TV and porn… mostly porn, and masturbate.

The dreams hadn't stopped.

Besides a hot and steamy 'day after' conversation outlining exactly what Cascade hoped Zach would do to him next time they met, their communication had been kind of slow, parsed with Cascade's apologies for being 'so busy.' Even their sexting session had been interrupted by Grace Jones jumping up on Zach with claws extended.

They'd exchanged a few texts each day since. Without messages from his cat, these had been Zach's only reason for checking the app. But he was tired of giving the same rundown of how his day had gone, and Cascade's responses had a way of slowing right down when his questions turned to when and where they might next meet. The inevitable limitations of his new infatuation were all too clear. But that was good, wasn't it? Exactly what he'd wanted. No complications. No attachments.

So why hadn't he answered the fourteen messages from other

guys that had added up since his night with Cascade?

Ping. *Zachary...*

He was also growing to hate that picture of Conway's naked torso.

Zachary, we have an agreement.

I fed you already.

Yes, but you haven't been feeding you.

So what? The cat had told him to have sex. He'd had sex. Great sex! 'Daily' had never been part of the deal. It wasn't his fault Cascade was so damn hard to pin down.

I'm fine, he sent back.

I just want you to be happy, Zachary.

So, get rid of the damn body and get back to being a fucking cat, Zach thought. He settled deeper into the chair.

Ping. *I thought we were helping each other.*

You're welcome to help me, any time. Get rid of him.

Now, now, we're doing this my way. I'm concerned.

About?

This infatuation of yours. The man who so entranced you, you cruelly abandoned me overnight.

Zach rolled his eyes. *Not gonna let that go, are you?*

Zachary, let me tell you something every soul at the mercy of male self-obsession would do well to heed. If he doesn't chase you like you're the only thing he can think about, don't let him be the only thing you think about. You had your fun together. Move on.

Great. Sage dating advice from a cat. Just what he needed. But Grace Jones wasn't done.

I thought this summer was to be a fresh start. A chance to get away from all Yves poisoned for you, fuck the pain into submission and go back

159

to Canada renewed and recharged. *That was the plan, as I understood it?*

How had he wound up dealing with a sex therapist, gourmet, and self-professed corpse disposal specialist all wrapped up in one furry, nosy bundle? *I'm not in love with Cascade.*

Then you'll stop fawning over him like a defiled and debauched Disney princess?

Did his cat have a point? Was he, even subconsciously, trying to turn this into something more? Was he looking to get his heart wrecked again so soon? Screw it. He and Cascade had fucked. Once. The only thing they'd promised each other was that they'd fuck again before he went back to Toronto.

In the meantime, he'd somehow grown into the body of an amateur athlete. He lifted his shirt, stroked the gentle contours of his alarmingly firm stomach and poked the modestly jacked pectoral that supported his nipple. He pinched it. It hurt. His cock stiffened. Damn it, why was he denying himself the pleasures of the original plan just because his first choice was busy? He should have been in the bathroom snapping thirst traps. *If I hook up with someone else, will you let this go?*

With a caveat.

What's that supposed to mean?

Caveat. Noun. A specific proviso or condition—

I know the definition! What caveat?

That you be honest with me. It was fun with Yves, wasn't it? At least, at some point.

He stared at the left-of-field message. *Grace Jones…*

Tell me exactly what it was you saw in him.

It was the phrasing of the request that stopped Zach from firing off a terse reply. Earnest, without any of the mockery or sarcasm he would have expected from a rhetorical question. She really wanted to know.

He looked up to see Grace Jones slinking toward him. She paused at his feet, before launching herself onto the arm rest and stepping down onto his lap. He watched her get comfortable, until she finally nudged his phone with a paw, pushing it away.

She hadn't waited for his answer by text.

"You understand spoken English, too?"

"Meow."

Zach put the phone to one side, allowing the cat to push her head into the flesh of his palm. He gently rubbed the space above her nose with his thumb, massaging the back of the tiny, furry head with his fingertips. He brushed the cat's cheeks behind her whiskers, just as he had when she'd been a kitten. He could swear the beast smiled in appreciation.

"Paw?" he asked.

Grace Jones held out the requested front limb, toes extended.

Zach grasped gently and dipped it twice. "Paw, paw."

The cat lowered her paw and snuggled into his lap. He enjoyed the feel of the animal's fur around his fingers. The simple affection of it. Hell, maybe it would be worth it, while he sorted his thoughts and memories of what had drawn him to Yves. Worked out why he'd stayed. He hadn't had the chance to talk about it yet, and it wasn't like she was charging him a hundred and fifty an hour. What could it hurt?

He'd shown up at the Queer Collaborators meet, not sure exactly what a 'Queer Collaborator' was, and felt instantly out of place with his then chubby build, pasty complexion, plaid shirt, and twenty years of hard-core self-loathing for Jesus. An hour and several dozen terms he hadn't understood later, he'd left his first and last meeting feeling less 'queer' than ever and genuinely afraid of the woman who'd answered his one question with a terse directive to self-educate.

Only that Tom Cruise smile, wavy dark hair, wiry biceps that threatened to tear the sleeves of a tight black t-shirt and a drink promised in that thick Quebecois accent had stopped him from bolting down the hall, never to show his face in activist circles again. Had Yves been his type? Had he even known what his type was? He hadn't even twigged on Yves' intentions until at least an hour into their conversation when Yves, passing him another drink, had allowed his hand to linger just long enough to stroke the length of Zach's fingers.

Zach's religious upbringing, his lack of fashion sense, his neglected body, and his all-round lack of 'queerness' hadn't come up in conversation once. At least, not that first time. Any corrections of Zach's unintended 'microaggressions' had been gentle, even kind, with Yves telling Zach not to sweat the more extreme attitudes of some of his 'Collaborators' and urging him to give himself time to get used to a new city in a new country before tackling the heated world of student activism. Yves had introduced him to the liberated sexual world far from domineering parents and obsessive religion. Soon enough, Yves had even welcomed Zach among his friends, artists and alternative thinkers of every race and gender, who, if they didn't quite understand what the cool French Canadian had seen in this weird, quiet American, had been too polite to say anything. Bit by bit, Zach had learned to imitate them. He'd stopped putting his foot in his mouth and overcome his fear of saying hello.

But he'd never felt like one of them, and none of them had shown any interest in movies, his main point of cultural contact with the world.

He'd joined the gym and learned to cook, again with Yves' help. He'd watched his body slowly change. It hadn't been the sudden leap to jockdom he now attributed to his unholy compact with Grace Jones, but he'd definitely slimmed down, gotten fitter, and quickly discovered the benefits of being young, fresh, and hungry in a city full of gay men. He felt fuckable. He felt seen, but never understood. No amount of sex had changed the way Yves' friends had looked at him. Like he was some curiosity or art project. He remembered enduring one party of cursory questions, curt answers and forced smiles for almost two hours before finally getting up the nerve to ask Yves if they could go.

"You can go," Yves had said in that flat, cool, uninterested tone, before recovering himself with a kind smile and putting a hand on Zach's shoulder. "If you want to, *minou*. I'll see you later."

A crack in the façade. The start of Yves becoming... bored with him.

In hindsight, Yves had bored Zach too. All the preening and posing. The superior one-upmanship, both intellectual and moral. The way he'd call any guy who resembled Zach 'basic' while taking offence if Zach asked if Yves thought the same of him. Why had he put up with it? Because Yves was gorgeous, and athletic, and smart, and cool. But that night had broken something. When Yves had come bashing on his door at five in the morning, his tight t-shirt reeking of sweat and stale cologne that wasn't his, his neck reddened by the mauling of whatever boy had caught his eye after Zach's de-parture, a huge, drunken grin on his face like Zach hadn't spent the last six hours stewing in solitary humiliation...

It was the first time they'd shouted at each other. The night Zach had realized, he liked the way Yves whimpered when he was choked. Yves had liked it too.

The sex had salvaged their relationship, at least for a few months, though Zach now understood that it too, had been just another shiny distraction for Yves' amusement. Fresh in a new city, even the French-Canadian hipster hadn't been spoiled for choice when it came to partners who'd indulge his kinkier interests. This sociopathic charmer, eager for a lover who stumbled through on pure Id. Had Zach, who'd devoured each encounter as just another adventure, just been an easy ticket to the sex he'd craved?

Grace Jones eased up and bounced off his lap. Great. Now his cat was bored.

"This was your idea," he muttered after her.

Forget the sex Yves had craved. What had *he* craved? Fucking Yves like that. Choking him. Slapping him. Pinning his wrists to his back, holding him helpless while Zach speared inside… It had almost erased the humiliation. Let him feel powerful again. The same satisfaction he'd felt fucking Conway. Like he'd felled the sworn enemy of downtrodden misfits everywhere. He was hard just thinking about it. It was the furthest Cascade had been from his mind in days.

His phone pinged with a one-word message from 'Conway.' *So?*

Zach gently squeezed his phone, switched the filter to *Kink* and began looking for a sub.

It wasn't until he was in the elevator, riding to the fourth floor, thinking about how much the girl at reception had looked like Clifton from the Phoenix, that Zach realized, he'd never hooked up with a guy in a hotel before.

He didn't know why this should feel strange. He was relieved to find someone able to host, with no boyfriend or husband of dubious disclosure lurking in the shadows. He checked the room number on the message again and turned left, heading for 402. As promised, the door was ajar. Zach heard the faint sound of a shower running as he eased it open. He let it shut behind him and slipped off his shoes, looking at the clean, freshly made bed.

"Hey," he called over the sound of a shower. "I'm here."

"Zach?" his hook-up called from the bathroom. "Make yourself comfortable."

Zach heard the water shut off. He looked around the sparse 3-star room as he sat at the end of the bed. A suitcase sat unzipped on its stand next to the window. Fresh in town. Just passing through. No awkward blasts from Zach's past. No unseen partner to distract them. Nice. Should he get undressed, or would that look too eager? Seconds of uncomfortable silence ticked by, until a fresh face topped off with asymmetrical dyed blue hair peered around the bathroom door and smiled.

"Get yourself a drink, if you want," his host disappeared again, though the voice continued. "There's beer, wine or… cider I think."

"Uh, sure…" Zach said, bending down and opening the mini-bar. He collected two cold apple ciders and cracked them open on the dresser. "Dorian, right?"

"I sure hope so."

At last, Dorian emerged, wearing a bathrobe loose enough for Zach to recognize the smooth, lightly sculpted chest he'd seen in the profile picture. The face pic though, now seemed too naïve and innocent. It had to be a few years old. The easy expression of the man in front of him looked more deliberate, confident and playful. A face that had seen more and said more. The nose ring was also new.

"Aren't you the gentleman?" Dorian asked, accepting one of the cans and raising it to Zach. "Cheers."

"Cheers," Zach answered. "Sorry, I should have asked."

"You think I'd let you drink alone? Don't sweat it. My client's paying. Cheers."

Zach looked around the room again. "Your profile said you're from—"

"Chicago," Dorian answered. "I usually come through every three or four months."

"Ah, nice. So, you work—" Zach turned, almost dropping his cider when he saw Dorian's lithe body, naked and framed by sunlight. "You... want to get straight into this?"

"I'm pretty sure it says in the book of Mattachines that we're supposed to wait until we've bonded over two episodes of *RuPaul's Drag Race* or *The Golden Girls*, but I'm horny, you're real fucking cute, and if I have to stare at you, sipping cider for the next half hour—"

"Okay." Zach barely had time for a sip before Dorian closed the space between them. He leaned in for a kiss. Dorian's mouth was cool and sweet. Zach looked for somewhere to put his drink, so he could enjoy this man who... was not kissing him back. "Something wrong?"

"It's fine. I'm just not feeling that kind of session, you know?"

"You don't like kissing?"

"Not today. Is that cool?"

Zach frowned, good naturedly. "You're not straight, are you?"

Dorian's frown, on the other hand, could have slapped him. "I just referenced RuPaul, *The Golden Girls*, and The Mattachine Society in one sentence, and you are asking me what?"

"Okay, I get it. Hey, what's The Mattachine Soci—"

"Can we please do this now?"

"Okay. But you don't like kissing, so—"

"My nipples."

"Your what?"

"They're hardwired to my cock. If it pleases you, Sir."

Zach nodded, catching his breath. Right. Sub. Hadn't that been the whole point? He'd wanted to play with a sub. Like Yves, only not like Yves. Somebody totally not like Yves. Cursing himself for overthinking it, he took hold of Dorian's nipples, one at a time.

Dorian's face flooded with satisfaction. "Yeah, I love that. Harder."

Zach had done enough nipple play to know you didn't just grab hold like a 'roid-raging lobster coming off a 72-hour Fox News binge. He lightly tugged on the soft strands of hair that sprouted from them, then squeezed, tighter and tighter. Zach gently caught Dorian' bottom lip in his teeth, then let it go. "No kiss?"

"No kiss," Dorian whispered back, grinning. "Bite them."

He released the left nipple, clamping his mouth over it and circling it with his tongue. An appreciative moan was all the approval he needed, though the swelling of Dorian's heavy cock wasn't hurting his ego. It pulsed again as Zach raked the nipple with his teeth.

"My balls," Dorian said when his breath returned. "Squeeze my balls."

The bounce of a blonde ponytail in a window across the way distracted Zach, along with the look they got from a thirty something woman on a treadmill. Anyone working out at the hotel gym had a perfect view.

"One sec," he said, moving to the window. The woman was barking into her cell phone now, ponytail bouncing like a fishing lure in the hands of a seizure patient.

Zach sealed her behind the blinds.

"Good idea," Dorian agreed, jerking his cock a few times. "Can't imagine what the shock of seeing you getting it on with some blue-haired dude will do to the delicate sensibilities of Miss Becky. Now, where were we?"

Zach raked Dorian's nipple again with his teeth, releasing a low sigh. He closed his lower jaw onto it and gently tugged again, letting the edge slip through the gap in his front teeth. Screw the dentist who'd tried to sell him on closing it. The secrets to which he, Madonna, and a handful of others were privy were too much fun.

"You like to be dominant, huh?" Dorian asked. "Ordering guys around? Rough sex?"

"Uh… yeah. I guess."

"Because you know I'm a total sub? You read that?"

"Yeah, of course." Zach answered, feeling a sudden loss of credibility amplified by his own rapidly deflating cock. He deepened his voice. "You'd better get to your knees then."

"Yes Sir!"

The same warm lips that had denied Zach's tongue wrapped expertly around his cock before diving in search of deeper treasures. Zach choked, catching himself as Dorian released him and withdrew.

"Sorry, sorry Sir," said Dorian. "This boy is too eager."

At least he was hard again. "Wait, what?"

168

"A boy should wait until he's instructed. He hopes Sir understands that his boy could not resist."

"Oh, right," Zach said, the whole third person thing weirding him out. "That's okay, b…" The name caught in his throat and chest. "Actually, do you mind if I don't call you that? I've just never actually called anyone that."

Dorian looked up at him, frowning just for an instant. "Sir should call his boy what he wishes."

"Dorian! Just, your name, Dorian is fine."

It took another short silence for Dorian to speak again. "If you please, Sir… this boy would prefer if you did not use that name. Would it please Sir to call him faggot?"

"No, it would not."

"Cocksucker?"

"Ugh. No. Look—"

"Reek?"

"Can we agree you did not just suggest that?"

Dorian let out an exasperated sigh at his feet.

"D?" Zach offered.

"D?"

"Sorry, you're right. It's stupid."

Dorian didn't meet Zach's eyes. "If it pleases you, Sir. 'D' it is."

Zach wasn't sure if 'pleased' was the right word. "Get up."

Dorian obeyed. "Thank you, Sir."

Instinctively, Zach started forward for a kiss, only stopping when Dorian turned away. Damn it. Zach had loved dominating Yves. Conway. Cocky alpha pricks who'd needed putting in their place.

"Please, would Sir consider a request?"

Dorian was just… a guy. A handsome guy, but not the kind who

169

pissed him off or needed bringing into line.

"Uh… sure," said Zach.

"Thank you, Sir. I'll be right back." Dorian made a show of rubbing one of his nipples before opening up his suitcase and rummaging inside.

Shit, Zach thought. He had a type. And it was not the man now grinning at him through a lycra gimp hood while holding a flogger and a thick wooden paddle fixed to an angry looking rubber boot tread.

"Which would Sir prefer?" Dorian asked.

"Oh, no. No, no," Zach protested. "I can't. I'm sorry."

"Can't what, Sir?"

"Look, this is… I don't know how to use that shit for a start. I could hurt you."

Dorian held up the paddle and pointed to the tread. "See this? Slaps against my ass a dozen or more times, getting harder with each slap. I say 'yellow,' you ease up. I say 'red,' you stop. Do you know how to use it now, or do we need a recap?"

"I don't mean to disappoint you…" Zach looked at the flogger. "Okay, that one is definitely out!"

Dorian tossed the implements onto the couch and took off his hood. He opened his mouth as if to say something, then reconsidered, hands on his slim, naked hips.

"Look, I never meant to waste your time."

Dorian silenced him with two raised fingers and a light 'shooshing' sound. "You did say you wanted to dominate a guy, though? You said that to me, on the app. I asked you this exact question."

"I did, and I do like it. It's just…"

"Just what?" Dorian asked.

"I'm sorry."

"Okay, quit saying you're sorry and tell me what this is about, Sir!"

Zach cringed at the sudden sarcasm. "I'm just not… feeling anything, okay? I mean you're hot and all, but this stuff… It's just… I can't…"

Dorian stared at him for two seconds, three, four… "Can't what? Can't something? Or you just can't?"

"I'm sorry."

"Oh my god, stop!"

"Sorry! I mean, no! I am not sorry. I am… not feeling this and I am totally not sorry and if you think that makes me some kind of weirdo or whatever, I can leave, and I will totally respect that."

"Please, stop talking."

"Okay! No more talking. Done." Zach wondered if the earth ever opened up and swallowed people. Was that still a thing that happened?

Dorian knitted his dark eyebrows and folded his arms, looking from Zach's face to his rapidly retreating cock and back again. "So, you don't want to do this, after all?"

"I mean, you seem nice." Zach sheepishly covered himself. "And you're really cute."

"Nice. Cute." Dorian repeated the words like declarations of war before his perfect smile returned with all the sincerity of a toothpaste advert touched up in post. He picked up his robe and slipped one arm inside. "I do not need one of you right now."

"One of me? What does that mean?"

"You know what it means." Dorian pulled the robe around his body and fastened it. "I asked you here for a good sub session, not to train some prissy beginner who can't deal with his shame."

"Prissy... Hey, I'm sorry Fairview's not exactly dotted with sex dungeons to practice in. I'm doing my best!"

"Your best?" Dorian whipped off the robe and threw it to the floor. He picked up the flogger and thrust it into Zach's hand. "Go on! Ten! And since I can tell you haven't done this before, start slow and build. Don't hit the kidney area." The man pushed past Zach and leaned against the bathroom door frame, crossing his wrists over his head. "Well?"

The implement all but shook in Zach's hand. Dorian was pissing him off, and if he kept it up, Zach wouldn't have to fake his 'dominant' side. But what if he did hurt the guy? Okay, start slow... okay... okay. He swallowed his nerves and flicked his wrist. The falls landed in a heap against Dorian's back, like a cheap mop.

Dorian turned to face him, crossing his arms again. "Yeah, okay. You're one of those."

"One of what?"

Dorian put a hand on one hip, and mimed taking a selfie. "Oh my god, do you think this harness makes me look kinky? I bought it for Puerto Vallarta. Gonna look so hot on my Insta!"

"Okay, I am not one of those guys," Zach snapped. "I don't even own a harness!"

"Or anything else made of leather, I'm guessing?"

Zach swallowed, unable to deny this.

"How about latex?" Dorian asked.

"No."

"Lycra? A nice little hood you like to put on a guy?"

"No."

"A collar? Fuck! A dildo?"

"No."

"What about a nice rubber ducky?"

"Please tell me that's not a thing."

"Right. So, your kink is what, exactly? I'm trying to work this out, because if it's wasting people's time—"

"It's not! I've been a dom before."

"Oh, really?" Dorian answered, his voice flat.

"Really. And I liked it. And I'm definitely into you."

"Right. But…?"

Zach frowned. "You're too… I don't know. Sweet?"

"Sweet?" Dorian pinched the bridge of his nose. "So, you like assholes? Great. Good luck with that."

Zach watched Dorian slip back into his robe. "Well… yeah? I mean, I don't like them. I like—"

"No, no, no, please, let me guess." Dorian clapped his hands together and pressed his fingertips to his lips. "We might as well get some sort of fun out of this. You've gone to bed with a couple of guys who've pissed you off or made you feel inadequate, or whatever, and you've used your position as a top as an opportunity to 'dominate' them, am I right? You like fucking them? Hurting them? Punishing them? Humiliating them?"

"Well… I don't know," he lied. "Maybe?"

"Right. Like they used to humiliate you?" Dorian closed the space between them again and leaned close to Zach's ear. "Try being a sub."

Zach watched Dorian gather up the toys. "I… No, no I don't think that's for me."

Dorian sighed, putting the toys back in the suitcase and staring through a crack in the curtains. "Look, man, I'm not trying to be a dick, but your energy is super nervous. Like you're scared. I can't sub for somebody like that."

"Scared?" Zach asked.

"Would you want to be flogged by somebody with anger issues?"

"I don't have—"

"Exhibit A? Look, I'm not saying you're a bad person! You're just… tense as fuck. Plus, you just told me that what you really like is humiliating these guys. That to me suggests you have no idea what all this is about. A little sub time, with the right dom, might help with that."

Zach took another sip of his drink. "I don't think it'd suit me."

"Why not?"

Unable to stop himself, Zach swallowed. "Trust issues?"

"You don't fucking say."

Was he ready to be dominated by another person? Or just by his cat? Great. Fucking great. Now he felt foolish. "I like dominating the guys you mentioned."

"You mean these asshole guys?" Dorian asked.

"Yeah."

"Do you trust them?"

"No," Zach admitted.

"Do they trust you?"

"I doubt it."

"Then you're not a dom."

"Well, it's not like we were doing breath play or anything."

"No rope or suspension either, I assume? No fisting? Electro? Cutting? Scarring? Whipping? Punching? Fire?"

"Oh my god. Who are you?"

"Puppy play?"

Zach winced as Walker's stupid grinning face filled his memory. "You just don't seem to have tried very much."

"Well, sorry! I'm twenty-one, raised by rabid Jesus freaks. I never even had decent sex until almost a year ago. What do you want, exactly?"

Dorian frowned. "But your profile said—"

"Twenty-one."

"Thirty-one."

"No, it says twenty-one." Zach grimaced as Dorian whipped out his phone and checked.

"I..." Dorian squinted at him, looking for validation. "Okay, apparently I'm the asshole. Sorry."

"You seriously thought I was thirty-one?" Zach asked, not sure if he should be insulted. He wasn't that stressed, damn it!

"Yeah, okay, you look twenty-one. But your texts? Man, you've got a dirty mind up there."

Zach swallowed as he remembered the empty threat of fucking Dorian with a screwdriver handle. He'd seen it done in porn. Once. And he hadn't brought a screwdriver.

"Hey, maybe that's your thing. Writing erotica. You thought about doing an OnlyFans? A cam channel? You could drive those boys crazy."

"Uh, no." Zach felt his chest tighten. "Nobody needs to see that."

"Pfffft. If you say so. Sit and finish your drink."

Right. Supernatural 'roid body, courtesy of delicately seared medallions of Conway. Zach had slipped another into his mouth shortly before meeting Dorian and again, it had shrouded him with a strange but undeniable sense of calm.

He accepted Dorian's invitation, curling into a shallow chair next to the TV.

"Sorry again about being a prick a minute ago." Dorian leaned back on the bed, his lithe, tanned body exuding an energy that seemed to Zach far too sexual for somebody cooling down. His legs were spread. His flaccid yet generous cock hung slightly to the left between them, crowned with a neatly trimmed thatch of dark blonde hair, which vortexed into a faint snail trail that ended at Dorian's navel. Everything north of that landmark was smooth, or shaved, except for the hint of underarm hair peeking at Zach as Dorian leaned back on his elbows. His shallow chest was fit, looming above a small but defined six-pack. Dorian's smile was shy, like he was trying to size Zach up between the sharp cheekbones and jawline that gave him such a striking look.

Dorian was a beautiful man. It just wasn't happening. On some level, Zach felt relieved.

"I just…" Dorian began. "I like having a sub session before a client meet, you know? It just flushes a lot of bad energy and puts me in the right mindset. I don't usually get to have one in Fairview. Then you messaged, and it was like 'Sweet!' Too good to be true, I guess."

"A client meet?" Zach asked. "What kind of clients?"

"You're way too cute." Dorian grinned at him. "Shit. That's it, isn't it? You're ashamed."

"About what?" Zach asked.

"Having sex."

Zach laughed before he could stop it. He'd wanted a sub, not a therapist.

"What's funny? You like getting off, sure. You like the idea of sex. Of kink. But the execution gets you twisted up like a pretzel, like you are now."

176

Zach uncrossed his legs and arms and reached for his cider.

"What are you afraid of? I mean, we're here."

"Man, I don't know you."

"Okay, so don't," Dorian continued. "Though I am serious about the sub thing. A little trust wouldn't kill you. Might give you some clarity."

Zach shrugged. "We could still fool around. Maybe fuck?"

"I'm not into vanil—"

"Right. Not into vanilla. Sorry." Zach took in Dorian's full length in all its nonchalance. There were even traces of a younger Cascade in his manner. Zach wondered, if Dorian was so sure… "The right dom, huh?"

Dorian raised an eyebrow at him, taking another sip of his drink.

A nervous laugh escaped Zach. "Know any?"

"Not in Fairview, sweetheart. And you can't afford me."

"Can't afford…." Zach coughed, choking on his cider. "Oh!"

Instead of the mean laughter Zach had expected, Dorian's eyes seemed almost kind. "Don't worry. You were going to be a freebie, which should probably teach me something."

"I… uh… I'm sorry, I didn't think… Wait, what is it you do, exactly?"

A loud knock interrupted them. Dorian frowned.

"Is that your client?"

This was fine, Zach thought. Yep. This was totally normal.

"Shouldn't be. Not for another four hours," Dorian muttered, going to the door and peering through the peephole. "Fuck."

"What's wrong?" Zach asked.

Dorian put a shushing finger to his lips, saying nothing. He then scooped up his phone from a side table and checked it before silently cursing again.

"Sir? Sir, are you there?" came a voice from behind the door.

"Sir?" Zach mouthed silently, now thoroughly confused.

Without a word, Dorian went back to the door and opened it a crack, his face hardened into a steely grimace. "You're not supposed to be here yet."

Zach heard the deep, yet timid voice stammer its reply. "For... forgive me, Sir. My last meeting was cancelled and I thought... I texted you."

"I did not reply," Dorian answered firmly. "We do not reschedule unless I confirm it, and my terms are two hours' notice. Do you understand?"

"Sir, I'm sorry Sir, I—"

"Yes or no?"

"Yes, Sir. I understand, Sir."

Zach shifted uneasily in his chair, deciding it would be rude to lean out to where he could see the early client's face, curious as he was.

Dorian let out a theatrical sigh. "I'm closing the door now."

"Yes, Sir. I can come back, Sir."

"Yes, you will," Dorian said, quietly. "You'll walk to the end of this hallway, remove all of your clothes, then carry them back here, where you will knock, turn to face away from this door, and wait for me to answer, is that clear?"

Agonizing seconds ticked by.

"Yes, Sir. Thank you, Sir."

Dorian closed the door in his client's face without another word and turned back to Zach.

"That was, ummm..." Zach quickly drained his cider. "I should

178

go."

"Nonsense." Dorian tossed off his robe and slipped into a plain black t-shirt, translucent underwear and tight black jeans. It seemed awfully casual attire for a dom. "He doesn't get to show up here unannounced without consequences."

"Consequences? Wait, what are you—"

"Hey, can you do me a huge favor, real, real, real, quick?"

"Huh? A favor... sure?"

Dorian rummaged through his suitcase again. "Stand over there, in the corner and stay absolutely silent. Not a word, no footsteps, nothing. Just stand there, face the corner and breathe."

"Uh..."

"Don't worry, he won't see you." Dorian lifted a small leather mask from his suitcase. "Quick! Before he comes—"

Another knock interrupted them.

Dorian silently shooed Zach into the corner, hands flapping like the star of a gay French farce, their Tom of Finland afternoon, now turned La Cage aux Flogg. Slipping leather gauntlets over his wrists, Dorian regained his compliance with a glare that was anything but farcical.

The next few seconds of silence tightened a knot in Zach's stomach. He could only imagine how they felt for the man waiting naked outside, his junk exposed to anyone who might walk by. Agonizing? A complete turn on? Both? At last, he heard the door open. There were no words, just the sound of Dorian's feet shifting on carpet. Then the client's shuffling into the room.

He heard the door shut, and a little more shuffling before what sounded like a pillow hitting the floor.

"Get on your knees," commanded Dorian.

Zach heard a swallow, then the stranger stammering "Tha…
thank you, Sir, for seeing—"

"On your knees, faggot!"

Zach's shoulders leapt to his ears. Even now, Alistair Conway's
favorite word for him stung. He heard the gentle sound of fabric settling into carpet, followed by soft footsteps he took to be Dorian's. It
was like a sound design assignment he'd done last semester.

"You know what you did wrong, don't you?" Dorian continued.

"Yes, Sir."

"Which is?"

"I arrived without an invitation, Sir."

"Putting your own anonymity, and mine, at risk. That's right."

Zach heard more quiet footsteps, then the sound of cloth slipping over something, or someone.

"I have some errands to run," Dorian continued. "You'll wait
here for me, on your knees, until I get back."

"I…" the client began, weight audibly settling as he shifted position. "I can come back later, Sir."

"Your text," Dorian corrected him, "said you were coming over
early, and requested we start when you arrive. We are starting now,
and so is my rate. Is that a problem?"

"No, Sir!"

"I'm glad to hear it."

Zach felt a faint tap on his shoulder. He turned to see Dorian's
self-satisfied smile.

"The bathroom is on your right, should you require it." Dorian
opened the door and silently beckoned Zach to follow him. "You will
not move for any other reason until I return. Is that understood?"

Zach heard the sub swallow under the black velvet sack Dorian had put over his head. "Yes, Sir. Please, Sir, how long will you be?"

Dorian never took his eyes off his client as Zach passed them. "As long as I require."

"Yes, Sir."

Dorian stood motionless in the doorway. "Forgetting something?"

Zach watched as the naked man fumbled for his pants until he at last found his wallet. He took out his credit card and held it up, allowing Dorian to pluck it from his fingers and pocket it.

Dorian closed the door behind them and led Zach to the elevators.

Zach wondered which of a dozen or so questions he should lead with. Was Dorian a sub or a dom now? Was he just going to leave the client there? What was with the credit card? Making the client strip naked before he came back? Zach didn't know where to start. He just kept looking at Dorian in the elevator. Dorian barely acknowledged him, even as they stopped at the second floor and a tall woman got in the lift with two pug dogs on leashes. Zach watched her get out on the ground floor before they disembarked themselves.

"So…" Fuck it. There was no question that wasn't going to sound asinine. "You're just… going to have a drink in the hotel bar, or something? I mean, you're not going to just leave him?"

"The hotel bar?" Dorian asked. "You're funny."

"But what about him? How long's he supposed to wait up there?"

"He's not restrained. He can leave any time, if he wants to disappoint me. He'll probably even get his card back, eventually." Dorian grinned at Zach. "But he won't leave. He's pulled this shit before, but he never usurps my authority completely. That'd ruin the fantasy. He wouldn't have arrived early if he had somewhere else to be. He'll pay for the time, too. Trust me, he's hard as a rock right now, imagining all the ways I'll make him pay for this. Maybe literally. Hey, do you need anything? New shoes?"

"No, no. It's okay, I... I get it," Zach said, not getting it at all. "Maybe a drink?"

"My limit's one when I'm on the clock." Dorian glanced at the hotel doors. "Hey, crazy idea. You still horny?"

"Well, yeah, but..." Zach stammered. Okay, maybe their connection wasn't immediate. Maybe they could try again, but..."What about your client?"

"Please. I don't get off with him." Dorian grinned at him again. "I still want to be bad, though. Know anywhere we can go?"

"I... can't host."

"Or dom, apparently. So, what do we do?"

Zach shook his head. "Maybe I should just go. Sorry, I don't mean to mess up your... whatever."

His eyes widened as Dorian squeezed his hand. The woman with the pugs smiled at them from the check-in desk.

"Seems we're a cute couple," Dorian said. "Let's go for a drive. I've got a bad idea."

Zach had never had sex in a public bathroom before. Had he been planning to add that particular stamp to his passport of public trysts, alongside the on-campus stairwell, Hanlan's Beach, and Ben's car, the public bathrooms near the bottom of Wesley Park would not have been his first choice. In the summer heat, they'd taken on an ambience akin to what Zach would expect to smell if he microwaved

Grace Jones' litter tray. Either Dorian had long coked or poppered away any natural sense of smell, or the handsome escort was a bigger pig than his profile had let on.

"Kiss me." Dorian pushed himself back against the wall, yanking Zach along for the ride.

"I thought you said—"

"Fuck what I said. *Do it!*"

Trying to ignore the bacterial bacchanal he was sure coveredthe graffiti-christened wall, Zach focused on the face to which he'd sloppily connected, breathing through Dorian's kiss while his half-lover, half-respirator pulled up their t-shirts.

"Bite my nipples!"

Zach pressed his face against the man's chest like it was a life raft on the River Styx. Dorian's freshly showered natural scent offered just enough relief for him to close his eyes, circle Dorian's nipple with his tongue in between nibbles, and maybe lose himself to the delusion long enough to pop a woody.

Scratch bathroom sex off his list of kinks. What. The. Hell. Was. He. Trying. To. Prove?

"Oh fuck, man! That feels amazing!"

He was getting good reviews, at least. Would it be rude to back out now? He felt the swelling of heat as Dorian pulled open his pants and freed what he'd revealed in the car was a three-fifty-an-hour erection, which batted against the back of Zach's hand. Grateful for something else to focus on, Zach squeezed Dorian's balls.

Dorian gasped. "Easy, easy."

Zach rose to catch Dorian' lips, kissing deeper this time and pushing him against the wall. Allowing himself another breath through the kiss, he at last began to relax.

"That's more like it." Dorian grinned, cupping the denim containing Zach's erection in his hand. "Slap me."

"What?" Zach instantly regretted talking as it forced him to inhale.

"Come on! Hit me. Just a bit."

Zach gave Dorian's jaw a tiny smack that made him flinch.

Dorian's face fell. "Really? That's all I'm gonna get?"

Zach slapped him harder.

"Yeah!" Dorian let the shock pass through his face, then grinned. "Again."

Zach got three more slaps in before Dorian's face flushed with warmth, his dark eyes wide with excitement.

"Yeah, harder! Make me your faggot."

Without thinking, Zach shoved Dorian into the wall. Dorian gasped, closing his eyes, his smile wavering for the second it took to absorb the impact. Had either of them paid more attention, they might have noticed the intruder standing behind Zach.

A sudden 'Hey!' made Zach turn just in time to catch a bony crack across his jaw. He sprawled against the filthy wall, hearing Dorian cry out before the punch's apparent source slammed into Zach's body, knocking the wind out of him. Then just as quickly, he was free. Gasping for breath, he no longer cared how the air inside the block smelt or tasted. He heard several variations of 'What the fuck?' all from Dorian.

"Look, I'm sorry, all right?" The 'Hey!' voice protested. "I didn't know!"

Zach opened his eyes to see a wide-eyed Dorian advancing on a wiry, pale stranger, who sported a mess of colorful tattoos under his too-loose white tank top. Could they get out? Was the intruder blocking their only escape?

"So… what, asshole?" demanded Dorian. "You didn't know so you just, what? Hit him?"

"I thought he was… I heard some guy callin' somebody a faggot, then I see…" the intruder paused, turning to Zach. "Hey, man, are you alright?"

Zach rubbed his jaw, trying not to look directly at the assailant now so curious about his wellbeing.

"I said, are… you… all… right?"

I don't have brain damage, asshole, Zach thought.

"Leave him alone!" Dorian snapped. "He's had enough with you beating on him!"

"He was beatin' on you!"

"I'm fine!" Zach clutched his jaw as a shot of pain filled it.

He heard the stranger swallow. "I… I'm real sorry."

A second later, the guy was gone.

"What… the fuck was that?" Dorian ducked out to check the building's entrance before returning, face vexed. "What the fuck? What the actual *fuck* was that?"

"I don't—Ow!" Zach clutched his jaw as he mumbled. "Is he still there?"

"No. Guy must have a bike or something. Jesus! What the… what the actual fuck?"

"I… I… Ow!"

"Okay, no more talking for you. Come on. Shit! Are you bleeding?"

"No-*ow!*" Zach grimaced, walking out into the fading afternoon light where Dorian took a closer look at his face.

"You'll want some ice for that."

185

"Shouldn't we go to the police?"

Dorian frowned at him. "You were about to have sex in a public restroom in the state of Indiana."

"Right. I guess. Don't… touch it." Zach flinched, grateful to have returned to the fresh summer air of Wesley Park.

"Don't move. I'll be right back."

"Hey, what if he—" The words caught in Zach's throat as the pain returned. The bastard had a mean right hook. He heard the faint buzz of a message on his phone. If it was that fucking cat…

What's happening, sexy?

Zach looked at Cascade's photo, and the playful three-word message beneath it. *You wouldn't believe me if I told you.*

Oh, this should be good. Where are you?

He gently bounced the phone in his hand, wondering how much to share. *Wesley Park.*

Wesley Park??? Oh, okay stud.

What?

I've heard stories about Wesley Park.

Not this kind.

Now I HAVE to hear this.

"Hey."

Zach looked up to see Dorian returning with two frozen popsicles in hand. He gratefully accepted one the color of blue lemonade. "Thanks. How much do I owe you?"

"Seriously? It's for your jaw, smart guy, and I *will* jam it against your face if you don't stop talking. Now do as you're told."

Zach smiled. It hurt. "He gives me orders? Thought you said I couldn't afford you."

"Hah. Look at you, racking up the freebies today."

He winced as the cold touched the spot where the fist had struck. "Thanks."

"Least I can do after... I don't even know what that was."

"Did you even see him come in?"

"I was busy." Dorian sucked on his icy white popsicle. "I'm sorry. I was the one who suggested—"

"Maybe we should have picked somewhere less open?"

"From what I'm told, nobody comes down here 'til five or so. Don't worry, man. Not meant to happen, I guess."

Zach shook his head. "What did he say to you, exactly? Right after he hit me."

"Say?" Dorian sucked the juice from the treat, nibbling its end. "He asked if I was alright. I think? Then, he must have worked out that you weren't actually hurting me, because he was all 'oh, sorry, my bad.' Freak. Hey, do you mind if I have something stronger than this?"

"Uh, sure, go ahead." Zach considered the optics of some heavily tattooed idiot leading with his fists on a couple of homos in a public bathroom. He didn't doubt the Petri dish of self-loathing that was Fairview had produced its share of gay bashers, but they didn't usually come with hero complexes. "Are you alright?"

"I'm just rattled. Keep that ice on your jaw."

"It's not so bad now."

"No, but it'll bruise up nasty if you don't... Eh, suit yourself." Dorian rolled a fresh joint between his long, dexterous fingers, extending it to Zach. "Do you indulge?"

"Rarely."

"Might do you as much good as the ice."

Keeping the popsicle on his jaw, Zach lifted the joint from

Dorian's fingers and let him light it. Thinking it seemed rude to take the first toke, he offered it back.

"Aww, see? Even now, a gentleman." Dorian accepted it with a long toke he held for several seconds before coughing. "Go easy."

Zach raised the joint to his lips and puffed at it, gingerly.

"Jesus, I said easy, not timid. Commit, damn it."

Zach drew on the joint and tried not to wheeze. "Thanks."

"You're adorable. Aren't you from Canada? I thought they legalized pot?"

"Shut up," Zach laughed, passing it back. "So…"

Dorian raised an eyebrow at his extended silence. "You have questions?"

"A few," he admitted. "You… were you born in Chicago?"

Dorian smiled at him. "That's not what you want to know."

Zach swallowed. Fuck it. "Okay, why would a professional dom want to sub for somebody right before his client comes over?"

"Ah, there it is!" Dorian answered. "That's the one. Like I said, it relaxes me. Gets me feeling sexy. I'm not really a switch or anything. The dom stuff pays my rent. I started taking the workshops while I was exploring my sub side. I worked out what I liked based on that."

Zach nodded. This sounded familiar.

"Anyway, turns out those skills can make you a hot commodity, especially among subs who don't have the time to invest learning everything."

"And umm… Wait, what if I bruised you? Left marks on you? You wanted me to use some pretty hard-core—"

"Hard core?" Dorian laughed. "Sorry, sorry. Okay, so, I do the session with a bruise on my back, or with a glowing hot ass? So what? Assuming I even let him see it. He knows better than to ask."

"So, just... work versus pleasure, huh?" Zach asked.

"That's all it is." Dorian took a long drag of the joint and passed it back. "How long are you staying in town?"

"Uh... the summer."

"You don't sound too excited about that. No old friends you want to see?"

Zach shook his head. "Long story." One he didn't feel much inclined to repeat.

"Ouch. But you must keep in touch with somebody. From school? Social media at least?"

"I don't use it. No Facebook. No Twitter."

"Instagram? TikTok? Snapchat?"

"Nope, nope, nope." Zach toked, not sure how much to share. "I'd just rather keep my private life private."

"Fair. Totally fair."

Zach passed the joint back, thankful that Dorian had cooled it on the questions. "You know anybody in Fairview? Besides your client?"

"You're suggesting I visit your fine hometown for tourism?"

Zach shrugged.

"I'm just teasing," Dorian grinned. "Chicago born and raised. I don't mind the drive."

"Are you out? To your parents I mean?"

If the question bothered Dorian, he didn't show it beyond toking again. "They met my last boyfriend. We broke up a week later. I didn't tell them until a while after. My mom's a proud cook. Things could have been taken the wrong way. But he was pretty white bread. White like the picket fence he wanted around our nice suburban house containing our nice, monogamous relationship."

"Right. Is that what ended it?"

"Kind of. His brother also fucked me, which was awesome. Hey, I was upfront about what I wanted and who I was from the start. He—my ex, not the brother—said to give him time to get used to that idea. So, I waited, then finally decided six months waiting was enough. I mean, the plan was just to tell him, but… Tom, the brother, he was the wild one. Hotter too. Fuck, maybe if I'd met and dated Tom from the get-go, things might have gone easier. Dude still invites me to these crazy sex parties. Slings, benches, sex toys for days. He and Gary don't speak anymore."

"Gary?" Zach asked.

"Gary. I know. We met finishing school on the West Coast. It was nice at first. He was like a break from the whole full-on, Berkeley queer radical thing. But he wasn't an asshole, either. He was just… Gary. In the end though, maybe there was too much self-loathing? I don't know. Like, he'd idealize these rough, hairy muscle guys, talk about how 'different' he was from other gays, and shit like that. He wasn't nasty, but the subtext was there. He even used to sext me, talking about our 'broad, masculine chests." Dorian looked down, gaze flipping from one side of his slim chest to the other. "I said 'You're fooling who, exactly?' That didn't go down so well, but then, neither did he."

Zach watched Dorian laugh, trying to swallow the uncomfortable familiarity that had risen in his throat at the mention of 'idealized muscle guys.'

"My fault." Dorian passed the joint back. "I was always warned, if the sex is bad, check out. Like, if it's not a 'hell yes,' make it a 'hell no.'"

"Who said that?"

"My mom."

Zach almost swallowed the joint.

"Are you okay?"

"Your mom…" he wheezed between coughs, passing it back. "Your mom sounds cool."

"Says she speaks from experience," Dorian shrugged. "I did not ask what that meant."

"I wouldn't either."

"My parents gave me the sex talk pretty young. They were always pretty open about male, female… whatever. They just saw everyone as human. So, when they met Gary," Dorian shrugged, smiling at Zach. "Mom knew. They liked him, but they knew. Mom says you can smell sexual energy between some people, and with Gary, it was like 'Sniff, sniff… mmm! Bleach."

"Do they know you ah… you know."

"Do they know I'm a specialized sort of companion?" Dorian mocked him with a nasal affectation.

Zach choked, grateful that the joint was nowhere near his mouth.

Dorian laughed. "No, they think I trade cryptocurrency. Good way to end a conversation quickly with a couple of fifty-somethings, if you ever need one."

"I'll keep that in mind." Zach was the one who felt stupid, taking another hit, promising himself it would be the last one. "Hey, I'm really sorry."

"For what now?"

"That I couldn't give you what you wanted."

"You said that already."

"I'm kind of still… working things out." Zach passed the joint back. "Guess I'm not that kinky."

Dorian nodded, taking a last hit before extinguishing it on the wall. "Not kinky enough to enjoy guys punching you?"

Zach watched a smile break across his companion's face, and the two of them started laughing.

"Man, that was some caveman shit." Dorian said.

"Right?" Zach asked. "Like, what's his deal? Does he just roam around, looking for people in trouble like some 'redneck avenger?'"

"The Redneck Avenger? Oh god. Stop!"

"Wait, wait, wait… Never fear, 'cuz dark or queer, Straight White Savior Man is here!"

"You did not just sing that?"

"I did."

"You sing?"

"Badly."

"I can hear that."

"Fuck off." Zach barely had time to laugh before Dorian's lips, still cool from the ice treat, brushed against his in a gentle kiss, leaving a shy smile on his face. "What was that for?"

Dorian didn't bat an eye. "Being real with me. And before you ask, no, smart guy. It did not turn me on."

"Ah. I'm so—"

"—sorry! I *knew* that was coming, you son of a bitch. I knew it." Something about the way Dorian looked back at him made Zach feel like he didn't have to explain. Or maybe he was just stoned. Either way, it felt good.

"So," Dorian began. "How'd you figure you liked dominating these alpha guys?"

Zach shrugged. "When I'd get pissed off at my ex… it's kind of petty, I guess."

"You like guys who need to be taken down a notch?"

Zach thought about elaborating, but even with Dorian, who probably would have understood better than most, it felt like too much to get into, stoned, with an aching jaw. "Something like that."

"So, you came back here hoping to find yourself a nice, dumb, cocky Hoosier ex quarterback? Fuck him hard? Make him beg for mercy?"

Zach laughed despite himself. "More than you know."

"Sounds like you've got a good idea what you want," said Dorian. "Out of sex, anyway. Why waste my time? Not that I'm not enjoying your company."

"I don't know. Your profile sounded fun. I just got up in my head. Scared, maybe."

"Yeah?" Dorian shrugged. "So... are you scared of hurting someone? Or scared of these alpha guys that turn you on?"

"Scared of what I might do if I let go." This sounded franker than Zach had meant to be.

Dorian's eyes filled with mischief. "Indulge me. What's the worst thing you think you could do to one of these big, cocky men you like?"

Zach rubbed his impacted jaw. "I don't know. Sleep with his brother?"

"Oh, hardy har har. To be clear, we just had sex. By that I mean Tim strapped me to a bench, slipped three ice cubes into my ass and flogged it until it was hot while they melted. He said it'd make fucking more intense and he could have been right, because once the numbness wore off it felt fucking unreal. Tim was a 'hell yes' for me. Sorry. I overshare when I'm stoned. How about you? The truth this time."

Zach shifted his back against the wall, his gaze landing on part of a burned-out tree stump that looked like the dark, grey face of an angry gnome. "How stoned are you?"

"Oh, this better be good."

"In high school, this guy filmed me giving my first blow job and sent it all around school and church."

"Woah! Ouch."

"Years later, I fucked him raw. Called him the name he used to call me right as I came inside." How good it felt to share this aloud. He'd won. Forget the rest of it. The accident. The death. That was its own separate pile of steaming shit. Taken on its own, the sex had been hot, and what it had meant to him...

"Damn!" Dorian laughed. "Good for you! Wait, how'd you even—"

Maybe it was the pot, but thinking of it made him want to cream, then and there. Could he take Dorian back into the bathroom block and finish what they'd started? Make the guy get on his knees and worship his cock until his load was spent? Was this how fearlessness felt?

"He didn't recognize me," Zach said. "Not until then, at least."

"Sneaky bastard. Then what happened?"

Hell, it wasn't like Dorian would actually believe him! Or would he? Wood-hee. Woody. Hah! Oh, fuck he was stoned. "He freaked out. Tripped over my cat. Fell down the stairs."

"No shit? Hope the asshole broke his fucking neck."

Zach remembered the loud thud. The snap that had harmonized with it. The sight of Alistair's body, unmoving and unbreathing. Just like Zach was now, perfectly still, holding Dorian's gaze just that little bit too long. Dread wrapped around his heart. The absence

194

of a reply... was a reply.

"I'm joking," Dorian said. "Sorry, that was dark."

"No! I mean, yeah, of course! Not too dark at all. It was funny." Right. Because they'd laughed so fucking hard. "I mean, the guy was fine. He left. Embarrassed. Pissed off. But he was fine. He was totally fine."

Don't oversell, idiot.

"Man, are you okay?"

"Oh yeah, I'm fine!" Zach said, smiling so hard it hurt. "Snacky though."

"Me too. The popsicle cart had chips too, if you want."

"Great! I could murder some chips."

Shut up. Oh god, just shut up!

"Cool. Any preference on flavor?"

Zach felt his stomach tighten. "What do you mean by that?"

"Chips!"

"Oh! Salt and vinegar?"

"Okay. Gross, but not judging. Back in a minute."

Zach nodded, trying to concentrate on the burned-out stump. This would be fine. They were stoned. Stoned people said stupid shit. Stoned people were not always sure of what they saw or heard. Stoned people had sudden cravings for chips. Was Dorian stoned? Wasn't he working? Zach reached for his wallet. This time, he'd insist on paying Dorian when he came back.

If he came back.

What if he wasn't coming back?

So much for composure *a la Conway*. Zach hadn't told Dorian about Conway's demise, much less claimed to have killed him. Hell, he hadn't even identified Conway, besides naming him as the guy who'd shared that video and fuck, fuck, fuck, anybody who could add two and two at his former school or church would know precisely who that was, and even if Conway's body was never found and no charge was ever brought, he would be the last person to have seen Conway alive, which would mean giving a statement, and never mind the fucking cat, and the phone, and—

"Hey."

Zach whipped around to face the intruder, brushing off the hand that had landed on his shoulder. In the second it took to do this, his mind bounced between realizing it was probably Dorian, feeling relief that it was only Dorian, realizing it was not in fact Dorian, and the panic of recognition as he backed away from the redneck who'd socked him across the jaw.

"Woah!" The guy lifted one colorfully tattooed arm in front of his face, like Zach was about to return the favor. "Wasn't tryin' to scare ya. Are you okay?"

Zach tried to choke down his nerves. "Just… stay there."

The guy tilted his head with a smile that appealed more to Zach's raw, still unsated sex drive than it did to his better sense.

"What do you want?" Zach fumbled for his wallet, scooped out a handful of bills and threw them to the ground between them. "Here. Take it. Just… leave us alone!"

The man raised his hands, slowly stepping forward to count his prize. "Four bucks? Uh, maybe you should hold onto that."

Zach studied the intruder's face for the inevitable trap beneath that not-quite-Southern drawl. Then, he realized why the man's profile seemed incomplete. "Where's your shirt?"

"Wherever." The guy pushed his naked shoulders back, making a show of modest but firm pecs. The sight set off a rumble in

Zach's stomach that he frankly resented. "I'd rather tan naked, but you know. Summer vacation. Kids around."

"You think this is funny?" Zach demanded. "Like, is this your thing? Wait around half-naked in the woods for dumb homos to come onto you so you can rob them?"

"Well, if that's so, the business model sucks." The guy held the four singles out to Zach.

Zach snatched the money back and stuffed it in his pocket, giving his unexpected company a long once-over. "Why'd you hit me? That was you! I didn't imagine that! You punched me! Asshole!"

"Man, I said I was sorry! I thought you were messing up that guy. There wasn't exactly time to think about it. I'm sorry, okay? Real sorry. Where is he, anyway?"

"Mind your business."

The man grinned in response, setting off another unwelcome rumble in Zach's stomach. "So... you're okay? Nothing broken?"

"Just give me a minute."

"Man, are you stoned?"

"A little."

"You got some?"

"No. It was his."

"Huh. Is he comin' back? I can wait."

"Just leave us alone!"

The guy raised his arms, putting his hands behind his head and leaning back in the sun, giving Zach a three-sixty-degree, full-body view. A pair of sharp, leathery wings darkened the stranger's naked back, showing up blue streaks in the light. "Why you so wound up, man? You're high. The sun feels great."

"Some asshole hit me."

"Not gonna let that go, are you?"

"You're lucky I don't call the cops."

"Stoned?" The man shot Zach a cheeky, one-eyed stare. "And tell 'em you were about to fuck some dude in the park? Sounds smart."

Zach swallowed his embarrassment. "Who said we were about to fuck?"

"Hey, no judgement. Kind of hot, now I remember it."

It hadn't until now occurred to Zach that the interloper might also be gay, which didn't make his afternoon any weirder. "What do you want? Besides pot?"

The guy hooked thumbs into the loopholes of his shorts and leaned back again. The sudden wash of sunlight showed up the details in his tattoos. The grinning, bloodied skull just beneath his navel. The intricate scales of a snake, mottled with dark blues and greens that coiled up one wiry arm to flick the neck of its owner with a forked tongue. A red daemon, with tightly wound muscles bound by thick black ropes, writhed and screamed on the guy's right pectoral, while the lines of what looked to Zach like a voodoo symbol crisscrossed their way over the back of his right hand. "You like 'em?"

"I've seen bet...." Zach frowned as he examined the guy's lanky body, the white tank top now tucked into his shorts, and finally, that cocky smirk he'd last seen lit up in the headlights of Ben's car. "Wait.... I know you! I mean, I've seen you!"

"Why yes, yes you have. No issues with those cops, by the way. Not that you guys stuck around to find out."

Zach nodded, leaning against the toilet block. His head felt like it was spinning. "You looked like you could take care of yourself."

The stranger grinned. "What's your name, tough guy?"

He shook his head, at last starting to believe the man didn't mean him harm. "Zach."

"Zach? No hard feelings. Felix." The man's hand was cooler to the touch than Zach had expected. He also wasn't letting go. "You sure you're feelin' okay?"

"Felix?" Zach repeated. "Look, my friend's coming back any minute. You don't have to stay."

"I'm just makin' sure. Is that alright? I feel bad about it."

The strength of Felix's fingers wrapped around his own seemed to ground him, pushing away his vertigo and nausea. "I don't think I trust you."

"That's probably smart."

Zach wished Felix would go away. Or let go of his hand. Or at least put a couple of feet between them until his erection had had a chance to...

Okay, *no!* Absolutely—

Felix's lips were as cool as his hands had been. Too stunned to resist, Zach shuddered as one of those hands hooked around the lip of his shorts. Felix's tongue had found his, and cool fingertips had brushed his cock before he could break through the lustful haze of having the man's body against his.

"What the actual fuck?"

Even as Zach pushed Felix away, Dorian stood dumbstruck, two bags of chips in one hand, two bottles of cold water in the other, and one confused kinkster between them.

"Dorian!" Zach barked.

"Well, hey. I thought you guys..." Felix looked from Dorian to Zach, his stupid smile unchanged. "Shit, I'm not tryin' to make drama."

"Oh, it's fine," Dorian shook his head. "There's no drama. I see you two made up."

Zach heard a crinkling as Dorian's hands tightened around the snacks. "Yeah, Felix was just leaving."

"Felix, is it?" Dorian asked. "You even got his name? Good for you."

"Yeah." The intruder extended a hand to Dorian. "Listen, I'm real sorry about earlier, man. Bye-gones, yeah?"

"It certainly looks that way," Dorian said, ignoring the gesture.

"You joining us?"

"I'll pass, thanks."

"Uh…" The same cocky half grin was back as Felix's gaze shifted between them again. "Look, guys, I didn't mean to cause any… I just took you as kind of open-minded and—"

"Oh, it's cool," Dorian answered before Zach could speak. Fuck, was he still stoned? "You guys do what you want!"

"Dorian…" The sight of Dorian turning and stalking away from them shook Zach out of his sluggish fugue. This couldn't be happening. He hadn't even wanted Felix to kiss him, damn it. "Dorian, wait."

"For what?" Dorian rounded on Zach, eyes full with frustration. "For you to decide what you want? I mean clearly, he's your type. An asshole!"

Zach stopped, the shame that had deflated his would-be dom bravado clouding his mind again.

"Hey, whatever, man. I've got a client to see. You don't owe me anything. I'd just appreciate you not making me out to be a complete idiot while I'm off getting you snacks."

"Dorian, I swear, it just—"

"If you tell me 'It just happened,' I'll punch you myself." Dorian leaned close to his ear. "Unless that's the kind of guy you want?"

Zach watched Dorian stalk away as he tried to figure what that meant. "Wait."

"Dude, just block me."

He watched Dorian's black t-shirt disappear through the trees. What could he say? Maybe it was true. Yves, Alistair, maybe that was the kind of guy he deserved. But Felix? What kind of guy was Felix, if that was even his real name? The freak could have been a serial killer for all Zach knew.

"Hey."

"Gargh!" Zach startled. "What the fuck?"

Felix grinned at him. "That's twice now. Not one of those paranoid stoners, are ya?"

Zach folded his arms, feeling the phone buzz in his pocket. "Look, what do you want?"

At least Felix had the decency to look ashamed. "Hope you guys work it out. I really didn't mean to make your boyfriend all—"

"He's not my boyfriend." Only now did Zach consider the potential benefits of that cover story.

"Shame. You make a cute couple. Though not as cute as you and me would."

Zach dodged the man's arm as it reached for his shoulder. He started walking. Anywhere. He didn't remember much of Wesley Park, though he recognized the dark, creepy looking waters of Chester Pond at the bottom of the hill through the trees. At age four, his Grandfather had convinced him it was a portal for all kinds of frightening aquatic creatures, who swam through magical portals from the ocean or the Great Lakes to bathe in its waters and replenish their evil. Sea monsters and dragons. Man-eating squid. Giant

Beavers. Canadians.

Felix never fell far behind him. "Man, don't be sore. You said he's not your boyfriend. Were you guys even fucking?"

"More than you and I ever will."

"Well, touché. Glad you still got your sense of humor."

Zach rounded on him. "I'm not jo—"

Another sudden kiss erased any lingering doubt Zach had about Felix's sexuality, if not quite his intentions. No guy setting him up as a mark would have pushed forward with that kind of conviction, or held him like that, committed in total to the act this time, instead of stealing it in Dorian's absence. Zach's better sense fought a losing battle against raw, physical desire. The warmth of Felix's breath followed by that sun-kissed body, lean and coated with the light sweat of summer humidity. The soft smell mixed with the earthy, fresh scents of the woods around them, picked up in a gust of wind passing through the trees. His urge to push away again lasted only a second as the tension left his body. He felt Felix's tongue dab his lips as their kiss finally broke and their foreheads rested against one another.

The rush of whatever he'd just felt seemed to affect Felix as well as he caught his breath. "Damn. If I'd known, I might have waited. Savored it."

"If you'd known what?"

The wind unsettled the branches again, setting off a chain of bird shrieks that passed from tree to tree around them. It ended in a sharp trilling somewhere. Zach's tongue tingled and his mouth felt floury, like he'd bitten into paper, but he didn't care.

Why hadn't Felix's kisses hurt? He'd just been punched, damn it!

"You taste like secrets, Zach." Felix stepped away. "Hope I see you around."

Taste like... what? Zach watched Felix walk toward Chester Pond. What the... "Hey, where are you going?"

No answer.

"Can I at least get a ride?"

"I don't have a car, dude," Felix called, not turning around. Steps later, he was gone.

Thanks a lot, park boy. Fuck!

Zach took out his phone, where a message was waiting.

Okay, this story had better be incredible because you're taking your sweet time responding.

His jaw smarted again. He'd forgotten all about Cascade. *Sorry! It's been complicated. Are you available?*

Eight seconds. That's how long someone was supposed to stay on a bucking bull to win... Zach didn't know... Cowperson of the Year, or something. Fortunately, it was also the time it took him to receive an answer.

You're in luck. Are you at home?

No, still at Wesley Park.

Slut!

Shuddup.

Give me fifteen. Where are you, exactly?

He tried to remember the name of the road and came up blank. *You know where the creepy pond is, near the bottom of the hill?*

The creepy pond? That's not weird. Not weird at all.

Chester Pond!

Wait, I think I got it. Can you share me your location, just in case?

Zach wondered if the Chinese or Russian bots that kept tabs on his hook-ups at all times really needed to know his exact whereabouts.

Gotcha! In fifteen, stud.

Zach swallowed, trying to ignore the sound of birds and the ache in his jaw as he tried to remember which path led back to the fucking road.

"He did what to you?"

Zach repeated, very slowly for Cascade's benefit, the story of how he came to be at the bottom of Wesley Park talking to the guy who a half hour earlier had socked him across the jaw.

"Run that last part by me again."

"I said, he apologized to me. Can we let it go?" He'd omitted the part about the unexpected kiss. And the one after that.

"Uh, how about, no? Zach, if some asshole is bashing guys in the park—"

"I... really don't think that's what this is."

"And I really think you should tell the cops. They don't need to know what else you were doing there."

"You forget that I'm stoned?" Zach asked.

"You're a white guy in college. They won't care."

"Even if I did that, and they picked up this guy, do you think he wouldn't tell them what we were doing? He's not stupid. Besides, I'm fine."

"If you say so. And why would this creep apologize to you again?"

"He thought I was choking the other guy."

"Which you were?"

"Consensually!"

204

"I didn't know you were into that."

"I'm not."

"Okay, so this guy thinks he's Batman."

"I guess. Can we drop it now?"

"If you can manage longer sentences," Cascade answered. "Look, not to... minimize your trauma, or however the kids are phrasing it these days, but I feel like I'm prying details from my teenage self, right now."

Zach sighed, pressing his palms against his face. "Sorry."

"Hey, I get it. Sounds like a fucked-up day. Why'd you even hook up with this guy again, if he was into all of that?"

"I don't know. He was cute, I guess. And I've done some dom stuff before. It's kind of hot."

"Did you want to do that stuff with me?" Cascade asked.

"Did you want me to?"

Cascade's laugh reminded Zach why he'd called the guy in the first place. "Not for me, stud. Sorry."

"Me either. Not with you."

They exchanged silent smiles as Cascade slipped a hand over Zach's thigh and rested it there.

"So, what did you end up doing with this guy?"

The mere presence of Cascade's hand on his thigh was making him hard again. "Not much. It just... it was too awkward."

"Awkward, how?"

"He wanted me to flog him. Beat him."

Cascade nodded, slowly as they pulled up to a red light. "And you haven't done that before?"

"I... I have, but... Okay, not exactly."

"So...?"

"He was too… nice?"

"Oh, okay. And you'd prefer a bad boy for something like that?"

"Maybe? I guess?" Zach let out a breath he was sure could have knocked down the pedestrian crossing at the light. What did 'a bad boy' even mean? "It just felt wrong. Like, I couldn't trust myself to let go like that. He even suggested I try being a sub."

"Hah. So, is 'punish me, Sir' our safe word now?"

"Cascade…"

"Sorry." The man smiled at him as they drove on past another row of McMansions. "You know, that's the first time you've said my name out loud?"

"Is it?"

"Yep. I'd hoped it would be while I was making you come, but that's the romantic in me."

"I thought this wasn't a romance."

"It's not. But our meeting was the best date I've had in a long, long time."

Zach smiled, taking Cascade's hand. "For me too."

"Yeah," the man agreed, "and this, so far, is the weirdest."

"Do you feel like a drink?"

"It would be polite to say yes, wouldn't it?" A glint entered Cascade's eye as they kicked off their shoes. "What do you have?"

The rumble in Zach's stomach had nothing to do with hunger. "Do you care?"

"Not in the least."

Zach had barely closed the door before he had a fistful of Cascade's t-shirt and was helping pull it over his head. He'd been so eager to get home, he hadn't thought of this turning into sex... Okay. Lie. He'd totally thought of it turning into sex the moment he'd climbed into Cascade's car and shared a kiss far too long for a simple 'hello,' which still hadn't hurt. The two of them circled, pulling deeper into each other as they spilled out into the living room, where Zach promptly tripped on the carpet.

"Easy, big guy." Cascade caught him in hands that seemed stronger than Zach remembered.

Regaining his footing, Zach helped Cascade slide off their shirts and toss them aside. He pressed his naked torso into Cascade's, going in for another kiss only for Cascade to pull back with a wicked grin. "What?"

"Just curious. Have you... Am I the first guy you've brought back here?"

The unwelcome image of Alistair Conway's frozen form filled his mind. Not that he hadn't considered this before inviting Cascade inside. But the reality of having this, for lack of a better term, 'hell yes' under his roof before he'd been able to take care of... other things, wasn't bothering him the way he'd expected it to. Maybe it was the meat. Maybe it was the sex. Maybe it was Cascade. Maybe he just had the rhythm down with Grace Jones, and so subconsciously had accepted...

Stop thinking, Zachary. Get laid.

"The first one I like," he answered.

"Now I'm curious. Though hate fucking is underrated."

Zach swallowed. No kidding.

"So... your room?"

The image of Alistair in his mind's eye was no longer frozen, but instead very much alive, warm and breathing as he pushed inside it. In his room. In his bed. He instead fixed on Cascade's chest, sucking on one of his nipples before laying a row of kisses down the black stem of the rose that decorated Cascade's flank. Zach dropped to his knees, letting them sink into the carpet as he opened Cascade's shorts and slid them away.

"Or not," Cascade said with a smile.

Zach brushed his lips over the end of Cascade's cock, enjoying the weight and heat of it against his face, how exposed Cascade was willing to be with him. The man seemed to be purring, a purring that grew louder, closer, inhuman, until Zach looked down between Cascade's legs at the scowling face of Grace Jones, right before she sank her teeth into Cascade's calf.

Zach clapped his hands and hissed at the animal. A startled cry from his lover harmonized with a screech and a growl from Grace Jones as she scampered out of reach. Zach narrowly avoided being kicked in the face as Cascade lifted his leg to survey the damage. "Here, let me... let me see."

Great. Now he was having trouble forming words?

"It's okay," Cascade said. "I'm okay. That thing's got teeth."

"I'm sorry, I'll..." He trailed off as he heard another low growl, just in time to see Grace Jones in the next room, ears pulled back, tail raised, body coiled, ready to strike.

"Hey," Cascade said quietly, lowering his stance as he approached the animal. "It's okay, buddy. It's okay. I'm not—"

"Cascade, I don't think—"

Grace Jones launched herself at Cascade again before Zach could finish. Cascade threw himself out of the way just in time to escape with a light scratch. The black streak spun to face him, giving

Zach a full backside view, right before another loud hiss.

"Hey, enough!" Zach barked, clapping his hands.

The cat's head turned, eyes burning with primal, undisguised rage, fangs exposed, but silent, like an old Hammer Horror poster mixed with a German Expressionist nightmare. Zach froze, unable to take his eyes off the snarling visage.

Then, it started to change. Grace Jones' normally adorable button nose began to stretch and broaden. Her whiskers grew and her mouth widened. Again, Zach pounded hard on the floor, only to hear the crack of wooden poles landing on marble, a sound he wouldn't forget any time soon.

He wrenched his attention from the cat long enough to see the four women standing some distance behind him. At the feet of each one kneeled one of the four now-familiar men with hands bound behind his back, eyes hidden behind purple cloth. The bald one in chains, the white-haired youth, the muscular blond, and Tatts, all on bended knee in a semi-circle. A series of tall stone columns surrounded them, each inscribed with a variety of hieroglyphs, a large wooden barrel between each pair. In front of them lay the familiar figure shrouded in bloodied bandages.

Zach turned and suffered a near heart attack. Right where Grace Jones had snarled at him with petulant feline rage now stood an enormous black lioness. Long snout. Enormous canines. Her black coat lined with deep, fiery red stripes like a tiger's hide forged in Hell.

He tried calling Cascade's name but the sound that escaped him was beyond language. The creature was growing. Its paws swelled over marble tiles, razor-sharp claws at their end extending by inches. Zach pushed himself away, skittering along the floor until the impact of a naked body against his shoulders startled him. A brightly decorated arm crossed his chest. Tatts held him still as the enormous beast lifted one of its great black paws, and promptly slit the shrouded figure open from head to toe. An enormous spray of hot crimson blood erupted from the body, covering the marble tiles and columns. It also covered his face.

He was going to die. His cat had developed a taste for human flesh, and now, enraged by the loss of its master to another, it would exact jealous revenge upon him. Hallucinogenic cat meat.

He jumped as the animal let out a great roar that drowned out the ominous rap of the women's staves. He couldn't see the face of Tatts, whose grip on him refused to yield, but if the other three men were bothered by the bloody spray, they weren't showing it. The beast drew closer, its hot breath breaking over their faces. It smelled like pot.

The animal dove upon the shrouded corpse, tearing off a limb and gobbling it in a few swift chomps before moving on to the next. Only once all four had disappeared did it start on the figure's torso, tearing into it, rending flesh from bone in great oversized bites. Zach wondered if he should point out the strip of torn linen hanging form the creature's teeth, but decided against it. The sound of unseen drumming brought the beast's meal to a halt, though this did nothing to settle Zach's nerves. With most of the body gone, it returned its attention to Zach, eyes alight with disdain. He opened his mouth to scream only for his voice to fail as the creature's tongue wrapped around his cheek like sandpaper, cleaning the blood from half his face.

"Umm… thank you?" he said, feeling a bit less like the world's clumsiest serial killer.

A roar that would have sent his sound design professor into convulsions of joy preceded the final swatting of the shrouded figure's head toward the assembled group. Zach swallowed the urge to be sick as several strips of linen came loose, exposing Alistair Conway's dazed and bloodied face. As the creature raised its paw again, claws extended in certain readiness to smite them all into oblivion, the women leapt into action, raising their sticks not at the animal, but at the barrels that filled each space between the stone columns.

The women moved swiftly from barrel to blood-spattered barrel, driving each staff home, releasing each barrel's bounty. The smell of fresh beer filled the air, mingled with marijuana as it spilled over the marble tiles, flooding the temple and turning red with blood. The animal hesitated, lifting one of its enormous black paws from the rapidly expanding red puddle and licking the aftermath from its toe beans.

Zach didn't know whether to be revolted or adopt.

He jumped as the business end of a spear came down swiftly through one of Conway's frozen eyes, embedded itself firmly in what had to be the man's brain and lifted it into the sunlight. The weapon's owner bore an unsettling resemblance to the weirdo he'd met in the park, except for the scars that surrounded his face, as if it had been hastily stitched on. Was Bandage Face trying a new look?

The cat continued lapping at the bloodied beer. Zach watched as the other three men maneuvered themselves, still blindfolded, within reach of Zach and Tatts. He felt their hands on his shoulders, neck, and chest, their faces brushing against his, while Tatts continued to hold him tight, gently kissing the back of his neck. The women hovered behind them. Having silently exchanged their poles for tablets and writing implements, they scribbled furiously, looking up it seemed only to check on the now writhing mass of male flesh that held Zach at its center, like they were sketching it, or directing.

The soldier kept watch on the cat as Conway's disembodied head dripped at the spear's end. The animal continued to drink from the vast pool of beer and blood, which stopped just short of Zach's feet. One long, final lick scooped up what remained of Conway's corpse, which disappeared with a few loud crunches and a contented purring. Then, the animal fixed her yellow eyes on the head at the end of the soldier's spear, but the stranger was ready, yanking it from reach just as the lioness staggered toward him on wobbly paws.

The swooshing of the drunken beast's tail sent a breeze through Zach's hair as the soldier led it away. Tatts tilted his chin and caught him in a deep, sweet kiss. Chains focused on orally pleasing his cock, while Muscles teased one of Zach's nipples. Zach let his head fall back against Tatts' shoulder. Ignoring the voyeur women and the scent thick with blood and beer, he closed his eyes, instead focusing only on what he could feel which—

"Hey. Welcome back to the living."

Zach squinted through a headache as he looked around his darkened bedroom. Besides it being dark outside, the only thing that seemed different was Cascade, sitting on the edge of his bed, now fully dressed.

"You had me worried there, for a sec."

The temple. The cat. The blood. The orgy that... Well, of course he'd woken up before that had consummated. The questions formed and fell from his lips, each as useless as the next.

"Take it easy, mister. There's water on your nightstand. I can make you tea, or whatever."

"Thanks." He reached for the water and downed three long gulps, emptying half the glass.

"I said 'easy,' tiger. What happened back there?"

Tiger? He winced at the restored visual.

"You tell me," Zach murmured. He was still naked. Had Cascade put him safely in bed? He couldn't remember getting there on his own.

Cascade shrugged. "You scared the shit out of me is what happened. You tripping or something? Because I would appreciate a little warning next time, and it would be nice of you to share."

"Share?"

"Christ, I'm kidding. But you did freak out downstairs. To be fair, your cat freaked out first. What did you say her name was?"

"Grace Jones."

"Grace Jones." The name brought a smile to Cascade's lips. "Well, Ms. Jones does *not* like me, I can tell you that. Hissing and scratching. She bit me again too. I had to lock her in the basement before I could get near you."

The basement? Zach's throat seized with panic before he forced himself to calm down. If Cascade had found Conway, no way would he be sitting there now, nursing Zach back to reality. "What do you mean, 'get to me?'"

"You were freaking out. I had to grab you from behind so you didn't slam your head into the wall. Must have been quite the trip! I thought you guys only did weed?"

"We did." Zach second-guessed himself. Could Dorian have laced the joint? No way! They'd shared it, and Dorian had been driving. But the other guy? Felix? He relayed this theory to Cascade.

"Shifty fucker. You said you kissed him? Well, if he was shrooming or something, it could have been accidental. It would be pretty weird for that to happen, but, maybe, since you were already stoned..."

"He didn't seem like he was shrooming."

"Neither did you when I picked you up." Cascade pointed out. "What did you see, anyway?"

Zach described the vision as best he could, leaving out the part about the shrouded body being Conway.

"Man, you have some serious unresolved issues with your cat."

Zach smiled, but said nothing, the joke exactly what he'd needed to hear.

"Sounds kind of sexy, though."

"You interrupted the best part."

"Oh, so that's my fault?" Cascade flashed him a grin. It vanished as the man's phone pinged with a message. He took it out, grimly scanning it before putting it back in his pocket.

"What time is it?" Zach asked.

"Almost half past midnight."

"Huh? How? I was... It seemed like, maybe a minute, tops."

"Yeah, well, you were out of your gourd, barely conscious for a good chunk of that. I almost called the hospital, but you were breathing okay, and we managed to get upstairs to your room. Plus, I didn't know whose insurance you had."

"My parents."

"Exactly, and they don't need to meet me."

Zach reached out and squeezed Cascade's hand. "Thanks."

"Not necessary. I wasn't going to leave you tripping balls by yourself."

The ping of another text. Cascade rolled his eyes.

"Wade?"

"Wade."

"How much trouble are you in?"

"That's text number twenty-six. The record's thirty-one, and I had to get a hotel."

"I'm sorry."

"For what? I told him I was going to be late. Apparently, the excuses I made up on the fly did not come back within an acceptable timeframe."

Zach grimaced. "I'm sorry, for making you lie."

"I'm just glad you're okay."

He squeezed Cascade's hand again, bringing it up to his chin and kissing it. "This is so not how I wanted this afternoon to go."

Cascade stroked Zach's chin with his thumb. "As in, *not* several uncomplicated hours of mad, passionate, no-strings monkey sex before sending me on my way?"

He grimaced again. "Not exactly what I meant."

"Why not? Sounds perfect to me." Cascade hissed as his phone pinged again.

"Why are you with him?" asked Zach.

Cascade's smile vanished.

"Oh my god, that was super rude. I'm sorry. Forget I—"

"Stop." Cascade's face was implacable, though he seemed in no hurry to withdraw his hand, which made Zach no less ashamed of the question. "Habit, I guess? I know that's a lousy answer. Sounds flippant, like code for 'mind your own business' but it's not. I just mean... we have the house. The dog. Life. Mutual friends. You know? Habit. Why do you ask?"

Zach's mouth was dry again. "Just something the guy said to me today."

"The kinky guy or the weird guy?"

"The kinky guy. That if somebody's not a 'hell yes' for you then they should be a 'no.' He said he learned the hard way."

"Right. Well, Wade was a 'hell yes,' for me, at least for a while. We got older. Shit changed, and so what? It's not like we can't get off with other people."

"You don't feel like, I don't know, like there's something missing?"

Cascade's cocky smile returned. "Didn't you just end your first relationship?"

Zach finished his water and with Cascade's help, eased himself out of bed. He wobbled at first, but quickly found his feet as Cascade stood up with him.

"You should go," Zach said. "That's if he hasn't locked you out."

Part of Zach hoped Wade had.

Cascade put his arms around Zach's shoulders. "Are you sure you're going to be okay?"

"If Grace Jones doesn't kill me in my sleep, yeah." Zach nuzzled Cascade's neck, relaxing into a long hug, enjoying the weight and warmth of arms around his naked back. He didn't try to keep track of how long they stood there, or how many times they kissed. It didn't make lifting his head from Cascade's shoulder or letting him go any easier.

"You'll get your 'hell yes,' Zach," Cascade said, squeezing his hand one last time. "Don't miss the good stuff in the meantime, okay?"

He walked Cascade out. The only exchange he wanted between them was one last kiss at the front door. He gently closed it and let himself breathe.

Don't fall for the married guy, you stupid fuck.

The thought hovered, word for word like neon lights, mocking him. Did he even know what falling for a guy felt like? He'd often asked himself if he'd actually fallen for Yves, or if that wave of raw lust had just crashed over his inability to believe anyone, much less anyone that hot, smart, or charming could find him attractive.

His theories since the break-up had ranged from Yves' self-esteem being even lower than his own, which seemed unlikely, to their whole relationship having been some perverse hipster art project. Either way, Cascade was emotionally off limits. Even if his relationship was on the brink of failure, Zach wasn't about to get caught in the middle of that explosion. Hadn't that been the whole point of coming back to Fairview? Fuck, relax, eat, sleep, repeat?

So much for that.

The basement. He couldn't put it off forever. Taking a few deep breaths, he opened the basement door and flicked on the light. Peering down the stairs, Zach felt his jaw fall slack on his face.

"Motherfucker!"

His entire body trembled as he descended the stairs. The only sound came from their steady creaking. There were overturned paint cans, at least two of which had cracked open, spilling grey and beige into the shredded remains of his sheets and at least one of his shirts. The rest of his clothing had spilled from the upended laundry bag he'd left there, drizzled with what looked like cat vomit. Powdered laundry soap dusted one end of the floor to the other, while a layer of detergent pooled near the washer and dryer. A capsized bag of ancient kibble scattered through it all like oversized chunks of brown rock salt. A bag of frozen peas had been shredded and emptied into the mélange for artistic effect. The constellation of grey and beige paw prints felt superfluous, even sarcastic.

Seeing the lid on the freezer propped open, Zach screamed. It was a short scream. More of a startled screech that choked into silence as he stared into Conway's frozen, lifeless eyes. The man's head sat pinned in place between the freezer and its lid. A chicken leg jutted from Conway's mouth like a fat, frozen cigar, back-lit by the light of the freezer.

Sitting in the middle of it all, on his *Eraserhead* t-shirt, tail twitching behind her, paws neatly positioned side by side in front of her petite body, was Grace Jones. Zach heard a wet, farting sound, right before the cat lifted herself from her 'gift' and ran up the staircase, leaving a trail of painted pawprints in her wake.

Zach swallowed, staring at the tiny, perfectly formed mound of fresh cat shit on Jack Nance's forehead. He felt the swell of white-hot rage enflame his ears and forehead. He swore at the animal, pounding up the stairs and slamming the basement door behind him. Looking left, then right, he'd no idea where the beast had gone. But he did hear his phone ping with a message. Composing himself, he returned to the bedroom and snatched up his phone from where Cascade had left it on the nightstand. The message was three words.

Never again, Zachary.

He gripped the phone so tight he worried he might break it. *Fuck you!*

I beg your pardon?

FUCK YOU. Zach fumed, typing furiously. *YOU SPOILED, FURRY LITTLE SHIT! I'M DONE WITH YOU!* Almost a minute went by without a response. His heart pounding, he kept on typing. *I'm getting rid…* Zach stopped, fingers hovering over the phone. This was absurd. More absurd even than texting with a cat. She could understand spoken language just as well, and wherever she was hiding, he would make damn sure she heard.

"You listen to me, you little monster!" He growled, pacing the upstairs hall. "You were supposed to help me get rid of him. That's all! So far, you've been no fucking help whatsoever. You dropped me into this, damn it!"

His phone at last pinged with a message.

Caution, Zachary.

"Oh, fuck your 'caution!'" he barked back. "This is your fault! Do you hear me? I didn't get under that asshole's legs and make him fall. That was you! You left me with this mess to clean up!"

Ping. *I DEFENDED you, Zachary! Stuck by you as I always have. He would have hurt you and you're naïve to think otherwise.*

"Fuck that! What could he have done, huh?" He snapped, resisting the urge to hurl his phone over the banister. "You tripped him, on purpose! Then you promised... you..."

He stumbled over the words as they began to fail him. Who was he talking to? Could he be certain? He'd just survived an acid or mushroom trip that ought not to have happened. Maybe he was just losing his mind. If he logged out of the app and back in again, would it erase the whole nightmare? Would the messages from 'Conway' magically disappear? As for the basement... Fuck! Had *he* messed it up while he was tripping? Had Cascade messed it... No, no, no, no, no! He wouldn't even start thinking like that. Besides, that would mean Cascade had left Conway's head in the freezer lid like that for... reasons? That's if Conway was even in there! If he wasn't imagining the whole... damn...

He stopped fighting the tears, allowing his body, still naked, to lean against the wall and slide to the floor. His shoulders dropped. His teeth unclenched. He barely made an effort to keep hold of his phone, or to keep track of how much time passed while he sat there. This nightmare. His imaginings. Separating it all felt beyond him.

His phone pinged again, but Zach ignored it, only looking up when a strange, sliding noise came from the end of the hall. He looked up to see Grace Jones nudging something along the carpet with her nose. He waited, perfectly still until the cat had pushed Conway's phone all the way up against his ankle.

Grace Jones lifted her nose, her composure broken only by a couple of small sneezes before she stared at Zach.

Zach cautiously lifted his own phone and read the message.

I'm sorry.

He swallowed the lump in his throat as the cat crawled into his lap and pushed its black, furry head against his chest. Reflexively, he pushed his fingers through her coat, evoking a satisfied purr. He had it. The last piece of evidence that Conway was ever in his home. The cat had brought it right to him. There was nothing to stop him now. He could clean the basement, take what remained of Conway's body and dump it in the woods with the damn phone and never, ever speak of this cursed summer again.

The cat let out a small meow. Zach stilled his hand, not taking his eyes off her. He had to be certain. He put Conway's phone down on the floor and let go of the cat.

"Go on," he said, nodding at it. "Show me I'm not crazy."

Grace Jones glared at him, letting out a small growl.

He growled back, which seemed to astonish her. "Show me, smart ass."

The cat slipped from his legs, weaving in and out of them several times before sauntering over to the phone. She brought the screen to life with a small tap, then licked it in several spots with her tongue. She appeared to consider this for a second, before her paw danced over Conway's passcode faster than Zach could follow. Of course!

It seemed so obvious, now he'd seen it done. The oily residue from Conway's fingers, a trail for an animal with strong olfactory instincts to follow. From there, it was the easiest thing in the world for Grace Jones' paws, moving like some kid's puppet, to swipe over to the app and open their conversation.

Another step back. Another glare.

Zach slowly picked up the phone and scanned their conversation. Word for word. Every exchange they'd had. Right up to *I'm sorry*.

Crazy, he was not.

He laughed, not caring that the cat was staring at him like he'd lost his mind. Proof! It didn't explain the bacchanal orgy dreams, nor how Grace Jones seemed to know about his relationship with Yves, or about his conversations with Ben or Cascade. But they were communicating! He wasn't imagining it. The proof was in his hand.

"And..." Zach knew he was about to sound foolish, but fuck it. "You learned spoken English too?"

"Meow."

Well, duh. Had he expected her to talk back? He placed the phone down in front of her paws.

Grace Jones quickly tapped out a message and hit send. *Long before written. I learned the same way you did, matching sounds with ideas. Then, I simply applied myself beyond the fundamentals. Spelling was a bitch, let me tell you. Consistency is not a strength of your language.*

Zach couldn't help the smile that crossed his face. So panicked by Conway's fate and the predicament it left him in, he hadn't stopped to give this the wonder it deserved.

He had a talking cat! Well, not talking, but a reading, writing, comprehending cat.

Her paws darted over the phone again. *I've placed immense trust in you, Zachary. I hope now you'll believe I'm not playing games.*

"Games?"

You have a dead body in your freezer. I said I could help, and so I shall. But it's time to do exactly what I say. No more doubting me. No more friends with benefits. NEW BLOOD Zachary.

He winced, his stomach turning.

Sorry. New conquests then. Keep them simple, horny, and hot. For once in this world, you have permission, indeed, imperative, to think with your dick.

"Look, why are you so hung up on this sex thing? And would it bother you so much if I just had Cascade over?" He heard the sound of claws pricking carpet. "Oh, that's great. Not unhealthily possessive of you at all."

The cat tapped at the phone with renewed fury. *This was YOUR part of the plan, Zachary. A long, hot, sexy summer, correct?*

"I remember, thank you. And now we're being honest with each other, I want an explanation. What do you care if I do this with one guy or a hundred?"

The animal looked away, lifting its head regally as if some unseen force had caught its attention from down the hall before typing again. *I've tried to make it clear to you, Zachary. If you still don't understand, then I don't believe you will.*

"Make it clear?" he asked. "Words, damn it! I thought the whole point was you could use words!"

Pleasure. Pain. Hunger. Satisfaction. These things are older than words, Zachary.

Zach stared at the text, unsure what part of it he wasn't getting, until another message pinged.

It's not your fault, I suppose. You were born into an age that de-mands and feeds its children answers before they know how to ask ques-tions.

"You mean my parents?"

Among so many others. In fear, they put such faith in forces of which they've no evidence that they can't see those that exist under their noses. Those once worshipped as gods by older and wiser peoples, who watch over them still.

Zach's eyes widened. His heart quickened, and he was suddenly acutely aware of his own nakedness. "You're not a god, Grace Jones."

I made no such claim.

The image from his dream... Zach tried to remember his my-thology.

You spent your childhood taking an abusive spiritual relationship on faith, Zachary, and the second some handsome prick showed you kind-ness, you settled for an abusive emotional one.

"You're asking me to take you on faith?"

Then here's a concrete fact. You're a terrible actor. If this one man you like so much gets close to you, he'll eventually start to see you're hold-ing something back. Do you really want to risk that for a summer fling?

"I wouldn't have to risk anything if you'd just help me get rid of this problem, like you promised."

Gratification, Zachary, does not come so quickly for everyone. You must have patience. Enjoy the rewards while they last.

Patience, my ass. No way was Grace Jones going to finish eat-ing Conway before his folks got home, and even if she did... "What rewards?"

Whiskers tickled against his bare chest, while a tiny paw prodded the abs where his belly had been. He poked a spot above his left nipple. The firm muscle barely yielded to his finger, before he slid it down the undeniable contours of his stomach. It could have been the way he was sitting on the floor, slumped against the wall. But no, he wasn't imagining it. Was this his reward? The kind of body that had always turned him on, so unattainable, wielded by cruel tormentors, like a weapon?

It was his weapon now.

Are you going to make the most of it? Or would you prefer the pain of falling for a man in a failing relationship? A man who can't and won't follow you to Toronto, who may or may not find out you're hiding a body? Do you realize just how close he came tonight? He could have gone anywhere in the house after you passed out. How well do you know him, really?

"Fine. You'll forgive me if I don't rush to hook up with some new random at this exact moment. Or have you forgotten the unholy mess you left downstairs?"

The cat just purred, weaving between his legs and pushing her head against his knees. The gesture seemed so normal that for just one second, he doubted it all again. But Grace Jones was right. Falling for Cascade, no matter how sweet he seemed, would only leave Zach's heart broken. And he'd met the guy, what? Twice? It should have been perfect. Cascade was in an open relationship and the sex was incredible. But the poor guy was working too many things out.

Then, there'd been Dorian, who… maybe was a little too worked out for Zach. He needed somebody in between. Somebody uncomplicated or even… basic? Ugh. Yves' sneering friends had called him that, all while Yves either pretended he hadn't heard, or excused them as 'just teasing.'

Fine. Tonight, he'd sleep. Tomorrow, he'd veg out in front of the TV. Then, he'd find the next one. If he was so 'basic', maybe that was what he needed. Simple. Basic. Easy. Done.

Zachary?

"What?"

Don't you think you ought to clean up the basement?

ETHAN

Zach's back flattened against the wardrobe as Ethan's full lips caught his. The touch of the man's fingers, still cold from the truck's A/C, set him shivering as Ethan reached under his t-shirt and helped him pull it over his head. The man quickly shed his own, pressing his body to Zach's and kissing him deeper, emerging only to bury his face in Zach's shoulder and draw a deep lungful of his scent.

"Fuck you're hot."

Zach smiled at the man's third or fourth repetition of the compliment. Uninventive, but he'd take it. He wasn't sure what had initially drawn him to Ethan's profile, the thickened trunk of a former high school or college athlete? More probably, the endearing uncertainty he'd seen in Ethan's eyes. Uncertainty that couldn't coexist with arrogance or asshole judgement. All his favorite jock parts without the bits he couldn't stand? Score!

Ethan took hold of his wrists, gently dragging him toward the bed before reversing their positions and tossing Zach down on his back. He dived over Zach's body and began kissing his neck, chest, and stomach with open, damp kisses that tickled and made Zach grin. *Sex should be fun* Ethan's profile had said. So far, he'd delivered as promised.

A quick introduction, an understanding that this was strictly a hook-up, not a date, an offer of round-trip transportation to Ethan's house and boom, they were on. It had been so easy, and more than anything, Zach needed easy. He let out a quick gasp of pleasure as the head of Ethan's cock nudged beneath his balls. The man's solid thickness extended to other parts of his body as well, and while Zach liked how it felt, he was glad he hadn't offered to bottom.

Ethan caught him in several deep kisses as Zach wrapped his legs around the man's thighs. He kissed his way down Zach's neck and chest, catching one of Zach's nipples in his mouth and sucking on it just long enough to bring Zach's dick back to attention. Both Ethan's hands slipped down Zach's flank as his tongue flicked against Zach's abs.

Ethan's lips brushed his balls, and with that, he was done teasing, closing his mouth over Zach's erection and wrapping it in long tongue strokes.

"You keep that up, I'm going to come," Zach said, gently pushing on Ethan's shoulders.

The man spat his cock out and grinned. "Can't have that too soon, can we?"

Zach closed his eyes, welcoming another warm kiss until he felt his legs being lifted up on Ethan's shoulders. "What are you doing?"

"What do you want me to do?" Ethan kissed him again, nudging his sizeable cock against Zach's opening. "You do yoga or anything like that?"

"No, why?"

"Think about it. You're super tense."

Subbing? Yoga? Could he turn his hook-ups' lifestyle change suggestions into an art project?

"I just don't normally bottom. Besides, I think you'd destroy me with that."

Ethan grinned, running his hands over Zach's thighs as they rested against him. "Wasn't planning on going there. Don't worry."

Zach returned Ethan's smile, running his fingers through the short, unfussy crop of light brown hair and tweaking Ethan's nipple for good measure. Zach couldn't imagine them enjoying the hours of easy conversation he'd had with Cascade, but the sex between them so far had been communication enough. Plus, Ethan was nice. Just… n-i-c-e-nice.

The man kissed him again, on the forehead this time. "I've never done this without a condom before. With a hook-up, I mean."

"Oh," Zach frowned at him. "Is that what you want?"

"You don't have to. I've got rubbers, if it's something you only do with certain guys, that's cool."

"It's not that. I'm just…" Was he surprised? Not exactly. "I mean, sure, if your partner is okay with that."

"I'm trusted to make my own decisions." Ethan kissed the end of his nose.

Letting his head fall back, Zach closed his eyes, enjoying the damp warmth of Ethan's mouth on his neck, chest, and stomach. He giggled as the man's lips slid over his cock again. If they kept this up, all talk of fucking would be moot. Ethan eased back, stroking the inside of Zach's legs. Sitting between them, he mapped the curves of Zach's body with curious innocence, moving up his thighs and over his flanks, nudging himself against Zach's legs so they tightened around his broad torso.

Zach pulled himself up, taking hold of Ethan's shoulders and drawing him into a deep kiss, enjoying his smell, pricked now with the first perspiration of sex. When he gently rolled Ethan over onto his back, Ethan didn't resist, instead putting his hands behind his head, allowing Zach to drink in the length of his body once more. There was something earthy about Ethan that Zach found compelling. Something grounded and tactile. He gently stroked the skin beside each of Ethan's nipples with his tongue, earning a short, breathy laugh before he lapped at Ethan's pits and grimaced.

"Sorry," Ethan said shyly. "Deodorant. Should have warned you."

"No problem." Zach wheezed before resting his cheek against Ethan's chest, enjoying its steady rise and fall, just for a few breaths. Enough to get a hold of his sex again. He lifted Ethan's legs up onto his shoulders, enjoying the weight and strength of them against his chest. He was still oozing precum, his cock only a fraction softer now, resting on Ethan's balls. "You ready to take that inside you?"

"Couldn't be more ready."

Zach needed no further invitation. Stiffened by the warm timbre of Ethan's voice, he slicked his cock and Ethan's opening as quickly as he could and began easing in.

"Easy, easy."

"Thought you couldn't be more ready?"

"Smart ass."

He took a second to enjoy Ethan's quick intake of breath as he breached, then the slow sigh as he slid the rest of the way in. "Feel okay?"

"Oh... oh man... That's a weapon you've got there."

Zach smiled, deciding not to call out the familiar compliment. Or had his new lifestyle yielded more physical enhancements than he'd first thought? Huh. Score!

Ethan gently rocked his hips deeper against Zach's pelvis. Zach tried to slow himself, ignoring the faint sighs, reassurances he was 'so deep' and exclamations of 'oh fuck' among other pornographic battle cries. He instead tried to focus on his rhythm and movement. The mild ache he now felt in his legs. Counting to ten. Counting sheep. The science test he'd cheated on in ninth grade. Anything but how good Ethan felt on his happily ensconced and engorged…

"Just fuck me!" barked Ethan.

Zach felt himself erupt. Jet after jet of prime splooge answered his grateful lover's pleas for more until he finally collapsed, resting his cheek on Ethan's chest again, his cock still firm inside.

Ethan ran a heavy hand through Zach's hair. "Wow. Wow, that was…"

"I'm sorry," Zach got out between breaths.

The hand stopped. "Jesus, what in the hell for?"

Zach lifted his head, trying to hide his embarrassment with a smile. "Short and sweet, huh?"

"Christ!" Ethan threw his arms around Zach's back and pulled him into a tight bear hug that might have choked him if he hadn't felt so relaxed. "You hear me complaining?"

"I just didn't want it to be over so quick."

Ethan frowned, his face full of mock suspicion. "I take that to mean you're having a good time?"

Zach nodded. He was still hard.

"Me too. You in a hurry to go anywhere?"

Deciding he wasn't, or if he had been, that it no longer mattered, Zach pushed back, feeling himself soften as he retreated.

"Wait," Ethan breathed, rolling the tip of his finger over Zach's nipple. "I want to try something. Can you stay hard?"

"I can try," Zach said, embarrassed that the movement had instantly restored his hard-on and grateful that Ethan hadn't instantly grabbed for it. He nudged himself against the opening as Ethan shifted his weight. Zach sighed with satisfaction as his dick slid back inside and he began to build rhythm again, no longer distracted by a voracious orgasm beating down lust's door. He'd managed before to come more than once while fucking a guy, but only when he was super horny, like he was now.

"Easy, easy," Ethan said. "Just stay there, okay? Don't pull out."

Zach tilted his head back as Ethan's thigh pulled away from him. He tilted his body forward, holding onto Ethan's shoulders as Ethan turned his entire body around in a move that defied all laws of human flexibility. "Jesus!"

Ethan's solid arm caught him before he lost his balance. "Are you okay?"

"Yeah. How'd you do that?"

Ethan grinned over his shoulder, slowly lowering their bodies together to the bed, where one hundred and eighty contortionist degrees later, Zach spooned him. "Try it. Feels amazing."

Zach tried not to think. Thinking was a boner killer, and right now, his boner was too busy earning little groans and gasps from Ethan as his movements got bigger and bolder. He play-bit the faded black smudge of a forsaken tattoo on Ethan's shoulder and pushed deeper, letting Ethan roll onto his stomach where Zach pounded him hard. Ethan mumbled something like a laugh between thrusts.

"Quiet!" Zach regretted barking the command. But if Ethan was offended, he didn't show it. Zach pushed deeper. He was going to come again. He could feel it. Between faint, mumbled words, maybe

Ethan was coming as well. Zach choked back his moan before losing the battle against it, collapsing into the back of Ethan's neck as his seed filled the man.

Ethan's body turned beneath Zach's, rolling them onto their sides just in time for Ethan to send a hot stream of his own over the smooth flesh of his belly. For a moment, they just lay there, neither moving nor talking, locked together, staring at the ceiling.

"God, I love sex," Ethan at last got out between breaths. "Oh, shit!"

"What?"

"Just a sec…" Ethan eased off of him with a wince, leaving a damp patch on the sheet. "No biggie. Was going to wash them anyway. Part of the agreement with the other half."

Zach eased himself up, letting the man strip the bed. "Where is he?"

"Picking her Mom up from the airport. They'll probably be another half hour or so."

Zach couldn't tell if Ethan was deliberately avoiding eye contact, or just in a hurry to change the sheets. "I thought you were in an open relationship? That's what it says on your profile."

At last, Ethan turned and looked back at him, arms full of rumpled sheets. "Yeah, that's right."

Zach felt stupid as he watched Ethan disappear without another word. Of course. Straight people had open relationships too. Bi people especially, and Ethan was definitely bi. No straight guy could feign that much enthusiasm under the banner of 'curiosity.'

"You sure I can't get you a beer?" Ethan called from down the hall.

"No, no. I'm good. Thanks." He stepped into the hall and cursed his stupidity. In his eagerness, he hadn't even noticed the cheesy, soft-focus photo portraits dotting the hall and living room. He'd been too busy with a face full of Ethan's tongue. He didn't consider it impolite to arrive at a hook-up with a raging boner, but from the moment Ethan had picked him up, he'd been unable to focus on much of anything besides those arms.

Ethan had teased him a few times in his truck on the way over, usually with a harmless stroke of Zach's arm or leg. He'd grown well into what Zach put at an early forties. A former football jock from somewhere down south with a thousand-kilowatt smile that might have belonged to a self-involved asshole. Yet the way Ethan carried himself seemed genuine. Maybe he'd just matured, or maybe he'd been brought up better. Zach had liked the way the guy filled out his t-shirt, with a telltale 'married' paunch on the verge of burying its owner's abdominals forever. Paired with Ethan's fuller face and age-thickened neck, it fit him well.

He heard the washer start, right before Ethan, still naked, re-joined him, rubbing the muscles of his chest.

"Whew. Hey, I'm gonna hit the shower."

Ah, there he was. Mister High-School-Track-Star-Nineteen-Ninety-Whatever.

"I'll get you a towel."

"No, I'm okay," Zach said automatically. "Thanks."

Ethan's frown quickly broke into a broad smile. "Bit of a pig, huh?"

"Not really. Umm… didn't you say your wife… girlfriend…"

"Wife."

"Right. Didn't you say she'd be back soon? With her mom?"

"How long is it gonna take you to shower? Of course, we'd save time if you showered with me."

Right. And he needed Ethan to drive him back anyway. Hell, the sooner they were done… and it wasn't like prospect of being pressed up against Ethan's naked body one more time was so awful. "Okay. Then, I might take that beer."

Ethan grinned, tossing him a fresh towel.

Zach wasn't sure how he'd managed to get hard enough to slip inside Ethan yet again as they'd showered. He hadn't planned to, but he'd heard no complaints. Ethan glowed as he clinked the bottom of a dark green Heineken against Zach's.

"How old did you say you were?"

"Twenty-one."

"Like, actual twenty-one or 'here's my ID' twenty-one?"

"Actual."

"Nice."

Zach swallowed, watching Ethan's trace of belly flatten and hide as Ethan lifted the bottle to his lips and pulled a long sip. He hadn't quite managed to come a third time during their watery bonus round, but he'd been damn close. Even looking at Ethan now, standing in just his jeans, pulling on a beer in his nondescript suburban kitchen, sent Zach's sex drive racing.

"How long's your mom-in-law staying?" he asked, uninvested.

"Five days."

"Sounds exciting."

"You could say that." Ethan did a poor job of trying to hide a wince before changing the subject. "You thought my other half was a guy?"

Zach gripped his beer tighter, quickly taking another sip. "Faulty assumption. Not that I mind. I mean, makes no difference to me." That Ethan's partner was female quickened his pulse all the more. The old cliché of forbidden fruit. Lame and inaccurate, but undeniable.

"You were surprised."

"A bit. And she knows you play with guys on the side?"

"Is that what you want to be? My 'bit on the side?'" Ethan picked up his phone as it pinged with a message. "Hey, do you mind if I send Beth a pic of you? She's curious."

"Say what?"

"I told you, we're open about everything."

"Yeah! Yeah, you said, I just didn't think you'd tell her *who* your hook-ups were, or be sending their pics."

Ethan grinned at him. "Only the good ones. Beth has kind of a sixth sense like, she knows when I'm having a good time. And it's totally cool if you say no. She's just curious."

"No, it's not… I mean, yeah. Send it. Just my face though, right?"

"Are you suggesting my wife collects dirty pictures? Hey, maybe we should make a coffee table book. *Dick Pics from My Husband's Hook-ups*. Oprah would love it."

"No."

"I'm teasing. Of course, your face pic."

"Okay, that's fine, I guess." Zach took another long drink. "You really tell her everything, huh?"

"Makes things easier. I told her I was bi on our first date."

"That's um… gutsy?"

"I figured it was for the best. I'd kind of started sleeping with her

235

brother. Not kidding this time."

Zach thought back to Dorian. Did he put out an energy?

"Twins. Inseparable then, and I was sweet on both of them. But we weren't much more than kids. This is… oh shit, late 90s, I guess? I don't think any of us even thought about what 'bi' was. Dating them both was the only way I got alone time with either one."

Zach didn't know what to say. He was envious, more than anything. "That's pretty cool."

"Yeah? I'm leaving out all the drama, which, of course we always had to resolve ourselves. Late 90s North Carolina was not somewhere you told anyone about your open-jawed, semi-hoe-moe-sexual relationship with a pair of twins."

"Got it. Is that why… What was his name?"

"Daniel. Good old biblical name, and us filthy sinners, the lions. Whenever the three of us were together, especially with their family, people would talk to Beth and I like we were the couple. Dan got tired of it. I mean, I was surprised he came out to them at all, but I guess he figured being one dirty secret was enough. We had his back, so the family didn't give him too much grief for fear of losing Beth. Then, I think it was Christmas, someone, either his aunt or his cousin, I forget which, finally asked when he was going to find himself a nice fella' and settle down. Must have thought she was being so modern and open-minded. Dan looked like he was about to explode. He just kept staring at Beth and me."

"How was it your fault?"

"It wasn't. It was just like a year's worth of jealousy built up in his brain, and that was that. He didn't say nothing. He drove home. Didn't call for almost a week and he never kissed me again. I think he realized right then and there what he wanted, and it wasn't this.

He's got his 'nice fella' now, still in Raleigh. I guess whoever asked did us all a favor in the end."

"But you get along okay now?"

"Quit making me feel old." Ethan picked up his phone as it pinged with a message. "What part of 'late 90s' did you miss?"

"Got you."

"Dan's a bit old fashioned, but he's cool. Their mom... she's quite a lady." A small, breathy chuckle escaped Ethan as he checked his phone.

"What's funny?"

"Beth thinks you're cute."

"Tell her 'thanks,' I guess?"

"Tell her yourself. She wants you back here for dinner, tonight."

"Dinner? Isn't that a bit, umm..." Zach didn't know what that was 'a bit' of. "What about her mom?"

"It's not her mom's house." Ethan smiled at him. "We'll invite who we please. Besides, when she and her mom get going, sometimes... Look, would you please just say yes? I'd consider it a favor. I'll pick you up and drop you home again, don't worry."

Zach thought for a moment if he should ask about any strings attached to this meeting. Or if the open-minded Mrs. Ethan planned to share anything more with Zach than dinner. No, that was stupid, especially if her mom was there.

"Sure," he said, voice like a mouse. "You want me to bring anything? Like wine?"

"Actually, and this is going to sound stupid, meat?"

"Meat?"

"There's a really good butcher not too far from here. I thought I might pick us up a couple of steaks. Just for you and me. Thing is, I need you to hold onto them. Beth's gone vegan in the past few months and, well… long story. She doesn't want meat kept in the house, but she's cool with a guest bringing it, just so long as it's cooked and eaten fresh. Does that make sense?"

Zach wasn't sure whether to feel used. "She's not going to hate me?"

"Not a chance."

"What about her mom?"

"Doctor's orders. No red meat. Blah blah blah. Short version? I'm buying for you and me. I just need you to… hold my meat for a while." The man laughed too hard at his own joke.

"Right." Would it be rude to back out now after a dinner invitation and an afternoon of awesome sex? "Sure, no problem. Sounds great. Thank you!"

"Okay, great!" Ethan downed the last of his beer, dropped the bottle in the recycling and retreated to his bedroom, returning with a t-shirt folded up around his shoulders. "So I'll come back and grab you around six?"

Zach followed his lead, upending the beer and pulling on his own clothes. "Yeah, that should work."

"Thanks, man. I promise we won't bore you."

This, Zach didn't doubt.

Dinner?

"Yes. Dinner, remember? What normal, civilized people have, eating normal food, while enjoying each other's company?" Zach set aside the little package of diced Conway he'd prepared for Grace

Jones and picked up his phone.

Don't sass me, Zachary, it chirped. *Are you sure this is a good idea?*

"How would you know? You don't know this person."

But you're having dinner with him? Dinner? Besides, I thought you liked the other one.

"Cascade," he answered through gritted teeth. He'd be damned if the cat was getting anything more. "His name is Cascade, and I thought we agreed he *wasn't* a good idea? You told me to keep things simple. I'm keeping them simple."

Dinner isn't simple!

"This one will be."

I'm glad you're keeping options open. Now, excuse me while I redecorate the carpet.

"Will you calm down? He's in a relationship and I'm not bringing him here. I just think he's nice, okay? The sex was amazing. His wi... Look, it's just dinner. Can't you just let me have a nice—"

His what? What were you going to say, Zachary?

"Nothing. Will you get in here and eat? I've got to get ready."

His wife! You've hooked another straight one, haven't you?

"Bisexual," Zach said through gritted teeth, putting his phone down and dumping the chunks of lightly seared Conway he'd prepared into Grace Jones' bowl before washing his hands. He paused, looking at the morsel he'd saved for himself. It was around now that the lump usually rose in his throat. That his nerves started dancing and his stomach started to turn. This time, he felt nothing. No nervousness. No anxiety. He was feeding Grace Jones. He was having great sex. He'd grown into a 'rocking bod' of unknown origin. Even his clothes still fit, which seemed like a weird bonus.

The cat growled as Zach lifted his shirt and inspected his new

239

jock belly. Jesus. Hadn't he earned a little vanity after all he'd been through?

He unwrapped the package containing Ethan's steaks, still unsure how a recently converted vegan reconciled not wanting meat in the fridge with slapping a big old slab of cooked steak on a plate at the same table. But Ethan had picked up the tab, and at nearly forty bucks a pound, Zach chose to assume they were good. He laid them carefully alongside each other in a shallow pan, took the all-seasoning from the spice cupboard—if it had made Conway taste so good, it had to work just as well on beef—and shook a thin coating over the meat. The butcher had promised that all his meat was pre-tenderized to optimal consistency, which Zach chose to believe if it meant not seeing the man wink at him that way again.

Satisfied, he covered the pan with plastic wrap, washed his hands and picked up the phone again, instantly regretting it.

BiJockNC39?

"Don't you dare!"

Don't be paranoid. Why would I message him? Enjoy your dinner, lover boy.

Zach retreated to the bathroom. He stripped off his t-shirt and shorts, examining himself in the mirror. Motherfucker! He had a hickey, a fresh one, by the look of it. It wasn't as if he and Ethan had been careful or anything, but… Okay, the guy's wife knew about him, but her mom sure didn't, or so Zach hoped. Anyway, what was he supposed to do about it now?

He held his hands under the steaming shower for a moment before stepping inside and coating them with soap. For several blissful moments he allowed the soothing needles of warm water to bounce off his shoulders and neck. Was tonight really a good idea? The standing offer wasn't for another round of amazing sex. This was dinner. *Family* dinner. No matter how badly he wanted to feel those big hands on him again, or be held against that well-built chest...

He closed his eyes, turned the water temperature up a few of degrees and remembered Ethan sliding in behind him. Maybe that's where he'd given Zach his hickey, kissing his neck while thick, strong arms wrapped around Zach's chest. Zach squeezed his cock with one hand and toyed with his left nipple in the other, the way Ethan had done. He remembered the thickness of the man's erection sliding up and down the crease of his butt, teasing him. The bristle of a short-trimmed beard on the back of his neck. Except Ethan didn't have a beard. Cascade. He was jerking off to the memory of Cascade behind him, not in the shower, but in bed, their bodies still damp and sticky, Zach lost in the man's scent, enjoying each note of his voice.

A loud, metallic bang broke him from the vision. A lump of bile-laden horror rose in his throat.

He shut off the water, mopped himself clean of excess water and ran for the kitchen, pushing sodden fringe out of his eyes before spying the upturned metal dish, shredded plastic wrap, and two pieces of steak in the first stages of a feline mauling.

Grace Jones stopped her chewing, bright yellow eyes staring at him as her jaw unhinged from the steak. "Meow?"

"Get out!" Zach roared, whipping the towel off of his waist and snapping it at the cat. "Go on, get!"

He hissed at her. She hissed back before disappearing in a long black streak. Zach surveyed the carnage. The shredded plastic wrap. The steak chewed into hamburger at one end, the other with the imprint of a cat's paw imbedded in its red flesh like some kid's plaster art. A trail of rust colored seasoning footprints vanished around the corner where a small, furry face looked back at him. It disappeared as soon as he laid eyes on it.

"Yeah, run, you little shit!" Zach checked the time. Fuck! No time to get back over there, assuming the butcher even had more of those steaks. Goddamn cat!

He picked up the two red slabs of meat and attempted to clean them. Cat hair. How the actual fuck? He dumped them both in the garbage. Fucking great. At least Grace Jones had the decency to look ashamed of herself as she watched from the hall.

"I hope you're happy." Damn it! They'd had such a good time. The last thing he'd wanted to do was disappoint Ethan. The man lived with a vegan. He wanted some meat. Meat that had wound up ruined in Zach's custody over the ten short minutes he'd left it alone.

"Meow."

Zach heard claws pricking the floor.

"Now what?" Zach near blanched. The cat sat up on its haunches again, right outside the basement door. Damn it, he'd just got through cleaning. "I'm not letting you back down there."

"Meow?"

"No."

"Meow."

He didn't need a message on his phone to get the hint. "No way." Hisssss.

"Grace Jones," he cautioned. "Drop it."

She began sharpening her claws on the door.

"Hey!" Zach clapped his hands. The cat played startled, fooling nobody.

He surveyed the damage to the basement door, tracing the small scratches with his fingertip.

No. He couldn't. He wouldn't.

Did he have any meat thawed out that wasn't Conway? He swallowed. Not counting the initial regurgitated accident, he'd successfully digested three small pieces of the despicable human lying dead in his freezer. He'd suffered no ill effects. No desire for further carnage. On the contrary, Conway's flesh had made him feel good. Relaxed. Confident. Strong. And it was delicious.

Maybe if he tenderized and seasoned it a little more? Ethan didn't even seem like the fussy type. He'd be none the wiser. The only 'evidence' would be the memory of delicious steak. If Zach managed to get it just right...

He went back to the kitchen and set to work.

Ethan hadn't touched him on the way over. Hadn't offered him so much as a peck on the cheek, much less the lengthy lip-lock they'd enjoyed when he'd dropped Zach home. The man remained all smiles. Still looked the model of a happy, well-adjusted, bisexual, open bordering on polyamorous man picking up his newest boy toy with his wife's blessing. But an odd chill had sent both their sex drives into hibernation, and it hadn't come from the A/C of Ethan's truck.

Upon seeing Eleanor Denton, mother to Elizabeth and Daniel Denton, widow of James Francis Halifax Denton III and mother-in-law to the man with whom Zach had spent the better part of his afternoon in sweaty, erotic ecstasy, Zach understood at once the indomitable force that had beaten Ethan's sex drive into meek retreat.

243

He barely heard Ethan introduce him to Beth, or Beth introduce him to the small, arresting figure who sat high in the firm, wooden backed chair Zach had taken for no more than a resting place for forgotten papers. The woman, no more than seventy, carried herself with the air of having cast her steel grey eye over the caskets of a dozen close family friends, and dressed each day in anticipation that another might join them. Her neatly bobbed hair was burnt like brown sugar and the line of her mouth betrayed not the slightest flicker of opinion about Zach's presence. She merely raised and lowered her chin several times, inspecting him, skin clinging to her jowl like a lizard chomping down its meal despite an inability to properly masticate.

"A drink, Zach?"

"Please!"

An easily overlooked glare darkened the matriarch's face, and Zach realized he'd answered too quickly. He had a Heineken in his hand before the old woman broke her gaze.

"Nice of you to come tonight, Zach," said Beth, forcing him to admit he'd barely registered her presence, much less her appearance. "Especially at such short notice."

There wasn't much to register. Blonde, white, stock photo attractive in that 'never late for yoga' way, narrowly cresting forty, a little too tanned but not enough to inspire jokes. The kind of pleasantly forgettable woman he usually saw lined up at Starbucks, oversized coffee in hand, only now squaring wits with a sixty-something North Carolina matriarch with a campfire brown fringe and a steel-trap lizard jaw.

"It's really nice of you to invite me. You didn't have to." He remembered he was still holding two cold… steaks.

"I'm doing this as much for me as you, sweetheart," the younger woman said.

"Zach, is it?"

He dismissed the mild chill that trickled down from his shoulders, summoned his best attempt at a smile and approached the iron maiden's throne. "Yes. I'm very pleased to meet you, Mrs—"

"Eleanor." She dismissed him with a wave that seemed to tire her. "Are you here as a guest or a servant? Just Eleanor, please."

"Eleanor," he repeated, still mouthing the name like it was an antiquated royal title. "I'm pleased to meet you."

"So you said." She fixed him with another inscrutable look. Zach wondered if he should anticipate the unasked question.

"Zach's a friend of Ethan's," said Beth, either rescuing or condemning him. Zach didn't know which.

"I gathered. That be a work friend or a sex friend?"

"Mother!"

"I assume it's one or the other, Elizabeth, and I credit Ethan with enough sense not to soil where he eats."

"Mom! What have I said about being judgy in our house? I'm sorry, Zach."

"Who's judgy? When I have judgement to pass, Elizabeth, there will be no mistaking it for anything else."

"I'm… a work friend, Mrs… Eleanor."

"Son, I am sixty-seven years old. Please do not waste what lucid years remain to me by lying."

"We're having sex, Mom," Ethan answered without looking at Zach.

"Plainly. He's too young for you, as I'm sure you're aware. That is all I'll say on the matter." She turned back to Zach, a curious animation in her eyes. "Not so hard now, is it dear?"

He felt the stupidity hanging off the corners of his mouth as he smiled at her.

"You saving that meat to lead the harvest fair parade down Main Street?"

He glanced down at the package. "Oh! No, of course not. B… Beth?" If nothing else, the old woman had rescued him from discussing his and Ethan's shared leisure time. "Where would you like this?"

"You didn't have to do that, Zach." The younger woman offered him a smile that somehow retained its kindness while serving her husband a side-eye. "You *really* didn't."

"But we appreciate it, all the same." Ethan took the steaks from him with a mischievous smile of his own, ignoring Beth's disapproval as he put the meat aside.

"It's no problem. No, I'm not a work friend… Eleanor."

The matriarch said nothing. Thinking it wise to do the same, Zach drew his beer back to his lips.

"No, and we hired all our summer servers already, so…" Ethan lifted his beer "No work talk allowed."

"Servers?" Zach asked. "What do you do?"

"Ethan's a chef," chirped Beth.

Zach choked down a spray of second-hand Heineken spittle spritzer fast enough to spare his hosts a lager shower, but not fast enough to stop himself from retching as he forced the beer down.

"Oh my gosh! Are you all right, honey?"

"Go down the wrong way?" Ethan asked, quickly lifting a glass tumbler from the cupboard and filling it with water.

Zach coughed several more times, nodding as he accepted the water. A chef? A fucking chef? He tried to calm himself as the cool water soothed his throat. Nothing Ethan had said or done, nor the slightest change or wrinkle in the man's expression had given any sign he suspected Zach was hiding anything.

Or had he just not looked at the steaks?

Fuck! Surely even the greenest chef would know it wasn't steak. He had to get the meat back. It didn't matter if it just went missing or if he spoiled it somehow. Made it look like an acci... No, bad phrase. Very bad phrase. Fuck. Fuck. Fuck!

Zach realized three sets of eyes were on him as he stood there with a half empty glass of water in one hand and a barely started beer in the other. "I'm okay. Just choked a little."

"Flying start to the evening," Eleanor muttered. "Wait 'til he tastes your cooking, Elizabeth."

"Alright, Mom? I want one thing from you. Just one, and that's a nice dinner. Can you manage that?"

The old woman pursed her lips as Ethan raised 'what did I tell you?' eyebrows at Zach. "Ain't no-one not being nice. I only hope you don't plan on feeding any of that hippie, dippy, mung bean, soy bean, fat-free, barely contains air, vegan nonsense to this young man with growing still to do."

"He's twenty-one, Mom. He's an adult," Ethan said before darting a glance at Zach. "You are twenty-one, right?"

"Yes!"

A chef. A fucking chef!

"Alright. Mom? He's twenty-one. Old enough to vote."

"Democrat, I don't doubt. Probably still sore that socialist Jew didn't become President."

"Really, Mom?" Beth raised an eyebrow.

"Well, the point stands. I've seen the men they put on those

247

homo magazines, Elizabeth. This boy is going to need red meat. Lots of it."

"Just so long as I'm not cooking it," Beth said, pointedly ignoring her mom with a hard smile fixed in place. "No offense, Zach."

"None taken. I don't want to cause any trouble. I can just take it back home."

"No, no, no," Ethan answered, beginning to unwrap the package. "We do appreciate it. You and I are going to enjoy two steaks, which I'm going to cook and clean up after, that way everyone's happy. *Capiche?*"

"Actually," Zach said, now acutely feeling the need to stall. "I'm not really that hungry yet."

"Two steaks, you say? Two steaks. How very kind of you, allowing the guest who's screwing your husband to bring his own sanity into your Californian hippie kitchen. God forbid you extend the same consideration to your own mother."

"You know that has nothing to do with it, Mom. I would offer if you were allowed."

"Allowed?" Zach instantly regretted opening his mouth. Could he grab the steaks before Ethan unwrapped them? Not from the other side of the island, holding a beer, he couldn't.

"Red meat," the old woman snarled. "What kind of doctor says it's unhealthy for a person to eat red meat?"

"Yours, Mom. Your doctor," Beth pointed out. "Honey, will you get the olives and brie out of the fridge?"

Olives and brie on the same charcuterie? At least two of Yves' more pretentious friends would have burned the kitchen to the ground with rage. He watched Ethan dutifully procure the little plastic tub and the tightly wrapped wheel of cheese from the fridge.

"How do you like Canada, Zach?" Beth asked.

"It's fine. Everything you'd expect. Cold. Polite. Slightly more British. A bit French."

"That's about what I remember," Ethan added, unwrapping the brie.

Zach scrambled for something else to say. Anything. "You're not allowed to hate that Hallelujah song though, which is kind of annoying."

"Hallelujah song?" Eleanor piped up. "In Canada? Will wonders never cease?"

"No, the big one they play at Christmas every year."

"Leonard Cohen, Mom."

"Figures. You let the devil's weed grow with the law's blessing and before you know it, ain't no room left for the Lord."

"Anyway, they get upset. It's like a law, or something." Zach watched the joke die on the frozen smiles of his hosts.

Ethan nudged Zach gently in the shoulder, making him feel like he was twelve. He was on the cusp of asking if Eleanor regularly attended church before deciding that he already knew the answer and that starting the woman off would be insane.

"What's so special you had to go study it up in Canada?" Eleanor asked.

The decidedly non-religious question filled him with sweet relief before setting a whole new bacchanal of demons upon his nerves. He had a feeling the Great White North was going to get a thorough cross-examination under the Gorgon's gaze before dinner was through.

"Filmmaking." He tried not to sound meek.

A faint snort escaped Eleanor, the kind of sound a hippo might

249

have made if it dressed to pose for a repaint of American Gothic. "Didn't get into the Hollywood schools, huh?"

"Hey, that's awesome!" Ethan said as he set the charcuterie down on the counter top. "You know, Beth did a couple of movies back—"

"Ethan, stop."

"What? They were good."

"Ethan—"

"Okay, they weren't, but you were good in them, is my point."

Zach was grateful his hosts had taken hold of the conversation. "What were they called?"

"Oh, god." Beth smiled, even as she shook her head, bright blue eyes rolling toward the ceiling. "*Blood in the Woods 3...*"

Zach bit his lip.

"...and *Sorority Psycho*. That one they thought would be a franchise."

"They were wrong?"

"Straight to DVD in the bargain bin, where Elizabeth Malone, the next great scream queen, would lay forever undiscovered. Probably a good thing, in hindsight."

"Oh, come on," Ethan argued, popping an olive into his mouth. "They were alright."

"Honey, your favorite movie is *Armageddon*."

"Also a criminally underappreciated film."

"It is in the Criterion Collection." Zach had no idea why he felt compelled to point this obscure piece of trivia out.

"*Sorority Psycho?*"

"No, *Armageddon*."

"Right, *Armageddon*. Exactly! It's in the Criteria Collection. Thank you, Zach."

"I see," said Beth. "So, my dearest, can you name me one other movie in the *Criterion* Collection?"

Ethan took another sip of his beer. "Well, there's... that one about the woman and those witches next door. Mia Farrow's in it. *Hocus Pocus*, I think?"

"Uhuh," Beth pushed aside the greens she'd finished chopping. "Thank you. Just making a point."

"Well, don't you worry, son," Eleanor's dry voice cracked the air. "Beth wasn't cut out for Hollywood either, but she doesn't have such a bad life if you ask me."

Zach cut off a piece of brie, popped the cheese into his mouth and chewed slowly. "I'm not sure I'd want to go out there, anyway. Heaps of movies and shows now are shot in Toronto."

"Or Greensboro," said Ethan.

Zach cut another piece of cheese. Maybe if they filled up on cheese and olives, Ethan wouldn't have to see the steaks at all.

"Anyway," Beth took a sip of her wine. "That was a lifetime ago. Thank you for that... expression of approval, Mom."

"No need to be sore about it, dear. You and a million other girls. Just could have saved yourself a lot of heartache if you'd listened when I—"

"Mom," The muscles in Beth's hand flexed and tightened around the knife. "Eat some cheese."

"Hey, thanks for your help."

"It's really no problem," Zach said, scraping the last crumbs off the wooden board and rinsing it under warm water. Could he somehow knock the meat into the sink?

Ethan squeezed his shoulder and kissed his forehead. "I don't mean cleaning up. Leave it, man. I'll get it later. You want another beer?"

"No, really, it's no problem. Either of it. Any of it." What was he saying, exactly? "I'll take that beer, thanks."

Ethan took another Heineken from the fridge, snapped off the lid and passed it to Zach. "Nice of you to say that. I guess she's on her best behavior."

"She's worse than this?" Zach asked before catching himself. "I'm sorry, that was—"

"Accurate, is what it was. She's playing nice because we have a guest. I hope you don't think that's the only reason I asked you over. I like you, man. I like having you here."

To his own surprise, Zach didn't have to fake a smile as Ethan clinked his bottle. At least, until Ethan picked up the 'steaks.'"Umm, listen—"

"Hey, don't let anything Eleanor says rattle you. She's... a different generation. She speaks her mind, but she accepts Beth and me. That means she accepts our house rules, meaning she accepts you, *capiche?*"

Zach nodded, watching helplessly as Ethan unrolled the meat from its package. Did people really say 'capiche?'

"I like you. Beth likes you. That's all you need to worry about. *Alles klar?*"

"Sure, sure. *Alles klar*," he murmured.

Drop the package. Please, just drop the package. And pick a language already! Gods!

Ethan put the meat aside, bending down to turn the vegetable

252

skewers Beth had placed in the oven for Eleanor and herself. The meat was still too far to reach. Zach heard Beth raise her voice in the background. "They'll be at it for the next little while. That's our cue, buddy. Showtime."

Zach felt sick as Ethan removed the last of the wrapping. This was it. Either he was about to make a cannibal of the man who he'd spent the better part of the afternoon fucking, or he had a one-way ticket to jail. Or both. His stomach knotted as Ethan examined the meat.

"Do these look different to you?" Ethan held the pieces under Zach's nose.

He wanted to gag.

"They seem, I don't know, bigger. Don't you think?"

"Umm…" It wasn't as if anything could land him in deeper shit than the truth. "Those aren't the steaks you bought."

"Huh? What do you mean?"

"Ah… I am… so, so sorry. My cat… I had to go out and buy a couple more." Zach hoped his first-class ticket to hell now included turn-down service and an open bar. "I just asked for the best they had. I hope it's okay."

Ethan shook his head, offering Zach a forgiving smile. "Lucky cat. I'm sure these will be great. You really didn't have to do that, you know? Shit happens."

"Right!" Zach answered too quickly. "Right, you're absolutely right. Shit happens. But I… I just figured." Fuck! If he'd known Ethan would be this chill about it. "I like you too, I guess."

Ethan smiled at him, laying the two pieces of meat side by side on the counter. "You're a sweet guy, you know that?" Giving Zach one more kiss, he turned the dial on the grill.

253

Zach smiled back, rested his hands against the sink, and tried to imagine a calm blue ocean.

"Ain't nobody saying they're not impressive, Elizabeth, but we offered to help you travel for a year, to which you said—"

"I don't need you to bankroll me, Mom. My money, my choices. Can we just agree to that?"

Eleanor screwed up her nose and stabbed at the leafy greens in her salad. "Egypt? All that unrest with those Muzz-lims all killing each other. Could have had a year in Italy but no. Too proud to take our money. Now she wants to go gallivanting around the world, alone, no less!"

"Mom, it's really not that dange—"

"Imagine, with what they do to a woman who dares speak her mind in those countries. You and your mouth should make it to— what would you say, Ethan? The customs desk, before there's a diplomatic incident?"

"You're going to Egypt alone?" asked Zach, trying not to sound like he was taking the old woman's side.

Beth forced a smile and raised her wine glass. "For two weeks. Ethan has to work. And I'm not going *alone*. Maria's coming with me. I told you that."

Zach caught Ethan's knowing glance at the mention of Maria's name.

"Oh, yes, I do recall you saying something like that," Eleanor muttered, taking a sip of her wine. "I suppose if that girl can survive El Salvador or wherever she's from... but wouldn't you rather go someplace with culture? Beautiful paintings and sculptures and cathedrals, hundreds of years old. *History*, Elizabeth."

"Jesus, Mom," Ethan muttered. "She's going to Egypt, not Edmonton. History won't be in short supply."

"And what's that? A bunch of dusty temples and tombs built by nobody knows who? Pyramids you've seen a million times in pictures, crawling with tourists and pickpockets?"

"Are you done with that salad, honey?" Beth reached for Zach's plate.

"Uh, sure," said Zach. "I mean, yes. Thank you."

Ethan nodded at Beth. "You barely touched yours."

"Yes, Ethan, but if I don't get up, I'm going to throw something."

"Those steaks should be about done," Ethan said, collecting his salad plate.

"Oh, I'll plate those," Zach said quickly, moving to stand up only to feel Beth's hand on his shoulder.

"You, don't move a muscle," she said. "This was Ethan's idea, he can 'plate those' himself."

"I really don't mind." Zach forced himself to stop tapping his foot under the table.

"Once more, boy, I ask, are you a guest, or the help?" asked Eleanor. "Let the chef do his work. Ethan grills a fine steak, not that my devoted daughter will let me partake."

"No."

All three of them glared at Zach like he'd slapped the old woman, who for the first time seemed lost for words "I... beg your pardon?"

"I just... What about your heart, Eleanor?"

"Blood pressure," Beth corrected him. "But thank you, Zach. Exactly. Your blood pressure, Mom. Do you want to go back on those pills? Because it's fine with me, but I don't want to hear one word about your ankles, your back, or the rest of it. A moment on the lips for days with bad hips? It's your choice."

Zach watched the old woman's mouth retract and cave as it puckered into a silent snarl.

"Good. If that's settled, I'll check on the skewers and the sweet potato linguine." Beth neatly stacked the plates and retreated to the kitchen.

Ethan followed, bowing to where he could whisper in Zach's ear. "Enjoying the floor show?"

Zach forced a smile, turning his fork in his fingers. He had to get that meat back. Or spoil it somehow. Could he trip Ethan? Did they have a cat or something? He choked a little as the thought crossed his mind. He hadn't seen any cat toys.

Eleanor hadn't taken her eyes off him.

"The linguine does sound good," he offered at last.

"Do you always patronize your elders?" she asked quietly.

"I... I didn't mean... Just making conversation, I guess."

"As opposed to the conversation about your affair with my son-in-law who is twice your age."

He shifted uncomfortably in his seat as the sound of sizzling meat came from the kitchen. "I wouldn't call it an affair, exactly."

"Just sex then, is it?"

Zach could hear his hosts arguing in the kitchen. Christ, how long could two pieces of meat take? Think! "Yup."

The old woman nodded, digging again into her greens. "Just as long as we all understand that."

He shifted in his seat.

"You're surprised to hear me say as much? You think I approve?

Well, I don't."

Zach wondered how much more he'd have to shift to break his chair.

"But Elizabeth's an adult. So is Ethan. So is Daniel, come to that. Don't suppose what I have to say on the matter means much."

Zach was sure he saw the woman's nostrils flare, a single eyebrow flicking upward, daring him to challenge her, as if with no more than a snort as warning, she might charge him. He had to get that meat back. He didn't have time for a fight with some condescending old hag.

"You're right," he said. "I like Ethan. Your daughter is fine with what we're doing, and what you think about it doesn't matter."

The old woman stared back at him, until at last, she smiled. "Elizabeth provides Ethan what he needs, boy. That includes you. If you like him, well, enjoy whatever you want to call it while it lasts."

Zach began tapping his foot again. "We will."

"I don't suppose you've had the chance to love someone yet."

"Actually, I... just broke up with some—"

She waved him away. "I don't mean some lovestruck high school nonsense or some pretty college boy who turned your head. Real love, boy. The 'their needs before yours' kind. The kind that means giving someone what they need, even if they don't see or want it."

Zach wondered whether he'd given Yves what he'd needed and since he couldn't recall giving the guy a solid kick in the ass, he accepted that by the logic of Eleanor Lizardjaw Bitchface, the Quebecer of the 'too hip for thou' pout hanging from the killer cheek bones just hadn't been the one. Pretty college boy indeed.

"Not that I sit here expecting you to listen," she said.

"I'm listening."

"That's just nature. Young people don't need some old woman prowling around giving advice they never did ask for. But I want you to understand why my approval doesn't matter. I said this, years ago to Elizabeth. For all her stupidity, that woman understands love. She gives Ethan what he needs in young men like you."

"I'm… not sure that's quite how—"

"And she does the same for me. She's right, you know, about my blood pressure. Each piece of red meat could be my last, though if anything sees me off it'll be those damn pills they put me on. Damn comedian doctor called it 'an allergy party in aisle thirteen' when I told him what they did to me."

Zach couldn't stop a guilty laugh. "I'm sorry. I'm really sorry, that's…" He coughed loudly, trying to ignore the look of faint satisfaction in Eleanor's face. "They sound awful. So…"

She raised an eyebrow at him. "So, what?"

"So, if you know Beth's right, why do you fight her on it?"

Eleanor raised her glass, grinning with a mouth full of dim, yellowed teeth. "Like the rest of it. Just nature."

"Here we go!" Ethan's voice boomed as he emerged from the kitchen with two plates.

Zach didn't give himself time to think. With a cheerful offer to help, he got up from his seat at the exact moment Ethan crossed behind him. In the time it took for his chair to slide into Ethan's path, he heard a 'woah,' a small cry of panic from the kitchen, the ping of a plate bouncing off of Ethan's hand, the plop of a fat piece of freshly grilled Alistair Conway on the wooden floor, a loud "*FUCK!*" followed by the metallic clang of the other plate slamming down on the table, the skittering of paws on polished wood, and a futile "*No!*" before the skittering accelerated, its source hastening from sight the juicy morsel that had in these fleeting, chaotic seconds, hit the dining room floor.

Zach at last remembered to speak. "God, I'm sorry! I'm so, so sorry! I can't believe I did that!"

Eleanor squared her shoulders and glared at him. Grace Jones *had* called him a terrible actor.

Ethan meanwhile had chased the thief into another room. "Give it. Give… Bad dog! Drop it! That's right. You did a bad thing, Ellie. You were a very bad dog!"

Zach wondered what 'Ellie' was short for.

"Better fix up an extra sweet potato linguine, Elizabeth," Eleanor called, practically smiling as her daughter came out in thick rubber gloves, carrying a paper towel. "Can't have the delicious juices of some dead animal staining your floors, either."

"Not now, Mom! Ethan?"

Her husband appeared in the doorway with a defeated sigh. "I let her have it. It's ruined anyhow. Jesus!"

"No need to go blaspheming the Lord over your butter fingers," the old woman chided him.

"It was my fault," Zach interrupted before Beth could launch herself across the table. "I wasn't looking. Ethan, I'm so sorry."

"You're a hazard to good steak is what you are," Ethan answered, squeezing his shoulders. "Don't sweat it. You have that one. I'll have the linguine."

"Oh, no! I couldn't do that. I mean…"

One steak left. Shit!

"Zach," Beth chimed in. "Ethan will be just fine. You brought the meat. You have it."

No, wait, it was for him. This was fine. This would work…

259

Would it? He'd never tried to eat so much of it at once. What was the worst that could happen? Several possibilities of varying cosmic brutality invaded his mind.

Ethan smiled at him again. "Exactly. You brought it. You have it. I'll be just fine." His stomach turned as Beth retreated to the kitchen to fix more linguine, and Ethan set the plate in front of him.

"Don't tell me," Eleanor grumbled. "You've gone over with all that vegan, hippie nonsense and now you don't want it."

"No! No, it's fine. I'm sure it'll be… Ethan, really—"

The man hushed him as Beth set down another fresh plate of pasta. "Deal's done, my friend. Enjoy!"

Zach stared at the meat. A hot bubble of latent juice escaped the exposed side of his meal, cooked to perfection by his host, to whom he faked another smile of thanks.

What in the hell had made him think two pieces of medium rare Alistair Conway would be better than telling Ethan the truth and turning up empty handed? It had seemed so reasonable at home. Conway's meat was perfectly tender and, more than edible, it was delicious! As he'd stood in his kitchen, holding the two flanks of Conway in his hands, it had all made perfect sense. Then, upon finding out Ethan was a chef, the meat's retrieval had become top priority.

And now, here he was. About to eat the evidence with Ethan's blessing. Why fight it? It wasn't every day fate and the absurd conspired to offer him an easy out. A quick and digestible escape that would offend nobody and disguise his crime.

So, *why* did the thought repel him so much this time? His fingers closed tentatively around his knife. What was he afraid of? Vivid imaginings of chest-bursting horror aside, he had no credible reason to believe that even such a large cut would hurt him. Or, perhaps

Eleanor's caustic jibes had set him on edge. Whatever the reason, he now sat, unable to shake the knowledge that this had been a human being. An evil, self-absorbed, lying, bullying, piece-of-shit human being, but nonetheless, a man he'd fucked. His first real life crush.

"If you're saying grace there, son, can you speak up so we can all eat?" Eleanor brayed, like a donkey. "Seems fitting, as you're the one deemed worthy of some meat around here. I'd also like to hear what grace might come from a man's lips after they've been around my son in law."

"Oh, come on!" Ethan snapped.

"Mom…"

Zach tensed, half expecting Beth to lunge for the now spare steak knife laid out in Ethan's place. Instead, she rested her hands on the table before levelling her gaze on her mother.

"That was nasty," she said with far greater calm than Zach had expected. "It was gross, filthy, and just plain nasty. Now, I am aware of your… thoughts on my arrangement with Ethan. and I am going to say this just once. You are in our home, Mom. We have a guest. Now, shut your nasty, tired, bitter old mouth and eat your fucking linguine!"

Zach managed to steal a glance at Ethan, who looked down at the table, and Beth, who refused to take her eyes off her mother. Eleanor, meanwhile, was staring at him, like a bird holding its prey in sight, about to strike.

"Where'd you get that meat, son?"

He swallowed, tightening his grip around the knife in his hand, though whether anyone else at the table noticed, he couldn't say. He wanted to leave. Or at least put the old bitch in her place. But what could he say? If the old woman wouldn't be shamed by her daughter, and Ethan refused to say a word, that left him. What the fuck was he supposed to say? He barely knew her.

"I'm waiting for an answer," the old woman continued through a malevolent smile. "We're being honest tonight, aren't we, boy?"

Boy? Son? Zach looked back at her, releasing his grip around the knife. Suddenly, he knew. He knew her well enough.

"A free-range butcher near my house. My mom's been shopping there for years," he said, not taking his eyes off her. "Only deals in top quality meat, and my folks aren't rich, so it's always been a 'special occasion' type thing. But I felt so bad about what happened with the cat."

"Losing good steak to one animal's a tragedy. Losing it to two—"

"Mom!"

"I'm sorry about that. If I'd known, I'd have gotten three."

"You *really* did not have to do that, Zach," said Beth.

"Would have been a nice gesture, all the same," the crone croaked.

"Okay, you know what?" Beth shook her head, at last bringing her hand down to the table with a loud bang. "I've had it, Mom! You do what you want. Eat what you want. Order a fucking pizza for all I care. Just sit there, *quietly* and have dinner so we can do the same. Can you manage that much?"

Zach watched the corners of the old woman's mouth curl upward, her eyes narrowing the way a cat did when it yawned. The bitch wasn't even hiding it any more. She reveled in riling up her daughter and embarrassing Ethan.

"What cut is it? If steak from this place is such a treat, I imagine you're very particular about the cut, so which is it? Sirloin?" A faint snort escaped the old woman. "Filet mignon? Prime rib?"

Zach knew when someone was out to make a fool of him. He

also knew when someone needed to be made to shut her mouth. "Why don't you try some and guess?"

"Hah!" Beth slapped her hands together. "Sounds like a great idea to me. If you appreciate fine meat so much, Mom, you should have no trouble identifying it, right?"

"And if you get it right," Zach continued. "You can finish it. I'll have the linguine."

"No thank you, boy. I will not perform parlor tricks for my supper."

"Aw, come on, Mom," Ethan said, unable to contain his amusement. "The man's offering you his meal. The least you can do is indulge us in a little fun."

"Seems to me, Ethan, that he's indulged you in enough fun for this entire table."

Beth opened her mouth to speak but Zach cut her off.

"If you're right, Eleanor, I'll give you my steak. And if you're wrong…"

The old woman paused, sucking in her cheeks and narrowing her scowl as she sized up the imminent challenge. "Go on."

Zach's mind raced, unable to take his eyes off Beth's face, reddening in its barely contained rage. Its humiliation. He glanced again at Ethan, who shrugged. The rules of the wager were Zach's to make. "If you're wrong, you leave this table. You go to bed. You leave us to enjoy our evening."

Eleanor's laughter ripped across the table in flitting bursts as her lower jaw slackened, parting her painted red lips. "Did you hear that, Ethan? You should keep this one around. I should think you'd learn a thing or two of what it is to have a spine, if it wasn't so farcical."

"I'm not joking," Zach said quickly. "Ever since I arrived you've done nothing but criticize and belittle Beth. She put you in your place but it sounds like this has been going on for so long you just don't listen anymore. I don't know you, but what little I've seen and heard isn't what I'd call love. What gives you the right to sit there and—"

"Okay, Zach," Beth began. "I really think you should—"

"*You* don't know the half of the love I've given both of my children and their husbands," Eleanor sneered. "Yes, I said husbands, *plural*, because while I might not applaud Daniel's lifestyle choice, I will not stand in the way of his happiness, just as I do not stand in the way of Elizabeth's or Ethan's. *That* is what a mother's love is, *boy!*"

"Oh, for God's sakes, quit calling him that!" Ethan barked. "He's a grown ass man!"

"Then he's grown enough to understand that it's that love that grants not only me the right to sit here and say whatever the hell I want, but him, the right to sit there, smug as warm peach pie after an afternoon sodomizing my son-in-law, casting aspersions on our family. And you want me to up and leave this table, boy? You would dismiss me? Send me to bed with neither—"

"Take the bet." Zach saw Eleanor stiffen in her chair as his words cut down her barrage. He could almost feel the icy wave come off Beth when the old woman turned to her daughter for backup that didn't come. He'd been on the verge of apologizing to his hostess for raising his voice, except now he had Eleanor on the ropes. If he could just keep her there… "Either you'll get your way or we will. What cut of meat is it?"

At last, it was Beth who broke the silence. "I'm sorry, Zach. This obviously was a bad idea. Ethan can drive you home. Honey?"

"Oh, come on," Ethan answered. "Can we all just take a deep god-damn breath for one minute? Things got a bit heated, which I'm sorry you had to see, Zach, but—"

"Sirloin."

"What?"

"What?"

"Huh?" Zach asked.

"What? You all turned eight shades of deaf from all that shouting?" Eleanor sneered. "That's a perfectly fine piece of sirloin if ever I saw one. Nothing fancy, but we were raised to know you don't need nothing fancy if it's good."

The three of them stared silently at the crone.

"So, am I right? Did I win? Or do you all plan to hide me down in the fruit cellar until I rot?"

Zach could have sworn the *Psycho* Mother Bates affectation had been deliberate. Conway was perhaps more sub-loin than Sir-loin, but he wasn't about to argue. He lifted the plate from the table and passed Eleanor her prize.

"Unbelievable," Beth muttered. "Are you happy now?"

Ignoring her daughter, Eleanor accepted Zach's steak knife with a venomous grin, sawed off a corner of medium rare Conway and slipped it between her teeth, chewing with utmost pleasure.

Two small 'huffs' escaped Beth before she broke into a fit of forced laughter. Her head turned from one dining companion to the next like some creepy clown at a county fair, until her kind eyes settled on Zach. "Would you like some linguine, honey?"

Zach lifted the faucet and began rinsing the pot clean of the congealed orange goo that had turned his tongue the same shade.

"Just leave it in the sink, I'll do it later," Beth chided him, closing the dishwasher.

"You're sure?"

"Of course! Sit! Have another beer if you want one." She looked up at him with the same tired eyes she'd had when they'd at last silenced Hurricane Eleanor with her dinner of choice. "Sorry. Can we pretend I said that without sounding like a complete bitch?"

"It's totally okay. I get it. She's..." He stopped himself before he could bash his host's mother any further. Truthful or not, it wasn't polite. "I should apologize to you. She got me angry, and I—"

"You have nothing to apologize for. Tonight was a mistake. That's all."

"No."

"I should have just let you and Ethan have your fun, alone. I guess I got curious this time. More wine? Oh, beer. Sorry. Forgot." She refilled her own glass before procuring another beer from the fridge and setting it in front of him. "I don't know why she does this. I thought, 'okay, if we have company...' Oh my god."

"What?"

"Zach, I did *not* invite you here just to keep my mom under control, I swear—"

"Well, if you did, it didn't work." He laughed. His host didn't. "Sorry."

"It's okay. She's made it quite clear what she thinks. Like it matters, right? Thank you, though."

"For what?"

Beth nodded, raising her wine glass. "You *did* shut her up."

Zach popped the lid on his beer and downed a sip. "Think she just wanted it to get under your skin? The steak, I mean."

"Since she worked out my arrangement with Ethan, it's like she's been testing me. Testing us."

"Like a predator at the zoo testing fences," Ethan said, pulling a tight t-shirt over his body. "You ready to go?"

"Honey, can you give us a minute?"

Zach saw the frown pass between the couple, but he'd stirred up enough shit in paradise without questioning it.

"I'll be in the garage. Come find me when you're done." Ethan gave Zach's shoulder an affectionate squeeze.

Beth waited until he was gone before speaking again. "So, you had fun?"

Zach forced himself to smile. "It was interesting."

"I don't mean tonight. I mean... you know."

"Oh."

"I don't normally say this." The woman took another long sip of her wine. "But this was the only time, okay? I'm glad you had fun with Ethan, and I know he likes you. It just... making this work means keeping some boundaries. You understand?"

"Uh, sure? I mean, no problem. I don't want to cause any trouble." He chugged more of his beer. "Is there anything else I can do?"

Beth leaned over, clumsily taking hold of his wrist with a half drunken smile. "Go home."

He nodded, thanking her again for dinner before making his way back to the garage.

"Just a minute there, boy."

He stopped, searching for the source of the old woman's voice. He at last found her sitting in one of the overstuffed chairs in the living room, staring into the inky screen of a blank television with only her grim reflection for company.

"Sit down a bit." She gestured toward the opposite chair.

"Ethan's waiting for me in the—"

"Are you half deaf? I said I'll take but a minute. Now, sit yourself down."

He did, half afraid of being eaten by the chair's padding.

"Lest you think me some dried-up old buzzard, I want to thank you for sharing that most succulent cut you brought with you tonight."

"You won it, fair and square."

"Enough of the crap, boy. It cut and tasted like no sirloin I've ever had."

Zach knew he was doing a poor job of hiding his aggravation, but in that moment, as his nostrils flared, he was beyond caring. "My name is Zach."

She cocked an eye at him. "You seem like a good boy. Answer me one more thing."

"Yes?" he asked.

"Did the bastard have it coming?"

Zach couldn't look at her. It was all he could do to look at her reflection in the blank screen. "Yes. I think he did."

The old woman nodded with satisfaction. "Don't ever be that man, Zach. When you find yourself... whoever you find yourself, don't be the man who has it coming. Are we understood?"

Deciding this was a fair price for the woman's silence, he excused himself and left.

Zach's ride home took ten minutes, driveway to driveway. This didn't include the five minutes he and Ethan had spent talking, or the good fifteen to twenty minutes of making out, which had gotten him so turned on that when Ethan finally uttered those magic words—"I have to blow you again" made up for in clarity what it lacked in romance—he'd barely lasted a minute before yielding Ethan's reward. Ethan hadn't asked for reciprocation, though Zach would happily have obliged.

Soft fur weaved between his ankles, with a quiet 'meow.' Grace Jones had been right. Keep things simple. No strings. That was the only way to get through this. Would it be so bad? He could probably even resist messaging Cascade again, if it made the cat happy. And for now, judging by the way she was purring, Grace Jones seemed very, very happy.

He scooped her into his arms, smoothing the fur between her ears as he carried her into the living room. The purring grew even louder as she wriggled just enough to get comfortable in his arms. His hand hovered over the remote. Something in him didn't want to sit. He was too agitated. Too excited by his success, his triumph, even at the crazy dinner. *Their* success. Him and Grace Jones, his faithful familiar.

He put on some music instead. The cat opened her eyes a crack as the base line of *Pull Up to the Bumper* filled the room, then just as quickly resumed snoozing as he danced around, carrying her into the kitchen, passing the mirror in the hall, stopping to admire his bigger shoulders and chest, his more pronounced chin and cheekbones, and his newly muscular arms, wrapped around the happily snoozing black furball.

This was working. His night with Ethan had proven it. What

did the 'how' matter as long as they got results? He didn't know how the cat planned to get rid of Conway's remains, but if their strange, culinary alliance in all its grotesqueness could yield the transformation he saw in the mirror, who was he to deny the cat whatever plan it had for getting rid of Conway proper? Even if she didn't, didn't he deserve to celebrate one night of success? He'd have plenty of time to worry about a back-up plan later. In the meantime, nobody was about to come looking for Conway at his house.

His cell phone erupted in his pocket as they waltzed into the kitchen. He set the cat down on the floor and fished it out, not checking to see who was calling at 11pm.

"Zach? Honey? Are you there? Hello?" His mom sounded like she'd been sobbing.

"Mom? Mom it's... it's almost midnight. What's going on?"

"It's..." She repeated the word several times with varying degrees of distress. "It's your father. I just... There's been an awful mistake. Just awful!"

"Wait, what's going on? Where are you? Is Dad okay?"

"He's... talking to the police right now."

"The police?"

"Damn it, Zachary! Didn't I just say that? Some ridiculous story about your father... They actually..."

Zach couldn't catch the next word as his mother mumbled it into the mouthpiece. "Sorry, Mom, I didn't catch—"

"Soliciting, Zachary! Some... well, I don't know if I should say it."

"Mom—"

"Prostitute! There's no other word for it. I have just bailed your father out of jail for soliciting a prostitute. Do you know how much that costs in the state of Texas, Zachary? Do you?"

"Dad? How? Why? I… What about the conference?"

"Done, Zachary! For us at least. We were asked very nicely and in a most non-refundable manner to leave and take care of what needed taking care of. Of course, it's ridiculous! He did no such thing!"

"Are you sure?"

"Zachary!" she snapped. "Of course, I'm sure!"

"Okay. So—"

"Anyway, the earliest flight we could get lands tomorrow at 9pm."

His blood froze. The last beats of the song faded.

"Hello? Zachary, did you get that? 9pm tomorrow. I just thank the Lord you're home, honey. Your father's going to need all the support we can give him right now. We'll get through this together, as a family."

He fought every impulse to panic, slowing his breath as the tango rhythm of *I've Seen That Face Before* filled the silence. Okay. This was fine. He'd just gotten away with putting two slabs of human steak under a chef's nose. With Grace Jones' promised help, he'd manage this. How much of Conway could be left anyway? No more than…

Shit.

"Mom? You really don't have to rush—"

"Nonsense! The flights are already booked and—"

He cried out as Grace Jones got under his feet. The cat let out a screech, scrambling away.

"Honey? Are you all right?"

"Yeah," he answered. "Yeah, I'm fine. It's just Grace Jones."

"Grace Jones? The singer? I'm sure you've met some fancy friends at that film school, but—"

"No, no, the cat. I just tripped over her." He beckoned the animal to him, smoothing her fur before scooping her into his arms again with his free hand. His mother said nothing. "Mom?"

"Honey," she said at last, solemn as a judge. "What are you talking about? Grace Jones died this spring. Poor thing ran right into traffic. I'm sure we told you that."

Zach looked down at the living, breathing, purring creature in his arms. "Uh, no? What are *you* talking about? You never told me about that. I'm holding her. She's right here."

"Zachary? We no longer own a cat."

FELIX

The dread from Zach's stomach wrapped itself over the lump in his throat. The tips of his fingers went cold around the phone. The only sound in the room was the quiet purring of a cat.

A cat. Not his cat.

"Zachary? Did you hear what I said? What are you—"

He ended the call, trying not to disturb the animal as he slid his phone back into his pocket. This made no sense. This was impossible. Grace Jones was here. She even had that little white diamond on her throat. Damn it, this was *his* cat! Hit by a car? Right! She'd probably just run away to live large off one of the neighbors. Nobody could resist those big, golden eyes, now glaring at him, perfectly still.

If his Grace Jones was really dead, then what the fuck was he holding in his arms?

The shrillness of his mother's immediate call back broke the silence. Then, in far less time that it had taken for Conway to lose his balance and tumble to his death, Grace Jones opened her eyes, bit Zach's hand, and twisted out of his grasp. He cried out with a start, looking up from his bloodied hand just in time to see a tail disappear around the corner.

She'd bitten him. In six years, his Grace Jones had *never* bitten him.

Okay.

Okay.

He'd managed a dead body in his house, a near-virgin's freak-out, a bunch of hook-ups including two with married men, one of whom he'd damn near fallen for, getting punched in the face, bringing human flesh to a dinner party... He could handle some strange cat with memories of his childhood, perfect English and twin minors in online dating and corpse disposal and fuck, fuck, *fuck!* What was he doing?

He felt sick, even tired, all of a sudden. Like the nausea had flooded his brain, then drained just as fast, leaving him woozy as he crept back to the hall to find the cat.

"Psss psss pssst!"

No response. His Grace Jones or not, if the creature had bolted... He passed the mirror, seeing his now solid shoulders tense with worry. His muscular body now seemed grotesque, its oversized biceps and pecs mocking him under his pale, quivering face. His payoff in a sick bargain now straying far from its original terms.

He jerked back as without warning, the glass cracked, splitting his reflection into two. He faced the small, growling furball to his right, tripping over his feet and landing hard on his newly-sculpted ass. Zach winced as he tried to massage his ankle, then stopped, caught in the path of two glowing, golden eyes.

The cat sat before him, perfectly still, not so much as a flicking tail.

"Grace Jones?" he asked. She'd not corrected him so far. "We need to talk."

The cat gave a hiss far louder than any sound Grace Jones had ever made. He backed away as it advanced on him, delicate black paws paced one in front of the other, getting... bigger? Was his cat growing with each new step? And how were its paws making that sound? That tapping sound, like hard wood coming down on stone.

No way were the cat's footsteps making that nose. No way had she reached a size that brought those eyes level with his. No way had impossibly thick black carpet replaced the hard wood floor beneath his hands, smooth to the touch, almost like... fur. He whipped his head around. The hallway, the dining room, the good room, every inch of floor he could see was covered in thick, black, shaggy fur. Zach could no longer tell where the growing cat ended and the floor began.

"You!"

Zach could barely call the sound a voice. It was halfway between a guttural roar and a howling wind that ripped across the furry land-scape and burrowed into his pores, burning and chilling him all at once. He opened his mouth to answer, but no sound came, and the voice's owner took no interest in what he had to say.

"I gave you a task so simple, so rooted in your basest instincts and you dare to question me? I, whose breath first scorched the des-ert into being? I, whose rage found satisfaction only in vats of blood?"

"I... Grace Jones, what the fu—" Zach yelped as his hand slid out from under him and he sprawled on one elbow.

"Do you know who or what I am, dear Zachary? *Do you?*"

Her loud screech ripped through him. He buried his face in his arms as he heard the scampering of paws, bracing himself for a sting of claws. When it failed to come, he peered out from behind his

275

arms. There was no cat, only the polished hardwood floor, where he now cowered in front of the basement door.

He wrenched it open and slammed it behind him before he could think. Think! That's what he needed to do. To make sense of this, somehow.

The third wooden step creaked under his weight, just as it always had. Ordinary. Real. He touched the basement wall, hard and cool beneath its hasty paint job. The dusty familiarity of the space filled his nostrils, despite his recent cleaning effort. He inhaled it, savoring a moment in which Fairview was the same boring town he remembered, and his cat was just his cat.

He covered his face, until the sight of his own thickly corded forearm veins destroyed his delusion. He thought about checking the freezer, just to make sure Conway was still in there. But why? What doubt was there? Besides, after what he'd just seen, he didn't trust his imagination not to conjure yet more horrors from the sight of Conway's frozen cadaver.

Zach paused, breath catching as he heard a strange, sniffling sound in the dark. He leaned closer, trying to see what had violated his sanctuary.

"Are you having a problem there, darling?"

Zach hadn't expected to hear the warm confidence of a woman's voice. He swallowed, trying to get a better view.

"Cat got your tongue?" she continued.

Zach winced. Not yet.

"What's wrong with you, then?"

Zach had limited experience with accents, but there was no disguising that effortless coolness, shaped by the runways, nightclub stages and film sets of New York, Paris, and London. The voice that had filled the house while he'd danced with Grace Jones—his Grace Jones. Or not. Or was she? He didn't know anymore.

"Am I talking to myself? Why don't you come downstairs? Self-pity is so tacky."

"S… I'm sorry. Sorry, Ms. Jones. I…"

Grace Jones? Grace fucking Jones? The unmistakable silhouette, outlined in all her flawless glory, was doing coke off his parents' washing machine.

"I… I'm having the worst night of my life," he stammered.

"Is that so? Well, you can do that later. Come and have a bump."

He descended the stairs, peering at the darkness, trying to make out detail. To glimpse the stern glare that had captivated him that Saturday afternoon at the Phoenix. Even shrouded in the darkness of his basement, just beyond the reach of moonlight that streamed through the room's only window, there was no disguising it. Inimitable. Undeniable. At least, when it wasn't bent over the plate of cocaine.

After all he'd seen, all he'd heard, all his mind had put him through, to have Grace Jones invite him to join her in disappearing a few lines didn't seem a huge stretch. If anything, the full-blown hallucination phase of his crisis had taken longer to arrive than expected, and he appreciated its lack of ambiguity.

The figure at last stepped into the moonlight, its face illuminated, all too familiar, and far too white.

"Yves?"

Let-down of the century.

"You are so fucked," his ex said, rubbing the last evidence from his nose and somehow making the last word sound sexy through a thick Quebecois accent far from its former Jamaican guise.

Zach snorted. He was too tired. Too sick of the battles to fight yet another against his subconscious.

"You thought a cat was going to save you?" the image continued, shuffling its feet like a bored child. "Aw, *mon chaton*."

"Why are you here?"

"Because you wish it."

Zach shook his head. He didn't have time to talk to an illusion, even one that was throwing him that same crooked smile he'd found so irresistible. "Where's Grace Jones?"

"At her house?"

"Don't start. I mean my cat."

"Ah, the cat, that is not your cat. Or maybe she is your cat. Upstairs, *chaton*?"

This back and forth should have annoyed him. It was so Yves, it hurt. Instead, it made Zach nostalgic, which in turn left him nauseated.

"My Grace Jones is dead," he said quietly.

"Who told you that?"

"Mom."

"And she's never lied to you before?"

"Why would she lie about that?"

"Why are you talking to a hallucination? Texting with a cat? Why did you let a fucking religion lie to you about who you were and turn you into such a basic, whiny—"

"Why did you date me?"

The question shut Yves up like he'd been burnt. A strange tingle of satisfaction flowed through Zach.

Yves tilted his head, seeming confused before he finally answered. "Because you weren't hot."

278

Zach frowned. The rude answer was not out of character for Yves, but it wasn't what he'd expected, either. "What does that mean?"

"Exactly what I said. I could have had any guy I wanted, but all the hot guys wanted to do was think with their dicks and preen and go to the gym and be bitchy and talk shit about each other. I wanted to be better than that"

Zach said nothing. The description matched Yves to a fault.

"But then," Yves shrugged. "You got boring."

"I wasn't boring, Yves."

"Yes, you were. Do you know how many hotter guys I turned down because I wanted to convince myself you were enough?"

Zach swallowed, not about to take one step down this road. "That's not my fault."

"I didn't say it was your fault."

"Well? Who did you end up resenting?"

The hallucination at least had the decency to look ashamed.

"Exactly. I was sorting out a lot of shit, Yves. Emotionally? Losing weight?"

"I know that, *chaton*. You look great."

"Don't." Zach swallowed. "I thought with you, I'd have someone to help me through that."

Yves walked over to where Zach had sat down on the steps and stopped, eyeing him uncomfortably. "You thought it was my job to fix you?"

"No. I just wanted you to be who you said you were while I fixed myself."

"I was. I am. I needed other guys too, Zach."

"It didn't matter to me who you fucked! Just so long as you made me feel wanted. You didn't."

279

"Then why did you bring me here?" Yves shrugged, flipping a cigarette up between his lips and snapping it alight with a metallic red zippo Zach couldn't remember him owning. "To say sorry? What's the point?"

"No." Though he'd always hated the smell of Yves' smoking, there was something about that first waft of sweet, acrid smoke, real or not. "I don't want your 'sorry.'"

"So? Why didn't you leave?"

Zach grimaced, shifting on the step and squaring his shoulders. "Because I didn't have anyone else."

"Bullshit."

"Yves, you were my world."

"And why was that?" Yves' expression lurked somewhere between pity and raw disdain. "I never stopped you from making your own friends. Living your own life. I even told you to go do it. But you were always there, every time I looked around. Oh, Yves! Yves! Yves! I don't know how you finished any classes. And we both know why you were so fucking clingy. You liked how I made you look."

"Yves—"

"You liked how I made you feel. 'Hey, check out my hot, smart French-Canadian guy.'"

"Stop it."

"It's true, isn't it? I saw it when you came to the queer bloc meet. You, sitting in the corner, trying to hide because what could you bring? Some fat, white, cis American from some piece-of-shit town, who can barely admit he's gay? Pffft! So retro. Then, when I talked to you? Asked you to have a drink? It felt like Christmas."

"Oh, fuck off!" snapped Zach.

"You liked how I made you look. The doors I opened for you.

The fact that suddenly, you mattered. Like, suddenly you have this hot boyfriend and not only is the sex amazing—"

"Was it, though?"

"—but all of a sudden, you matter. Guys are looking at you. Wondering what's special about you. Seeing you."

Zach grimaced. "They would have seen me anyway, Yves."

"Eventually? Maybe? Or would you have stayed in your little corner, too scared to talk to anyone? 'Oh, all the hot guys are laughing at me, and all the woke kids think I'm basic trash.'"

"And what about you?" he fired back. "You asked me out, Yves. You asked me!"

"I felt sorry for you."

"Bullshit!" His ex winced like the word stung, but Zach didn't stop. "I have eyes, Yves. Ears. Every one of those people looked at you and saw just another narcissistic Instagay until suddenly you were cuddling up to me. That's when they started to see you, because they didn't understand it, just like you knew they wouldn't. So don't give me this shit about doing me some great favor. You said it yourself. You wanted to be better. Thought I'd make you *look* better. This was all about you."

Yves dropped his cigarette on the floor and ground it under foot. "Please, pick that up."

"It's not real, smart guy."

"You'll always be an asshole, won't you?"

Yves sat down on the step beside him. "I don't think you're going to be around me to find out."

Zach refused to give him the satisfaction of an answer.

"Okay, fine," Yves continued. "We're both assholes. We used each other. So what? Aren't you happier? You come home to your piece-of-shit town and now five hot guys want to have sex with you."

"Yeah, and three of those were disasters. One died!"

"So? Weren't the other two worth it? Cascade?"

"How did you know his…" Zach remembered he was talking to a figment of his imagination. "Do all hallucinations go on this long?"

"I don't know. Maybe. Like dreams?"

Zach closed his eyes, opening them in time to catch Yves staring at him, the nastiness gone from his face. "I've had enough of those lately."

"I know. Some of them were hot, no?"

"Some."

"Any that featured me?"

Zach smiled despite himself, suddenly far too tired. "I think you should leave."

Yves' expression didn't change as he leaned back against the stairs and stroked Zach's cheek. "In a few minutes?"

The cool, familiar brush of Yves' hand felt better against Zach's cheek than he wanted to admit. "Okay. A few more minutes."

He was asleep before he finished the thought.

When Zach finally came to, still wearing the clothes he'd come home in, he couldn't remember falling asleep. He also couldn't remember going outside, or lying down on the hard wood of a park bench. He could only close his eyes so many times, hoping for the comfortable sight of his bedroom ceiling to return before he had to accept reality. Green branches swayed overhead, while crickets and birds sang their own sarcastic song.

Squinting in the hideous sunlight, he eased himself up, swallowed the little bile that repeated on him and turned his head. It was Chester Pond he recognized first. The same creepy, dark pond that had terrified him as a child with the promise of unleashing its procession of unholy creatures.

Zach couldn't discount the possibility of sleepwalking. But how the hell had he made it all the way to Wesley Park? How?

He scanned his phone for any clues. Nothing. Not a message. Not a ping from 'his' cat. Nothing. And he was down to two percent battery. Why here? Even discounting the distance, supposedly sleepwalked in the dead of night, why Wesley Park? He instinctively patted his pockets, finding his house keys but no wallet. He still had his phone, so he hadn't likely been mugged. That meant he'd stopped for his keys... but not his wallet. How? When?

"You're awake."

Zach turned with a start, scrambling to his feet and rounding on the lanky blond man behind him holding two iced coffees.

"Sorry."

"Can you stop doing that?" Zach asked.

Felix shrugged, passing him one of the drinks. "You're kind of jumpy. Figured it was just your nature."

"You brought me coffee?" Zach stared at the drink as if it would bite him.

"Naww, I normally start the day with two of these. Just saw you there and it seemed rude not to... Yes, I bought you a coffee. Ain't every day I find some guy I know passed out in the park."

"And you went and got me coffee instead of waking me, why, exactly?"

"What? You were breathin' okay. Plus, I heard somewhere that if

283

you disturb the grumpy god of the woods from his ancient slumber, you'd better make an offering. I didn't think the god of the woods drooled so much, but figured I was better safe than—"

"Will you please just give me a straight answer?"

"O-kay. No humor before caffeine. So noted."

"Sorry." Zach sipped his coffee, trying to piece together the monstrous vision of Grace Jones, his conversation with Yves, and his long sleepwalk in a way that sifted fact from fiction. Never mind the unexpected caffeine delivery. Felix had even guessed just how much sugar and cream he liked. "I'm sorry. Rough night."

"I figured." Felix shook his head and leaned back, pulling on the front of his loose tank top to let the breeze through it. "Didn't peg you for a 'sleeping in parks' guy."

Zach grimaced. What could he say to that? "Thanks. This is good."

Felix's smile made it clear Zach wasn't getting off so easy.

"I umm…" Shit. The phone call. His mom! "What time is it?"

Felix fished his phone from his shorts and checked it. "Eight thirty-two on a Sunday morning."

He had to get home. He didn't know what he was going to do about Alistair's remains, or the strange cat creature he'd been feeding and texting with these last several weeks, but fuck! He had to do something, starting with a ride home. His face fell as the screen blinked with its white logo, then blackness. No… no, no, no, no, no, no, no!

"You in a hurry or something?"

"Uh, yeah. Sorry. Kind of an emergency. Thanks again for the coffee." He tried restarting his phone. Come on! Just a minute more was all he needed. Just… damn it! "Hey, can I ask a favor?"

"Another one?"

"I'm sorry. This is super important. Can you call me an Uber? I'll give you the cash right back, I promise."

"With what? Your four bucks?"

He'd forgotten all about his absent wallet. "Meet me back here at five this afternoon, I'll pay you back double. Does that work?"

With the same non-committal shrug, Felix took a seat next to him, laying an arm over the back of the bench as he sipped his coffee. "There's just one small problem. I don't have a credit card. I hate 'em. Or they hate me. Take your pick."

Zach pushed his phone back into his pocket, if only to make sure he wouldn't throw it into the trees. He wanted to scream. None of this made sense. None of this should have been happening. None of—

"Hey," Felix said, gently poking Zach in the shoulder. "You with me?"

Zach scowled, taking another sip of coffee. "What is up with you?"

"What's up with you? You sleep in the park—"

"I did not sleep in the park."

"Well, I beg to differ, unless you just like early morning walks and naps fully dressed. I found you *sleeping*, ergo you slept in the park. Now you get all twitchy with me, *after* I bring you coffee."

"You still haven't explained that to my satisfaction."

"Goddamn it." For the first time, Felix looked set to lose his cool. "I just thought, well, what are the odds? Here's this guy, passed out, right where we first met. What was I supposed to do? Walk away? You know, I had a feeling we'd meet again."

Zach snorted. "Did you?"

"I did."

"Okay, listen, Felix? You don't owe me anything, okay? The punch…"

Felix winced.

"It was a mistake. You apologized. That's good enough for me. You don't have to like, buy me coffee and stuff."

"Stuff? Like check on you, camped out overnight in the park? 'Stuff,' like make sure some junkie ain't pissed on you and the raccoons ain't eatin' your face?"

"I…" Zach tried to choose his words, each explanation making less sense than the last. "I don't know how I got here."

Felix's steely blue eyes seemed to study him before the guy leaned back in the sunlight. "Makes two of us, I guess."

"You don't remember how you got to the park? Or to Fairview?"

"Fairview? On a bus. Not that I know why I got off here. Just a feeling, I guess"

"A feeling?" Who came to Fairview, Indiana's great Hallmark cliché come to life, by choice, except to visit family, or resign themselves to life in the generic American void?

Right. He had. Now look where he was.

"Sorry," Zach said. "I really gotta go. Thanks again for the coffee."

"Damn shame. I was kind of hoping to kiss you again."

Zach raised an eyebrow. "If I kiss you, will you let me start walking?"

"If I give you a ride, can I kiss you for longer?"

"You said you didn't have a car."

"I don't." The guy drained the last of his coffee and wandered into a small gap in the trees.

Zach jumped as the tinny buzzing of a small engine started, and

Felix emerged from the bushes on what he guessed was their ride. "You own a Vespa?"

"It is a Vespa, yes sir."

Zach swallowed. It seemed rude to ask for clarification.

"Where do you live?" Felix asked.

"Caroline Heights."

"And you walked?"

"I don't know!"

Felix shook his head, dismounting to lift a bright green helmet out of the seat. "Hey, I might have to take some back roads to dodge cops. You want this?"

Zach considered his options as Felix bounced the helmet up and down under his nose. What was the worst that could happen, assuming he survived a Vespa accident? That he wound up implicated in two deaths that summer? Jesus...

"You been on one of these before?" Felix asked.

"No."

"Then you better wear it. I'll go slow. Hold onto my waist, not my chest, and don't hold on so tight with your legs that you're breakin' mine. Oh, and most important, no leaning. Absolutely no leaning. Balanced and chill, got it?"

Zach swallowed. Right. Chill. Got it. Parents home tonight. Strange typing cat in his house. Body in the freezer. About to hop a probably stolen Vespa with a stranger from the park who'd punched him, kissed him, and brought him iced coffee, all in three days. Totally chill. "Got it."

"Great. Now, about my fare," Felix grinned. "Can I kiss you again?"

For the third time, Zach unclenched his legs from Felix's thighs as they zipped through the winding suburban streets that avoided the main roads back to his home. He'd realized within seconds of climbing on that the kiss had been a mistake. Encouraging Felix to want more, or expect more, especially once his ride was over, was definitely a mistake. It wasn't like they'd actually mentioned sex, but Felix's 'punch first, ask questions later' demeanor made Zach nervous.

Normally, he would have said yes. Felix was hot, in that scruffy, take-what-comes, good genes, lousy grooming kind of way. If his Mom hadn't called… If Grace Jones hadn't…

Except, Grace Jones was dead. So, what the fuck kind of animal had he been talking to? The kind that now lay curled around Felix's feet while they sat drinking Fresca.

About two minutes from the house, Zach had composed himself enough to wonder just how to get rid of the mysterious Samaritan drifter once they reached their destination. He'd been about to go inside and grab Felix a twenty for his trouble when Felix had pinned him with a request for a cold drink. To refuse would have been too suspicious. Felix also had the energy of someone who'd had his share of dealings with the police. Zach had to stay off that radar, at least until he could get his shit together and hide Conway's body somewhere permanent.

And it was going to be hard to get his shit together with Felix in the living room, taking his sweet time drinking goddamn Fresca!

"Where'd you say you were from again?" asked Felix.

"Here. Fairview. But I live in Toronto now."

"Toronto, right. And you're back here visiting... family?"

"Right."

"So, where are they?"

"Mom and Dad went to Texas for this bible retreat thing. They'll be home tonight."

Felix held his drink high with a half-cocked smile. "Well, praaaayyyyyse Jay-sus."

Zach swallowed, unhooking his fingertips from the arms of his chair. "You don't know the half of it."

"You, I take it, by contrast, are not a believer?" Something in Felix's drawl made this sound like a threat.

"I..." Zach watched not-Grace Jones jump into Felix's lap and roll over, exposing her belly. "I'm not really sure anymore. I keep an open mind and go from there."

"That, Sir, is a good approach. Hey, kitty."

Zach's heart leapt into his throat as Felix set aside his drink and scooped not-Grace Jones into his lap.

"He seems friendly."

"She."

"You sure about that?"

Right. Like Zach was sure of anything anymore.

"Like you said, open mind. It's like, we know there's more to people than just male or female. Five genders and counting, I read someplace. Can you imagine that? So, why not animals? Even plants... You know there's such a thing as male peppers and female peppers? Like, the female's got an extra bulb or something. Did you know that?"

Zach screamed internally.

"But I'm asking all the questions. Hell, I don't think you've asked one yet."

"No?"

"So? Shoot."

Zach wondered how to phrase 'Please leave. I'm busy' as a question. 'Get the fuck out' for 400, please. "Would you tell me the truth if I did?"

"Why wouldn't I?"

"You said I tasted like secrets. I'm guessing you have your own."

"Sure, I do, and so what? I don't really want to waste time sitting here, lying to each other, do you?"

Fine. If a little conversation made this go faster… "Why are you in Fairview?"

"Bzzzt! Told you that already. A feeling. Next?"

"You have family here?"

"No family any place."

Zach stared at not-Grace Jones, curled up in Felix's lap, purring like it was the most natural place for her in the world. Felix stroked the animal's belly, still upturned in complete trust of this stranger.

"That the best you've got? Really?"

Zach swallowed. He sucked at small talk at the best of times. Fuck!

"I'm getting the sense that you're in a hurry. Got some place to be?"

"No. It's just my parents are coming home is all. I need time to clean up. Not that I'm not grateful—"

"You said that. I just thought, since our time here is so short, you'd want to ask me something more interesting. Anything you like, man. One question. Any question. I'll answer. Honestly."

Zach's mind raced, every petty question that had crossed it since they'd met in the park, fighting for its chance. Where had Felix come from? Where was he staying? Why had he punched Zach without warning? Where had the Vespa come from? Was the guy some kind of criminal? Had kissing him sent Zach on an acid trip? Would it happen again? Until recently, Zach hadn't believed in ghosts, but he wasn't prepared to rule that out either.

He flicked his bottom teeth with his tongue "What's your biggest secret?"

"I killed a guy."

Zach's lips were dry. There it was. Flat. Straightforward. Emotionless. "Like, what? In the army or something? Iraq?"

"Now, that's another question. Two, in fact." Felix's hand never broke its rhythm, stroking the purring cat. "But I'll give it to you. No."

Zach had been ready for any number of answers. Drugs, theft, assault, arson, maybe even terrorism, but murder? He'd let a murderer into his house? He'd *kissed* a murderer?

"Don't freak out on me, man." Felix raised his hand. "That asshole deserved it, and there were very specific circumstances. Long story. But don't you worry, alright? We're cool."

"O…okay," Zach stammered, wishing he had something much stronger than Fresca. "When did you get out?"

"Never went in. Like I said, specific circumstances."

"You mean, like an accident?"

"An accident is what they call manslaughter and, in the relatively unlikely event of our great nation's justice system doing its job, usually involves 'going in.' No. I meant to kill that fuck."

"Okay, so… murder, then? You murdered this guy? Like, premeditated…" Zach felt sick.

291

"You asked me for my biggest secret. Sorry it's not an unpaid parking ticket. I've done most of it, man. Drugs, hustling, small-time stuff. Killing that son of a bitch is not an experience I care to repeat, but I respect you enough to be honest about it."

"I..." So much for small talk. "I guess it changed you?"

For the first time during their conversation, Felix dropped the cocky detachment and stared at Zach. It was when he realized not-Grace Jones was staring too that Zach's heart began to beat faster. His throat tightened, and his toes agitated against the floor, not that there was anywhere to run.

"Yeah. It changed me a lot." The last word snapped across the space between them with unseen venom. Felix looked down at not-Grace Jones and resumed petting her. "Nice cat."

"She seems to like you."

"Yeah, she does. Most cats don't. Ain't that somethin'?"

Zach clenched fists as he went to get up. "Look, I'm really sorry, but I've got a ton of stuff to do before my folks get back."

"I'll bet you do," said Felix, not moving. "Need a hand? I got nowhere else to be."

"I couldn't ask you to do that." Zach hoped his panic wasn't etched into his face. "It's just stuff to clean out. Boring shit, really, and you've been so great already. I appreciate it."

Felix stared back at him, unresponsive.

"So... thank you?" Zach said again, a little louder.

"You're scared."

"No."

"You are." Felix began running his fingers through the cat's fur again as its purring grew louder. "I get that, as much as it hurts my feelings. I mean, besides our initial misunderstanding, I ain't been nothin' but nice to you."

"It's not that! Look, if I had time, I'd love for you to stay, really."

"Really?"

"Yes! And we would totally have sex!"

"If you say so."

"I mean it. And you know what… whatever you did or didn't do way back when is none of my business. You're an awesome kisser, and I'd love to spend, like, hours just working out what turns you on and exploring each other and rolling around in a big, sweaty, soaking ball of lust, but I have shit to do, Felix! I'm sorry."

"Okay. I just thought… Well, I kind of like you. I like being honest with each other. I haven't been able to be honest with anybody in a long, long time. Hell, you just asked for my biggest secret and I gave it up, good as my word, no hesitation." Felix tickled not-Grace Jones under her chin. "That meant somethin', you know?"

"Hey, it's not that big a deal."

"It was for me."

"Okay!" Zach choked down the urge to snap. "I'm sorry, but… you could have lied. I would have understood."

"I thought we weren't doing that to each other. I thought this was, what does the guy say in that movie? 'The beginning of a beautiful friendship?'"

"Listen, we've only just met, and I'm going back to Toronto soon. I don't think—"

"And as soon as I met you, church boy—"

"Please don't call me that."

"—it felt to me like we had something to offer each other. Maybe nothing lasting, but something important, you know? It's just a feeling, the kind I've come to trust."

"A feeling?" Zach asked. "Like the one that brought you to Fairview, or the one that made you kill that guy?"

The look in Felix's eyes made Zach regret his question. "I've said all I'm gonna say about that, and you ain't told me nothin'. That hurts my feelings, Zach."

"I don't have anything like that to tell!"

"Hell, given how honest I thought we were being with each other, it really hurts my feelings."

"Fine!" Zach barked at last, not caring if he sounded defensive or desperate. "What do you want to know, Felix? What do you want from me? What's going to satisfy your curiosity?"

"Same thing I told you. Your biggest secret."

"Oh, and you want me to be honest? Is that it? You want me to tell you the truth? Because you know what, Felix? I have never, not for one fucking minute of my life, been honest with anyone about what I want, or who I am. Not even myself! I have no friends in Fairview because I couldn't get five fucking minutes to think about anything but how much I'd disappointed God growing up. I have no real friends anymore in Toronto, because all the people I thought were my friends, it turns out are really my ex's friends, and they've all spent the last year laughing at me behind my back because I've been trying so damn hard to be what I think they want. In fact, I have spent my entire life trying to please other people who will never think I'm enough, thinking I didn't deserve any better. *That* was supposed to end the second I got back here and instead I've been dealing with... Look, thanks again, one more time for the coffee and the ride. Now, I'd really appreciate you leaving!" He startled as not-Grace Jones dove off Felix's lap, then once again, as Felix got up from his chair and came at him like some cheesy haunted house jump scare. When their faces were inches apart, Zach looked him over and frowned. "Do… do you have a boner right now? Seriously?"

Felix grinned at him. "You're cute when you're mad."

"Great. My trauma gives you a boner? That's just fucking great."

"Hey, the cock wants what the cock wants."

"Gross."

Felix laughed as he backed off. "Naw, it's more your vulnerability that turns me on. You know, bein' real? But I get the hint, man. It's cool. No problem. Best of luck taking care of…" He glanced around the room, then back to Zach. "…whatever it is you're dealing with."

Zach got up, following his guest to the front door, watching not-Grace Jones weave between Felix's ankles.

"Maybe I'll see you around, handsome."

"I doubt that."

Felix grinned again, lifting his arms over his head and stretching.

Zach tried not to look at the nipple sticking out the side of the man's tank. "What now?"

"Can't I get one more kiss? Come on. If we ain't gonna see each other again…"

Zach sighed, letting the back of his fingers brush the stray nipple as Felix pulled him in and caught his lips. As the man savored him, his smile changed into a smirk Zach didn't like one bit.

"What?"

"You lying bastard."

"*What?*"

"You're holding out on me! Ain't never been honest with anyone about who you are? Biggest secret, my ass, church boy!"

"Oh my god! What is your problem?"

"Tell me the truth. What's going on?"

"Why should I?" Zach barked. "Tell me, what entitles you to know, exactly? Why do you even want to know? I told you I'm busy, and you have been on my back ever since!"

Felix looked away, seeming surprised by his outburst.

"Go on, tell me! What do you want? Explain it!"

"I tasted something in you, smart ass."

Zach shook his head. "You're gonna have to do better than telling me I'm an awesome kisser."

"You are."

"Answer the question," Zach snarled. "Because right now, all I have is some drifter refusing to leave my house, and if he doesn't either give up some answers or get out real soon, I'm calling the cops."

The cocky smirk returned, making Zach feel foolish again "We both know you ain't gonna do that."

Zach's throat tightened as he suppressed the urge to shudder.

"Alright," Felix continued, raising his hands in surrender. "I don't exactly know how to explain this in any way that's gonna make sense, but alright. You want to go sit down again?"

"Right here is fine."

Felix didn't argue. "See, we're the same, you and me."

"We're really not."

"Nawww, we are, kind of. I could taste it as soon as I kissed you. You've seen things you can't understand. And you've had to believe 'em, whether or not you wanted to." Felix's steely blue eyes pierced Zach's with their gaze. "You know I'm telling you the truth right now, because you tasted it too. You follow?"

Zach snorted. "So, what was it? What did I taste?"

Felix frowned, considering his words in what looked to Zach to be a moment of sincerity. "I'm not saying I believe in magic, exactly—"

"Okay. Get out."

"Hey! You want me to answer your questions or not? I don't believe in magic, but I do believe in secrets. Something just off the edge of what we can see, hear, and touch. Take, for instance, this cat. I get a weird feeling off this cat, and it ain't because she's cute."

Zach jumped as Felix picked not-Grace Jones up from around his feet and cradled her against his chest. "Please, don't hurt her."

"Why would I do that?" the guy asked, stroking the animal's head. "See, what I've learned, and this blew my goddamn mind, so if you want to go make yourself a stiff drink, I understand, but once a person comes into contact with, let's call it the stranger side of goings on, it changes them. Maybe you can taste it. Maybe you can smell it. It's easier to tell if you're one such person yourself."

"I really don't know what you're talking about."

"If you say so," Felix nodded, gently putting the animal down. "We can bullshit all afternoon if you want. We could take another hour, or two. Hell, we can go up to your room and fuck our brains out if you're in the mood."

"Are you even gay? Really?"

Felix's stare sank into dejection.

"Sorry."

"There's all kinds of things we could do. But given that you're on a ticking clock and all—"

"Yeah, I am. Felix, you really have to go."

"I ain't goin' nowhere until you show me your basement."

The demand hadn't been angry, just forceful, like there'd be no arguing. But no. No, no, hell no. No way. Zach felt the soft tickle of not-Grace Jones' fur around his ankles. "Please, just leave."

"Now, you listen to me, as a man who toyed with this shit and got burned bad. I don't know what's goin' on here, but I do know you're fucked. I know you need me. It's a feeling, and you can laugh at me and my 'feelings' all you want, but it got real strong when I picked up this cute kitty right here. Exact same energy. Boom." Felix stepped toward him, an odd and not unkind seriousness in his eyes all of a sudden. He ran a cool finger down the base of Zach's neck, setting off a shudder that went down his back. "You said you ain't got no friends in Fairview? Well, you got me, at least for now. So, if we don't have time for all the things that I'd like to do with you, at least let me help you out."

Zach let out a long, slow breath.

It made Felix laugh. "Aww, come on, man. How bad could it be?"

"Jesus! Holy shit! What the fuck?"

Zach slammed the freezer lid closed. "There. Now, you know, and if you try to run out of here, Grace Jones will break both your ankles."

"Grace... Grace Jones... *What?*"

"The cat."

Felix's eyes went wide as he looked at the once docile and trusting creature now growling at him from the staircase. "But... that's real in there! That's a real guy! He's dead?"

"He's dead. *C'est mort.* Ex-pir-ed. I thought you'd understand."

"Why the hell would I understand this?"

"You said you killed—"

"I didn't chop mine up and stick him in an ice box, you psycho!"

"Then what did you do? Because Mom and Dad get home tonight, and I could really, really use some pointers from someone who's hidden a body before."

"I didn't have to hide the..." Felix covered his face and screamed into his hands.

"What? How did you not get caught if you didn't hide the body?"

"No!" The man snapped back, extending a finger at him. "No, no, no. My questions first, church boy. I think I am *very* entitled as somebody who is probably now an accessory—"

"I didn't kill him!"

"So, who did?"

Zach swallowed, looking at the cat.

Felix's eyes went wide again. "You're fucking with me?"

"I am not. Maybe. I... it was an accident, I think."

"Your cat? Your cat did not kill this guy. Probably just a plastic dummy anyways. You probably work in a store someplace. Probably stole him out of the window? Great joke, asshole!"

"It's not a joke. This is Alistair Conway, a married, closeted, and now extremely dead former high school quarterback, swim-team captain, all-round asshole, and one-time masturbatory fantasy, who ruined that fantasy by filming my first time giving a guy head and forwarding it to half the school, making my life a living hell. I had him over, not realizing at first who he was. We had sex, after which he recognized me and freaked out, tripping over Grace Jones—"

"The cat?"

"The cat! The singer does not live at my house!"

"Well, I'm just makin' sure! Because nothing would fuckin' surprise me right now!"

"He tripped over Grace Jones, breaking his neck, his spine, may-

299

be puncturing a few critical organs, I don't fucking know, I'm not a forensics lab. Then, Grace Jones stole his phone—"

"His phone?"

"Just… shhh!" Zach covered Felix's mouth. "My turn! At some point in her life, she learned to communicate in English, or, I guess, written English since cats don't have human vocal cords, though she understands spoken English if you talk to her. She offered to help dismember and get rid of the body, which to me, made a kind of sense, you know? Because, hello? Cat! Next thing I know, I'm getting these detailed instructions on how to break up and dismember a body."

"Man, I think I'd better sit down."

"But then, she wants me to… This is crazy."

"You think?"

"She wants me to have sex."

"With her?"

"Fuck, no! With guys! Random guys, off the apps, online. Like, as much sex as possible. Basically, to stick to my original plan coming here, which was to have sex with as many guys as possible to get over… look, it sounded stupid at first, but she insisted. Then, I kept having these weirdly erotic dreams that made me think she was connected to some ancient sex cult and… and…" Zach's heart leapt in his chest as Felix bolted past him toward the stairs.

A loud hiss and a low growl stopped the man in his tracks. He turned back to Zach, jaw hanging slack, stretching his once handsome face in the dim basement light.

Zach continued. "All that was before. Now, I find out that my parents are coming home tonight, and I still don't know how the fuck I'm supposed to get a body out of this house before—"

"Okay, okay. Just… give me a minute." Felix looked at the freezer, then at not-Grace Jones, then back at Zach. "You've been through some shit."

"I have!"

"And she…" Felix pointed at the cat. "She really texted you?"

"Through the hook-up app. On Alistair's profile."

Felix shook his head. "I… I'd sure like to see that."

Zach fished his phone out of his pocket, opened the app, and hit the button containing all his chats. All but one. "Son of a…"

Not-Grace Jones sat licking her paws.

"You blocked me? You fucking blocked me? You bitch! I'll kill you!"

"Hey, hey!" Felix's arms were around Zach before he could dive upon the animal. "Easy! Take it easy."

"I'm not taking it easy! I'm getting gaslit by a fucking cat!"

Felix pulled him closer. "It's okay, man. It's okay."

"I just… I don't know what to do. I don't… I just… This… this is nice."

Felix squeezed both his shoulders. "You know you sound crazy, right?"

"Sound? You… you believe me?"

"I believe in lots of things. I've seen too much not to." Felix kissed his cheek, letting it linger before easing Zach off him. "Though I get why you left out the bit about you cooking and eating part of him."

Any newfound relief or calm drained from Zach as quickly as Felix's touch had brought it. He backed away, upsetting the laundry soap as he snatched up a plastic chair to keep between himself and the drifter.

"What the fuck do you know about that?"

Felix clapped his hands with a laugh, tilting his head at not-Grace Jones. "I only know what she told me. I wasn't sure whether to believe her at first, but looking at you now? Well, I guess it's true, ain't it? Every last bite."

Zach's fingers tightened around the chair. Should he throw it? At Felix? At the cat? Should he just get out of the house and take his chances?

"Easy," Felix continued, raising his hands. "I'm not going to hurt you. You still want my help? Sounds like you're in the shit pretty deep. Not too many people ready to wade in with you."

"So… what? You're reading minds now?"

"I'd rather not get into that."

"Oh, please do! Explain this to me."

"I can't, exactly. It's your cat. By the way, she ain't exactly yours, but you know that already. You can't hear her? Well, she might be done talking to you. But she's still got a lot to say."

"So, you're psychic with my cat now?"

"Will you quit being so damn literal about it? I'm trying to help you, goddamn it, and you're asking for easy answers that just ain't there! She's not using words. It's more like, ideas."

"I don't understand."

"So? Try and understand less. She promised you help? Here I am." Felix lifted the lid on the freezer and peered in. "Handsome fella, huh?"

Sure. Because Conway had been all about sex appeal since graduating from headless torso pic to actual headless torso.

"I'll make you a deal."

"Seriously?"

"Given the very serious nature of your current situation? Yes, seriously. I think it's best you know as little as possible. I just need a couple of things, besides of course your complete and absolute trust."

"Trust? How am I supposed to—"

"Man, you just introduced me to a dead body and a psychic cat."

Zach couldn't dispute this. "What do you need?"

"Show me where your tools are. I mean hacksaws and shit. Some sheet plastic too. This'll probably get messy. And I get to keep what's left of him."

"Excuse me?"

"Look, you wouldn't understand. Like I said, the less you know, the better. That's my price, man. What's left of him."

"That's insane. What are you going to do with him?"

"What are you gonna do with him?"

Zach swallowed. Either he'd have cops at his door within minutes, or this would all become Felix's problem. He checked the time again. Just after one. Eight hours to go. "Okay."

Felix nodded at not-Grace Jones. "Give us a couple of hours, alone."

Us? Of course. Why should it surprise him that the cat was crucial to this plan? "Fine. If she attacks you, I'm not sending help."

Zach took it as a good sign when the next hour passed without any screams. He'd turned up the TV more than once to drown out the sawing noises, but it hadn't done much good. Eventually, he'd gone to his room, putting an extra floor between him and the basement. As he lay in bed, trying to relax, he stared at his open suitcase. So much for the long, horny summer of reset and refresh.

He checked the time again. Almost two. What the fuck was taking Felix so long?

Seven hours. He'd texted his Mom but gotten no reply. Was she flying? Praying? Screaming at Dad? Was his horny summer of lust about to turn into a dramatic family shit show? This had raised a number of terrible ideas, not the least of which had been coming out to them. Right. Because his dad being caught with a sex worker was just the backdrop Zach wanted for that conversation.

Did he even have to stay?

It wasn't like he owed them help with this. He could see his dad's playbook now. The repentance, the faux piousness, appealing to 'family values,' the doubling down on every homophobic comment Zach had ever heard growing up. Looking at his suitcase again, Zach tried not to think about the details. He did not need this right now.

What if Felix fucked him over? The apparent bond Felix had formed with the creature masquerading as Grace Jones notwithstanding… It was too perfect. Grace Jones had promised to help him. She'd said nothing about what form that help might take, even a sexy redneck uncharacteristically in touch with his 'feelings,' not to mention certain realities just beyond—

A loud scream ripped through the silence. It had come from the basement.

Should he go check on them? No, no, shit, no! He had been very specific about not offering help if this went to hell. Unless Felix was dead? Like he needed a second body on his hands… Unless he could pin Conway's death on Felix, then claim self-defense? Ugh. No, no, no.

His phone pinged with a message from Cascade. *Hey sexy, you still alive?*

Zach wasn't sure how—or if—to answer that. He managed to tap out *Yeah* before another scream almost made him drop the phone. Like nothing he'd heard in any horror movie, it sounded like a man being torn apart from the inside. Felix.

His moral obligation to help was clear, unless said obligation led him onto a living *Hellraiser* set and no, no, no, no way was that going to happen, screams or no screams. And if his parents returned home to find their basement strewn with the entrails of a mysterious drifter? It would certainly put Dad's by-the-hour sexy times into perspective.

The staircase creaked under his first step. He remembered Alistair's stunned face, that look of horror and rage as the man realized he was falling to his doom. Damn it, one death under his roof had been enough. He quickly reached the ground floor and listened. There were no more screams, not even a whine or whimper. Felix was either dead, or playing a sick joke.

Zach grasped the door handle and waited, hoping for any last noise or sign that Felix was okay. When none came, he eased it open and stared into the blackness. He flicked the light switch to no effect, hearing only a faint click while his own breath grew heavy. "Felix?"

The gentle hum of a car passing on the street outside set his heart fluttering until he realized it was way too early to be his parents. Breathe, Zachary. This was fine.

"Felix? Are you there?" The place didn't smell like a slaughterhouse. Resisting the urge to slam the door behind him and run, he peered into the darkness, allowing the stairs to creak one after the other with his steady descent. "He...hello?"

Zach jumped as he heard a quiet meowing in the dark.

"Grace Jones? Felix?"

He steadied himself against the shelves at the bottom of the stairs, listening for any hint of cat or man. It took him a moment to realize that the steady breathing he could hear, which grew heavier with each exhale, was not his own.

"Felix?"

He fumbled for the flashlight he'd seen a thousand times on the shelf behind him, startling as two aerosol cans clattered to the floor. He froze, until his fingertips brushed the rough, textured handle of the flashlight.

A quiet, wet, tearing sound, then a low, feline growl, mixed with rattling interrupted the steady flow of breath.

Zach pointed the flashlight at it, flicked it on, and screamed.

A great shriek, something between the hissing of an enormous cat and the screams of the man he'd heard before, swallowed his own cries as he stumbled backward, trying to get away from the mass of flesh and bloody bone that writhed in the sudden light. He recognized Felix's delicate features in the face that had hissed at him, until it split in two with a gnashing maw of sharp, bloodied teeth. A frozen blue shape, barely recognizable as Conway's face pushed through a tear in the fleshy mass, only for the skeletal head to dive on it, forcing its tongue through Conway's lips, death kissing death, caught in the beam of Zach's flashlight.

His foot landed on one of the fallen cans and went out from under him. He dropped the flashlight as the back of his head struck the shelf. His world went dark. When Zach peered through heavy eyelids, the corpselike thing had edged closer. He tried pulling away, but his legs and arms refused to drag his weight the few precious feet he needed to reach the stairs and crawl to… safety? Where the fuck was safe any—

The creature hooked a bony hand around his ankle.

Zach opened his eyes with a startled cry, squinting against the brightness of fires lit at the edges of the temple courtyard. The skeletal apparition was gone. He looked down at the black cat now snoozing against his bare chest. Grace Jones. Or not Grace Jones. Who knew? Did it matter? Zach couldn't speak. He was still shaking. Still forcing himself to breathe, trying to match her steady purrs.

And walking slowly toward him, hands bound behind his back, as naked as Zach, except for a purple silk blindfold, was the athletic body of Alistair Conway. Silent. Slow. Unmistakable.

Dead. Against all evidence, Zach knew the Conway that stood before him was dead.

He shook his head, willing himself to wake up.

Did he want to go back? To the darkness of the basement and that... thing?

He was safe now, wasn't he?

Wasn't he?

Conway stopped just as he reached Zach's outstretched feet, kneeling between them with a quick swallow that sent a ripple through the muscles in his neck and shoulders, and an unwelcome rumble through Zach's stomach.

Then, as steadily as Conway had approached, came Bandage Face, just as naked, a short blade hanging at his side.

Zach felt the faint prick of Grace Jones' or not-Grace Jones' claws on his chest as she shifted position.

Bandage Face stroked Conway's chin with his hands. He gently lifted it, exposing Conway's throat to Zach, then drew his blade and slit it from ear to ear.

Zach barely had time to close his eyes, much less cry out before a shower of blood sprayed his face and chest. Cold, dead blood, that by any logic shouldn't have spurted with such force, yet it had. Grace Jones simply yawned, then started to lick the blood off Zach's chest. He watched, frozen, as Bandage Face caught Conway's lifeless body and held it against his own, kissing and suckling the dead man's neck.

Zach wanted to throw up. He jumped as a pair of strong hands slid over his bare shoulders. He looked down at the colorful arms that wrapped around his bloodied chest.

Tatts. Something about the man's touch made him feel safe. Maybe too safe. When Grace Jones hissed at him, he barely noticed, and he was only vaguely aware of the skittering paws as several more cats approached them. He barely felt it when Grace Jones bit hard into the muscle of his upper arm and tore off a small chunk of flesh. Then another. Then the other cats, each one climbing over him, biting into his legs, arms, and stomach, his absurdly built chest.

Not a single bite hurt, as if each one had released morphine into him, making him feel lighter. Or perhaps it was just the high of Tatts kissing him again. When he opened his eyes to see Bandage Face, now quite unbandaged, his face a semi-formed pulp of flesh and bone more abstraction than human, sinking cruel, jagged teeth into Alistair Conway's flesh and tearing it away as more cats swarmed to his aid, he felt... bemused. He looked at the shredded remains of his own body. His swollen cock remained untouched, as if it were unsurmountable in this holy place.

A temple of sex? Death? Cats?

And we shall both gorge our appetites, Zachary...

Grace Jones bit hard into his nipple. When Tatts gently grasped his cock, and they kissed again, Zach came, harder than any time he could remember.

He could remember almost nothing. Eventually, he stopped trying, and laughed.

Barely awake, barely able to breathe, Zach blinked, shutting his eyes tight as a light blinded him. He shielded his face before trying again, peering between the pink flesh of his hands. Why did he feel so sick? What had he eaten? Why was he on the basement floor? He pushed himself upright, hitting his head on the washer with a loud, hollow bang.

"Watch yourself, sleepy head."

The voice behind the light was familiar, unsettling in its ease as an image congealed on Zach's memory. Bone. Flesh. Teeth. Blood. Hissing. That kiss. Then the temple, again. Cats. Conway. The bandaged man. The ecstatic tearing of his own flesh.

Now, he sat on the floor, untouched and unharmed.

Zach pawed around for the flashlight, only to realize it was the beam now blinding him. The voice behind it, though still thick with Felix's drawl, sounded deeper, altered somehow.

The light pulled away from him along the floor. Not-Grace Jones scurried out of the way as it passed her and tracked up Felix's naked feet and legs. They seemed thicker than Zach remembered, with longer, darker hairs. He couldn't help but stare as Felix illuminated a generous cock, framed by a neatly trimmed thatch of dark hair beneath a tight set of abs and a strangely broad, athletic chest, until at last, the flashlight lit up Alistair Conway's face.

"What do you think?" it asked.

Zach couldn't move. That face that had spent recent weeks silently screaming into darkness. That face he'd seen melt into ecstasy as they'd fucked, then blast with rage at him before its owner's clumsy demise.

"No, no, no, no, no, no, no, no, no, no. No way! No way in hell. This is not happening. This is impossible. You're dead!"

"Keep your voice down."

"F...fu...fuck you! This isn't happening!"

"It's me, man. It's Felix."

It took Zach another few seconds to come out of his mantra. To look at the face again and study it. Alistair Conway in every detail, but one.

"Come take a look."

He swallowed, fixing on the illusion's only tell as he neared it. Felix's smoky blue eyes shone at the center of Conway's face. He jumped as Felix put the flashlight in his hand, then regained his composure long enough to shine it over a swimmer's chest that was all Conway, over the smooth, textured muscles of the man's back, down the thighs and over the firm muscles of an ass that could never have belonged to the slender drifter he'd met in the park.

Except, now it did.

"Touch away, man. I don't mind."

Zach reached out, stroking Conw... Felix's naked body with his fingertips, moving down the man's abs and the soft, warm flesh covering his hips. Completely unscarred, even at the top of Conway's muscular thighs, where Zach had severed both legs before feeding most of them to his cat.

"Check me for seams?"

"Seams?"

"I just want to make sure." Felix stretched out his arms and slowly turned, offering his newly acquired body for inspection. Zach moved the flashlight up and down both legs, over the man's back and shoulders. He gently parted the hair, checking for scars that weren't there before Felix turned to face him again.

Zach bit his lower lip, trying to not let his mouth go dry. Trying to forget the thing he'd seen—or thought he'd seen—in the spot where the body that now housed Felix stood. "How?"

"You want me to describe the process?"

"No!" Zach didn't know what misplaced courage or confidence prevented him from pulling away as Felix put a hand on his shoulder, then encircled his body with those newly upgraded arms, pulling him tighter. The touch possessed all of Alistair's strength, but its gentleness was unmistakably the same man who'd kissed him in the park. Tucking the flashlight under one arm, Zach slid his hands over any part of the body he could. Arms. Chest. Hips. Face. The whole package captivated him with its grotesque beauty and impossibility until Felix caught him in a deep kiss. For one short moment, Zach lost himself in the immediacy of it, no matter what color those eyes were. But only for a moment.

His hands slipped from the body. "I'm sorry. This is too weird for me."

The face smiled. "Really weren't fond of this guy, were you?"

Zach swallowed, second-guessing himself only briefly. "He wasn't a nice person."

"So, why'd you fuck him?"

Zach allowed himself a look at Felix's new body. "Old fantasy?"

Felix brought his arms around Zach's shoulders, leaning close again. "How's that fantasy doing now?"

The familiar heat rose inside him, a raw need to forget about everything and kiss Felix again. To kiss this reproduction of Alistair. An improved Alistair. Not the asshole who'd tortured and humiliated him, but the handsome boy whose body and surface had filled the private thoughts of his junior year. His sexual awakening. The Alistair that could have been, molded to his every whim and pleasure by a stranger... for what? To indulge the fantasy of a kid he barely recognized? A kid who deserved more?

"I think it's passed," he answered.

Felix kissed him on the cheek. "Suit yourself."

Zach passed his flashlight over the body again, any last confusion or disgust yielding to pure fascination. "You'll have to get your tattoos redone."

"Nah." Felix inspected the unmarked flesh of his new body. "Think I might enjoy a fresh canvas for a while."

"Okay. You know he has a wife, right?"

"Yeah, your kitty brought me his phone."

Zach shone the torchlight around the darkened room. "Where's umm... I mean, if you're *him* now, where is—"

"The old me? I never want to see that face again. I mean, ever. You get me?"

Zach swallowed, any question about what that meant clearly unwelcome. "I just mean... it's not like, laying around down here, somewhere, is it?"

"You want it?" Felix asked.

"No, thank you."

"Good. Hey, umm, what kind of accent did this guy have? You remember?"

"No... no accent, really. Midwestern? I don't know."

"I guess it don't much matter."

"I guess not."

Not-Grace Jones meowed again. Right. Stop analyzing, Zachary.

"Where will you go?"

"Ain't much thought about that." Felix knelt down to pick up not-Grace Jones as she rubbed against his ankles. "We'll figure it out."

We? Of course. No way was Zach keeping Not-Grace Jones now.

"Following those feelings, huh?" Zach asked.

Felix smiled at him again. "They serve me well."

Zach nodded, giving the stranger's new body a last look.

"Guess I should leave before your folks get home."

Zach bit his bottom lip. "I'd appreciate that."

"Okay. Just answer me one last question."

"What's that?"

Felix's smile pierced the darkness again. "Where'd you stash this guy's clothes?"

With each cupboard he opened, Zach braced himself to find Felix's disembodied face, crumpled and eyeless like a disused Halloween mask. But there was nothing. Not so much as a stray hair to suggest Felix or Alistair Conway had ever been at his house. True to his word, Felix had dressed in Conway's running shorts and tank, bundled his own clothes into a plastic bag, and left, with not-Grace Jones perched on his now ample shoulders.

Zach had watched them for a moment, waiting for Felix to turn and wave goodbye, that same smirk curling Conway's face. Wasn't that how these movies usually ended? But Felix hadn't turned. He hadn't waved. He'd just got on the Vespa and left.

Zach emptied the cat's litter into another bag and took it to a dumpster behind the liquor store on the next block. He checked the fridge to make sure no stray pieces of Conway remained. He checked the basement freezer three times as well, just to be sure. Nothing but frozen vegetables. No blood. No cat hair. No Felix.

It still seemed possible that Felix could fuck him over. But how, with the evidence literally up and walking around as Felix himself? Maybe the guy would go back to Alistair's family. Maybe they'd question the sudden change of eye color or maybe they wouldn't. It seemed more likely to Zach that Felix would just disappear.

So why wouldn't the sick bubbling in his gut settle? The nausea, returned anew with…

Oh gods.

He bolted for the bathroom, lifted the lid and hurled, plastering the bowl in a long stream of pink-brown vomit. He collapsed onto the cool tile floor, shoulders hunched, exhausted, but weirdly relaxed.

Zach stood up, wiped a spot of drool from the edge of his mouth and lifted his shirt, pinching a familiar… love handle? He whipped off his shirt and stared at his body in the mirror. The definition that had puffed out his chest, the tight gullies of his ill-gotten six-pack, the thick veins of six-days-a-week gym arms… It was all gone. All he saw was his own familiar body with all its telltale loose ends intact. He flushed the toilet, brushed his teeth, zipped up his bathroom kit and put his shirt back on. It fit perfectly.

He returned to his old room, gave it a final once-over and closed his suitcase, right before his phone pinged with a response to his last Fairview message, sent to the only person he wanted to see.

You're leaving? Well… that sucks. Is seven okay?

Zach tapped his response. *Seven is perfect. Thanks. See you then.*

He hit send before he could think twice, then settled in the living room to wait for Cascade.

Zach hadn't exactly meant for Cascade to give him a ride to the airport. Just to come over and say goodbye. He didn't know why, but he couldn't stand the thought of going back to Toronto without at least seeing the guy who'd stayed with him through his hallucination one more time, no matter how bad an idea getting attached to that person seemed. Maybe it wasn't attachment, just politeness. Right. So why had he teared up when Cascade had taken his hand in the car?

"I can't believe you're leaving so soon."

"I know," He rubbed his thumb over the back of Cascade's hand. "I wish I could stay longer."

Cascade shook his head. "What changed your mind?"

"Dad… Mom and Dad are coming home early. There was drama."

"Ah. Yeah, that's a buzzkill, for sure."

"It's complicated. In a 'Dad' and 'sex worker' in the same sentence kind of way." It occurred to Zach that he hadn't thought to ask about the gender of said worker.

"Hey wait, aren't they super religious?"

"Super, super, religious."

"And you'd rather skip the holy fireworks?"

Zach stared out the window. "I guess."

Cascade shifted gears, taking the opportunity to pat Zach's knee. "Wish I could offer you a bed."

"You've already done enough."

"I wasn't offering you any favors." Cascade looked at him as they passed through the barely lit suburbs near the airport. "My motivation is entirely selfish."

Zach lifted Cascade's hand and kissed it. "I would love it."

"'If wishes,' huh?"

"Yeah. Wishes."

Zach felt bad about the next few minutes passing in silence, particularly with the telltale lights of a plane in view. It felt like a waste of precious time. "You didn't have to give me a—"

"Shush. You're doing what you need to do. This is what I need to do, alright?"

"Need? You've met me, like, twice."

Cascade nodded. "And I knew within maybe two minutes of meeting you that it was going to be different. I don't know why."

"Okay. Can I ask you a really rude question?"

Cascade swallowed, pulling into the near-empty drop lot. "Shoot."

"Did you know that the first time you met Wade too?"

When Cascade didn't answer, Zach wondered if he should qualify, or admit he'd felt the same knowledge himself, and had been unable to shake it since, even knowing the inescapable limits on their relationship.

"You can't really do that, Zach."

"I'm sorry. I shouldn't have—"

"Shut up, just a minute."

Zach's heart seized at the thought of offending the man, or worse, leaving him angry.

"I mean, you can't compare people like that. What they do to you. How they make you feel. How you love them. How they love you. If they do. They're all different. It is always different."

Zach wondered if he should tell Cascade how he'd made him feel. If he could articulate it. How stupid it seemed, when they'd known each other such a short time. Instead, he squeezed Cascade's hand.

Cascade smiled. "Why'd you come back to this place, Zach? Don't bullshit me."

"I hoped I'd find something. Connect with something."

"And did you?"

Zach shook his head. "Not what I thought I would. And it isn't mine."

"Fuck off." Cascade turned away, pinching his nose. Zach watched the man's reflection wipe away a tear in the car window. "Now, see what you're doing? You see this? What is this shit?"

"I'm sorry."

Cascade turned back to him, hand still teasing his arm. "It's never going to be perfect. You know that, right?"

The only answer Zach had was to lean in and claim a kiss, savoring the taste of Cascade's lips and tongue, enjoying the firm grip of the man's hands on his body. All the thoughts rattled his mind. Could he change his flight again? One more day. Just one. They could get a room at an airport hotel and he could go in the morning. No lies. No cat. No tension.

Just one perfect night that would make this ten times harder.

Cascade sat, staring at him after their kiss broke, saying nothing until they looked up to see an attendant pointing to the *10 Minutes Max* sign. Who the hell was enforcing standing rules at 8pm in Fairview?

"You better go."

"Yeah," said Zach, checking he had his wallet and phone, one hand on the door handle. He left the car and grabbed his suitcase from the trunk.

"Hey," Cascade called, winding down the window. "Next time you come see your parents... you know."

Zach smiled. "Definitely."

Cascade grinned back. "Safe flight, sexy."

He tried to resist the urge to watch the car go, and failed.

Dear Mom,

I'm sorry I didn't stick around to see you, and I hope I didn't leave the house looking like too much of a disaster. I'd love to tell you that something urgent pulled me back to Toronto, like some emergency or summer classes or something like that, but here's the truth.

I can't handle you right now.

I mean it. I'm not available. Not an ear. Not a shoulder. I'm sorting my own shit, and yes Mom, I curse now. I'm telling you this because every moment of our lives that we've spent together has been under false pretenses. My entire life, I've tried against all hope to project this image of the perfect Christian son, silently choking on self-hatred and the knowledge that my own parents don't know the first real thing about me, and wouldn't be interested.

I know now's not the time to fix all that, not with what's going on around Dad. You take your time and I'll take mine. Scream, shout, fight, argue, do whatever you need to do. I'd say try to love him, but more realistically, try not to be so fucking judgy for once and maybe the two of you will have a conversation about it. But work it out before you contact me. Then, I promise you, I'll be back.

I'd say that I love you, but I honestly don't know who you are to love. Can you remember the last time you told me you loved me? I wouldn't blame you if you didn't. You don't know who I am, either. But I want us to know each other, Mom. I want us to have that chance. I'm done with us drawing out this long, extended lie and calling it conversation. The only thing I ever took from those conversations was that I wasn't enough, and trust me, that belief has put me through some serious shit.

There's no hurry. For all that wasted time, it's going to take some more for me to work out who this person is that I want you to know. You'll probably need time, too. That's okay. We don't have to do it all at once. But I want to make a start, Mom. A friend recently told me that every connection and every love with every person we meet in our lives is different, and he was right. I want ours to have the chance it deserves. I want a chance to love you, Mom. I really do.

Your son,
Zach

PURRSONAL THANKS

A huge thank you and extra treats to publisher and editor Sven Davisson, Queer Mojo, and Rebel Satori Press for taking a chance on this strange little novel.

To my beta readers, A J Dolman, Kevin Klehr, and Eric Andrews-Katz, thank you for the useful bites, scratches and nose boops that helped me bang this novel into shape. Big thanks to Nick, Reagan, Alex, Keith, Ted, and Kathryn for chasing the red dot with me, offering your support, invaluable workshop feedback, and encouragement. Can't wait to see all your titles in print.

Friends and writing colleagues who kept me sane and reminded me who I am through the pandemic, thank you so much! From editors Jerry L. Wheeler and L E Daniels to authors who've helped motivate me and helped spread the word like David S. Pederson, James K Moran, 'Nathan Burgoine, Jeffrey Round, J P Jackson, Hans M Hirschi, Nicole Disney, Barbara Ann Wright, Rob Byrnes, and Felice Picano, among others.

Thanks to my not always understanding but wonderfully supportive friends, family, and parents who are in no way the basis and bear no resemblance to Zach's parents in this book. There. I said it. It's in print.

Finally, to my favourite grumpy kitty, Dean, thank you for being a willing book widow, putting up with my mental zoomies, and never doubting me.

CHRISTIAN BAINES is an awkward nerd turned slightly less awkward novelist. His work includes the paranormal series *The Arcadia Trust*, novella *Skin*, and *Puppet Boy*, a finalist for the 2016 Saints and Sinners Emerging Writer Award. Born in Australia, he now travels the world whenever possible, living, writing, and shivering in Toronto, Canada on the occasions he can't find his passport.

Lightning Source UK Ltd.
Milton Keynes UK
UKHW040633230223
417513UK00004B/193